Simon Scarrow taught history before becoming a full-time writer in 2005. This title introduces his Roman soldier heroes Cato and Macro, who first stormed the book shops in 2000, and have subsequently appeared in other bestsellers including CENTURION and THE LEGION (see inside for a full list of titles in Simon's Roman series). His 400-year-old house in Norfolk is in an area colonised by the Romans in the first century AD, and home to the rebellious tribal leader Boudica. The inspiration for his books comes when walking his dogs around the ruins of a Roman town just outside Norwich.

Simon has many other literary projects in hand including a young adult Roman series. He also develops projects for television and film with his brother Alex.

To find out more about Simon Scarrow and his novels, visit www.catoandmacro.com and www.scarrow.co.uk.

UNDER THE EAGLE

SIMON SCARROW

headline

First published in 2000
by HEADLINE PUBLISHING GROUP

First published in paperback in 2001
by HEADLINE PUBLISHING GROUP

This paperback edition published in 2012
by HEADLINE PUBLISHING GROUP

21

ISBN 978 0 7553 4970 8

Typeset in Bembo by Avon DataSet Ltd,
Bidford-on-Avon, Warwickshire

Printed and bound by CPI Group (UK) Ltd, Croydon, CR0 4YY

Headline's policy is to use papers that are natural, renewable and recyclable
products and made from wood grown in sustainable forests. The logging and
manufacturing processes are expected to conform to the environmental
regulations of the country of origin.

HEADLINE PUBLISHING GROUP
An Hachette UK Company
338 Euston Road
London NW1 3BH

www.headline.co.uk
www.hachette.co.uk

For Audrey and Tony,
best of parents and best of friends

THE ROMAN ARMY CHAIN OF COMMAND IN 43 AD

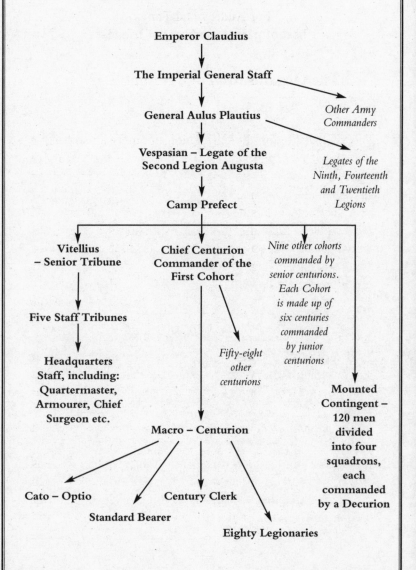

Emperor Claudius

The Imperial General Staff → *Other Army Commanders*

General Aulus Plautius

Vespasian – Legate of the Second Legion Augusta

Legates of the Ninth, Fourteenth and Twentieth Legions

Camp Prefect

Vitellius – Senior Tribune

Chief Centurion Commander of the First Cohort

Nine other cohorts commanded by senior centurions. Each Cohort is made up of six centuries commanded by junior centurions

Five Staff Tribunes

Headquarters Staff, including: Quartermaster, Armourer, Chief Surgeon etc.

Fifty-eight other centurions

Mounted Contingent – 120 men divided into four squadrons, each commanded by a Decurion

Macro – Centurion

Cato – Optio

Standard Bearer

Century Clerk

Eighty Legionaries

The Organisation of a Roman Legion

The Second Legion, like all legions, comprised some five and a half thousand men. The basic unit was the century of eighty men commanded by a centurion with an optio acting as second in command. The century was divided into eight-man sections which shared a room together in barracks and a tent when on campaign. Six centuries made up a cohort, and ten cohorts made up a legion, with the first cohort being double-size. Each legion was accompanied by a cavalry unit of one hundred and twenty men, divided into four squadrons, who served as scouts and messengers. In descending order the main ranks were:

The *legate* was a man from an aristocratic background. Typically in his mid thirties, the legate would command the legion for up to five years and hope to make something of a name for himself in order to enhance his subsequent political career.

The *camp prefect* would be a grizzled veteran who would previously have been the chief centurion of the legion and was at the summit of a professional soldier's career. He was armed with vast experience and integrity, and to him would fall the command of the legion should the legate be absent or *hors de combat*.

Six *tribunes* served as staff officers. These would be

men in their early twenties serving in the army for the first time to gain administrative experience before taking up junior posts in civil administration. The senior tribune was different. He was destined for high political office and eventual command of a legion.

Sixty *centurions* provided the disciplinary and training backbone of the legion. They were hand-picked for their command qualities and a willingness to fight to the death. Accordingly their casualty rate far exceeded other ranks. The most senior centurion commanded the first century of the first cohort and was a highly decorated and respected individual.

The four *decurians* of the legion commanded the cavalry squadrons and hoped for promotion to the command of auxiliary cavalry units.

Each centurion was assisted by an *optio* who would act as an orderly, with minor command duties. Optios would be waiting for a vacancy in the centurionate.

Below the optios were the *legionaries,* men who had signed on for twenty-five years. In theory, a man had to be a Roman citizen to quality for enlistment, but recruits were increasingly drawn from local populations and given Roman citizenship on joining the legions.

Lower in status than the legionaries were the men of the *auxiliary cohorts*. These were recruited from the provinces and provided the Roman empire with its cavalry, light infantry and other specialist skills. Roman citizenship was awarded on completion of twenty-five years' service.

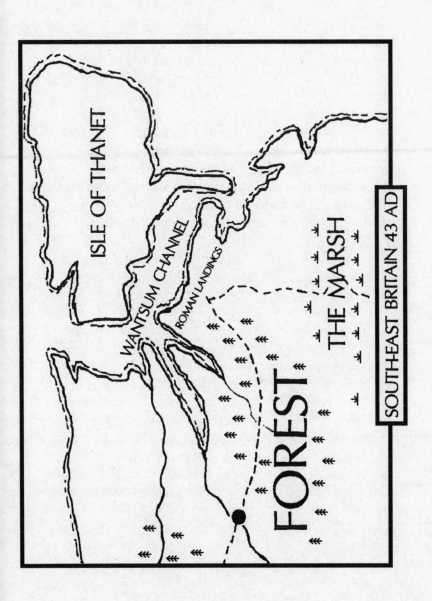

ISLE OF THANET

WANTSUM CHANNEL

ROMAN LANDINGS

FOREST

THE MARSH

SOUTH-EAST BRITAIN 43 AD

Prologue

'It's no good, sir, the bastard's well and truly stuck.'

The centurion leaned back against the wagon and paused for breath. Around him a score of bone-weary legionaries stood up to their waists in the foul-smelling ooze of the marsh. From the edge of the track, the general followed their efforts in growing frustration. He had been embarking on to one of the evacuation ships when news arrived that the wagon had run off the narrow path. He had immediately taken one of the few remaining horses and galloped it back through the marsh to investigate the situation at first hand. Weighed down by the heavy chest resting on its bed, the wagon resisted every effort to wrestle it free. There was no further help available now since the rearguard had finished loading and put to sea. Only the general, these men and a thin screen of the last remaining cavalry scouts stood between the wagon and the army of Caswollan snapping at the heels of the erstwhile Roman invaders.

The general let slip an oath and his horse raised its head in alarm from the nearby copse where it had been tethered. The wagon was lost then, that much was evident, and the chest itself was too heavy to carry back to the last ship waiting at anchor. For security's sake the key to the chest had remained with the quartermaster, now well out to sea, and the chest was so constructed as to make it impossible to open without the right tools.

'What now, sir?' the centurion asked.

The general looked long and hard at the chest, in silence. There was nothing he could do – nothing at all. Wagon, chest and contents were not going to move. For a moment he dared not contemplate that, since the loss of the chest would set his political plans back by a year at least. In that agonising moment of indecision a war horn blew close at hand. With terrified expressions, the legionaries started to wade back towards their weapons lying on the track.

'Stay where you bloody are!' the general roared. 'I haven't ordered you to move!'

The legionaries paused, even with the enemy close at hand, such was the depth of their awe and respect for their commander. With a last look at the chest, the general nodded as he made his decision.

'Centurion, get rid of the wagon.'

'Sir?'

'It'll have to stay here until we return next summer. Drag it a little further in so it sinks, mark the spot and then get back to the beach as fast as you can. I'll have them hold a tender ready for you.'

'Yes, sir.'

The general slapped his thigh angrily, then turned to mount his horse and set off back through the marsh towards the beach. Behind him came another burst from the war horn and the sound of swords clashing as the cavalry scouts fought it out with the vanguard of Caswollan's army. From the moment the Romans had landed, to their present flight back to Gaul, Caswollan's men had dogged them every step of the way, harrying stragglers and foragers day and night, and showing no mercy to the invaders.

'Right, lads!' the centurion bellowed. 'One last heave . . . Get your shoulders to the wagon. Ready now . . . Heave!'

Slowly the wagon sank further into the mire; dark brown marsh water flowing up through the seams in the bed of the wagon and rising up the sides of the chest.

'Come on! Heave!'

With a last combined thrust the men eased the wagon further into the marsh and, with a soft gurgling plop, the wagon disappeared beneath the dark water leaving a faint swirl rippling across the oily surface, broken only by the long wagon shaft.

'That's it, lads. Back to the ship. Smartly does it.'

The legionaries waded ashore and snatched up their shields and spears while the centurion hurriedly sketched a map of the location on the wax tablet hanging from his shoulder. When he was done, he snapped the tablet shut and joined his men. But before the column could move off a sudden pounding of hoofbeats on the track caused his men to turn, wide-eyed and afraid. Moments later a handful of cavalry scouts burst out of the mist and galloped by the infantry. One scout leaned forward across his horse's neck which ran with blood from a gaping wound in the man's side. Then they were gone.

Almost at once came the sound of more horses, this

time accompanied by the harsh cries of the natives the legionaries had grown to dread. There was a new triumphant edge to their war cries and a cold finger of dread traced its way down the spines of the Romans.

'Ready javelins!' The centurion called out and his men hefted their throwing spears back, waiting for the order. In the mist, the sounds of their pursuers swept towards them, unseen and terrifying. Then indistinct grey shapes appeared a short way off. 'Release!'

The javelins arced up and out of sight and crashed down on the reckless Britons with a chorus of screams from both man and beast.

'Form up!' the centurion cried out. 'At the command . . . quick march!'

The small column stepped out down the track towards the distant safety of the last evacuation ship, the centurion marching at their side, keeping an anxious watch on the mist that swallowed up the track behind them. The volley of javelins did not delay the Britons for long and soon the sound of hooves closed in on them again, slower and more cautious this time.

The centurion heard a thud and one of his men gasped in pain. He turned to see an arrow shaft protruding from the back of the rearmost legionary. Fighting for breath as his lungs filled with blood, the man fell to his knees and toppled forward.

'At the trot!'

The belts and harnesses of the legionaries jingled as they quickened the pace and tried to increase the distance between themselves and their invisible pursuers. More arrows whirred out of the mist, fired blindly at the

Romans. Still, some found their mark and one by one the column shrank in size as men fell on the track and lay, swords drawn, grimly waiting for the end. By the time the centurion reached the final rise, where the marsh gave way to sand and pebble, only four men remained with him. The faint sound of the seashore was the music of hope to their ears and a slight September breeze worked to thin the mist ahead of them.

All at once the path ahead was clear. Two hundred paces away across the shingle, a small boat waited in the surf. A little way out to sea a trireme lay at anchor in a gentle swell and, far out towards the horizon, the dark specks of the invasion fleet were fading into the gloom of dusk.

'Run for it!' shouted the centurion, throwing down his shield and sword. 'Run!'

The shingle scattered beneath their feet as they sprinted down towards the boat. Immediately the war horn sounded behind them as the Britons also caught sight of the sea, spurring their horses on to run down the surviving men before they could reach safety. Teeth gritted, the centurion hurled himself down the gentle slope, grimly aware of the sounds of their pursuers closing rapidly, but he dared not look back for fear that it might cause him to slow his pace. He could see a tall figure standing in the rear of the boat desperately urging him on, as the general's red cloak rippled out behind him in the gentle breeze. Fifty feet to go, and a sharp cry came from just behind him as one of the Britons thrust his spear through the rearmost legionary.

With every fibre of his body screaming out for life,

the centurion pounded across the wet sand at the sea's edge, splashed through the surf and hurled himself over the bows of the boat. Eager hands grabbed him under the shoulders and bodily pulled him down. An instant later, a legionary crashed down on top of him, snatching his breaths from the sea air. A pair of the general's burly bodyguards jabbed their spears at the pursuers who had reined in at the water's edge now the odds had been evened. But they were already too late and the boat quickly moved into deeper water as the oarsmen bent themselves to their work, rowing the boat back to the safety of the trireme.

'Did you manage to sink the wagon?' the general asked anxiously.

'Y-yes, sir . . .' panted the centurion, and he patted the wax tablet hanging at his side. 'There's a map, sir. Good as I could make in the time we had.'

'Well done, centurion. Well done. I'll have that now.'

As the centurion handed over the tablet he glanced round and saw that only one man had escaped with him. Only one. On the shrinking shoreline he could see a score of horsemen clustered round another of his men, foolish enough to be taken alive, and the centurion shuddered at the thought of what terrors lay in wait for the helpless legionary.

Every man in the boat watched in silence, until finally the general spoke.

'We'll come back, men. We'll come back, and when we do I promise you that we'll make those bastards regret the day they ever took up arms against Rome. I, Caius Julius Caesar, swear this on my father's grave . . .'

The Rhine Frontier

Ninety-six years later, in the second
year of the reign of Emperor Claudius
Late 42 AD

Chapter One

An icy blast of wind swept into the latrine with the sentry.

'Wagon's approaching, sir!'

'Shut the bloody door! Anything else?'

'Small column of men.'

'Soldiers?'

'Hardly.' The sentry grimaced. 'Unless there's been some change in marching drill.'

The duty centurion glanced up sharply. 'I don't recall asking for an opinion on policy, soldier.'

'No, sir!' The sentry snapped to attention under the glare of his superior. Only a few months earlier Lucius Cornelius Macro had been an optio and was still finding promotion to the centurionate hard to handle. His former comrades in the ranks were still inclined to treat him as an equal. It was hard to register a respectful attitude to one who so recently had been seen emptying his guts of a skinful of cheap wine. But, for some months before the promotion, Macro had been aware that senior officers were considering him for the first available vacancy in the centurionate and had done his best to keep indiscretions to a minimum. For, when all his qualities were placed in the balance, Macro was a good soldier –

when good soldiering was required – conscientious in his duties, reliably obedient to orders and he could be counted on to hold firm in a fight and inspire others to do the same.

Macro suddenly realised that he had been gazing at the sentry for a while and that the legionary was shifting uncomfortably under his scrutiny, as one tends to in front of a silently staring superior. And officers could be such unpredictable bastards, the sentry thought nervously, first whiff of power and they either don't know what to do with it, or they insist on giving bloody-minded and stupid orders.

'What are your orders, sir?'

'Orders?' Macro frowned for a moment. 'All right then. I'll come. You get back to the gate.'

'Yes, sir.' The sentry turned and hurriedly made his way out of the junior officers' latrine block, pulling the door to as the half-dozen centurions glared after him. It was an unwritten rule that no-one, but no-one, permitted their men to interrupt proceedings in the latrine. Macro applied the sponge stick, pulled up his breeches and apologised to the other centurions before hurrying outside.

It was a filthy night and a cold northerly wind was blowing the rain down from the German forests. It swept across the Rhine, over the fortress walls and was funnelled into icy blasts between the barrack blocks. Macro suspected that he was keenly disapproved of by his new-found peers and was determined to prove them wrong. Not that this resolution was working out terribly successfully. The administrative duties relating to the command of eighty men were proving to be a nightmare – ration-collection details, latrine rotas, sentry rotas, weapons inspections, barrack inspections, punishment ledgers, equipment procurement chits, arranging fodder for the section mules, taking charge of pay, savings and the funeral club.

The only help available for carrying out these duties came in the form of the century's clerk, a wizened old cove named Piso, who Macro suspected of being dishonest or simply incompetent. Macro had no way of finding out for himself, because he was all but illiterate. Brought up with only the most rudimentary knowledge of letters and numbers he could recognise most individually, but more than that was impossible. And now he was a centurion, a rank for whom literacy was a prerequisite. Doubtless the legate had naturally assumed Macro could read and write when he approved the appointment. If it came to light that he was no more literate than a Campanian farm boy, Macro knew he would be demoted at once. So far he had managed to get round the problem by delegating the paperwork to Piso and claiming that his other duties were keeping him too busy, but he was sure that the clerk had begun to suspect the truth. He shook his head as he trudged over to the fortress gate, pulling his red cloak tightly about him.

It was a dark night, made darker by the low clouds that completely obscured the sky; a sure sign that snow was on the way. From the gloom about him, Macro could hear a variety of sounds typical of the fortress existence that had been part of his life for over fourteen years now.

Mules brayed from stables at the far end of each barrack block and the voices of soldiers, talking and shouting, drifted out through the wavering light of candlelit windows. A bellow of laughter peeled out of a barrack block he was passing, followed by a lighter female laugh. Macro halted mid-stride and listened. Someone had managed to sneak a woman into the base. The woman laughed again and then began speaking in thickly accented Latin and was quickly hushed by her companion. This was a flagrant breach of regulations and Macro abruptly turned towards the block and laid his hand on the latch. Then paused, thinking. By rights he should burst in, loudly bellowing in parade-ground fashion, send the soldier to the guard-house, and have the woman thrown out of the base. But that meant completing an entry in the punishment book – more bloody writing.

Gritting his teeth, Macro released his grip and quietly stepped back into the street, just as the woman let out a shriek of laughter to prick his conscience. A quick glance about to make sure that no-one else was there to witness his failure to act and Macro hurried on towards the south gate. Bloody soldier deserved a good kicking, and if he had been in Macro's century that's how he'd have been dealt with; no paperwork needed, just a swift kick in the balls to ensure the punishment fitted the crime. Still, from her voice she could only have been one of those nasty German tarts from the native settlement that sprawled just outside the base. Macro consoled himself with the thought of the legionary concerned coming down with a bad dose of the clap.

Although the streets were dark, Macro moved instinctively in the right direction since no legionary base deviated from the standard design used in all camps and fortresses. In a matter of minutes, he had emerged on to the wider thoroughfare of the Via Praetoria and marched towards the gate where the street passed through the walls to the south of the base. The sentry who had interrupted Macro at the latrine was waiting at the foot of the stairs. He led the way into the gatehouse and up the narrow wooden staircase to the battlement level, where a lit brazier cast a warm red glow around the sentry room. Four legionaries were squatting close to the fire playing dice. As soon as they saw the centurion's head appear above the stairs they stood to attention.

'Easy lads,' Macro said. 'Carry on.'

The wooden door to the battlements sprang inwards with the wind as Macro lifted the latch and the brazier blazed momentarily as he stepped outside and slammed the door to. Up on the sentry walk the wind was biting and whipped Macro's cloak behind him, tugging at the clasp on his left shoulder. He shuddered and snatched it back, holding it tightly about his body.

'Where?'

The sentry peered out through the crenellations into the darkness and pointed his javelin at a tiny flickering light swinging from the back of a wagon approaching from the south. Straining his eyes as he stared into the wind, Macro could make out the outline of the wagon and, behind it, a body of men plodding along the track. At the rear of the column came the more orderly progress of the escort whose job was to stop the stragglers slowing the pace. Maybe two hundred men in all.

'Shall I call out the guard, sir?'

Macro turned towards the sentry. 'What did you say?'

'Shall I call out the guard, sir?'

Macro eyed the man wearily. Syrus was one of the youngest men in the century and, although Macro had learned the names of most of his command, he knew little of their characters or histories as yet. 'Been in the army long?'

'No, sir. Only a year in December.'

Not long out of training then, Macro thought. A stickler for regulations, which he no doubt applied in every circumstance. He'd learn in time; how to compromise between following strict procedure and doing what was needed to get by.

'So then, why do we need to call out the guard?'

'Regulations, sir. If an unidentified body of men is approaching the camp in force the guard century should be called out to man the gate and adjacent walls.'

Macro raised his eyebrows in surprise. The quotation was word perfect. Syrus clearly took his training seriously. 'And what then?'

'Sir?'

'What happens next?'

'The duty centurion, after assessing the situation determines whether or not to call a general alarm,' Syrus continued tonelessly, then hurriedly added, 'Sir.'

'Good man.' Macro smiled and the sentry smiled back in relief, before Macro turned back towards the approaching column. 'Now then, exactly how threatening do you think that lot is? Do they scare you, soldier? Do you think all two hundred of them are going to charge over here, climb the walls and slaughter every mother's son of the Second Legion . . . Well, do you?'

The sentry looked at Macro, looked carefully at the flickering lights for a new moments and then turned back sheepishly. 'I don't think so.'

'I don't think so, *sir*,' said Macro gruffly as he punched the lad on the shoulder.

'Sorry, sir.'

'Tell me, Syrus. Did you attend the sentry briefing before the watch?'

'Of course, sir.'

'Did you pay attention to every detail?'

'I think so, sir.'

'Then you would recall me saying that a replacement convoy was due to arrive at the base, wouldn't you? And then you wouldn't have had to haul me out of the latrine and spoil a particularly good shit.'

The sentry was crestfallen and he could not bear the long-suffering expression on his centurion's face. 'I'm sorry, sir. Won't happen again.'

'You see that it doesn't. Or I'll have you on double duties for the rest of the year. Now get the rest of the lads ready at the gate. I'll deal with the recognition call.'

Shamefaced, the sentry saluted and went back into the gatehouse. Soon Macro could hear the sounds of the guard rousing themselves and descending the wooden stairs to the main gate. Macro smiled. The lad was keen and felt guilty about his mistake. Guilty enough to make sure that it never happened again. That was good. That's how dependable soldiers were made – there was no such thing as a born soldier, Macro reflected.

A sudden blast of wind buffeted Macro and he retreated into the shelter of the gatehouse. Inside he positioned himself close to the glowing brazier and let out a sigh of relief as the warmth soaked into his body. After a few moments, Macro opened the small viewing shutter and looked out into the night. The convoy was nearer now and he could make out the wagon in detail as well as the individual men in the following column. A miserable bunch of recruits, he thought, not an ounce of spirit in them. You could tell that by the apathetic way they trudged along, even though they were in sight of shelter.

Then it began to rain, quite suddenly, large drops flung diagonally by the wind that stung the skin. Even that failed to increase the pace of the convoy and, with a despairing shake of the head, Macro began the formalities. He opened the main shutter, leaned his head out of the window and filled his lungs.

'Halt there!' he shouted. 'Identify yourselves!'

The wagon reined in a hundred feet from the wall and a figure beside the driver rose to reply. 'Reinforcement convoy from Aventicum and escort, Lucius Batiacus Bestia commanding.'

'Password?' Macro demanded even though he knew Bestia well enough, the senior centurion of the Second Legion and therefore very much his superior.

'Hedgehog. Permission to approach?'

'Approach, friend.'

With a crack of the whip the wagoneer urged the bullocks up the rise that led to the gateway and Macro

16

crossed over to the shutter that opened on to the inside of the fort. Down below, the sentries were clustered by the sidegate trying to keep out of the rain.

'Open the gate,' Macro called down. One of the soldiers quickly drew out the locking pin and the others slid the beam back into the recess. With a heavy wooden groan, the gates were pulled open just as the wagon reached the top of the rise, its momentum carrying it through the gate into the base. Looking down from the guardhouse, Macro watched the wagon draw up to one side. Bestia jumped down from the driver's bench and waved his vine cane at the sodden procession of new recruits passing by.

'Come on, you bastards! Move! Quickly now! The sooner you're in, the sooner you can get warm and dry.'

The recruits, who had followed the wagon for over two hundred miles, automatically began to mill round it once inside the gate. Most wore travelling cloaks and carried their few belongings in blankets tied across the shoulder. The poorest recruits had nothing, some didn't even have cloaks, and they shivered miserably as the wind drove the freezing rain at them. At the rear stood a small chain-gang of criminals who had opted for the army rather than remain in prison.

Bestia immediately waded into the growing crowd with his cane, beating a clear space for himself.

'Don't just stand there like a herd of sheep! Make way for some real soldiers. Get over to the far side of the street and line up facing this way. NOW!'

The last of the recruits stumbled in through the gate and followed the rest to take up an uneven line opposite the wagon. Finally the escort marched in, twenty men in step, who halted simultaneously at one word of command from Bestia. He paused for effect to let the implicit comparison sink in as Macro ordered the sentries to shut the gate and return to their duties. Bestia turned back to the recruits, legs astride and hands on hips.

'Those men,' Bestia nodded over his shoulder, 'belong to the Second Legion – the Augusta – the toughest in the entire Roman army, and you'd better not forget it. There is no barbarian tribe, however remote, who hasn't heard of us and who doesn't live in mortal fear of us. The Second has killed more of these scum, and conquered more of their land, than any other unit. We have been able to do this because we train men to be the meanest, dirtiest, hardest fighters in the civilised world . . . You, on the other hand, are soft, worthless piles of shit. You are not even men. You are the lowest fucking form of life that ever claimed to be Roman. I despise each and every last fucking one of you, and I will weed out every worthless piece of scum so that only the best join my beloved Second Legion and serve under our eagle. I've watched you all the way from Aventicum – and, ladies, I'm not impressed. You signed up and now you are all mine. I will train you, I will hurt you, I will make men of you. Then – *if* and when I decide you are ready – then I will let you become a legionary. If any one of you doesn't give me every last shred of energy and commitment then I will break him – with this.' He held the gnarled vine cane aloft for all to see. 'Do you shits understand?'

There was a murmured assent from the recruits, some

of whom were so tired they just nodded.

'What was that supposed to be?' Bestia shouted angrily. 'I can hardly fucking hear you!'

He moved into the crowd and grabbed a recruit roughly by the collar of his travelling cloak. Macro noticed for the first time that this recruit was dressed differently from the others. The cut of his cloak was unmistakably expensive – no matter how much mud was caked on to it. The recruit was taller than the rest, but thin and delicate-looking – just the kind of victim to make an example of.

'What the hell is this? What the fuck is a recruit doing with a better cloak than I can afford? You steal it, boy?'

'No,' the recruit replied calmly. 'A friend gave it to me.'

Bestia slammed his vine cane into the boy's stomach and the recruit doubled over and slumped to the ground, hands splashing into a puddle. Bestia stood over him, cane raised for another blow.

'Whenever you open your mouth you call me *sir*! Understand?'

Macro watched the young man gasp for air as he tried to reply, then Bestia swung the cane down on his back and the boy yelped.

'I said, do you understand?'

'Yes, s-sir!' the recruit cried out.

'Louder!'

'YES, SIR!'

'That's better. Now, let's see what else you've got.'

The centurion grabbed the blanket carrier and wrenched it free. The contents spilled out on to the muddy ground; some spare clothes, a small flask, some bread, two scrolls and a leather-bound writing set.

'What the . . . ?' The centurion stared down at the last of the contents. Then he slowly looked up at the new recruit. 'What's this?'

'My writing materials, sir!'

'Writing materials? What does a legionary want with writing materials?'

'I promised my friends in Rome I'd write, sir.'

'Your friends?' Bestia grinned. 'No mother to write to? No father, eh?'

'Dead, sir.'

'Know his name?'

'Of course, sir. He was . . .'

'Quiet!' Bestia interrupted. 'I don't give a toss who he was. Here, you're all bastards as far as I'm concerned. So then, what's your name, bastard?'

'Quintus Licinius Cato . . . sir.'

'Well then, Cato, I know only two types of legionary who can write – spies and those who think they're so bloody wonderful they're going to be officers. Which are you?'

The recruit eyed him warily. 'Neither, sir.'

'Then you won't need this stuff, will you?' Bestia kicked the writing kit and the scrolls towards the drainage gully in the middle of the street.

'Careful, sir!'

'What did you say?' The centurion spun round, cane at the ready. 'What did you say to me?'

'I said careful, sir. One of those scrolls is a personal message for the legate.'

20

'A personal message for the legate! Well, I . . .'

With a grin, Macro saw that the grizzled centurion was momentarily floored; he'd heard it all before, every excuse, every explanation – but not this one. What on earth could a recruit be doing with a letter for the legate? A first-class mystery, and one that had knocked Bestia off his perch. Not for long though – the centurion stabbed his cane towards the scrolls.

'Bloody well pick that stuff up and bring it here. Just arrived here and you're already messing the base up! Fucking recruits,' he grumbled. 'You make me puke. Well, you heard me. Pick it up!'

As the tall recruit leant down to retrieve his belongings Bestia barked out a series of orders, assigning batches of recruits to members of the escort to be guided to their units.

'Now, get moving! NOT YOU!' Bestia shouted at the lone recruit, who had managed to stuff his belongings back into his pack and had turned towards the safety of the others standing in the pouring rain. 'Over here! What are the rest of you staring at?'

The escort legionaries started to tell off their charges. While the recruits were cajoled and herded into groups, Bestia snatched the scroll Cato held out to him. Taking care to keep it out of the rain as much as possible, he read the address waxed on to it. He checked the seal as well, rechecked the address and paused a moment to consider his next step. He happened to glance up at the gate and saw Macro grinning. That settled it.

'Macro! Get your arse down here.'

Moments later, Macro was standing to attention in

front of Bestia, blinking as the rain dripped down from the brim of his helmet into his eyes.

'This seems genuine.' Bestia wagged the scroll under the junior officer's nose. 'I want you to take this and escort our friend here to headquarters.'

'I'm on sentry duty.'

'Well then, I'll relieve you till you get back. Get going.'

Bastard! Macro swore silently. Bestia had no idea of the letter's significance, or whether it was even genuine. But he dare not take the risk. Communications to legates took strange routes these days, even from the highest sources. Better to let someone else take the blame if the letter proved to be worthless.

'Yes, sir,' Macro replied bitterly as he accepted the scroll.

'Don't be too long, Macro. I've got a warm bed waiting for me.'

Bestia strode off to the gatehouse and climbed the stairs to the shelter of the sentry room. Macro glared after him. Then turned to have a good look at the new recruit who was causing him to make a long trek to the headquarters building through the driving rain. He had to look up to examine the lad who was nearly a foot taller than himself. Under the brim of the travelling cloak, a mop of black hair had been flattened into straggling trails by the rain. Below a flat brow, a pair of piercing brown eyes in deep sockets glinted either side of a long thin nose. The boy's mouth was clamped shut, but the bottom lip trembled slightly. Although the clothes were soaked and splattered with mud from the long journey from the depot at Aventicum, they were of a surprisingly good quality. As for the writing set, the books and this letter for the legate . . . Well, this recruit was something else. Clearly no stranger to money but, if so, then why the hell join the army?

'Cato, wasn't it?'

'Yes.'

'I'm also called sir.' Macro smiled.

Cato stiffened into an approximation of the attention position and Macro laughed. 'At ease, boy. At ease. You're not on parade until tomorrow morning. Now let's get this letter delivered.'

Macro gave the boy a gentle push away from the gate in the direction of the centre of the base, where the headquarters block loomed in the distance. As they walked, he looked at the letter in detail for the first time and let out a low whistle.

'Know what this seal is?'

'Yes – sir. The imperial seal.'

'And why would the imperial service use a recruit as a courier?'

'I've no idea, sir,' Cato replied.

'Who is it from?'

'The Emperor.'

Macro choked back an exclamation. The boy really had his attention now. What the hell was the Emperor doing sending an imperial despatch via a bloody legionary recruit? Unless there was more to this boy than met the eye. Macro decided an uncommonly tactful approach was required if he was to discover more.

'Forgive my asking, but what are you doing here?'

'Doing here, sir? Joining the army, sir.'

'But why?' Macro persisted.

'It's to do with my father, sir. He was in the imperial service before his death.'

'What did he do?'

When the boy didn't answer, Macro turned and saw that his head was bowed low and his expression troubled. 'Well?'

'He was a slave, sir.' The embarrassment of the admission was clear, even to a bluff fellow like Macro. 'Before Tiberius manumitted him. I was born shortly before.'

'That's tough.' Macro sympathised; freed status did not apply to existing heirs. 'I take it you were manumitted soon after. Did your father buy you?'

'He wasn't allowed to, sir. For some reason Tiberius wouldn't let him. My father died a few months ago. In his will, he begged that I be set free on condition that I continue to serve the Empire. Emperor Claudius agreed, provided that I join the army, and here I am.'

'Hmmmm. Not much of a deal.'

'I don't agree, sir. I'm free now. Better than being a slave.'

'You really think so?' Macro smiled. It seemed like a poor exchange in status: the comforts of the palace with the hardship of life in the army – and the occasional opportunity to risk life and limb in battle. Macro had heard that some of the wealthiest and most powerful men in Rome were to be found amongst the slaves and freedmen employed in the imperial service.

'Anyway, sir,' Cato concluded, with a touch of bitterness. 'I didn't have any choice in the matter.'

Chapter Two

The guards on the gate at the headquarters building crossed spears as the two figures squelched out of the darkness, one with the crested helmet of a centurion and the other a bedraggled youth. They stepped into the flickering light of the torches clamped into the portico.

'Password?' a guard asked as he stepped forward.

'Hedgehog.'

'Your business, sir?'

'This boy has a despatch for the legate.'

'Just a moment, sir.' The guard disappeared into the inner courtyard leaving them under the watchful eyes of the other three guards, all large men – hand-picked for the legate's company of bodyguards. Macro undid his chin strap and removed his helmet before tucking it under his arm in preparation for meeting any senior officers. Cato pushed back his hood and brushed his straggling hair to the side. While they waited, Macro was aware of the youth glancing keenly about himself even as he shivered. A spark of sympathy pricked Macro as he recalled his own feelings on admission to the army; the excitement tinged with fear as he entered a completely unknown world with its strict rules, its dangers and its harsh life away from the comforts of his childhood home.

Cato busied himself with wringing water out of his cloak and a puddle soon formed about the boy's feet.

'Stop that!' Macro snapped. 'You're making a mess. You can dry out later.'

Cato looked up, hands wrapped around a tightly squeezed section of the hem. He was about to protest when he was aware that all the soldiers were looking at him with grave disapproval.

'I'm terribly sorry,' he muttered, and let go of the hem.

'Look here, lad,' Macro said as kindly as possible. 'No-one minds a soldier being in a mess when he can't help it. But what they do mind is a soldier who fidgets. It drives the army mad. Isn't that right, boys?' He turned to the guards and they nodded vigorously. 'So from now on, no fidgeting. Get used to standing still and waiting. You'll find that's what we spend most of our time doing.'

The guards sighed in sympathy.

Footsteps approached from the inner courtyard as the guard returned to the portico.

'Sir, please follow me. The boy too.'

'The legate's going to see us?'

'Don't know, sir. I've been ordered to escort you to the senior tribune first. This way please.'

He led them through a broad arch into a courtyard surrounded by a covered walkway. The rain gushed down off the roof tiles into guttering that channelled it out of the building into the street. The guard led them round each side of the courtyard until they reached a further doorway opposite the portico. Through the door, the building opened out into a large hall with offices along each side, except for the far wall where a purple curtain hid the Legion's shrine from view. Two standard bearers with drawn swords stood to attention in front of the curtain. The guard turned left, paused outside a door and tapped twice.

'Come,' a voice called and the guard quickly opened the door. Macro led the way inside, beckoning Cato to follow him. The room was narrow, but it stretched back a fair distance to accommodate a desk along one wall and a rack of scrolls at the end. A brazier glowed just inside the door, filling the room with a warm fug. Seated at the desk was a tribune. Macro knew him by sight, Aulus Vitellius, a former playboy in Rome but now on the path of a political career which began on the staff of a legion. Vitellius was an overweight man with a dark olive complexion that betrayed a southern Italian background. As his visitors entered, he pushed his chair back and faced them.

'Where's this letter?' The voice was deep and tinged with impatience.

Macro handed it over and then took a step back. Cato stood mutely at his side, next to the brazier. A faint smile of contentment played on his lips as the warmth entered his body and the shivering stopped.

Vitellius cast a quick glance at the letter and then ran his fingers over the imperial seal, consumed by curiosity. 'Do you know what this is?'

'Boy says it's . . .'

'I'm not asking you, Centurion . . . Well?'

'I believe it to be a personal letter from the Emperor Claudius, sir,' Cato responded.

Cato's stressing of 'personal' was not lost on the tribune and the latter fixed the boy with an icy stare. 'And what do you think could be so personal that the Emperor would trust its delivery to you?'

'I don't know, sir.'

'Exactly. So I think you can safely leave this with me. I'll see that the legate receives it in due course. Dismissed.'

Macro instantly moved towards the door, but the young recruit hesitated. 'Excuse me, sir. The scroll?'

Vitellius stared back, dumbfounded, as Macro quickly grabbed the youth's arm.

'Let's be off, lad. The tribune's a busy man.'

'I was told to deliver the scroll in person, sir.'

'How dare you,' Vitellius said quietly, eyebrows closing together as reflections from the brazier flickered across his dark eyes.

For a moment Macro watched the exchange of expressions; the tribune struggling to contain his anger and the boy, afraid but defiant. Then the tribune's eyes flashed towards the centurion and he forced a smile on to his lips.

'Right then, in person it is.' Vitellius stood up, scroll in hand. 'Come with me.'

Vitellius led them down a short passage into an ante-chamber where the legate's private secretary worked at a desk to one side of a large studded door. He looked up as they approached and, seeing Vitellius, wearily rose to his feet.

'Can I see the legate?' Vitellius asked briskly.

'Is it urgent, sir?'

'Imperial despatch.' Vitellius held out the letter so that the seal could be seen. The secretary instantly knocked on the door of the legate's office and entered without waiting for a reply, closing the door behind him. There was silence for a moment and then the door opened again. The secretary ushered Vitellius inside and held up a hand to the other two. From inside, Macro could clearly hear a raised voice, punctuated by an occasional monosyllable from Vitellius. The dressing down was mercifully brief but the tribune managed to fire a cold, hostile glare at the centurion as he passed out of the office back towards the admin hall.

'He'll see you now.' The secretary waved a finger at them.

Macro silently seethed with anger at Bestia. That bloody letter would do for him. Having been ordered to act as the boy's guide to the headquarters, Macro was about to face the wrath of the legate for imposing on his precious time. If Vitellius, a tribune, could be shouted down only the gods knew what the legate would say to a humble centurion. And it was all the bloody boy's fault. Macro instinctively passed on the look he had received from Vitellius, then gulped nervously as he marched smartly through the door, past the smug expression of the secretary. At that moment he would rather have faced ten howling mad Gaulish warriors single-handed.

The legate's office was unsurprisingly spacious. The far side was dominated by a black marble-topped table behind which sat Titus Flavius Sabinus Vespasian –

scowling as he looked up from the open letter in front of him.

'Right then, Centurion. What are you doing here?'

'Sir?'

'You're supposed to be on duty.'

'Orders, sir. I was told to show this new recruit to headquarters and see you got that letter.'

'Who ordered you?'

'Lucius Batiacus Bestia. He's covering the watch until I return, sir.'

'Oh, is he?' A frown creased the broad brow of Vespasian. Then his gaze switched to the young recruit standing one step behind and to one side of Macro, desperately hoping that immobility was the surest route to invisibility. The legate's eyes quickly looked over the boy, assessing his potential. 'You are Quintus Licinius Cato?'

'Yes, sir.'

'From the palace?'

'Yes, sir.'

'Bit unusual to say the least,' Vespasian mused. 'The palace doesn't generate too many recruits for the legions, my wife excepted – even she's finding it hard to adapt to the squalor of a legate's private accommodation. I doubt you will find our ways much to your taste but you're a soldier now and that's that.'

'Yes, sir.'

'This,' Vespasian waved the letter, 'is a letter of introduction. Normally my secretary deals with such trivial matters because I have better things to do – like, for example, commanding a legion. So you can imagine how annoyed I might have been to have the tribune waste his time and, more importantly, mine, with such a matter.'

Vespasian paused and the two visitors withered under his glare. Then, he continued, in a more moderate tone. 'However, since this letter is from Claudius, as you no doubt know, I must defer to his power to bother one of his legates with petty details. He tells me that, in gratitude for your late father's service to Rome, he has made you a freedman and wishes me to appoint you centurion in my legion.'

'Oh,' Cato replied. 'Is that good, sir?'

Macro spluttered with rage momentarily, before regaining control and bunching his fists hard against his thighs.

'Problem, Centurion?' Vespasian asked.

'No, sir,' Macro managed to respond through clenched teeth.

'Now then, Cato,' the legate continued mildly. 'There is absolutely no possibility of me appointing you centurion, whatever the Emperor wishes. How old are you?'

'Sixteen, sir. Seventeen next month.'

'Sixteen . . . Hardly old enough to be a man. Certainly too young to lead men.'

'Begging your pardon, sir, but Alexander was only sixteen when he commanded his first army in battle.'

Vespasian's eyebrows shot up in amazement. 'You consider yourself to be an Alexander? What do you know about military affairs?'

'I have studied them, sir. I am familiar with the works

of Xenophon, Herodotus, Livy and, of course, Caesar.'

'And that makes you an expert on the *modern* Roman army does it?' Vespasian was enjoying the youngster's hubris. 'Well, I must say, I only wish all our recruits were so versed in the arts of war. It would be novel to have an army march on its brains rather than its stomach. Would be quite something, wouldn't it, Centurion?'

'Yes, sir,' Macro replied. 'We'd all be headaching instead of bellyaching, sir.'

Vespasian looked at Macro in surprise. 'Was that meant to be a joke, centurion? I don't hold with junior officers being funny. This is the army, not some Plautus comedy.'

'Yes, sir. Who, sir?'

'A playwright,' Cato patiently explained to Macro. 'Plautus adapted material from Greek theatre—'

'That's enough, son,' Vespasian cut in. 'Save it for the literary salons, should you ever return to Rome. Now then, I've decided. You will not be a centurion.'

'But, sir . . .'

Vespasian held up a hand to silence him and then pointed at Macro. 'You see this man? Now, he's a centurion. The man who escorted you here from Aventicum is also a Centurion. How do you think they came to be centurions?'

Cato shrugged. 'I've absolutely no idea, sir.'

'No idea? Well, just you listen. This man, Macro, has been a legionary for many years – how many, centurion?'

'Fourteen years, sir.'

'Fourteen years. And in that time he has marched halfway across the known world and back. This man has fought in Jupiter knows how many battles and minor engagements. He has been trained to use every weapon in the army. He can march up to twenty miles a day in full armour carrying his kit. He has been trained to swim, build roads, bridges and forts. He has many other qualities besides. This man led his patrol to safety when the Germans cut them off on the far side of the Rhine. Then, and only then, was he even considered for promotion to the centurionate. Now which of these things can you do? Right now?'

Cato thought back a moment. 'I can swim, sir – a bit.'

'Have you considered a career in the navy?' Vespasian asked hopefully.

'No. I get seasick.'

'Oh dear. Well, I'm afraid that swimming doesn't quite qualify you for command, but since we're going to need every man we can train for next year I will allow you to join the Second Legion. Dismissed . . . that's the army way of saying, please be a good fellow and wait outside.'

'Yes, sir.'

Once the door had closed behind the young man, Vespasian shook his head. 'What's the world coming to? Think we can make a soldier out of him, Centurion?'

'No, sir,' Macro replied immediately. 'The army's too dangerous a place for theatre critics.'

'So is Rome,' Vespasian sighed, recalling those who had rashly ventured an opinion on the literary output of the late Caligula. Not that matters were much better under his successor, Claudius. The new Emperor's chief secretary, the freedman Narcissus, had spies everywhere, busy compiling reports on the loyalties of every Roman who might pose the least possible threat to the new regime. The atmosphere in the capital was poisonous following the failure of Scribonianus' coup attempt and Vespasian had recently been informed that several of his wife's friends were among those already arrested. Flavia herself had only recently joined him at the base, anxious and fearful, and not for the first time Vespasian wished that Flavia would be more circumspect in her choice of social companions. But that's what came your way, Vespasian considered, when you married a woman who had been brought up in the highly political atmosphere of the imperial household. Like the young man waiting outside. Vespasian looked up from his desk.

'Well, Centurion, we'll see what we can do for young Cato. Is your century up to strength? Didn't you lose your second-in-command recently?'

'Yes sir. The optio died this morning.'

'Good, that simplifies things. Sign the boy up in your century and make him an optio.'

'But, sir!'

'But nothing. That's my order. We can't make him a centurion and I can't bend an imperial dictate too far. So we're stuck with him. Dismissed.'

'Yes, sir.' Macro saluted, turned smartly and marched out of the office, cursing under his breath. The position of optio was traditionally within the patronage of a centurion and was worth a good deal of money. He would just have to make sure the lad didn't last too long, one way or another. After all, a soft city type who didn't seem to want to be here could easily be induced to seek a discharge given the right kind of prodding.

Cato was waiting for him outside. The lad half smiled and Macro nearly kicked him.

'So what's to happen to me, sir?'

'Just shut up and come with me.'

'Yes, sir.'

'Lads, I'd like you to meet the new optio.'

In the darkened mess room the faces turned towards the centurion, lit in pale orange by the few lamps they could afford to burn. Once their gaze flickered from their centurion to the tall young boy at his side few could conceal their amazement.

'Did you say . . . new optio, sir?' someone asked.

'That's right, Pyrax.'

'Isn't he a little, well, young?'

'Apparently not,' Macro replied bitterly. 'The Emperor's decreed a new selection procedure for junior officers. You have to be tall and skinny and familiar with selected Greek and Latin histories. And those who have bothered to read the odd work of literature are given preferential treatment.'

The men looked at him blankly but Macro was too cross to offer any form of explanation. 'Anyway, here he is. Pyrax, I want you to take him to my clerk. Get him written in and issue him with a seal. He's going to join your section.'

'Sir, I thought recruits could only be written in by officers.'

'Look, I'm too busy right now,' Macro blustered. 'Anyway, that's an order. I'm making him your responsibility. So get on with it.'

Macro rushed from the mess and hurried back down the passage to his quarters. Piso was waiting outside his small office with some papers.

'Sir, if you could just sign . . .'

'Later.' Macro waved a hand at him and snatched up a dry cloak as he made for the outside door. 'Have to get back on duty.'

As the door slammed after him, Piso shrugged and returned to his desk.

Some time later, Cato was sitting bolt upright on the top bunk of a section room. Such was his height that on the top of his head he could feel the straw which lay under the roof tiles. He flinched, suddenly wondering if there were any rats in the rafters, and nervously twisted the small lead ingot that hung from a thong tied around his neck. It bore his name, his legion and the imperial seal. It would be with him until he left the army, or died in battle. Then it would be used to identify his body. Letting his chin rest on his knees, Cato wondered how he was going to get out of this appalling situation. The section room, with cramped bunks for eight men, was no better than one of the stables reserved for work horses at the palace.

And these men!

Well, they were animals. Pyrax had introduced him round the mess and Cato had been hard pressed not to reveal his disgust at the foul-smelling, boozy, farting, belching legionaries. They, for their part, had seemed unsure how to regard him. There was some resentment to be sure. Apparently an optio was a rank many were struggling to achieve. Nominally he was their superior, but he was in no way given to understand that he would be treated as such.

Conversation was limited to a discussion of who had screwed the most women, killed the most barbarians, spat the furthest, farted the loudest – that kind of thing. Stimulating to the senses maybe, but it left the mind a little cold. After what seemed a decent length of time, Cato had asked if Pyrax might be so kind as to show him to his room. Every face in the room had turned towards him, some wide-eyed and open-mouthed. Cato sensed he had somehow put his foot in it and decided that an early night would clear the air.

Chapter Three

Late the following afternoon, as dusk gathered around the fortress and the sharp winter air began to bite, an exhausted Cato hauled his feet into the barracks. The section room was quiet but, as he shut the door, Cato saw that he was not alone. He felt a twinge of irritation at this intrusion into the moment of privacy he had been looking forward to. Pyrax was sitting on his bunk darning a spare tunic by the fading light of the open shutter. He looked up as Cato crossed to his bunk and climbed up on to it fully clothed.

'Hard day, new boy?'

'Yes,' Cato grunted, not wanting to provoke any discussion.

'It only gets worse.'

'Oh.'

'Think you can hack it?'

'Yes,' Cato said firmly. 'I will.'

'Nah!' Pyrax shook his head. 'You're too soft. I give you a month.'

'A month?' Cato replied angrily.

'Yeah. A month if you're sensible . . . More if you're a fool.'

'What are you talking about?'

'There's no point in you being here. You ain't cut out for it – just a wet kid.'

'I'm nearly seventeen. I can be a soldier.'

'Still young for a soldier. And you ain't in shape. Bestia's going to break you in no time.'

'He won't! I promise you that.' Cato unwisely allowed himself a display of adolescent bravado. 'I'd rather die.'

'It may come to that.' Pyrax shrugged. 'Can't say many'd be sorry.'

'What do you mean?'

'Nothing . . .' He shrugged again and continued sewing as Cato glared at him, quite oblivious to the burning shame he had provoked in the youngster. Instead Pyrax concentrated on making sure that he kept the line of stitches quite straight as he worked along the seam. Cato watched without interest; he had seen the palace slaves at work repairing clothes all his life. All the same, spinning, weaving and sewing had always been the work of women and it was something of a novelty to see a man wielding a needle so adroitly.

Cato was sharply aware that his appointment as optio was causing him a lot of enmity. Already he seemed to have fallen foul of Bestia, the centurion in charge of training. Worse still, some of the recruits were openly hostile to him, particularly a group of men sent to the legion from a prison in Perusia, bound in chains for the entire journey. Their self-appointed leader was a thick-set, ugly man who excelled in the latter description, so much so that it was inevitable that he be named Pulcher – the beautiful. One day on the march Cato had found himself immediately behind Pulcher when the man had demanded a drink from Cato's flask of wine. It was a small thing, but the tone with which the demand had been made was so loaded with menace that Cato had handed the flask over at once. Pulcher drank deeply, then, when Cato asked for the flask to be returned, had passed the wine to his friends.

'You want it, boy?' Pulcher had curled his lips into a sneer. 'Then you take it.'

'Give it back to me.'

'Make me.'

Cato winced at the memory and his conscience once again demanded of him whether this was really the behaviour of a proper soldier. A proper soldier would have struck the man at once and taken the flask back. But, the rational side of his mind argued, a man would have to be built like a brick shithouse to take on Pulcher, with his solid limbs and hands like shovels. As if reading his expression, Pulcher had snarled and Cato instinctively stepped back, causing everyone to laugh. He had burned with shame, and still did, even though he told himself that retreat from superior forces was perfectly reasonable, intellectually virtuous in fact. A kindly soldier from the escort had retrieved the flask and tossed it back to Cato with a laugh. Pulcher spat in his direction before the soldier prodded him back into line with the butt of his spear.

'I'll see you in camp, boy,' Pulcher snarled, raising his chains. 'As soon as I get rid of these.'

Since their arrival at the fortress the army had kept the recruits busy and Cato hoped that Pulcher had forgotten about him. He had striven to keep as far from the man as possible, not even meeting his gaze, in a bid to become invisible. Now, he had returned to the barracks rather than remain with the other recruits after they had been dismissed at the end of the day. It was essential, he reflected, to make some friends quickly. But how? And who? The others had bonded into little groups during the journey from Aventicum – while he had been reading bloody Virgil, he angrily reminded himself. What he would give to begin that journey afresh, knowing what he did now.

Alone, and a long way from his friends back in Rome. For a moment misery welled up inside him and Cato's eyes stung with tears. He turned towards the wall and buried his face in the coarse material of the straw-stuffed bolster. He felt his chest shudder and suddenly felt angry, angry at himself, angry that he wasn't man enough to cope without tears and angry that nothing in his life had prepared him for this. All his smug Greek tutors and their stupid admiration for only the finest rhetoric and poetry – what bloody good were they now? How could poetry protect him from that animal, Centurion Bestia? At this moment he would have exchanged all his learning for a single friend.

Pyrax paused and looked up, needle poised above the tunic. He had heard the new boy turn over and recognised the stifled sob for what it was. Pyrax shook his head sadly. Most recruits were old enough and hardy enough to cope. Then there were boys, like this one, who really shouldn't be in the army. It might be the making of them, as some soldiers argued, but equally it might destroy them.

The boy sobbed again, muffled as much as possible by the bolster.

'Hey!' Pyrax said harshly. 'Do you mind? I'm trying to concentrate here.'

Cato stirred. 'Sorry. I think I've got a cold.'

'Yeah,' Pyrax nodded. 'Sure. Bound to happen in this weather.'

Cato rubbed his face on the corner of the rough military blanket, drying his tears and trying to make it look as if he was blowing his nose. 'There.'

'Better?'

'Yes, thank you,' Cato replied, grateful that someone was taking interest in him. Then he was immediately worried that his chance to talk to Pyrax alone might be stalled if anyone interrupted. 'Where are all the others?'

'Dice game in the mess room. I'm going to join 'em once I've fixed this. Want to come with me and meet the lads?'

'No thanks. I need some sleep.'

'Suit yourself.'

'Tell me,' Cato suddenly turned and propped himself up, 'is that Centurion Bestia as much of a bastard as he seems?'

'How do you think he got the name Bestia? But don't take it to heart, he treats all recruits the same way.'

'Maybe,' Cato said doubtfully, 'but he seems to have it in for me in particular.'

'What do you expect?' Pyrax said through gritted teeth as he pulled the end of a knot tight and then cut off the spare thread. 'You're in the camp for one night and you're promoted to a rank most of us have to wait years for.'

Cato watched the man closely before speaking. 'You resent it?'

'Of course. You've not proved yourself in any way. You're just a boy.' He shrugged. 'It ain't right.'

Cato flushed with guilt and embarrassment, glad that the dim light partially hid his expression. 'I didn't ask for it.'

'It don't make sense. Direct appointments are made for men with some kind of army experience but you? I'd dearly love to know the reason why.'

'It was a reward for my father.'

'Hah! That's a good one!'

The light had finally died outside and Pyrax put his tunic and sewing kit to one side. 'By the way,' Pyrax paused at the door, 'don't fall asleep in your kit. It'll need to be cleaned for the morning. Bestia hates untidy soldiers. If he has taken a dislike to you, don't give him any opportunity to make the most if it, eh?'

'Thanks.'

'Sleep well, new boy.'

'My name's . . .' Cato started to say, but the door had already closed behind Pyrax and the darkened room swallowed up the protest. He was still for a moment, and nearly fell asleep, but Pyrax's warning jolted him back to consciousness. He sat up, groping with his tired fingers for the buckles at the side of the leather jerkin. The drill instructors had kept the new recruits on their feet since that day's dawn had broken what seemed like an age before. He had been kicked out of bed while it was still dark and pushed outside into the street where the other recruits were being rounded up. Still half asleep, shivering in the chill of the pale dawn light and shrinking from the fine drizzle in the air, their breaths had risen in grey wisps as they were led to the quartermaster's stores where the external trappings of civilian life were peeled away and replaced with the uniform of a legionary.

'Excuse me!' Cato had called out. 'Excuse me.'

The quartermaster's assistant looked back over his shoulder. 'What is it?'

'Well, this tunic, it seems a bit big for me.'

The assistant laughed. 'No, mate. It's the right size. You're the one that's the wrong size. You're in the army now. One size fits all.'

'But look! This is ludicrous.' Cato held the tunic up in front of his body, it was far too wide for his thin frame, and his height drew the hem well above his knees. 'My legs will freeze. Is there nothing else?'

'No. You'll grow into it.'

'What?' Cato replied incredulously. 'I'm the shape I am. I'm not suddenly going to shrink and grow outwards. Now find me something the right size.'

'I told you. That's all there is, and you're stuck with it.'

The raised voices were audible right through the storeroom and all the other recruits and assistants paused to look in their direction. In the small office behind the counter, a chair screeched back on the flagstone floor and a burly man emerged angrily from the door.

'What's all the bloody shouting about?'

'Are you in charge here?' asked Cato, glad to see someone in authority he could make a complaint to. It was as bad as some of the shops in Rome. Everyone was using cheap help these days, staff who neither cared nor knew about their goods. He had been forced to complain about such matters to managers many times before when purchasing for the palace and knew the best approach to adopt. 'I was trying to explain to this man . . .'

'Who the bloody hell are you?' The quartermaster bellowed.

'Quintus Licinius Cato, Optio of the Sixth Century, Fourth Cohort.'

The quartermaster frowned for a moment and then laughed. 'Oh, I've heard all about you! Optio! Hah! Well then, optio,' he smiled. 'What seems to be the problem?'

'Look here. I just want this man to provide me with a garment my size.'

'May I?' The quartermaster reached out for the tunic, and Cato gladly returned it to him. The quartermaster made an elaborate show of examining the tunic, running his hand over the crude stitching and finally holding it up to the light coming in from the open shutters.

'Yes,' he concluded. 'This is a standard-issue tunic all right. Nothing wrong with it.'

'But—'

'Shut it!' The quartermaster flung the tunic back across the counter. 'Now take the bloody thing and don't waste any more of my time.'

'But—'

'And call me "sir" – you snotty little upstart!'

Cato opened his mouth to utter a horrified protest, but managed to bite his tongue at the last moment. 'Yes, sir.'

'Good. Now get the rest of your kit.' The quartermaster turned back to his office, then noticed that everyone had stopped to enjoy the performance. 'What the hell are you lot gawping at?'

The stores building instantly turned back into heaving activity as the new recruits collected their kit allocations. With a shrug, Cato folded the tunic and stood at the counter as the assistant piled his clothing and equipment on to the battered wooden surface. In addition to the tunic was a pair of woollen breeches, a yellow leather jerkin, a thick red cloak waterproofed with animal fat, boots shod with iron nails and a mess tin. The assistant shoved a slate towards him. 'Sign here, or make your mark.'

'What's this?'

'Receipt for your civvy clothes.'

'What?'

'You're not allowed to keep your clothes. You give 'em to me after you change into uniform. We sell them for you in the local market and give you the proceeds.'

'Absolutely not!' Cato said firmly.

The assistant turned back towards the office and opened his mouth to call out.

'Wait!' Cato stopped him. 'I'll sign. But do you have to sell them? I want to keep my boots and travel cloak.'

'Recruits have to be in uniform. Can't just wear any old thing. Anyway there's no room to store clothes. But I promise we'll get you a good price.'

For some reason Cato doubted he would see much of a return on his clothes. 'How can I be sure you'll give me the full sum?'

46

'Are you accusing me of dishonesty?' the assistant replied in mock horror.

Cato slowly stripped naked and pulled on the standard-issue tunic. It was as ill-fitting as he had feared, reminding him of the short tunics worn by the prostitutes back in Rome. The breeches were uncomfortable and had to be tied tightly above his skinny hips to stop them falling down. And they itched terribly. Almost as uncomfortable were the heavy military boots made of thick-cut leather and laced with tough thongs. The nail studs on the bottom made a clattering sound on the stone floor and some of the younger recruits were amusing themselves by kicking sparks off the paving, until the quartermaster tucked his head round the door and shouted at them to stop. When the boots were laced and tied Cato pulled the heavy leather jerkin over his head and fastened the buckles on each side. It was difficult, as the leather of the new jerkin was stiff. It was hard to bend forward and he could only just reach his laces with a great deal of straining. He noticed that, for some reason, his jerkin had a piece of white linen stitched over the right shoulder – a quick look round the room revealed that his was the only jerkin with a patch.

The main door to the stores building momentarily darkened and Cato looked up to see Centurion Bestia enter and stand just inside the room shaking his head pitifully as he surveyed the new recruits, tapping his silvered greaves with the tip of his cane.

'Stand still!' he shouted and the room instantly fell silent. As he slowly strolled down the length of the storeroom the recruits nervously fell back against the wall.

Bestia snorted derisively. 'Hah! I've never seen such a bunch of women! Right then, girls – outside now!'

The drizzle had cleared away with the dawn and the sun glowed through a slight haze. The air was just cold enough to be fresh to the skin and, all around, the fortress bustled with activity. Training raw recruits was something Bestia greatly enjoyed. Like every drill instructor, he had amassed a collection of useful invective for all occasions and comfortably slipped into the required role of rock-hard intolerance with subtle hints of a warm-hearted concern for his charges. In time they would come to regard him as a father figure – though perhaps not all of them.

As Bestia's eyes swept down the ranks they fixed on Cato, looming nearly half a head above the rest – his height emphasised by the fact he stood immediately to the left of Pulcher.

'You! Yes, you, Mister-I've-got-a-bloody-letter-from-my-friend-the-Emperor!' Bestia bellowed as he strode towards Cato and sharply poked his vine cane into the white shoulder patch. 'What the bloody hell is this?'

Cato winced. 'I don't know, sir.'

'Don't know! How long have you been in the army? Almost half a bloody day and you still can't recognise badges of rank!' Standing right in front of Cato, he glared up into the youngster's face barely a span apart. 'Just what kind of fucking soldier are you?'

'I don't know sir, I . . .'

'Don't look down at me!' Bestia screamed, splattering saliva. 'Keep your fucking eyes straight ahead! At all times. Do you understand me?'

Cato flicked his eyes up and stiffened. 'Yes, sir.'

'So what the hell are you doing with optio's insignia?'

'I am an optio, sir.'

'Bollocks!' Bestia shouted. 'We do not promote ladies overnight.'

'I was, in matter of fact, made an optio last night, sir,' Cato explained.

'So then, optio today, centurion tomorrow, tribune the day after . . . At this rate you'll make fucking Emperor by the end of the week! You take me for a fool, boy?'

'Er, excuse me, sir,' one of the drill instructors said quietly from behind Bestia. 'He *is* an optio, sir.'

'What?' Bestia jerked a thumb at Cato. 'Him?'

'Afraid so, sir. Direct commission from the legate. It's been entered on the new recruit roster, sir.' The drill instructor held out a wax board and pointed out Cato's name.

'Quintus Licinius Cato, optio.' Bestia read out loud. Then he turned back to Cato with clear menace in his eyes. 'So that's what the letter was about! Friends in powerful places, eh? Well, it won't help you. Optio you may be, but while you're on basic training you get the same treatment as the rest. Understand?'

'Yes, sir.'

'In fact,' Bestia leaned close to him, whispering, 'I'll treat you worse. You got the promotion – now you're fucking going to have to earn it.'

Then he spun round and strode away. He took up a position ten paces ahead of the front rank of recruits. 'First lesson, ladies. The attention pose. Your drill instructors have placed you in four ranks, exactly one pace apart from the man beside you, and two paces between ranks. Memorise your position. In future, when I tell you to form ranks you will go to the position you are now in, at once. The correct posture for unarmed attention position is this.'

Bestia dropped his cane and stiffened, his chest thrust out, shoulders back, head up, arms straight down with palms flattened against the sides of his thighs. He paused a moment. 'You all see that? Right then, let's see you do it.'

The recruits self-consciously did their best to adopt the pose while the drill instructors went down the ranks, making adjustments where necessary. Once they were content Bestia continued. 'Next thing. When standing at attention you must at all times fix your eyes straight ahead – whatever happens. And I *mean* whatever happens, ladies. If bloody Venus herself rides past accompanied by a thousand naked virgins and I see any one of you so much as flicker his eyes to one side, I will beat the living shit out of him. Understand? I SAID, DO YOU UNDERSTAND?'

The recruits flinched before nervously replying in an overlapping wave of yesses.

'Louder! I want to fucking hear you this time!'

'YES, SIR!' The recruits roared.

'Better . . .' Bestia smiled. 'Think of yourselves as a part of one body. You will move, talk and think as one from now on . . . Right then, over to the armourer for your weapons. Now, when I say, "Prepare to march . . . march!" you will lead off on your left foot and follow me keeping in position. I will call out the step and I'll keep it slow. Right then, ladies. Prepare to march! March! Left. Right. Left. Right . . . Left . . . Left . . . Left.'

Led by the centurion and flanked by the drill instructors, the recruits ambled off in a long straggling column. Cato tried to keep in time but found that the recruit in front of him, Pulcher, had a short stride, and Cato had to concentrate hard on shortening his pace so as not to collide. It took a considerable act of faith to believe that any army could get two such differently proportioned men to march at the same pace. Almost as if the gods had decided to prove the point Cato scraped his boot down Pulcher's ankle.

'Shit! Watch it, you bastard!' Pulcher turned angrily.

'You! No speaking in ranks!' A drill instructor shouted. 'You're on a charge! Get moving!'

The stocky recruit scowled once at Cato and quickly fell back into step. A moment later Pulcher hissed over his shoulder, 'You'll pay for that, mate.'

'I'm sorry,' Cato whispered back.

'Sorry ain't good enough.'

'It was a mistake.'

'Tough shit.'

'But . . .'

'Shut your fucking mouth, before you get me into any more trouble.'

Cato marched silently behind Pulcher, making sure that his feet kept a safe distance behind the man's heels.

The recruits looked confused, Macro reflected with a smile as he watched them from the chief armourer's desk. They had all received, and signed for, their issue of

51

helmet, mail shirt and dagger, and swaggered around the armoury the way he had seen thousands of new recruits do before. The thrill of wearing a soldier's uniform for the first time was ageless and the recruits looked at each other admiringly. Then, the armourers had started issuing the weighted wooden swords, large rectangular wicker shields and training spears. The recruits were staring at their weapons dumbfounded, holding them at arms' length in disgust.

'Always the same, isn't it?' Macro grinned.

'One-day wonders.' Scaevola complained. 'They never learn. What is wrong with young men today?'

'Same problem as ever. Even you were like them once.'

'Bollocks.' Scaevola spat from his toothless mouth. 'Now tell me, young Macro, what are you doing here? Don't see you from one year to the next. Last time we had a quiet drink, you were a bloody legionary. Now look at you. Centurion Macro. Bloody legion's gone to the dogs.' He looked up and caught sight of the twinkle in the centurion's eyes. 'If you've just come by to wind me up . . . ?'

'Not this time.' Macro smiled and raised his cup. 'Just to share some wine with a veteran, and exchange the odd scrap of news.'

'The odd scrap of news!' Scaevola said contemptuously. 'I know why you're here.'

'Oh yes?'

'It wouldn't be anything to do with the bloody inventory the legate's ordered, would it?'

'Of course not.' Macro reached over with the flask and topped Scaevola up. 'Why would I be interested in that?'

'You'd be the only one in the legion who wasn't.' Scaevola took a swig. 'Anyway, I'm not saying nothing. Orders.'

'Yes,' Macro repeated thoughtfully. 'Orders. I wonder where we're being sent? Hope it's somewhere warm for a change. I'm bloody sick of Germany. Freezing in winter, baking in summer and it's impossible to get any decent wine – cheaply that is.'

The last remark was pointed. The wine they were drinking was from Macro's last jar of Falernian, not the acidic Gaulish brew the local traders peddled. He hoped Scaevola appreciated the gesture, and also hoped that it might loosen the veteran's tongue. It wasn't just for curiosity – a centurion needed to plan ahead. It was useful to know where the Legion was being sent so that he could prepare for the transfer and buy in whatever he needed for the journey before the news broke officially and supplies were snapped up and the local traders charged premium prices. With a tip of his head Scaevola emptied his cup and Macro instantly refilled it. 'Wherever we go, I hope there's something decent to drink.'

'Fat chance!' Scaevola snorted. 'You'd better enjoy this stuff. Won't be much booze over there.'

'None at all?' Macro feigned horror.

'None.' Scaevola replied, then abruptly stood up and shouted over Macro's shoulder. 'There's nothing bloody wrong with that sword! Hold it properly!'

Macro turned on his stool and searched out the target of Scaevola's anger. Standing out, as usual, was that infernal new boy, examining his wooden short sword as he held it by the tip of the point.

'But, sir. This isn't a proper sword. It's wood.'

'Of course it's bloody wood.'

As Centurion Bestia pushed his way through the crowd of recruits to see what the fuss was all about he bawled out. 'What? You causing trouble again? What's the matter now? Sword the wrong size?'

'No, sir. It's wooden. Not a proper sword, sir.'

'Wooden? Of course, it's bloody wooden. It's not a proper sword because you're not a proper soldier. If you become a real soldier, then you get to play with the real thing.'

Bestia filled his lungs to address all the recruits. 'As some of you may have realised, like sonny boy here, the weapons you have been given are not real. Because you do not yet deserve the real thing. If we just handed out dangerous weapons to you ladies you'd be injuring each other in no time. The army does not wish to save our enemies the effort. Before you can hold a sword you must respect it. You must learn how to use it properly. Same goes for the spear. You may find your weapons heavy. That's because they're twice the weight of the standard issue. You are soft, idle scum and we need to build you up and make men of you. We can only do that by training and exercise, and there'll be plenty of it, ladies. So get used to the weight. Now then, the sword belt is fastened with the sword hanging to the right, NOT to the left – like I've got it. That's for officers only . . . Hold your spear in your right hand, shield in the left and get into four ranks outside . . . Now!'

The recruits placed their shields and spears down and struggled with the stiff buckles of their swordbelts before grabbing their equipment and fleeing towards the door.

'Excellent stuff this wine,' Scaevola hinted. 'Shall we have another?'

There was hardly any left in the flask and Macro made sure that Scaevola had the lion's share, saving the dregs for himself.

'What were we talking about?' Scaevola asked.

'Drink. You were saying there's no good drink where the Legion's going.'

'Did I?' Scaevola raised his eyebrows.

'I suppose that means the far east,' Macro carried on casually. 'Nothing decent to drink, just that crap they make out of fermented goat's milk, so I've heard. Or worse, it might even be Judea.'

He watched Scaevola's face for any flicker of response, but the chief armourer merely took another draught of wine and nodded. 'It might be Judea . . . It might not.'

Macro sighed with frustration – getting information out of the canny old veteran was harder than getting the clap off a vestal virgin. He decided to attempt a new line of enquiry.

'Well, have you indented for any lightweight tunics?'

'Now why would I do that?' Scaevola frowned. 'Why on earth would I indent for those?'

Macro took a deep breath, fighting back his growing irritation at Scaevola's smug avoidance of the one answer he sought. 'Look here, Scaevola. Just tell me what you know. Just one word. Just the name of the place we're going. Just the name of the province will do. And I promise I won't tell another soul. You have my word.'

'Sure.' Scaevola smiled. 'Until someone comes up to

you with a flask of wine and tries to loosen your tongue. I have my orders. The legate wants to keep it quiet for as long as possible.'

'But why?'

'Let's just say that the men won't be best pleased when they find out where we're being sent.' Scaevola drained his cup. 'Now I must get back to work. Vespasian wants the inventory completed as soon as possible.'

'Well, thanks,' Macro said bitterly as he rose from the table. 'Thanks for nothing.'

'Not at all!' Scaevola beamed. 'Drop by any time.'

Macro didn't reply as he turned and made for the door.

'Oh, Macro!' Scaevola called after him.

'Yes?'

'If you do drop by, feel free to bring some more of that wine along.'

Macro ground his teeth and stamped out of the armoury.

Chapter Four

Vespasian was wearing the full dress uniform of a legion commander as he mounted the podium at the side of the parade ground. The silvered greaves, breastplate and helmet caught the light of the midday sun and shone brilliantly. The red crest and cloak lifted to a faint breeze. Behind him stood the standard bearers carrying aloft the golden eagle of the Second Legion and the image of the Emperor Claudius – a rather over-flattering likeness, thought Cato, who had last seen the Emperor spluttering food while attempting to conduct a conversation at an imperial dinner. Below the eagle hung a bottom-weighted square of red leather upon which the words 'Augusta' had been embroidered in gold letters.

The recruits faced the podium in four ranks with Bestia and his drill instructors five paces to front. All were standing silently, spears and shields grounded to the sides, as demonstrated to them shortly before. Chests were thrust out, chins raised and shoulders squared, even though Cato couldn't help feeling slightly ridiculous with what seemed to be an over-large wicker basket to one side and a child's wooden toy to the other. But still the sense of occasion filled his breast as he gazed solemnly at the podium where Vespasian was making the ritual offering of two cockerels to the gods. He washed his hands in the ceremonial bowl, dried them on a silk cloth and turned to face the assembled recruits.

'I, Titus Flavius Sabinus Vespasian, Legate of the Second Legion, Augusta, by gracious decree of the Emperor Claudius, pronounce favourable omens on those here assembled for the purpose of enrolment in the Second Legion, and do hereby request and require those here assembled to undertake the oath of allegiance to the Legion, to the legate, to the Senate and People of Rome as vested in the body and person of the Emperor Claudius. Legionaries, raise your spear and recite the oaths with me . . .'

Two hundred right arms swept straight up and sunlight glinted on the shimmering spear tips.

'I swear by the gods of the Capitol, Jupiter, Juno and Minerva . . .'

'That I will faithfully execute the orders of those placed over me . . .'

'By the will of the senate and people of Rome . . .'

'As embodied in the person of the Emperor Claudius . . .'

'Furthermore, I swear by the same gods . . .'

'That I will defend the standards of my legion and my century . . .'

'Unto the last drop of my blood. This I swear!'

As the last echoes died away, all was still for a magical moment and Cato felt a lump rise in his throat. The oaths had made him a different man. He was now set aside from the rest of society, in a new order of existence. He could be ordered to his death on the legate's whim and he would be compelled to obey. He had pledged his life to protect an inanimate lump of gold atop a plain wooden staff. Cato doubted the sanity of the oath he had taken. It was wanton irresponsibility to pledge unquestioning obedience to any man that fate, nepotism or merit placed over him. Nevertheless . . . there was something else, an overwhelming gush of excitement and a feeling of belonging to a group imbued with the mystique of an exclusively male society.

At a gesture from Vespasian, Bestia ordered the recruits to ground spears.

'New recruits to the Second Legion,' said the legate. 'You are joining a unit with a proud tradition and I demand that you honour that tradition every waking moment for the next twenty-six years. The months ahead of you will be hard, as I'm sure Centurion Bestia has already told you.' He smiled. 'But they are crucial in making you into soldiers I can be proud to command. A legionary is the highest trained, hardest fighting man in the known world – and that means we must mould you into a very special kind of person. Years of experience will see to the rest. As I look down at you, I see countrymen and men from the cities. Most of you are volunteers, some conscripted. Your past is your own affair, not the army's. Whatever you were in civilian life you are soldiers now and that is how you will be judged. You are fortunate men. You have joined the Legion at a time when it is about to make history.'

That made Cato's ears prick up.

'In years to come you will be celebrated as conquerors, as men who dared to challenge one of the last great mysteries at the edge of the known world. Think on that, and let it be your inspiration while you train. You are in good hands. You could find no better person to train you than Centurion Bestia. I wish you luck and have every confidence that you will succeed.'

Back to the clichés, Cato groaned inwardly.

'Carry on, Centurion.' Vespasian nodded to Bestia and then left the platform followed by the standard bearers.

'Yes, sir!' Bestia turned to face the recruits. 'Well, ladies, that completes the enrolment. You are all mine now. And training begins immediately after the midday meal. I want you back here then. Any later and I'll stripe your back with my cane. Dismissed!'

The entire afternoon had been spent on basic drill without a moment to sit down and Cato's legs and arms ached abominably from the strain of holding his heavy training equipment. He desperately wanted to sleep, to rest his body and drift away from the hard world he had been forced into. But sleep would not come. Strange surroundings, reflections on the day and anxieties about the future all combined in a whirling bout of mental activity that drove sleep away. He turned on to both sides to try and find the most comfortable arrangement afforded by the uncomfortable bunk, but either way the hard wooden slats could easily be felt through the worn woollen cover of the mattress. His sleeplessness was compounded by the frequent roars and cries from the dice game that was going on in the next section room. Not even the thick bolster pulled over the head could do much to keep the noise out.

But finally sleep came, despite all, and Cato had slowly rolled on to his back, mouth opening in a snore – when a pair of hands roughly shook him back into consciousness. His eyes flickered open to see a thick mop of oily black hair, dark eyes and broken teeth in a mouth stretched into a cruel grin.

'Pulcher . . .'

'On your feet, you bastard!'

'Do you know what time . . . ?' Cato began lamely.

'Fuck the time. We've got business to settle.' Pulcher grabbed Cato's tunic near the throat and hauled him down from the bunk on to the floor. 'I would've got here sooner, but Bestia put me on latrine fatigues, thanks to you. You really did drop me in the shit, didn't you?'

'I-I'm sorry. It was an accident.'

'Well then, let's call what I'm about to do to you an accident. Then we're quits.'

'What do you mean?' Cato asked nervously as he scrambled up off the floor.

'Just this.' Pulcher pulled a short-bladed knife from inside his cloak. 'A little cut to remind you not to fuck with me again.'

'No need!' said Cato. 'I promise I'll keep out of your way!'

'Promises get forgotten. But not scars . . .' Pulcher tossed the knife up and caught it by the handle – the point aimed at Cato's face. 'On the cheek, that way you'll remind others not to mess with me as well.'

Cato glanced around the room, but he was trapped in the corner with nowhere to run to that Pulcher couldn't reach first. A sudden roar of laughter from the next room attracted his eyes to the wall.

'You shout and I'll gut you here and now!' Pulcher hissed. Then he shifted his weight forward.

Cato could see the attack was imminent and, in desperation, lunged forward, grabbing at the wrist behind the blade with both of his hands. Pulcher had not been expecting the terrified boy to move first and tried to withdraw his hand – too late. The boy's grip was surprisingly strong and no amount of shaking and jerking could free his knife arm.

'Let go!' Pulcher snapped. 'Let go, you little piece of shit!'

Cato made no reply and, instead, suddenly sank his teeth into Pulcher's forearm. Pulcher cried out and instinctively smashed his free hand into the side of Cato's head, knocking him back against the bunk. There was an explosion of white inside Cato's skull before the room swirled back into vision. Pulcher was looking down at a dark oval patch on his arm where Cato's teeth had broken the skin.

'You're dead!' Pulcher stooped into a crouch, knife at the ready. 'You're fucking dead!'

Suddenly a broad shaft of light from the corridor flowed into the room as the door was swung open.

'What the hell is this?' Macro growled. 'Is this a fight?'

Pulcher drew himself up. 'No, sir. Just showing the boy how to handle himself in a fight. We're friends, sir.'

'Friends?' Macro repeated doubtfully. 'Then what happened to your arm?'

'Lad got carried away, sir. Didn't mean no harm. Ain't that right?'

Cato rose from the floor. His first instinct was to tell the truth. Then he realised that this wasn't the soldier's way. If he was to earn any respect from his new comrades he couldn't afford to be seen as running to authority for protection. Besides, if he covered for Pulcher now then maybe the thug would have cause to be grateful to him. Any advantage was worth securing at this stage.

'Yes, sir. That's right. We're friends.'

'Hmm.' Macro scratched his chin. 'Well, if you really are friends then I'd hate to be one of your enemies. Right, optio – I want a word with you in my quarters right now, so I'm afraid your friend here will have to leave.'

'Sir!' Pulcher replied smartly. 'I'll see you tomorrow, Cato.'

'Yes . . .'

'We can continue our practice then.'

Cato smiled weakly then Pulcher turned and left the room, leaving an amused Macro in his wake.

'So that's your friend, is it?'

'Yes, sir.'

'I'd be a little more careful in my selection of friends if I were you.'

'Yes, sir.'

'Now then, we need to talk. Come with me.'

Macro led the way down the corridor to the administration section of the barracks block where his quarters were situated. Cato was ushered, with a friendly wave, into the centurion's office where two desks were set against opposite walls. The larger desk was completely clear while the smaller was covered in neatly arranged piles of papyrus and waxed slates.

'Over there.' Macro pointed to a trestle chair by the larger desk and Cato sat down quietly while the centurion found another chair and placed it behind the desk.

'Drink?' Macro asked. 'It's good stuff.'

'Thank you, sir.'

Macro poured them each a small cup from a large jar and then eased himself back into his chair. A good deal of wine had already passed his lips that day and he felt uncommonly good-natured. Experience should have told him that today's good nature is tomorrow's skull-crunching hangover – but the gods of wine and memory never were on speaking terms.

'I need to talk about your duties, as far as being an optio is concerned. For the moment I just want you to help Piso with the paperwork. There's no way I can let you give orders to the other men in the century – they'd die laughing. I know you outrank them, officially, but you just have to accept that you can't act as an optio for the moment. Understand?'

'Yes, sir.'

'Given time, once you've trained . . . then we'll see. But for now I need a clerk more than I need a second-in-command. Piso will show you what you need to know in the morning.'

'Yes, sir.'

'Now I expect you could use some sleep, you'll need it. You can go.'

'Thank you, sir.'

'I will arrange for Piso to show you the ropes after training ends tomorrow.'

'Yes, sir. I'll look forward to it.'

Chapter Five

The time passed quickly, to Cato's consternation. There simply did not seem to be enough time in the day to do all that the army required of him. Apart from the relentless drilling at the hands of Bestia, Cato had administrative duties to carry out each evening, and then he had to ensure that his equipment was thoroughly cleaned for the next morning. Bestia had the eyes of a hawk and any speck of dirt, broken strap or missing buckle was instantly spotted and resulted in fatigues, or a thrashing with his cane. Wielding a vine cane was something of an art, Cato had discovered. The trick was to inflict as much pain with as little lasting damage as possible – soldiers were supposed to be disciplined, not hospitalised. Accordingly, Bestia restricted his blows to the fleshy parts of the legs, shoulders and buttocks. Cato had occasion to sample Bestia's expertise one day when he had failed to fasten the chin strap of his helmet. Bestia had pounced on him, ripping the helmet off – almost taking one ear with it.

'That's what will bloody happen to you in battle, you stupid bastard!' he shouted into Cato's face. 'Some bloody German will rip your fucking helmet off and smash his sword through the top of your skull. Is that what you want?'

'No, sir.'

'Personally, I don't give a toss about what happens to you. But I will not let the tax-payer's investment in you go to waste just because you're an idle bastard. You we can replace, but a dead soldier means lost equipment and I will not let you give the quartermaster any excuse to get on my back!'

Bestia swung his cane and, before Cato could respond, there was a sharp blow to his left shoulder and his arm went numb. The nerveless fingers loosened their grip on the wicker shield and it fell to the ground.

'Next time you forget to fasten your helmet, it'll be your fucking head.'

'Yes, sir,' Cato gasped.

At the start of every day the recruits had to assemble fully dressed and fully equipped as the dawn trumpet calls blared out across the fortress. Kit inspection was followed by a breakfast of porridge, bread and wine, dolloped into their mess tins by a resentful cook's assistant appointed to rise with the recruits. Then came parade-ground drill. Marching in step, halting, turning, changing face at a word of command. Every mis-step, wrong turn or mistimed movement brought forth a stream of invective from Bestia and his drill instructors and the slash of a vine cane. Eventually the recruits could respond instantly to his commands and training proceeded to the next stage – formation changes. From close order to open order, line to column and back to line. Learning how to march in wedge formation and tortoise formation – and all this while carrying the heavy training equipment.

After the midday meal it was even worse as the drill instructors moved their squads on to fitness training. For the first month, each afternoon was spent marching round the outside of the base, again and again and again until the burnished winter sun dipped into the wispy grey of dusk and, at last, Bestia led them back through the main gate at the same unrelenting pace. In the first weeks, numerous recruits fell out of line only to be promptly pounced on by a drill instructor and thrashed back on to the end of the column.

After the incident in the barracks, Cato made strenuous efforts to keep away from Pulcher and he was quite content to let the other man believe it was through fear. And fear it was, fear tempered by a logic which told him that there could only be one outcome from an open confrontation with Pulcher – being beaten to a pulp. To Cato's mind it made little sense to satisfy one's pride at the expense of one's body. If Pulcher thought him less of a man because Cato denied him the opportunity of beating him up then that was the measure of Pulcher's stupidity, and of any man who felt the same. And yet others did feel the same. Cato slowly became aware of the pitying glances directed at him by other recruits, and the way in which they drew back from him in the few spare moments between training sessions.

'You're going to have to fight him,' said Pyrax one evening as they sat on a bench in the century's mess room.

Cato took a swig of the rancid wine he had bought to

share with Pyrax. The foul liquid rasped down his throat and he coughed.

'You all right?'

Cato nodded. 'Just the wine.'

Pyrax looked down into his cup and took a thoughtful sip. 'Nothing wrong with it.'

'Perhaps if I fight him when I'm drunk I won't notice the pain,' Cato wondered. 'He gets to win easily, I get a few knocks and then it's all over.'

'Maybe. But I wouldn't count on him letting it go at that. I know the type, once they know they've got you beaten they can't resist coming back and doing it again and again. But you keep avoiding Pulcher and people are going to start wondering. I say face him, take a beating – but don't give in too early. Try and stick it to him. Land a few painful blows and he'll leave you alone. Maybe.'

'Maybe? Is that the best I can hope for? Accept a swift kicking on the off chance that Pulcher may decide to leave it at that? What if he doesn't?'

Pyrax shrugged.

'Oh thanks! That's really helpful.'

'Just telling you how it is, son.'

Cato shook his head. 'There must be some other way. Some way of confronting him without a fight.'

'Maybe,' Pyrax shrugged. 'But whatever you do just get it over with soon, before too many people think you're a coward.'

Cato stared at him a moment. 'Is that what they're saying?'

'What d'you expect? That's what it looks like.'

'I'm not a coward.'

'If you say so. But you'd better prove it.'

The door opened with an icy blast and several legionaries entered the mess. In the wildly flickering glow of the mess brazier, Cato recognised them as men from another century. They looked round and then, very deliberately, sat on a bench on the far side of the room. Pyrax quickly downed the last of his wine and rose to his feet.

'Must be off.'

'Why so early?' asked Cato. 'There's plenty left in the flask.'

'True. But I've my reputation to think of,' Pyrax added coldly. 'Remember what I said – do whatever you're going to do, but do it soon.'

Once Pyrax had left the mess Cato brooded over his wine for a while, and then, when he looked up, he momentarily caught the eyes of one of the new arrivals. The man instantly glanced away and carried on talking in low tones to his friends. It was hard not to think that they were talking about him, that they had come to this mess out of curiosity to see the coward who had been appointed an optio.

Cato stood up and, pulling his cloak on, hurried from the mess. The air was freezing and the night sky was threaded with fine clouds rimmed in pale silver from a half moon. Quite beautiful, he thought and paused for a moment to savour the stillness of the moment. But all too soon his mind turned back to the need to confront Pulcher and with a curse he stamped off towards his quarters.

* * *

Nor was Pulcher the only thing troubling his mind. Aside from the relentless drilling during the day Cato had to devote most evenings to learning his duties as an optio. The centurion's secretary, Piso, had been ordered to train the new recruit in the art of military administration. And an art it was, as Cato quickly came to realise. Piso was responsible for the century's records; a file on each legionary itemising every aspect of the soldier's life as far as it affected the Legion. Medical records, leave granted, military awards granted, disciplinary breaches and the appropriate punishments, deductions from pay for food and repayments on equipment issued.

One evening, shortly after the conversation with Pyrax, found Piso and his protégé working in the warm fug of the century's office. The brazier glowed and the wooden fuel crackled pleasantly as the two men examined Cato's latest attempt at writing in the arid style beloved of the army. Piso grunted appreciative noises as he read over the brisk but irrefutably logical requisitions and nodded approvingly at some of the well-turned phrases calculated to provoke a sense of urgency, or implying that an authority well above that of a lowly century clerk was indirectly responsible for the request.

The doorlatch clattered and Macro came into the room rubbing his hands and making straight for the brazier. He stretched his arms out and smiled as the heat soaked into his palms. A vague smell of wine betrayed the fact he had just returned to barracks from the centurion's mess.

'Cold night, sir.' Piso smiled.

'Bloody cold!' Macro nodded. 'How's our new boy working out?'

'Fine, sir. Just fine.' Piso exchanged a look with Cato. 'In fact, he's going to make an excellent clerk one day.'

'So you think young Cato is ready to step into your shoes?'

'I didn't say that, sir. There's still quite a bit to learn. But he's got a talent for it and no mistake. We were just looking over some of his requisition statements. Would you care to have a look, sir?'

Macro shook his head. 'Another time. When I'm not so busy. Anyway, I'm sure he's doing as well as you say. And so you should, what with all that education you've picked up.'

'Yes, sir,' Cato replied, wondering slightly about the change of tone in Macro's voice. 'It's proved to be very useful, sir.'

'Yes.' Macro stared at him silently for a moment, his expression unreadable. 'Anyway, that's not why I'm here. It's about time you got some field experience. There's a detachment being sent to a local settlement tomorrow morning. The local chief sent a Roman tax-collector packing after cutting out his tongue. Seems the chief's related to some troublemaker trying to make a name for himself on the other side of the Rhine. Anyway, Vespasian's sending the Third cohort to arrest the chief and confiscate all precious metals and stones to compensate the tax-collector. One of the centurions of the Third got kicked unconscious by a mule this afternoon and the optio's already in the hospital. I've been ordered to take temporary command of his century – you're coming with me.'

'Oh! Will there be a fight, sir?'

'Doubt it. Why?'

'It's just that we haven't trained with real weapons yet.'

'Don't worry about it. Borrow some kit from one of our lads. Shouldn't need it though – as soon as those Germans see us coming they'll do everything they can to get rid of us. We just go in, make the arrest, requisition whatever we can find and leave. Should be home by nightfall.'

'Oh . . .' Cato could not keep the disappointment from his voice. He had hoped that the excursion might keep him out of Pulcher's reach for a few days at least.

'Don't worry, son,' Macro said kindly, having misread Cato's expression. 'You'll get to see some fighting one day, I promise. But it's good that you're keen to get stuck in. No good being a soldier unless you enjoy your work.'

Cato smiled weakly. 'Yes, sir.'

'Right then!' Macro clapped him on the shoulder, shoving him backwards good-naturedly. 'See you at dawn by the north gate. Full armour, cloak and provisions for the day.'

'Yes, sir. If it's all right with Piso, I'd like to get an early night, sir.'

Macro turned to his clerk, eyebrows raised.

'Certainly!' Piso smiled. 'If the centurion pushes those men like he pushes us you'll need all your energy for tomorrow.'

After the door had closed behind Cato and his

footsteps could be heard fading down the corridor, Macro turned back to his clerk.

'What do you think of him?'

'He's got a knack for paperwork; neat hand and a good memory.' Piso paused for a moment.

'But . . . ?' Macro filled in.

'I'm not sure if he's cut out for army life, sir. Seems a bit too soft.'

'You ever met anyone from the palace who wasn't? Too much good living – that's their trouble. Most of 'em wouldn't last five days in the army, but so far that lad's kept up. What he lacks in fitness he makes up with determination. You know, I think we might be able to make something out of young Cato after all.'

'If you say so, sir.'

'I say so, but you don't think so, eh Piso?'

'To be honest, no, sir. Determination's one thing but fighting requires quite different qualities. I don't think he's got what it takes.' Piso paused. 'There's a rumour going round that he's a coward.'

'Yes, I've heard. But you know how it is with rumours – there's nothing in most of 'em. We have to give the lad a chance.'

Piso was struck by a sudden insight. 'Then you *are* expecting trouble, sir?'

'It's possible, you know what the Germans are like, any excuse for a fight. But I doubt it will amount to more than knocking a couple of heads together. Still, it'll give me a chance to see how Cato reacts.'

'If what I've heard's true, he'll run.'

'Care to make a wager on that?' Macro smiled. 'Five

sestertii? I know you can afford it.'

'Yes, sir. But can you?'

'Five sestertii.' Macro ignored the gibe and spat on his hand. 'Five says that if there's trouble Cato doesn't run. Or are you too scared to take the bet?'

Piso delayed no more than a moment before slapping his centurion's palm. 'Five it is!'

Chapter Six

The night had been cold and, as the soft light of dawn struggled through the morning mist, the fortress of the Second Legion was revealed in a sparkling white frost. The men of the Third cohort were forming into their centuries in a businesslike manner as the air was wreathed in the steam of their breath. Five hundred men, in full armour and heavy cloaks, were gathered in faint filtered shafts of light, rubbing hands and stamping feet in an effort to generate a small bit of warmth against the biting winter air. Jeers and good-humoured insults were exchanged with passing legionaries from other cohorts fortunate enough to be remaining in the fortress for the day. The officers stood apart from the loose columns of men and Cato had no trouble locating Macro's stocky form.

'This your protégé, Macro?' said the man next to him.

Macro nodded.

'A little young for an optio, wouldn't you say?'

'We'll see,' Macro grunted, casting his eyes over the optio in his ill-fitting tunic and cloak. The centurion circled slowly, making a close examination of the young man's equipment, testing the buckles with a sharp tug, and tilting Cato's head back to ensure the helmet strap was fastened. 'You'll do. Right, while we're out of the base you stick by me and do whatever I say. No wandering off, no nothing without my say-so. Understand?'

'Yes, sir.'

'Now, join the front of the last century in line – that's the Sixth. Wait for me there.'

'Sir?'

'What is it?'

'How long are we going to stand here?' asked Cato, already shivering.

'You just can't wait, can you?' Macro shook his head. 'Not long now, boy, we're just waiting for the tribune.'

One of the other centurions spat on the frozen ground. 'Bet the bastard's still in bed.'

'Doubt it,' Macro replied. 'The legate's on his case. Seems he wants to test Vitellius. But this little trip's nothing more than an exercise in command. Even Vitellius would struggle to screw it up.'

'Macro, old son, never underestimate the incompetence of staff officers. They're born and bred for disaster . . .'

The exchange fell out of earshot as Cato made his way towards the standard rising over the Sixth Century. A few of the men eyed him curiously as he approached.

'You're Macro's optio?' the standard bearer asked.

'Yes.'

'He mentioned he had a new boy, but I didn't dream he was being so literal.'

Cato opened his mouth to reply before he got control of his feelings. Then he blushed and fumed silently.

'Just stick close to the centurion and me, lad, and you'll be all right.'

As Cato stood at the head of the century the other optios had been given the nod and were now moving down the ranks quietly ordering the men into column of fours, and dressing the lines so that in a short time the cohort was formed up, at ease, and ready to move off. Cato could not help but be aware of the growing sense of impatience as the men stood and waited. The sun had cleared the dawn mist lingering along the battlements and was washing the cohort in a weak orange glow.

And still they waited. For long enough that the cold began to take numbing advantage of their stillness.

At last the clatter of a walking horse sounded from the centre of the fortress and Cato turned to see a red-cloaked officer approaching, feathered plume bouncing from the crest of his helmet. At his approach, the group of centurions broke up and returned to their centuries. Vitellius trotted down the column and took up station at its head. A single word of command later and the lead century marched off, heading through the gate and on to the track beyond the walls. The succeeding centuries followed suit and, as the rear of the Fifth century moved forward, Macro counted off ten paces and then bellowed out the order to advance.

Cato's response, thanks to Bestia's harsh training regime, was automatic, and he instantly broke into the slow measured pace of the standard march two paces behind Macro and abreast the standard bearer. They passed through the gate, iron-shod boots echoing back off the stonework, and out into the half-tamed wilderness of the frontier province. The rising sun cast long shadows across the hoar frost to their left and numerous puffs of steamy breath swirled into the cold air. Underfoot, the ground was frozen hard where, weeks before, muddy channels marked the wagon ruts leading away from the fortress to the many frontier villages in the area. Despite the cold, Cato felt glad to be getting away from the Legion – a whole day without Bestia and Pulcher to occupy his mind.

The head of a column breasted a small rise in the land and, as the Sixth century followed down the reverse slope, Cato took a last look over his shoulder at the fortress stretching out across the landscape – a long stone wall with the red tiles of the headquarters building beyond. A settlement of bars, brothels and squalid hovels sprawled unevenly beneath the walls on the far side of the fortress. Looking ahead, a line of trees marked the end of the land cleared by the Second Legion and the beginning of one of the ancient forests that sprawled across Germany. Beyond the fringe of saplings struggling to recover some of the ground ravaged by the Legion's engineers, enormous pines and oaks reared up, dark and forbidding. Cato shivered, partly from the cold, and partly as he recalled the fate of the three legions General Varus had foolishly led into the depths of just such a forest nearly thirty years earlier. Over fifteen thousand men had been massacred in the gloomy twilight under the tangled boughs, their bodies left by the Germans to rot into the dirt.

As the column advanced down the track and the trees began to close in from the sides and overhead the men fell silent, some glancing anxiously into the depths beyond. Macro could well understand their feelings; there was something innately strange about this far-flung frontier of the Empire. The forests were unlike anything else in the known world, dark and impenetrable. Even the local tribes were afraid of them and told tales of how restless spirits of the dead were cursed to wander as pale wraiths through the shadows and green-filtered light. The track the cohort followed had been hacked through the forest by the Legion's engineers; the locals had preferred to trek round the forest before the Romans arrived. Even now some still refused to enter the woods. The engineers, it seemed, had also been afraid of the place, as the track made no attempt at a straight line and instead curled its way round the thick tree trunks, such had been their determination to get the job done quickly. A short while after the column had entered the forest no more than a score of men could be seen before or behind and Cato felt a trickle of sweat trace its way down his spine beneath his tunic.

'Sir?'

Macro turned his head as he crunched along the frozen track. 'What is it, boy?'

'How far exactly is this village, sir?'

'You mean, how much further through this forest?' Macro smiled.

'Yes, sir.'

'A few miles before the track clears the trees, then we should reach the village by noon. Don't worry about this place, it's harmless enough.'

'But if we should be attacked . . .'

'Attacked?' Macro scoffed. 'Who by? Not the poor sods we're visiting. Bunch of simple-minded farmers. And your nearest German war-band is well to the other side of the Rhine. So relax, boy, you're making the women nervous.' Macro jerked a thumb back at the legionaries of the Sixth century and those in earshot jeered loudly. Cato blushed and merely tried to pull his neck in as far as possible while keeping a close eye on the silvan shadows.

Once the initial oppressive spell of the forest had worn off, the soldiers stopped talking in hushed tones and the column wound its way through the trees accompanied by the usual loud banter of marching soldiers as they swapped jokes and exchanged insults. The deep boughs swallowed up much of the noise and what was left sounded flat and strange to their ears.

At last the column pulled free of the forest and marched out into a bright winter morning as an unobscured sun bathed the land in a warm glow. This side of the forest had been cleared and the cohort passed through primitive farmland dotted with the grim little peat huts of local German settlers, each one marked by a thin trail of smoke reaching up to clear sky. Most of the farmers had taken in their grazing animals and steam clung about the low outbuildings from which the lowing of cattle and the squealing of pigs could be heard as the soldiers passed. There were few signs of human life, the odd face at a door silently watching the column chinkling along the track, but nothing more.

'Friendly lot, aren't they?' the standard bearer commented.

'They don't seem much bothered by us,' Cato replied. 'I'd have thought they'd be a bit more interested. It's not what I imagined the Germans would be like.'

'What did you think they'd be like?'

'Big and aggressive – that's what we heard in Rome.'

'That's exactly what they are like when you're fighting them,' the standard bearer said with feeling. 'But these are just farmers. They're like all civilians when an army passes by. Just keeping their noses clean and hoping we don't have any cause to pay them any attention. Behind that door' – the standard bearer nodded towards a hut they were passing – 'and behind every door sits a family praying we don't stop. Soldiers are bad news for their kind.'

From the head of the column came the shouted order for the cohort to halt and each centurion instantly relayed it to his command. The men stood, silently waiting for the next instruction.

'All officers to the front!'

Macro, having the furthest to go, immediately broke into a trot and made his way along the side of the column towards Vitellius, rising above the First century on horseback. From the rear of the cohort Cato could see that the track passed over a low crest. The officers gathered around Vitellius, at the respectful distance infantry give to horses, as he issued his orders with occasional gestures for clarification. Once dismissed, the officers hurried back into position at the head of their centuries. Macro smiled as he saw the questioning expressions on the faces of the standard bearer and his optio.

'The village is just beyond that rise. The tribune wants to play it low key. He's only taking in the First century. The rest of us are to form up along the crest in sight of the village in case we're needed.'

'Why aren't we all going, sir?' Cato asked. 'Why split the command?'

'Because that's his order, lad,' Macro snapped, but then instantly relented since the optio had made a reasonable point. 'He doesn't want us to make the locals too nervous. We just make the arrest, seize the valuables and leave peacefully. If we all just march in there he thinks we might spook them into doing something foolish.'

'Something foolish?'

'Fuck knows what.' Macro shrugged his wide shoulders dismissively. 'I don't see a bunch of farmers deciding to take us on. Still, it's orders. Ah! Here we go. Back to your position, optio.'

At the head of the First century Vitellius led his men over the crest and out of sight. The following centuries moved to the right and left of the road along the crest. The centurions of the Second and Third centuries paced out the line and marked the positions for each century as they marched at right angles to the road. The gap left for the Sixth century straddled the road and Cato, sticking close to the standard bearer and Macro as ordered, found himself in front of the line of men, formed up four deep, that stretched out over a hundred paces on each side. Ahead, the ground sloped gently down to a village nestling inside a wide loop of river that emerged from the forest surrounding the cleared land.

Cato was surprised at the size of the settlement. He had been expecting a loose collection of mud huts inside a flimsy palisade. Instead there were hundreds of huts and larger buildings crammed within a high turf wall and water-filled ditch. The main gate was closed, flanked by two squat stone towers from which the narrow drawbridge was controlled. A little beyond the gate, the track opened out into a square in front of the largest building in the village.

It was a good half mile from the crest to the drawbridge and the First century had already covered most of the distance on the track while the rest of the cohort had formed up. There seemed to be little response in the village as the soldiers approached and the men waited peacefully as a few faces appeared at the wall to inspect their visitors. While the five centuries stood at ease word was passed that rations could be eaten and the men started feeding on the contents of their haversacks. Cato took out a strip of dried beef and gnawed at the tough but highly flavoured meat. The morning's march had made him more hungry than he realised and he worked his jaws furiously while gazing out across the panorama below.

Cato's eye was suddenly caught by a movement at the far side of the village. Three figures, carrying shields and spears, were running away towards the distant treeline. A greasy smudge of smoke eddied up from where Cato had first seen them as a small camp fire smouldered.

'Sir!' he called out to Macro. 'Over there!'

'What is it?'

'There, sir.' Cato pointed with his javelin. 'Those men running. D'you see 'em?'

'Yes, boy. I see them.'

'What should we do, sir?' Cato asked.

'Do?' Macro frowned. 'Nothing. They're too far away to do anything. Anyway, there's only three of them.'

'Should we tell the tribune?' Cato persisted.

'No point.'

They watched silently as the three armed men disappeared across the farmland towards the trees while Vitellius led his men across the open ground towards the gate and halted the century by the ditch in front of the towers. The tribune waved his arm determinedly and, after a short pause, the gate swung inwards to admit the soldiers. The century passed inside the village and, for a few anxious moments, disappeared from view amongst the huts before emerging into the village square. Vitellius halted the column and sent two men forward to the main door of the largest building facing on to the square. Before they could reach it, the door opened and a tall woman with long flaxen hair emerged. Although those remaining on the hill crest could hear nothing and see precious little from half a mile away, it was clear that some argument was taking place between Vitellius and the woman.

'I thought we were sent to arrest the chief, sir?' Cato commented.

'So we were, boy,' Macro said irritably. 'He shouldn't waste time. There isn't much daylight to waste in winter.' He stared up at the sky where the sun looked longingly towards the horizon. 'Don't much fancy marching home in the darkness.'

Cato involuntarily looked back towards the forest in the distance. The place had been unnerving enough in daylight, Jupiter knows what it would be like in pitch darkness. 'If it gets dark wouldn't it be better to go round the forest, sir?'

Macro shook his head. 'Too far. Besides we can make torches if we need to. You aren't scared, are you, boy?'

'No, sir.'

'Good. Stay that way,' Macro said with relief, hoping that his five sestertii were still safe.

Down in the village the argument was being forced to a conclusion as Vitellius waved his hand at the woman and two soldiers abruptly pinned her arms back. A squad forced their way into the large building, only to emerge a moment later with a large chest. Having deposited it by Vitellius they proceeded to the next building and forced an entry.

'Seems like our man has got away,' Macro remarked, and yawned elaborately. 'The tribune shouldn't have wasted time on the woman.'

'Unless she's the kind of woman the tribune takes a shine to,' the standard bearer muttered. 'You know what Vitellius is like with women, can't resist the impulse to chat 'em up.'

'He should do it on his own time then. Not the army's. And certainly not mine. And not on a bloody cold day like this.'

'Sir!' Cato interrupted. 'Look there! The gate!'

For some reason the gate was slowly being closed and, as Macro watched, the small drawbridge began to rise. A cold feeling of dread, far colder than the trickle of sweat on a winter day, etched its way down his spine. He shifted his gaze to the centre of the village, but Vitellius and his men seemed unconcerned and continued with the house raids. Beyond the far wall of the village a faint movement attracted his gaze. A shadow was emerging from the forest, as if the sun was setting sooner than it should. Then he realised it couldn't be, the sun was behind the cohort.

'Cato! Your eyes are younger than mine. What's happening over there – at the edge of the forest there!' He pointed urgently.

For a moment Cato wasn't sure, a sight haze had risen over the low ground and partially obscured the view. But a moment later the blurry shadow distilled into distinct shapes. 'I think . . . I'm sure, it's a body of men. Coming out of the forest, this way.'

He looked at Macro wide-eyed. 'Germans?'

'What else?' Macro replied dryly.

'But what about the others in the village?' Cato said in alarm. 'They can't see.'

'I know, boy. I know.'

More of the men saw the approaching danger and pointed it out to their comrades. An anxious murmuring swept up and down the line.

'Quiet, there!' Macro bellowed. 'Shut your mouths and stand still!'

The legionaries obeyed instantly the moment discipline was invoked. Puffing down the line came

Centurion Quadratus of the Second – the senior officer present.

'Macro! You see 'em?'

'Yes.'

'We'd better get down there and join the others.'

'We were ordered to remain here,' Macro replied firmly. 'Unless Vitellius signalled us to move.'

'But he can't see them.' Quadratus jabbed a finger towards the approaching Germans, in their thousands now as they poured out of the forest towards the village.

'If we go down there, then we'll all be caught in the trap,' said Macro. 'I suggest we try and attract their attention instead.'

Quadratus stared at Macro a moment and then nodded. He turned to face down the line and cupped his hands to his mouth. 'Standards! Signal recall!'

The remaining five standard bearers raised their standards high and began slowly circling the hanging pendants. Macro looked down at the village where the soldiers of the First century carried on seizing portable items of value, oblivious to the approaching catastrophe.

'Come on, come on!' Quadratus muttered. 'Someone look up . . . this way.'

Finally they saw a soldier gesture towards them with his javelin and Vitellius turned in his saddle. For a moment he sat motionless on his horse, then turned and frantically waved an arm. The soldier who had seen them rushed from the clearing and shortly after reappeared at the top of one of the gate towers. Even as he did so, figures emerged in the spaces between the village buildings surrounding Vitellius and his men. The century quickly formed up in close order and backed out of the clearing towards the gate. Some of the villagers ran forward and threw stones and lumps of wood at the retreating Romans. A sudden shower of javelins from the rearmost ranks rained down on the villagers, leaving half a dozen prostrate as the others fled back into the narrow alleys. The century was soon lost from sight behind the village buildings as it headed back to the gate.

From the hill, the Germans approaching from the forest were now in clear view and it was possible to estimate their numbers and speed of approach.

'Three, maybe four thousand,' Quadratus guessed.

Macro shook his head. 'Barely that I'd say.'

'Vitellius should have time to get out before they reach the village.'

'Easily. They're still nearly a mile from the far side of the village. Once Vitellius clears the gateway he should make the crest before they get anywhere near.'

'Then what?'

'Don't know,' Macro shrugged. 'We'll just have to wait and see what he orders.'

Cato stared at the two officers in disbelief. How on earth could they be so cold-blooded when their comrades faced imminent extinction right under their eyes? And after that, the rest of the cohort would be outnumbered ten to one. He felt a burning desire to turn and run, to shout out to all the others to do the same. But his body refused to move, partly out of shame and partly out of the dread of making the return journey through the forest alone. While he stood motionless, Cato's gaze continued to flicker between the approaching Germans and the village, watching for the progress of the First century. There was a sudden motion in one of the tower gates, the legionary sent there by Vitellius was seized by a group of men, a spear run through him and the body hurled into the ditch.

'Sir!'

'I saw it, boy.'

A series of flashes and glints marked the arrival of the First century at the edge of the village and a brief struggle was fought out for control of the gate. All the while the Germans swarmed nearer to close the trap.

'It's going to be a close thing,' mused Quadratus. 'Better get ready to make a fighting retreat. I'll get the other centuries back on the track. Macro, I want you to stand here and cover our backs until Vitellius arrives.'

'All right.' Macro nodded. 'But you'd better move fast.'

Quadratus made his way down the line shouting out the necessary commands, and one by one the centuries on the crest turned from line into column and marched back towards the track. At the same time, Macro ordered the Sixth ten paces down the slope to clear the head of the track for Quadratus. Down in the village, Cato could see that the First century had managed to overwhelm the villagers at the gate and legionaries were pulling back the thick wooden gate to make their escape. With Vitellius riding at their head, the First doubled up the hill towards the rest of the cohort. A small crowd of villagers followed behind, but quickly gave up once a fresh volley of javelins was hurled back at them.

Once the century was safely away from the village,

Vitellius spurred his horse up the slope to take command of the cohort. He reined in beside Macro, the horse snorting harshly over the frothy bit as a savage gash on its flank bled profusely.

'What the hell's going on here, centurion?' he shouted angrily. 'Where's the rest?'

'Quadratus has moved them back on to the track, sir,' Macro explained.

'What for? Scared of a few bloody villagers? I'm taking the whole cohort back in there and we're going to burn the bastards to the ground!'

'Sir,' Macro interrupted. 'If you care to look over there.'

'Eh? What?'

'Beyond the village, sir.'

For a moment Vitellius froze as the true peril of the situation was at last made clear to him. He studied the dark mass of Germans streaming towards the village and realised what the other officers already knew, that there was no hope of fighting against such odds.

'There's still some distance between us. If we can make the forest in time we can use a rearguard to hold them off.'

'I believe that's what Quadratus had in mind, sir.'

'Good. Right then you stay here. When the First arrives let them through and order them to join on to the end of the column. This century's the rearguard. Only pull back once the cohort is on the move.'

Vitellius took another look back down the slope, gauging the relative positions of both sides. 'They won't reach the village for a little while. With luck, we'll be able to keep far enough ahead of them. Right, centurion, you've got your orders.'

'Yes, sir.' Macro saluted as Vitellius wheeled his horse and rode over the crest towards the head of the column. Once he was sure the tribune was out of earshot, Cato turned to Macro.

'What's going to happen?'

'Just what he said. A quick march back to base. That's all.'

Cato feared that things were not going to work out as simply as that. A nagging feeling at the back of his mind suggested that the worst was yet to come and he silently cursed Macro for ordering him to join the expedition. Instead of the promised bloodless exercise and a reprieve from the attentions of Bestia and Pulcher, he was now faced by a horde of German savages. Barely four weeks into his military career, he reflected bitterly, and already people were queuing up to kill him.

The men of the First century struggled breathlessly up to the line of legionaries below the crest and were quickly ushered on to the track. When the last had passed through the ranks, Macro ordered the line to withdraw ten paces to their original position. The century was about to form up when a faint roar sounded from beyond the head of the column.

Bursting from the distant forest was another swarm of Germans, racing across the farmland to cut off the cohort's retreat. A quick glance was all that Cato needed. Even to his untrained eye it was obvious that the Germans would reach the track well before the nearest century was anywhere near it. Suddenly it was all clear to Cato – the three men running for the forest – the signal fire – the delaying action of the chief's woman. A very neat trap indeed, he conceded, just before the full terror of their plight set the hairs standing on the back of his neck. Looking to Macro for a solution, he was surprised to see the mask of the centurion's composure drop for a moment. He stared at the new threat, then quickly turned back to the first of the German swarms, now hardly three quarters of a mile from the far side of the village.

'Oh great,' muttered Macro. 'Now we're well and truly fucked.'

Chapter Seven

Once the cohort had left the base early in the morning the Second Legion settled into a normal day's routine. Bestia's recruits stamped around the parade ground trying to keep warm in between bouts of drilling, while the commander of the Fifth cohort took his men out of camp for the monthly route march that the army required of all its troops. This day the cohort was joined by the clerical staff from headquarters, grumbling bitterly that their excused-duties status was being ignored by Vespasian.

Watching from an upstairs balcony as the cohort, with the clerks sandwiched between the Third and Fourth centuries, filed down the Via Praetoria, Vespasian could not restrain a grin. The Second Augusta was his first legion command and he aimed to make it a success, even if that meant upsetting the headquarters' clerks. Every man and beast in the Legion would be made fighting fit in readiness for the following year's campaign. Moreover, due to the special nature of the operation outlined to him in the message sent by the imperial general staff, the men of the Second would need training in amphibious warfare. Soldiers, he knew only too well, had an innate suspicion of all things aquatic, let alone nautical. The settled garrison life the Legion had been leading for several years was not going to help matters, he reflected, sipping from a cup of heated wine. A rapid period of adjustment was required and the enforced exercise of the clerks was just the first phase in Vespasian's programme to prepare his troops for the following summer. From now on, route marches and weapons practice would be doubled and no soldier or officer would be permitted excused-duties privileges.

As the tail of the cohort tramped past, Vespasian left the balcony and returned to his private quarters, closing the shutters. Spread across a large wooden table were the inventories he had ordered, as well as a series of missives from Rome providing details of the Legion's relocation – the route they would take across Gaul; the supply depots on which the Second would be permitted to draw while on the march and notification of the amphibious warfare experts to be attached to his command for the duration of the campaign. The document that had set all this in motion was safely secured with his confidential papers in the chest under the table. From constant rereading, Vespasian knew the details by heart. Nevertheless, he removed the key from the chain around his neck and unfastened the lock. The despatch was folded round a scroll and the remains of the broken imperial seal of deep red wax were still fixed to the stiff parchment. Beside the scroll was another, smaller, document marked for his eyes only and written in a personalised code by the Emperor himself. Vespasian considered it for a moment with a pained expression, and then pushed it to the back of the chest before extracting the larger despatch. Flattening it out on the table top, Vespasian took another sip of warm wine and ran his eyes over the finely written script yet again.

The Second and three other legions, together with thirty cohorts of auxiliaries, were to invade Britain the following summer. The imperial clerk who had drafted the despatch had stated the plan as boldly and as simply as that. Then, perhaps a little remorseful about such a staggering degree of understatement, the clerk had struck a rich vein of loquacity and launched into an elegant essay on the significance of the planned campaign. Britain, he noted, had merely been reconnoitred by Julius Caesar; a successful invasion would rekindle the glory of Rome and once again remind the civilised world (and the uncivilised who dwelt without) of the potency of Rome, and its new Emperor.

Vespasian smiled at that. The Claudian accession owed everything to the support of the Praetorian Guard. But for them, the current Emperor would have been swept away in the bloodshed that followed the assassination of Caligula. Claudius might be Emperor, but his suitability for the post was something of an issue among the chattering classes of Rome. Even the plebeians were not entirely convinced that he was up to the job. This campaign plan – the conquest of Britain – was transparently intended to recast Claudius in the heroic mould. A quick victory, a glittering triumph and prolonged public celebration in Rome would firm up Claudius' hold on the affections of Rome's fickle masses.

The clerk continued his outline of the campaign by

stating that the forces allocated to the invasion would more than suffice. Intelligence reports from Britain suggested that armed resistance would be minimal and widely dispersed. The invasion force would quickly brush aside any opposition that might be concentrated and the rest of the campaign would be a simple matter of reducing tribal strongholds by diplomacy or force.

'By diplomacy or force,' Vespasian repeated aloud with a weary shake of his head. Only someone on the imperial staff could make it sound so simple. Any soldier with frontier experience knew just how unlikely it was that diplomacy would succeed. Vespasian doubted if the Britons could even pronounce the word, let alone understand the concept it entailed.

The Britons, according to the imperial clerk's liberal interpretation of Caesar, were an ill-disciplined rabble with a quaint line in chariot tactics. Their hill-forts amounted to little more than mounds of mud supporting flimsy palisades. Few casualties were anticipated and the invaders would have ample opportunity for personal enrichment as a result of the anticipated spoils of war – mainly, slaves. Vespasian was reminded to make that point quite clear to the rank and file of the Legion, who might otherwise be swayed by the superstitious rumours circulating about the mysterious mist-wreathed isle beyond the fringes of the known world. At this point, Vespasian guessed, the clerk became aware that he had rather over-gilded the lily and the despatch switched back into a more objective style. Vespasian was instructed to stamp down harshly on those who spread such rumours and to maintain the highest degree of discipline in the best traditions of the Roman army. The despatch curtly concluded with a schedule of troop movements for the coming months.

Laying the document to one side, Vespasian drained the last of his wine and stared down at the paperwork covering the table. It would be quite an adventure, to say the least. The assembling of a vast force, its daily provisioning and stockpiling of reserves for resupply following the landing, the construction of a fleet, the training of the army for amphibious operations – not to mention the small matter of the campaign itself and the establishing of an entirely new province with all the provision of infrastructure that implied. And for what? The despatch told of vast resources of gold, silver and tin found on the island. From what Vespasian had heard of Britain from the merchants who passed through the fortress, the island was a squalid affair. No cities, no culture, ugly women and preposterous hairstyles. Hardly the kind of place Claudius could proudly introduce to the rest of the empire. But it was a conquest and reputations were built on military success. Vespasian was keenly aware that his political stock needed building up if the ambitions he harboured in his heart were to become any kind of reality. Yes, Britain would do nicely, for all concerned – except the natives, he mused with a smile.

And speaking of natives, there were one or two local arrangements to finalise before the Legion handed over the fortress to the mixed cohort from Macedonia that had been assigned to replace the Second during the campaign. There were some tribal land disputes to settle and that nasty business with the tax-collector which the

Third cohort was presently sorting out. The tongueless tax-collector had filed a petition for compensation with the provincial governor and had stipulated that, unless the sum he claimed was paid in full, he would only be satisfied by the local chief's execution. Mindful that the local tribe had had a poor harvest this year and might need to buy in food over the hard German winter, Vespasian had offered to have the chief's tongue cut out in restitution. But the tax-collector, an uncouth Gaul with an appalling accent and no conversation – a situation unlikely to improve now – had insisted on his blood money, or the chief's death. And so Vitellius had been sent to deal with the situation, a task well in keeping with the tribune's taste for enforcing the Roman peace.

Vespasian found it difficult to warm to his senior tribune but couldn't quite discern why. The fellow was equable enough and popular in the mess. He drank hard, though never to the point of intoxication. He womanised indiscriminately and frequently – as any man should, Vespasian thought approvingly. Moreover, Vitellius loved sports and could drive a chariot as if he had been born with a set of reins in his hands. If he had a vice it was gambling, and even then he was good at it – intuitively knowing when the dice were for or against him. He had a knack for making friends, particularly the kind who were useful politically, and a bright future lay ahead of him. Who knew how far the man would rise? And with that question Vespasian put his finger on the nub of the matter – the man constituted a possible rival in future life.

And then there was that other matter. The coded message unwittingly delivered by that recruit some weeks earlier direct from the personal office of the Emperor, using the personalised cipher Claudius had agreed with Vespasian. It briefly informed Vespasian that someone at the fortress had been implicated in last year's coup attempt by Scribonianus. As soon as the plotter's identity had been obtained from the surviving members of the conspiracy, Vespasian would be told so he could see that the individual concerned disappeared quietly. Fine euphemisms, Vespasian reflected, smiling wryly as he imagined the techniques used by the imperial torturers to extract information and see that people disappeared as discreetly as possible. By way of comfort, the message assured him that at least one – yet again unidentified – imperial agent was present in the camp to assist Vespasian in any way the agent saw fit.

It was all a confounded bloody nuisance, given the exhausting preparations required for the Legion's involvement in a major offensive campaign. A soldier needed to concentrate on military objectives, not high politics, if the army was to operate effectively. And from now on he would have to view every one of his officers with a degree of suspicion, at least until some hapless soul in the Mammertine prison finally cracked and provided a name. Vespasian couldn't help hoping that the name would be that of Vitellius. Now that really would be a neat solution to most of his present anxieties.

Vespasian poured himself some more wine from the jar warming over the glowing embers in the brazier. He sipped carefully at the steaming liquid as he reflected that it was a shame that he hadn't managed to find a more dangerous undertaking for Vitellius than turning over a local village.

Chapter Eight

The tribune's horse came thundering back down the track. Slewing to a halt at the rearmost century, Vitellius thrust an arm out, pointing down the slope to the village.

'Macro! Get your men back there at the double!'

'Sir?' Macro was momentarily startled by the order. His eyes followed the direction the tribune was pointing, and passed rapidly over the village to where Germans were swarming across the flat farmland towards them.

'Just do it, Centurion!' Vitellius shouted. 'At the double.'

'Yes, sir!'

'And when you get to the village, go right through it and secure the far gate.'

'Yes, sir!'

'Stop for nothing! Understand?'

'Sir.'

As Macro turned to the Sixth century to bellow out the command, Vitellius savagely jerked the reins round and kicked his heels into the side of his horse, before racing back down the column which had smartly about-faced and was quick-marching back towards the village. Macro grabbed Cato's arm.

'Stick close. Whatever happens.'

Cato nodded.

'Right, lads, at the trot. Follow me!'

Macro led the century down the track, a small column of panting legionaries gasping out plumes of steamy breath as they looked to the far side of the village and gauged the distance of the German horde sweeping towards them. Even Cato could see that the enemy were sure to reach the far gate ahead of them. What then? A brutal fight in the filthy narrow streets and certain death. And death would be preferable to capture if only a fraction of what Posidonius had written about the Germans was true. Harness straps and scabbards chinked loudly and Cato, who had not yet perfected the technique of running in full battle-dress, struggled to keep hold of shield and javelin while preventing the sword scabbard from being caught between his thighs. Worse, Cato's one-size-fits-all helmet began to tip down over his eyes as he ran, requiring a regular backwards flip of the head.

Glancing back over his shoulder, Macro could see that the other centuries were now coming over the crest and breaking into a run down the slope. He nodded approvingly. The tribune had the good sense not to let them run all the way back to the village and face the Germans while fighting for breath. Macro glanced ahead at the village gate. A small group of Germans, bearing a motley assortment of antique weapons and the more harmful type of agricultural tools, waited uncertainly – quite surprised to see the legionaries hurrying back down the slope towards them. Macro was a few score paces away and saw the frightened expressions on the faces of those who had not yet run away. He filled his lungs with air and drew his sword.

'GRRRAAAARRR!'

Cato leapt to one side in astonishment.

'Keep running, you fool! That was to scare them, not you!'

Sure enough the remaining Germans, rather than face the roaring centurion, turned and ran back into the depths of the village, not even stopping to close the gates. Barely a glance was spared for the Roman body lying untidily by the gate as the legionaries burst in right behind the villagers, screaming with rage and enjoying the effect. Only Cato kept silent, grimly glancing at the roughly constructed huts hemming them in, and quite overwhelmed by the appalling stench of the place.

'Close up!' Macro bellowed over his shoulder. 'And keep shouting!'

The century turned a corner and ran straight into the first steadfast opposition – a dozen hairy men with shields and hunting spears straddling the roadway. Foolishly they had positioned themselves too close to the corner and were run down almost before Cato was aware of their presence. Those that were brushed into a side alley fell out of sight and survived. The others were trampled over and finished off by swift javelin thrusts as the century swept over them. Cato saw only one German go down, his face smashed by the edge of Macro's shield. The man screamed shrilly but the cry was instantly lost in the crushing press that carried Cato forward into the heart of the German village. All sense of fear was lost in the need to concentrate on retaining his footing while remaining as close to Macro as possible. At his side, Cato was aware that the standard bearer was shouting 'On! On!' at the top of his voice, lips drawn back in a grin. By the Gods, Cato thought fleetingly, these men were actually enjoying themselves. Fools! Did they want to get themselves killed?

Suddenly, they were running into the square in front of the chief's hall that Cato had seen from the hillside, villagers scattering before the howling legionaries.

'Leave them!' Macro ordered. 'Keep on! Stay with me!'

He led the century from the village square by the widest route, sure that it led to the village gateway facing the oncoming horde beyond. The way ahead was clear and the only sign of the locals were doors that shut hastily at their approach. Through a gap in the buildings, Cato saw that they were now close to the other gate, rising just above the intervening thatched roofs. Then he was aware of a new sound, the howling of a multitude that rose even above the screams of the legionaries. As they became aware of the noise the legionaries fell silent and the pace slowed momentarily.

'Don't slack, you lazy bastards!' Macro shouted. 'Come on!'

The legionaries sprinted forward in a last effort to secure the gate ahead of the approaching Germans. Cato followed the standard bearer and Macro in a final desperate dash up a slight rise between the stinking German huts and then slammed into the centurion's back as the latter slewed to a halt. Cato's shield slipped from his grasp.

'Shit!' Macro exploded.

'Sorry, sir! I didn't . . .'

'Form line!' Macro shouted, ignoring him. 'Javelins at the ready!'

Retrieving his shield, Cato straightened up and froze. Fifty paces in front stood the gate-house, doors wide open, and swarming through them with a blood-curdling roar, now that they had caught sight of the enemy, were the Germans. They were quite the most hideous creatures that Cato had ever seen; large of body with wild hair, faces disfigured by blood-lust, and their foul animal stench was overwhelming.

'Get to one side, son.' Macro swept Cato to the end of the first line of legionaries where the standard bearer had grounded the standard and drawn his sword. 'First two ranks! Release javelins!'

A dozen javelins were hurled forwards at a high angle and arced towards the Germans, disappearing moments later into the crowd raging down the roadway six abreast. As if a rope had tripped them, the front ranks toppled forward, some impaled on the Roman javelins, others stumbling over the wounded and being pushed to the ground by the pressure from behind.

'Next two ranks, release javelins!' Macro's voice repeated, loud, calm and clear. The second volley turned the front of the German charge into a confused mass of dead and wounded, with the uninjured frantically struggling to get free of the tangle. Macro weighed up the situation in an instant and waved his sword over his head. 'Come on lads! Let's have them! Charge!'

Then he was off, running straight at the Germans,

shield raised to cover his torso and short sword pointed straight at the throat of the nearest enemy. With a shout, the century surged after him and once again Cato found himself being swept helplessly along in this flood of madness. Unlike the front ranks of legionaries, Cato still carried his javelin and, rather than carry the awkward weapon into the heaving melee he decided to hurl it as far forward as possible before drawing his short-sword. But the javelin throwing he had practised on the parade ground bore no resemblance to throwing a javelin in battle conditions. As he drew his right arm back he almost impaled the legionary immediately behind.

'Oi! Watch it, you stupid cunt!' the man shouted angrily, thrusting the butt to one side as he barged past Cato. 'You'll do someone a fucking injury!'

Cato flushed with embarrassment and then quickly hurled the offending weapon forwards at an unfortunately low trajectory, which caused the javelin to glance off Macro's helmet and fly off horizontally over the heaving mass of Germans before dropping out of sight. Cato swallowed nervously as the centurion shot a look of rage back over his shoulder, swore at the top of his voice and then turned to take his anger out on the nearest available German. Cato quickly drew his sword and threw himself forward, trying his hardest not to appear responsible for the errant missile.

The rearmost legionaries were busy shouting encouragement to those further forward, pausing only to finish off any Germans betraying signs of life amongst the tangled bodies stamped into the filthy ground. Cato was shocked to see one or two Roman bodies in among them – men he didn't know. As the legionaries steadily pushed the Germans back towards the gate more Roman bodies appeared, some still staring in surprise at their dreadful wounds. Blood flowed from the wounded, dripping down on to the street where iron-shod boots churned it into the mud. As more Romans fell, the fighting line grew nearer and Cato steeled himself for the moment when he would have to step into the space left by a Roman casualty.

Pressed back against the gate, a handful of Germans desperately tried to broaden the fighting line to take advantage of their numbers, scaling the low walls of the surrounding huts. A shout from Macro brought down a volley of javelins from those legionaries in the rear ranks and the Germans fell back into the mob.

Cato saw the standard waving at the head of the century as the legionaries forced their way step by step towards the gate. Then Macro led a renewed surge that brought the Romans between the huge gate-posts.

'Stand here!' Macro ordered and, with a last thrust of his sword into the enraged German mob, he disengaged and forced his way back through the ranks of the legionaries holding the gateway. Inside he faced the remaining troops. 'You lot. Up on the wall. We need to clear a space in front of the gate. Use your javelins, stones – whatever you can get your hands on.'

As the legionaries scaled the earth ramps to either side of the gate Macro saw Cato and caught his arm. 'Optio! I want you and six men ready with that locking bar. When I give the word, you get it into the gate braces as quick as you can. Understand?'

'Yes, sir.' Cato answered, staring at a crimson gash on the centurion's sword arm.

'Good. Then see to it.'

Then he was gone, thrusting his way back through the lines defending the gateway, shouting encouragement to his men. Cato quickly stirred and saw that the nearest men were watching him, waiting.

'Right!' He tried to sound firm. 'You heard him. Sheath swords and down shields.'

Astonishingly – to Cato at least – they reacted to the order and, unencumbered by the large heavy shields, they reached down and took a firm hold of the rough-hewn locking bar. Cato leaned his shield against the wall of a hut, then he bent and grasped the front of the bar.

'Ready? Lift!'

Cato slowly straightened, gasping with effort as he strained to raise the bar on to his shoulder where it rested uncomfortably. 'Right then,' he said through gritted teeth. 'Over to the gate, easy now!'

They struggled forward, stepping carefully over the prostrate forms of Romans and Germans, and then stood waiting to one side of the gate where the fight seemed to be going the Germans' way. The thin ranks of legionaries were slowly being forced to give ground. With his height Cato could see the Germans beyond, snarling with rage, throwing themselves forward on the Romans.

Macro shouted. 'More fire from the wall there! Use everything you've got!'

The soldiers above desperately rained down the last of their javelins, together with rocks and stones torn from the nearest huts, on to the heads of the helpless Germans.

Instinctively those at the front drew back from the gate, away from the slaughter.

'Back!' Macro turned and shoved the nearest legionaries back through the gate. The remaining Romans hurriedly withdrew, presenting their shields to the enemy. The last men through grabbed the edges of the gate and frantically swung the heavy timbers towards the Germans. Outside there was a howl as the enemy realised what was happening and they rushed forward again, regardless of the stones being hurled down from the walls above. At their head raced a tall warrior, blind rage and hatred etched on to his broad features. As the gates swung out to meet him he lunged for the nearest Roman with his spear.

'No, you fucking don't!' Macro swung his sword down on the head of the spear, knocking it to the ground. Unable to check himself, the German tumbled into the rapidly closing gap and Macro head-butted him, flattening his nose with a sickening crunch. As the German howled, Macro kicked him free of the gate. 'Piss off, you bugger!'

The gates closed with a grinding thud and – before the order could be given – Cato and his men quickly heaved the bar up, over and into the holding brackets where it dropped solidly into place. An instant later the gates suddenly swung in against the bar, which groaned against the strain. Macro watched for a moment to make sure that they were secure and then, posting a guard at the base of the gates, he ordered the remains of the century up on to the wall.

The village wall was a miserable affair, erected mainly

110

to ward off marauding war-bands from the wilderness beyond the Rhine. The dirt from the ditch surrounding the village had been heaped up to form an interior rampart, faced with turf to hold the soil in place. A narrow walkway, surfaced with a corduroy of logs, ran along the top of the wall beside a chest-high palisade of sharpened stakes, chest-high to a normal man but neck-high to the stocky Macro, who rose on his toes to best view the scene in front of the gate.

A seething mass of Germans stretched out in front of and to the sides of the village, like two arms encircling the Romans trapped within. Immediately below Macro, the Germans were being driven from the gate by a fresh fusillade of stones and a respectful gap, littered with dead and wounded, formed in front of the thick timbers. Further back Macro could see that faggots were already being bundled together from a stock of firewood the villagers had left beyond their walls where it would not be a fire risk. Once those faggots were ready, it would only be a matter of time before the ditch was filled and an approach to the wall was completed. At least the century had bought some time for the rest of the cohort. Macro turned to look for any sign of the other centuries. Dull cries and the faint clash of weapons sounded from elsewhere in the village and, from his slightly elevated position, Macro could see other legionaries stretched out around the wall. The village was secure then. Good. Time to make a report.

Looking down at the carpet of bodies strewn over the street leading up to the gate Macro estimated that almost a fifth of his men were dead, or badly wounded. He

111

glanced up and caught the eye of young Cato, who instantly flashed his gaze over the wall with an expression of rapt attention.

'Cato! Keep your fucking head down, unless you want some German to use it for target practice!'

'Yes, sir.'

'Come here. Job for you.'

Hunched down below the palisade, Macro removed his helmet and wiped his brow with his uninjured arm. As he prepared to give the details of the report to Cato, he ran a finger along a dent across the top of his helmet.

'Wouldn't know anything about that I suppose?'

Cato blushed silently.

'I guessed not. But if anyone tries to spit me like that again I'll have the bastard's hide. Now then I want you to find the tribune. Find him as quick as you can and you tell him we're holding this gate. Tell him I've got about seventy effectives left and then ask him for orders. Understand?'

Cato nodded.

'Get going then!' Macro slapped him on the helmet.

The centurion watched Cato run down the ramp to the street and quickly pick his way over the dead and wounded. As he replaced his helmet, Macro made a mental note to have a word with Bestia if they ever got out of this mess. That boy definitely needed some more javelin practice. He sighed and cautiously peered over the palisade to see how the Germans were progressing with the faggots.

Cato's boots pounded down the street as he ran back

the way the century had come only a little while earlier. Alone, he felt vulnerable and he glanced nervously from side to side as he hurried between the squalid ranks of German huts and buildings. But he saw no-one until he had almost reached the square at the heart of the village. There he ran into a Roman picket guarding the approach. The two legionaries hefted their javelins anxiously at his approach, looking beyond him, but were relieved when Cato drew up, breathing heavily.

'Where's the tribune?'

'What's happening, Optio?'

'Nothing . . . need to find the tribune . . . message for him.'

One of the legionaries gestured over his shoulder. 'Back there, by the chief's hut. What gives at the other gate?'

'It's being held,' Cato called over his shoulder as he ran past.

When he emerged from the narrow street into the square Cato halted in surprise. Hundreds of Germans of all ages were milling around in the centre. Then he saw that they were being herded together by scores of legionaries who pushed with their shields and prodded with javelins to steer their charges into a compact group for easy guarding. Some were still being driven in from the surrounding streets as Cato pushed his way through to the chief's hut where Vitellius was giving orders to a centurion.

'. . . and if they put up any struggle, or try anything on, kill them all.'

'Kill them?' The centurion looked uncertainly at the

113

villagers, many of whom were wailing loudly. 'Kill them all?'

'That's what I said,' Vitellius snapped, and then sneered. 'Or haven't you got the stomach for it?'

'No, sir!' The centurion seemed surprised. 'Just think it'd be a bit time-consuming to kill them all, sir.'

'Then you'll just have to do it quickly.'

'Sir!' Cato interrupted. 'Message for you, sir! From Macro.'

'What the hell is this, soldier?' Vitellius shouted. 'How dare you come up and yell at me as if I was some market-stall trader! Now, you make your report properly!'

'Excuse me, sir.' The centurion coughed. 'But may I carry on?'

'What? Oh yes. You've got your orders. Get moving.' Vitellius nodded curtly at Cato. 'Now you.'

'Sir. Centurion Macro begs to report that he is holding the other gate and—'

'Casualties?'

'About twenty, sir. He has seventy effectives left, sir. The centurion begs to request if you have any orders for him, sir.'

'Orders?' Vitellius repeated vaguely. 'Right then. You tell him he must hold the gate. We've secured the walls and the interior of the village. Now we've got to hold out until help arrives.' Vitellius looked up at the slowly greying sky. 'We're expected back before dark. The legate will set out as soon as he realises we're in some kind of trouble. If we're lucky, that'll be tomorrow morning. Still, we're better off here than in that forest.'

'Yes, sir,' Cato agreed wholeheartedly.

'You tell Macro what the situation is, and that he is to hold the gate at all costs until relieved. Do you understand me, optio?'

Cato nodded.

'Now go.'

Chapter Nine

Around the German village the day gradually dimmed into the smudged grey of approaching dusk. Once the fighting had died down, the physical heat and frenzied mental preoccupation of battle drained away and the legionaries standing to on the wall shivered in the freezing winter gloom. To make matters worse, snow had begun to fall, large flakes that drifted down lazily in the still air. The initial ambush had failed and now the Germans withdrew out of javelin range and most stood hurling abuse at the village in their harsh tongue. Others busied themselves in constructing faggots and lopping branches off young pine trees to make crude scaling ladders. The Roman defenders watched anxiously from the wall, occasionally sparing hopeless glances in the direction of the Second's fortress, a mere eight miles away. More ominously, the legionaries of the Sixth century could see that a substantial tree had been felled nearby and was well on the way to being converted into a battering ram.

Macro had not been idle either. He had ordered some men to pile small rocks on the wall to supplement the few remaining javelins and another group to pile heavier rocks and earth against the rear of the village gates to absorb the impact of the ram. These were standard counter-measures but if the Germans managed to fully co-ordinate their attack then the thin line of Romans manning the village wall would inevitably be overrun, as Macro patiently explained to his young optio while the latter bound the gash on Macro's forearm.

'What then?' Cato asked.

'What do you think?' Macro smiled thinly as he stamped his feet. 'They'll be all over us, we won't have a chance. We'll be cut to pieces.'

'Keep still please, sir. Will they take prisoners?'

'Best not even think about that,' Macro said gently. 'Believe me, you'd be better off dead.'

'Really?'

'Really.'

'The tribune said Vespasian would send help as soon as he realised something was up. If we can hold out until then . . .'

'Big if,' Macro replied. 'But we might. Just make sure you do your bit.'

'I will.' Cato tore off the excess from the rough dressing and tied the ends firmly. 'There you go, sir. How's it feel?'

'Not bad.' Macro flexed his arm, and winced as a shaft of pain stabbed up to his shoulder. 'It'll do. No worse than I've already had.'

'You've been injured before then, sir?'

'All part of the deal when you join the army. You'll soon get used to it.'

'If we survive.'

'We might yet.' Macro tried to sound reassuring and then, seeing the gloomy expression on the youngster's face, he punched him on the shoulder. 'Chin up lad! We're not dead yet. Not by a long way. But if we do go, well then, there's not a lot we can do about it, so we might as well not worry, eh? Now then, let's see what those bastards are up to.'

A quick inspection of the German lines in the gathering gloom of the snowflake-speckled dusk revealed no significant changes and the dull thuds of axe blows on wood continued unceasingly. Satisfied that the village was safe for the moment, Macro turned back towards Cato.

'Just going to have a word with the rest of the lads. Keep them cheerful. While I'm about it, I want you to take a couple of men and see if you can find something to eat and drink. I'm hungry. Might as well have something while we wait for Herman to stir.'

A quick search through the nearest huts produced a good haul of dried meat, fresh bread and several jars of the local brew.

'Go easy on that stuff,' Macro warned, speaking from bitter experience. 'Make sure no-one gets a skinful or they'll be up on charges when we get back to base.'

Cato looked over the centurion's shoulder. 'Sir! The tribune . . .'

Vitellius and a bodyguard of four burly men emerged from the darkened street and mounted the ramp to the gate. Macro stiffened and was about to call the century to attention but Vitellius shook his head.

'Let the men rest, Centurion. They've earned it.'

'Yes, sir. Thank you.'

'How goes it?'

'Well, as you can see,' Macro swept an arm out to indicate the ring of Germans surrounding the village, 'we're not going to be able to hold that lot off with seventy men, sir. They've been making faggots and assault ladders ever since the last attack. And over there, they've nearly finished a battering ram. Once they bring that up . . .'

'I see.' Vitellius scratched his chin, as if in deep contemplation. 'You'll just have to hold them back, as long as you can.'

'Yes sir . . . How's the rest of the cohort?'

'Our position's not too bad. We control the wall and all able-bodied villagers are being kept under guard. Quadratus's century got the worst of it. That bitch – the chief's wife – opened an outflow grill. Twenty of them got behind Quadratus's men before she was discovered. Just picking us off while the men were keeping the Germans outside the village away from the wall. Lost almost half the century before we flushed them out.'

'You can rely on Quadratus, sir.' Macro smiled.

'Not any more, took a German pike in the guts. Went clean through him.'

'No.'

'Afraid so, centurion. And the Germans managed to take down his optio as well. That's the reason why I'm here. Can you spare someone to take over from Quadratus?'

Five paces away Cato's ears burned and his blood went ice cold in anxious anticipation. He summoned up all his will power not to look at Macro and instead gazed resolutely over the wall at the Germans gathered around the fires, their faces glowing red. Adopting what he hoped was the nonchalant pose of a veteran, Cato continued listening with a pounding heart.

'Hmm.' Macro pondered, looking around, and Cato could almost sense the weight of his gaze as it rested momentarily on his back before passing on.

'What about your optio?' Vitellius asked. 'Is he a good man?'

'Hardly a man, sir. Just a new boy. Can't afford to let him out of my sight. He means well but he's nowhere near ready for what you need.'

'Pity.'

The crushing weight of rejection wrapped itself round Cato's heart. He clamped his teeth tightly and fought back tears of humiliation.

'You have anyone else?'

'Yes, sir. The standard bearer's a good man. Take him.'

'All right then.' Vitellius nodded. 'You know the score, Centurion. Hold the gate at all costs. If we can get through the night Vespasian is bound to send help in the morning. I'm counting on you. Carry on.'

'Thank you, sir.' Macro brought his hand to his chest in salute and then watched as the tribune and his bodyguard picked their way over to where the century's standard drooped above the wall.

'Wanker!' he cursed softly. '*I'm counting on you*' – as if Macro didn't know his duty.

He cast a quick glance round to ensure the indiscretion had not been overheard. The stiff pose of the boy gazing fixedly over the walls was distinctly unnatural.

'Cato!'

'Sir?' The voice sounded aggrieved.

'Any sign of movement?'

'No.'

'Well, keep your eyes peeled.'

'Yes, sir.'

The tribune and his small squad walked back to the gate along the wall, the standard bearer in tow. Vitellius nodded curtly at Macro as he and his men passed.

'Take care, sir,' said the standard bearer.

'You too.' Macro smiled. 'We'll look after the standard while you're gone, Porcius.'

For a moment the standard bearer paused and looked longingly at the Sixth's standard, then with as little show of reluctance as he could muster he thrust the wooden shaft at Macro. 'Here.'

Then they were gone, disappearing into the cold darkness between the dingy German huts, leaving Macro holding the standard with its weighted banner hanging down from the horizontal cross-piece. For a moment Macro felt a strange twinge of excitement as the familiar awkwardness of the standard brought back the memories of his own year served as a standard bearer. He turned the shaft fondly and smiled at the reawakened sensibilities of a far younger man, tantalisingly visceral, then he was aware of Cato again.

'Boy!' he called out softly. 'Come here.'

Cato dutifully came to attention in front of his superior, face hardened with suppressed emotions.

'Relax, son. You've got a new duty. I want you to look after this.'

'Sir?'

'You heard what the tribune said?'

'Yes, sir.'

'And I trust that's all you heard. Now we've lost Porcius I need a good man to take charge of the standard for a while. Are you up to it?'

It was more of an order than a question, however gently said, and Cato felt elated as the bitter shame of a moment before was washed away. Without waiting to reply, he downed his shield and took a firm grasp on the standard with his left hand.

'It's a big responsibility,' Macro said. 'You know that.'

'Yes, sir. Thank you, sir. I'll guard it with my life.'

'You'd better. If Porcius finds so much as a scratch on it when he takes it back, he'll have your balls hanging from the tip the next time we go into action. Got that?'

Cato nodded solemnly.

'Stick close to me and, whatever happens, you hold on to that standard and you keep it high. Up where the men can see it at all times. Understand? . . . Now then, what's up?'

A sudden flow of movement through the men on the wall had caught his eye. All the legionaries were on their feet, shields and swords at the ready. Cato lifted the standard and followed Macro up to the palisade. Beyond the walls, the Germans had risen from their fires and were now moving in a black mass towards the gate. Irregular shapes in the crowd showed where men struggled with the faggots. Some carried torches that lit the faces of the nearest men in a flickering yellow-orange glare.

'Now, remember, lads,' Macro called out as he drew his sword, 'if they get in here then the whole cohort is finished. So give it your all.'

A loud shout rippled along the approaching German horde and quickly grew into a roaring cheer of anger and arrogance. Some of the legionaries shouted back their defiance.

'Steady!' Macro called out above the din. 'They're just wasting their breath! And we've got nothing to prove!'

Beside him, Cato stood rooted to the ground, transfixed by the approaching menace. For some reason, this mass advancing with fierce determination seemed far more threatening in the darkness. His imagination was busy amplifying every noise and every shape. Unlike that afternoon's mad charge through the village, the imminence of desperate conflict gave men space to consider their own courage, their own willingness to fight, and to vividly imagine the worst consequences of what might befall them. Cato shuddered and instantly cursed himself, quickly glancing round at the others on the wall.

'You afraid, lad?' Macro asked quietly.

'Yes, a bit.'

Macro smiled. 'Of course you are. So are the rest of us. But we're here now and there's nothing we can do about it.'

'I know that, sir. But it doesn't make it any easier.'

'Just keep a tight hold on the standard.'

The Germans held a steady pace until they were close

to the wall. Then a war horn cried out from somewhere in the night and from all round the village came more horns, and wild warrior roars crashed like a wave against the thin Roman line manning the flimsy palisade. In front of the gate, the dark forms swarmed up to the ditch and hurled the faggots into the deep shadows while others rained down a shower of arrows, spears and rocks on the defenders. With a shield raised over his head, Macro looked up to see that the pile of faggots was filling the ditch in two positions, one on either side of the gate. In a little while the ditch would be filled to a width that would allow the Germans to throw a stream of ladder-bearing men directly up against the wall. Worse still, heaving its way through the horde came the battering ram – the biggest threat to their position.

As long as the legionaries kept their heads, scaling ladders could be dislodged and pushed back, but a ram would inevitably break through the rough-hewn village gate. Then Macro and his men would have no defences to shelter behind and the Germans would overwhelm them by sheer weight of numbers. With reckless bravery, the Germans had quickly filled the ditch and, rather than making a direct assault, Macro was surprised to see them ramping the faggots up against the wall. Those Germans that fell were simply tossed on to the growing pile.

All at once the enemy horde parted in front of the gate and the battering ram, a stout pine trunk with branch stumps for handles, was carried up to the gate by a score of burly men. As the ram crashed against the gate timbers, the impact was felt by all those on the wall above. Macro peered down behind the gate as the second blow thudded home and he saw the crossbar nearly leap from its brace, only just held in place by the frantic efforts of the men he had left on guard. Several pegs were already starting from their sockets.

'This isn't good,' Macro muttered and turned back to look over the wall. Even as the defenders hurled stones down each casualty was instantly replaced and the rhythm maintained. 'This isn't good at all.'

'Isn't there something we can do, sir?' asked Cato.

'Oh yes! If we had Greek fire, we'd fry 'em up nicely.'

Cato dimly recalled what little he had read of the experimental weapon and found it hard to believe that the element burned with a national accent. But from the gleam of longing in Macro's eyes it would appear that the Greek variety was something quite special.

'Would German fire do, sir?'

'What?'

'German fire, sir.'

'What the hell are you talking about?'

'Well, sir, it's just that there were some large ovens still alight in one of the huts over there. Must be a bakery of some kind. No bread though. I suppose they must have been preparing the ovens.'

Macro stared at him for a moment. 'And you didn't think to inform me?'

'No, sir. You just ordered me to find provisions.'

'Right then, we need fire now, so see to it.' Macro replied, trying hard to hide his exasperation. 'Find the men who went looking for food with you and order them to bring coals up to the walls on their shields. Then get back here.'

Once Cato had gone Macro examined the inside of the gate from ground level. The pounding was already opening gaps in the heavy wooden beams through which he could glimpse the Germans beyond. Each new blow dislodged a shower of dust and debris from the wall above and Macro had to blink several times to clear his eyes. Hurrying back up to the wall, he detailed several men to use pitchforks to take straw from nearby huts and pile it on the walkway above the gate. It was not until the first detail returned, shields piled high with red glowing embers, that Cato realised what the centurion's intentions were.

'Get those on the straw!'

The sweating legionaries tipped the embers into the straw and, despite the slight dampness, smoke and small flames flickered into life. As the fire caught and sizzled, Macro pitched more straw on top and smoke began to billow causing the nearest legionaries to break into fits of coughing.

'Right then! Over the wall with it!' Macro shouted. 'Use whatever you've got, but get it over the wall!'

The Romans dived in with pitchforks, the few remaining javelins and even short swords and the burning bundles of straw, sparks crackling high into night, blazed down on to the hapless Germans with the battering ram. Shouts and screams of terror sounded from below and the pounding at the gate ceased. At the foot of the wall Macro could see the ram lying abandoned, almost covered in burning straw. The heat hit his face a stinging blow and Macro stepped back. No-one would be using that battering ram for quite a while, even if it failed to burn completely.

126

'Hah! Look at them run!' Cato beamed. 'They'll not be trying that again tonight.'

'Maybe.' Macro nodded. 'Maybe. But two can play that game. Look there!'

Cato turned to follow the direction the centurion was indicating. The ramps built by the attackers were finished and, as he watched, torches arced up from the German lines and fell in an explosion of sparks in among the faggots. Within moments the ramps were ablaze and bright orange flames licked up the village walls driving the legionaries back. One hapless soldier, fully illuminated by the flickering glare, was hit by several arrows and pitched forward into the blaze with a scream of terror that abruptly ceased. Cato shuddered, but before he could spare the poor man any more thought a small flame suddenly licked through a gap in the walkway.

'Oh no,' he muttered, then turned towards Macro. 'Sir! Look there!'

Macro looked down just in time to see another, larger, tongue of flame hungrily flicker through the walkway. The gate was on fire. Some of the straw must have landed too near the wall. 'That's just fucking great! So much for German fire.' He glared at Cato.

'We could try to put it out.'

'Shut up! It's too late for that.' The centurion's mind raced. All three fires on the wall had a firm hold and were burning ever more fiercely even as he watched. There was nothing they could do to put them out now. And if they stayed on the wall they would be burned as well as providing nicely lit targets for the German archers.

There was nothing for it. They must give ground until the fire died and they could move back up to defend the wall. But, with the gate already well ablaze and two more openings burning through the wall, in a matter of an hour's time the Sixth century's defence of this side of the village would collapse like a cheap tenement block. And that would be long before dawn and any hope of relief from Vespasian.

'Stand back!' he roared out so that all his men would hear him above the raging crack and roar of the flames. 'Off the wall!'

He waited until the last man had descended the gate ramps and then he took a final look towards the palisade, where sharpened stakes of wood hissed and steamed in the withering heat. Beyond the wall, the front ranks of the Germans were illuminated brilliantly and their triumphant faces wavered and shimmered through the heat-distorted air. Then he ran down to his men and formed the main body up in the street inside the gate, with two smaller sections fronting the stretches of wall ignited by the Germans.

'What do we do now, sir?' Cato asked.

'We have to wait – and pray that the fire lasts.'

Chapter Ten

The fire not only lasted, it raged, sending swirling streams of sparks high up into the night sky where they mingled and melted the falling snowflakes. Most of the sparks slowly glowered into nothingness, but some fell back to earth – landing on the angled thatch roofs of the village. Even as Macro was cursing himself for deciding to burn the ram, and thereby the gate he was intending to save from the ram, Cato drew his attention to the nearest huts. Smoke curled up from the roofs, and here and there an orange twinkle gleamed, then rippled into flames. Macro glanced round anxiously and saw that the huts as far back as fifty paces from the wall were catching fire. Unless they moved they would soon be trapped right in the centre of the blazing inferno to come. A sudden crashing sound drew his gaze to the front, where the entire gateway was collapsing into the roaring flames.

Beyond they could hear the Germans shouting triumphantly. They would be edging towards the blaze, itching for the moment when the fires had subsided enough to allow them to stream into the village and slaughter the cohort. But for now the flames showed no signs of subsiding, indeed the fire was growing ever more intense as it spread amongst the huts. The heat in the street was already intolerable and Cato found himself squinting to protect his eyes, buffeted by the wavering, stinging air. The centurion knew the time had come to retreat, a bitter truth to swallow – but a necessary one.

'All troops to me! All troops to me! Back down the street!'

The legionaries turned and quick-marched until they reached the limit of the fire where Macro ordered them to halt and close up once again. The men looked back in relief, glad to be out of immediate danger. The position they had occupied moments earlier erupted in a shower of sparks as a building collapsed across the street where they had been standing.

'Close one, sir,' muttered one of the men.

'We're not out of it yet,' Macro replied sourly. 'Fire's spreading fast. We'll fall back with it. If we're lucky, we can keep the fire between us and Herman.'

'Until we run out of village,' Cato said softly.

Macro turned quickly, on the point of shouting out some abuse, but the boy was right. 'Until we run out of village,' he agreed. 'Or Vespasian reaches us.'

The fire, let loose like an uncaged beast at some amphitheatre, raged across the village, hungrily devouring all in the path of its blazing jaws. Above it, the sky glowed orange and the snow falling from the sky melted into rain. Little by little the legionaries gave ground and, as they did so, Macro became aware that the blaze at the gateway was dying down far more quickly than it should. He frowned, uncomprehending. Then he saw Germans beyond the falling flames, throwing buckets of water on the ruins of the gate where smoke and steam mingled. As he watched, the men around him became aware of what was happening and a low murmur of despair trickled through the Sixth century. The Germans were clearly not content to leave the Romans to the eventual wrath of the fire, they wanted blood, and the street leading up to the gate was nearly clear of flames due to its relative breadth.

'Silence!' Macro shouted. 'We're not done for yet. Not as long as we can keep the fire between us and them. First two squads with me. Castor!' Macro yelled to the century's veteran. 'See to it that the rest tear down buildings along the street – anything that helps the fire line spread. Got that?'

'Yes, sir.'

'But you keep the line open for us. When you're done you call us back. We'll fall back through you.' Macro turned to the front two squads. 'All right, lads, listen. If Herman gets down the street we have to hold him back long enough for the others to do their work. Then we run like hell. Come on then.'

With Macro and Cato at their head, the two squads marched down the street and stopped as close to the ruins of the gate as the heat permitted. There Macro formed them into an unbroken shield wall and they waited. But not for long. The fire at the gate was quickly extinguished leaving a smouldering heap of ruined timber. The Germans stumbled across it, heedless of the residual heat, and resumed their chain of water jars where the burning building had fallen into the street. As the enemy laboured the Romans waited silently and Cato, in the second rank, held the shaft of the standard tightly to stop himself shaking too obviously. He glanced sidelong at the men around him, silent and still, eyes grimly watching the Germans working towards them.

Suddenly the Germans downed their jars and scrambled over the last blackened ruins between them and the Romans, voices raised in hysterical war-cries.

'Steady, boys!' Macro growled. 'Hold your line. We fight in formation.'

Cato could see over Macro's shoulder the first of the Germans, long hair streaming, running straight at them. Without slowing for a moment, he crashed into the wall of shields and was despatched by a quick thrust. With a gasp he fell dead on the street. But more followed, thudding against the shields, desperately trying to force an opening into which they could thrust their short spears. As the weight piled up, the legionaries gave ground. The first of their number fell, wounded in the side by a spear thrust. Streaming blood, he went down – his place instantly taken by the man behind – and his comrades were powerless to help as they gave ground and left him exposed to the Germans. With a savage cry, the man's throat was ripped open by a spear and the gushing crimson splashed up the shield wall.

Cato ducked as a spear-thrust was aimed at his own head and the standard dipped forward. The Germans eagerly lunged for it and one secured a grip on the banner.

'Hands off, Herman!' Macro shouted, thrusting his sword into the chest the German had foolishly exposed. Abruptly his grip was released and Cato snatched the standard back to the vertical, horrified by the shame of what had nearly happened.

For a second, Macro was able to glance back down the street and saw that the rest of the century had pulled down several buildings, piling the rubble and burning thatch across the street. It was almost time.

'Rear section! Fall back now.'

The men needed no urging and turned to sprint down the street towards the small opening left for them where Castor had some men poised with ropes to pull a wall down across the street. As soon as the Germans saw the rearmost men run back to safety they shouted their contempt and flew at the thin shield wall with renewed fury. Even Cato could see that the last section would be in perilous danger the moment it tried to disengage. But Macro was ready for the moment and, without warning, bellowed an order, 'Break and charge!'

With a shout, the legionaries pushed their shields out and hacked into the Germans before them. The unexpectedness of the move momentarily caught the Germans off guard and they checked and recoiled.

'Run!' Macro shouted.

In an instant the charge turned tail and the soldiers bolted down the street, Cato amongst them, cursing the awkwardness of the standard. As the street narrowed towards the point where the rest of the century was waiting, Macro faced the Germans once again, determined to make sure his men got away. The enemy were still reeling from the sudden turnabout in Roman tactics and, with a grim smile of satisfaction, he ran after the others.

But one German, more alert than the rest, hefted his spear above his head and hurled it after the retreating Romans with all his might.

Cato, awash with relief, was bolting towards the gap being held open by his comrades when he heard Macro shout.

'Ahhh! Fuck!'

Cato turned quickly. Ten paces up the street Macro had tumbled headlong, a spear right through his thigh. His shield had fallen ahead of him and his sword lay to one side. Beyond Macro, the Germans had recovered from their surprise and were running towards the stricken centurion. Macro looked up and saw Cato.

'Run, you fool!'

'Sir . . .'

'Save the fucking standard! RUN!'

In a moment of shocking stillness Cato saw the angry look on Macro's face; the Germans running down towards him; the fire raging in the buildings around them and the sky glowing blood red against the night. Then, before he was aware of any kind of conscious decision, he was running back towards his centurion screaming meaninglessly at the Germans.

Chapter Eleven

'Did you see Titus today?'

'Sorry?' Vespasian looked up from his travel desk. 'What did you say?'

'Your son, Titus. Have you seen him today?' Flavia tapped her finger on his shoulder. 'Or have you been too busy to notice that you have a son?'

'My dear, I really haven't had time.'

'That's what you always say. Always. All this wretched paperwork is taking up your whole life.' She looked into the document chest. 'Don't you think you should make time for the boy?'

Vespasian laid down his stylus and regarded her for a moment, heart heavy with guilt. After three miscarriages and one still-born, Titus had seemed like something of a miracle. The long labour had nearly killed Flavia and the child. Since his birth in Rome two years ago the boy had been treated like a precious vase, wrapped in wool and hardly ever out of his mother's sight. Vespasian had devoted much effort to being as supportive as he could, all the while conscious that time spent with family was time spent away from politics and career advancement – which was ultimately for Titus's benefit, he assured himself.

Accepting the appointment to the Legion had not been an easy choice. He had known Flavia was hugely reluctant to leave Rome, even as she dutifully urged him to accept the post. Like all wives with a respect for tradition, she had accompanied him when Vespasian had left to take up his command. While the fresh air was a pleasant change from clinging stench of Rome, it had not proved beneficial to Titus. Since they had arrived at the base the child had been down with one illness after another. The cold, damp climate was ruinous to a fragile constitution, and many months of long nights at the side of his cradle had exhausted Flavia. The thought of the loss of Titus filled them both with dread, but Vespasian had had the comfort of a full working day while Flavia had not. Removed from her social circle and isolated in the closed world of a military base with only a handful of other officers' wives, Flavia's world had turned inward on her son.

Titus, as is the way with infants, contrived to find every possible way to drive his mother, and her domestic slaves, completely frantic with worry. There was no shelf, table edge or door he had not managed to crash his head against, no chair or chest he had not fallen off and no rug or mat he had not tripped over. The boy's natural inquisitiveness meant that no safety audit of their quarters was ever completed thoroughly enough that Titus did not find something dangerous or unsavoury to stick in his mouth or poke in his eye or when the mood took him – which it frequently did – in the eye of some unfortunate slave. Now his nurses were having to contend with a fine range of needle-sharp teeth that closed unexpectedly on any exposed flesh that ventured within range.

Vespasian smiled at the thought that at least his son had spirit.

'What?' Flavia asked.

'Eh?'

'You're smiling. What are you thinking?'

'I'm thinking it's time I spent some time with my boy.' Vespasian pushed the travel desk back and stood up. 'Come.'

As they left the study and walked along the covered walkway that ran along the private courtyard Vespasian looked at the sky. Beyond the dull flickering light of the courtyard torches the freezing night air was brushed with the first flakes of snow. It occurred to him that Vitellius had not yet returned and the thought of the cocksure tribune marching back from the village in a miserable blizzard would have been gratifying were it not for the poor men he was commanding.

As the door to the little nursery opened, Titus's head swivelled round and, with a shout of pure pleasure, he jumped on to his little legs, pushing his nurse to one side, and ran across to his parents.

'Dada!' he squealed as he wrapped his arms around his father's legs and tipped his head back, wide-eyed and smiling. 'Pick up! Pick up! Pick up!'

Vespasian leant down and, firmly grasping the boy under the arms, swung him up above his head, provoking a fresh bout of excited screaming.

'How's my soldier? Eh? How's my little boy today?'

Vespasian smiled and turned to his wife. 'He's growing up fast. Not long now before he gets to wear his first toga.'

'He's still a baby!' Flavia protested. 'Still my little baby. Aren't you?'

Titus regarded his mother with a disgusted expression and pushed himself back from her tight embrace. Vespasian laughed and leant forward to ruffle the boy's unruly hair. 'That's my little soldier!'

'He's not a soldier!' Flavia said firmly. 'And he's not going to be a soldier, at least he's not going to be one for any longer than is absolutely necessary. If I have anything to do with it, he'll stay in Rome where I can look after him.'

'We'll have to let him decide for himself one day,' Vespasian replied gently. 'The army's a good life for a man.'

'No, it's not! The army's dangerous, uncomfortable and populated by uncouth louts.'

'Provincials like me, I suppose.'

'Oh, I didn't mean . . .'

'Only joking. But seriously, if Titus is to make a career for himself in the Senate then he must serve with the legions first.'

'You could see to it that he gets a posting near home.'

'We've been through this. The appointments get made by the imperial staff. I have no influence there, at least not at the moment. If you want him to be successful he must serve in the army first. You know that's the way it is.'

'Yes.' Flavia nodded sadly and kissed Titus on the

forehead. The infant sensed her mood and suddenly hugged her tightly, crushing his little face into her shoulder. 'I just wish I could have him at this age for longer.'

'I know. I really do. Maybe there'll be more children one day. When you're ready.'

Flavia stared up into his face, dark eyes full of painful memory that threatened to well up into tears. She blinked and then forcefully smiled away the tremble in her lip. 'Oh, I hope so. I want so very many of them. And I want them with you. You promise me you will be careful?'

'Careful?'

'This new campaign of yours in Britain. You will be careful.'

'Britain! How the hell . . .' Vespasian's brow creased angrily. 'That's supposed to be a secret. Where did you hear it?'

'From the officers' wives.' Flavia laughed at his expression. 'You men really do have a great deal to learn about keeping secrets, don't you?'

'Typical,' Vespasian muttered. 'Bloody typical. I swear my most senior officers to strict confidentiality and the next thing I know it's common gossip. Is nothing sacred any more?'

Titus laughed and shook his head violently from side to side.

'Now, don't fuss, dear.' Flavia patted him on the arm. 'I'm sure the secret's safe from everyone else. But don't let's change the subject. I was talking about Britain.'

'So, it seems, is everyone else,' grumbled Vespasian.

'You must promise me you'll be careful. I want your word. Right now.'

'I promise.'

'That's settled, then.' She nodded in satisfaction. 'Now give the boy a hug and put him to bed.'

Vespasian carried the child over to the cot in the corner of the room. Leaning down, he pulled back the soft woollen covers one-handed and removed the warming brick. As he was lowered into the cot, Titus moaned and tightly clenched his hands into the folds of his father's tunic. 'Not tired! Not tired!'

'You must go to sleep now,' Vespasian replied softly as he tried to prise his son's fingers loose. The boy's tiny hands were surprisingly strong and his father struggled to unpick them as the child's eyes welled with tears of anger and frustration. As the last fingers were worked free from the cloth round Vespasian's neck Titus suddenly bit his father on the knuckle. Before he could help himself, Vespasian swore out loud.

'Language!' Flavia hissed. 'Do you want him to pick up such words at his age?'

It occurred to Vespasian that any child brought up in a military garrison was going to pick up a rather wider vocabulary than was deemed appropriate in the polite social circles of Rome.

'That boy,' he continued after a moment, 'has quite a bite on him.'

'But that's good.'

'It is?' Vespasian looked down with raised eyebrows at the small teeth-shaped crescent on the back of his hand.

'Show's he's got strength of character.' Flavia pressed the still struggling boy down into the cot and drew the cover up over his body.

'Shows he's got sharp teeth,' her husband muttered.

With a last whine, Titus succumbed to a child's sense of routine and turned over on to his stomach, closed his eyes and, with a few meaningless mumbles spoken softly into his mattress, fell asleep. Both parents gazed down at him for a moment, wondering at the peaceful, perfectly rounded shape of his face, the final twitches of his curled fingers in the flickering glow of the oil lamps.

Someone hammered on the door. Titus stirred, eyes flickering open for a moment.

'Who the hell?'

'Just shut them up quickly,' Flavia hissed. 'Before they wake Titus.'

Vespasian opened the door on to the courtyard and was confronted by the duty centurion and a shivering legionary.

'Sir!' the centurion barked in best parade-ground manner. 'Beg to report . . .'

'Shhh! Keep your voice down. My boy's asleep.'

The centurion stood open-mouthed for a second, before he managed to force himself to continue in a whisper. 'Beg to report a fire.'

'A fire. How big a fire? Where?'

'In the direction of the forest, sir, towards the Rhine.'

Vespasian eyed the man impatiently. 'And you think that's worth disturbing me for?'

'This sentry says it's a big fire, sir.'

'Big? How big?'

141

'Dunno, sir,' the legionary replied. 'Can't see the fire as such, sir. Just a glow, on the horizon like.'

A nasty thought struck the legate. 'Third cohort back yet?'

'No, sir.' The centurion shook his head. 'No sign of them.'

'Right, I'm coming. You're dismissed.'

Flavia crossed over to him in small, quiet steps. 'Trouble?'

'Possibly. I'm just going to check. I'll be back soon. You get to bed.'

When Vespasian reached the tower above the eastern gate the parapet had already disappeared under a softly curved layer of snow. Beyond the fortress wall, a dull white landscape stretched out towards the distant fringe of the forest, only dimly visible through the swirling snow. Nevertheless, the duty centurion had been right to summon him; an orange glow reflected off the clouds beyond the tree-line. That had to be quite a fire, Vespasian mused. Moreover, a fire directly in line with the local German settlement.

He turned back to the duty centurion. 'Still no sign of Vitellius?'

'Nothing, sir.'

Worrying, most worrying. Yet what trouble could Vitellius have led the Third cohort into? According to the latest intelligence reports there was little indication of any rebellious sentiment brewing amongst the locals. Still, the cohort should have returned to base by now. And the intensity of the distant glow indicated a sizeable fire. Vespasian considered the damage his reputation would suffer if he sounded the alarm too easily, all too clearly visualising the mocking laughter of his men. But the thought was no sooner in his head than he quickly dismissed it. His pride came a poor second to his feeling of responsibility to the men of the Legion. He turned back to the duty centurion.

'Call out the horse squadron. I want them to scout the route taken by the Third cohort to the local village. They are to report back to me in person the moment they find anything. Then call out the Legion. I want all senior officers at headquarters immediately. Centurions are to have their men in full battle order and ready to move off in line of march. Except the First cohort. They stay and guard the base. Got all that?'

'Yes, sir.'

'Then go. And run!'

After the duty centurion had gone, Vespasian turned back towards the distant fire. Unless Vitellius had lost his way back to the fort, the fire had to be connected with the cohort's absence.

'Sir?'

When he looked up Vespasian saw the concerned look in the young sentry's face. 'What is it, soldier?'

'Do you think our lads are in trouble?'

Behind them the first call to arms shrieked out across the base, to be quickly taken up by others, and out into the night, silhouetted against numerous doorframes, poured the soldiers of the Second Legion. Vespasian forced himself to grin.

'They'd better be in trouble, or else I've just pissed

off four thousand men for nothing. And that wouldn't do, would it?'

Chapter Twelve

Cato was screaming at the top of his voice as he hurtled towards the two Germans closing on his centurion. At the last moment, he lowered the tip of the standard and swept it from side to side. The foremost German standing above Macro, poised for the kill, looked up at the shrill shouts and half turned to face the new danger. Macro didn't hesitate a second and smashed his fist up into the man's crotch. He doubled over and fell to his knees retching, and Cato tumbled over the top, rolling to one side. The remaining German looked quite startled and suddenly burst out laughing. Cato angrily rose to his feet and brandished the standard in his enemy's face.

'Don't you fucking laugh at me!'

For a moment the pair stared into each other's eyes, the German's expression quite cold and calculating now. Suddenly he feinted to Cato's right and, as Cato swung the standard round, the German ducked back and aimed a sword thrust at Cato's armpit. The army standard, like all army standards, was designed for show and not grace and the heavy headpiece swung so far round that the bottom of the shaft came arcing right into the face of the lunging German and stopped him dead. With a

145

stunned groan he slumped on to the ground. Cato, who had been facing the other way, came round – gritting his teeth at the prospect of a fatal wound – and stared in shock at the man collapsing to the ground.

'What?'

'Leave him!' Macro called out. 'Come here, boy! Get this spear out of me!'

'Sir?'

'Just do it!'

Cato took a firm grasp with his spare hand and Macro turned his leg for a better angle. 'Now!'

Cato pulled with all his might and the leaf-shaped spear tip came free of the leg with a gush of blood and torn tissue. Macro howled in agony just once and then, clamping his mouth shut, he painfully raised himself as Cato lifted him by the arm. The wound was bleeding badly, but happily the blood flowed rather than spurted – no fatal wound then. But the pain was the worst he had felt, quite mind-numbing, and it took a great force of will for Macro to swing his arm round the youth's shoulder as Cato helped him back towards the gap between the buildings where the rest of the century waited. Behind them, above the roar of the flames, Cato could hear pounding footsteps and he glanced back to see the Germans rushing forwards, screaming for Roman blood. He renewed his efforts, almost dragging the centurion along with him. Then they stumbled and Macro went down on his knees, crying out as it jarred his wounded leg. The faces ahead filled with despair – they could see that the two would never make it before the Germans were on them.

'Go!' Macro grunted. 'That's an order!'

'Can't hear you, sir.'

'Save the standard.'

At that moment Castor sadly shook his head and gave the order for the building to be pulled down. The legionaries hesitated until the veteran screamed the order out again and then the ropes tightened and the wall crashed down into the street bringing the blazing thatch with it.

'Oh shit!' Cato stopped, then quickly looked back. The Germans were almost on them. To his right was a stone wall with a stout wooden door. Quickly he lifted the latch, kicked the door inwards and bundled the centurion and the standard inside. He ducked through the opening and slammed the door shut, hurriedly throwing the locking bar into its cradle. A crunching thump echoed in the confined space as the first Germans arrived outside and pounded the door. It was dark inside, but light from the flames illuminated the edges of the shutters and gaps in the eaves. The one window in the room faced on to the street, but luckily it had been closed and bolted, and now it too shuddered under the impact of blows from outside.

'See if there's another way out of here,' Macro said as he examined his wound by touch. Blood was still flowing freely and he dare not spill any more than was necessary if he was to keep his wits about him. He undid his sword belt and removed the scabbard before fastening it above the wound as tightly as possible. The bleeding had slowed to an ooze when Cato returned a moment later.

'Well?'

'Seems to be some kind of barn, some hay at the back and a ventilation opening, but that's it.'

The pounding at the door was more rhythmic now and, as they both looked at the shuttered window, a long splint of wood flew back into the room where a dark point pierced the shutter. It wriggled, disappeared and moments later more splinters flew and jagged orange shafts of light pierced the gloom.

'We can't stay here.'

'No,' Cato responded. 'Look there!'

A yellow glow had appeared in the raftered thatch over their heads, and then another flaring violently into tiny flickering flames that quickly increased in intensity.

And all the time the shutters were being hacked to pieces.

'We'll have to use the ventilation window,' Cato decided. 'There's a ladder, but with your leg it might be difficult.'

'We haven't got any choice.'

'No. But we have to delay them as long as we can. Can you guard the window, sir?'

'Yes, but—'

'Please, sir, there's no time to explain.'

'Very well.' Macro nodded. 'Help me up and give me your sword.'

Taking the weight off his injured leg, Macro leaned against the wall to one side of the window while Cato disappeared to the back of the barn. Abruptly a large chunk of the shutter finally gave way and tumbled to the floor. Immediately a spear thrust inwards and then hands grabbed the edge of the window frame as a

German prepared to pull himself through. Macro slashed down at the nearest hand and the severed fingers jumped up into the air as the man drew back, screaming.

'Come on, you bastards!' Macro shouted. 'Who's game for some more?'

The attack on the door suddenly increased in frenzy and, solid though it was, the wood began to give way. Defending a window was one thing, but the door would be impossible.

'Cato! Whatever you're going to do, better do it right now!'

'Coming, sir!' Cato grunted, and then staggered towards the front of the barn carrying a twisted mass of straw on the end of a pitchfork. He dumped it between the door and the window and hurriedly spread it out. Then, reaching up to the roof, he used the pitchfork to pull down some of the burning thatch, raising his arm to protect his face from the tumbling sparks that came in its wake. Thick tendrils of smoke curled up. Then the flames took hold and, just as the door gave way, the front of the barn crackled with fire, shrouded in thick choking clouds.

'This way!' Cato called out and coughed violently as he inhaled the foul-tasting smoke.

Propping Macro up as best he could with the hand that was unencumbered by the standard, Cato half supported, half dragged the centurion over to the rear of the barn where a ladder led up into the darkness.

'You go up first, sir. Take the standard with you, but give me the sword. Shout once you're through.'

Macro did not argue with the lad's orders and turned

to make his way up the ladder, cursing his wound and the awkward standard in equal measure. The smoke from the fire was thickening downwards from the apex of the barn, catching in his lungs and stinging his eyes as he climbed the short, but agonising, distance to the ventilation window. He punched it open and quickly hung his head out, gasping for breath. From this raised position, Macro saw that this side of the village was being consumed by brilliant raging flames, rapidly spreading as the fire was fanned by a light breeze. The Germans were picking their way through the twisting alleys, trying to avoid the fire, heading for the open village square where the remains of the cohort were preparing to fight for their lives.

Immediately below was a small closed yard, where two pigs were dashing about in a fine panic. A mound of winter feed lay directly beneath and Macro hefted the standard up and through the window before letting it drop. From inside the barn there was a sudden crash as the door finally gave way and then a rush of feet and harsh shouts.

'Cato!'

'Go, sir!' the boy called. 'Go now!'

The Germans, coughing, were coming towards the rear of the barn, determined to hunt their Roman quarry down, and Macro hurriedly wriggled through the window. Working his way round, he lowered himself down the outside wall until he was hanging full stretch, and then released his grip. The landing was made softer than he had expected as one of the pigs had decided that the hay would make a good shelter from the chaos of the outside world. The last thing that a pig could reasonably expect was a heavily armoured infantryman crashing down from above. Nevertheless, the air was rent with a terrified squeal and a deeper human oath as both struggled to free themselves from the tangle. Macro kicked the beast to one side and sat on the hay, breathing heavily, but otherwise unhurt. The pig had not been so fortunate, its back was broken and the two forelegs worked pathetically to drag the beast over the soiled yard away from danger. And all the while it squealed and screamed so that Macro feared it must attract attention.

Inside the barn, he could hear the Germans shouting angrily as they slashed about in their search for Romans to slaughter. Then came a shout and, immediately after, the scraping of the ladder on the inside of the wall. Macro quickly pulled the standard close to him, swept armfuls of hay across his body and lay still. Through the strands across his face Macro stared anxiously up the wall as a dark head appeared against the orange sky. For a horribly long moment the German's head gazed down, then there was a harsh exchange of words and the head withdrew. Macro kept quite still, listening intently as the voices in the barn faded away, under the screams of the injured pig. When he judged he was safe, he sat up and shook off the stinking hay. One side of the yard seemed to give out on to a street and, from over the wall, he could hear Germans pounding by. The other side was comparatively quiet and, nursing his leg, Macro eased himself up and peered over. Immediately beyond the wall was a large area filled with wicker pig-pens – he could hear the animals grunting inside.

Macro eased back down and, waiting until the street fell momentarily quiet, he called out for Cato beneath the window.

No reply came. He called again, but still nothing.

Damn the boy. He should have followed up the ladder the moment the door gave way. But, with a twinge of guilt, Macro realised that the Germans would have been instantly led to the sound. Cato, he realised, must have know this and sacrificed himself to save Macro and the standard.

The pig's squealing had reached a new, nerve-wracking, pitch of terror and Macro kicked it hard in the side of the head.

'Keep the fucking noise down!' He swung the boot in again. 'Want me to get caught?'

But the pig just renewed its cries with increasing panic. Inevitably, some passing Germans paused in the street to investigate the noise. Macro did not hesitate. The standard went flying over the far wall and he frantically pulled himself over the top and slid down the side into a pile of dung scraped together from the nearest pens. Grabbing the standard and keeping as low to the ground as possible, he crawled between the pens towards the centre of the village, trying not to imagine what he might find even if he did make it back to the cohort.

Chapter Thirteen

When the door crashed open Cato's mind was racing. With Macro safely out of harm's way, he moved along the wall and dived into the huge pile of straw gathered in the corner, burrowing his way deep inside as the Germans advanced into the barn.

Then there were voices close by and, suddenly, a terrible screaming from somewhere just outside the barn. Cato immediately feared for his centurion, before common sense told him that no man could make a noise like that. One of the Germans laughed and then dissolved into a fit of coughing. The smoke in the barn was starting to catch in Cato's throat and he desperately strained to keep his chest still.

Something moved quickly through the straw and there was a dull clang as it struck the barn wall. The noise was repeated, closer this time and, with a feeling of cold dread, Cato realised that they were searching the straw with their spears. He forced himself to remain still, knowing full well that surrender was suicide. More spear-thrusts followed as the Germans hunted for their prey, painfully coughing in the thickening smoke of the burning barn. Someone shouted. Abruptly the search ceased as the Germans hurriedly withdrew from the blazing building.

Only when he was sure that he was alone did Cato cautiously pick his way out of the straw. The room was full of smoke, with only a small decrease in density at floor level. Staying low on his stomach, Cato crawled towards the front of the building where the straw he had lit shortly before was now reduced to glowing embers. Beyond the shattered doorframe the street was swarming with Germans. One voice shouted out a string of orders before they moved on towards the centre of the village. Cato waited until the last sound of the footsteps had gone before he rolled out into the street, coughing loudly and gulping down the fire-warmed night air. His lungs and his eyes stung painfully and it was only after he managed to clear the tears from his eyes that Cato could clearly see the street around him. Although the shouts of Germans could be heard above the crackle and roar of flames he was, for the moment, alone – except for the man he had knocked out earlier with the butt of the standard.

Approaching cautiously, Cato saw that the German was still out cold; a nasty black and blue lump had risen on his forehead. With Germans all around and Romans in short supply, Cato reasoned that a change in appearance would be a prudent move. He undid the clasp on the German's cloak and rolled the helpless man over to pull it free. As he draped it over his own cloak the malodorous mix of sweat, human and animal soiling and waterproofing grease was quite overwhelming, and Cato retched. He struggled for a moment to free the buckle holding his helmet on and then let the cumbersome weight of iron and bronze thud to the ground. There was nothing he could do about his army-cropped hair and, with a distasteful wrinkle of his nose he raised the cloak's hood over his head. With his sword sheathed under the cloak Cato snatched up the German's spear and shield. Looking down at himself he saw that the overall effect, while far from convincing, might at least allow him to look less like a Roman.

What now? The only direction that offered any possibility of safety was towards the village square and what was left of the cohort. But what of Macro and the standard? Cato hurriedly examined the now fiercely blazing barn for access to the rear, but the narrow passage down the side of the barn was filled with flames. The heat scalded his face and Cato recoiled from the passage entrance. Pulling the cloak tightly about his head and body, Cato took a deep breath and plunged headlong into the passage. The heat and light were tremendous and almost at once there was the smell of roasted waterproofing grease. Cato hunched further down and ran on, flames scorching his bare legs, then he was past the side of the barn, out of the fire. The entire cloak was smouldering and Cato hastily beat out the few patches that were alight.

The high wall at the rear of the barn was hard to scale, weighed down and tired as he was. Scrabbling breathlessly up the side, Cato just managed to raise his head above the uneven stonework. The yard behind the barn seemed empty apart from a large pile of winter feed.

'Sir!' Cato called out as loudly as he dared.

Something stirred in the winter feed at the sound of his voice and Cato felt his heart leap with relief. Then the air was cut by a scream of agony.

'Sir! Are you hurt?' Cato cried out anxiously, and then a vague shape twisted out of the winter feed and writhed in screaming fits of agony. A pig. Where was the centurion?

Cato released his grip and sank down beside the wall; young, scared and alone. Bitter tears of hatred at the way the fates had treated him pooled in his eyes for a moment. The roof of the barn suddenly crashed down into the hungry flames. Cato stumbled back as the instinct for self-preservation reasserted itself within him. Very well, he was alone, surrounded by the enemy and a raging fire, but he wasn't going to surrender his life to either without a struggle.

Quickly constructing a mental plan of the village with the relative positions of Romans, Germans and the fire, Cato decided on a direction and hurried away from the barn along the narrow passageway, eyes and ears alert for danger.

Pigs, Macro thought, might be induced to taste well in the hands of a good cook, but in their raw state they were barely tolerable at the best of times, and German pigs – never. As he crawled through the filth between their pens, where the urine and the more liquid variety of shit oozed into a badly dug drainage channel, he strove to keep his mind on saving the standard, which he kept as far from the filth as possible. A quite unbearable stench invaded his nose and overpowered his mind, so that he crawled on, swearing every imaginable oath at each pig he passed.

Macro crawled up to a large wicker gate. Through the crudely woven hazel he peered cautiously into the street beyond. A short distance to one side, the street gave out on to the market area, made up of roughly built stalls, now empty and bare in the depth of winter. The fire had not reached this part of the village and the locals who had escaped Vitellius's round up were carrying away the few precious possessions that time allowed, casting anxious glances beyond Macro to where flames licked high into the night. From what he had seen from the ventilation window, Macro estimated that a little distance beyond the market he would find the village square. The handful of villagers nearby were women, children and older Germans – none of whom seemed to pose too much of a threat. If he got by them as stealthily as possible he might be ignored. And then he would have a short march along the street to the rest of the cohort.

Painfully rising to his feet, Macro withdrew the peg that fastened the wicker gate. Sticking close to the side of the street, he kept the butt of the standard off the ground in a bid to remain as quiet and unobtrusive as possible. Progress was slow as he was beginning to lose any feeling in his wounded leg and, worse, loss of blood was making him feel faint-headed. Breathing deeply he forced himself on, into the market and down the side of the deserted stalls, unobserved or ignored by the villagers retrieving the last of their valuables and helping themselves to those of absent neighbours. It was not in their interest to attract attention any more than it was in Macro's and those who saw him simply eyed him warily as he passed.

Leaving the market, the sound of fighting grew louder and Macro paused for breath at a point where the street bent round sharply towards the village square. His vision was clouding badly and his head started to spin. Macro rubbed his eyes and bit back on the nausea and, gradually, clarity of vision and mind returned. A quick glance around the corner would tell him if the way ahead was clear. The centurion leaned his head out.

The German ran into him so quickly that Macro was only aware that he was suddenly flat on his back, gazing up at the orange sky, winded and gasping for air. To one side of him the German had fallen headlong, spear clattering on to the street. As Macro struggled to roll over and draw his dagger, the German reacted more quickly. In a trice he was on his feet, snatching up the spear and whirling round to plant the broad blade in his enemy's throat. Macro held his dagger out, knowing it was no more than a pathetic gesture of defiance.

'Thanks be to Jupiter!' the German said in perfect Latin.

'Eh?'

The German lowered his spear and offered him a hand. Macro just stared at the man as if he were mad.

'Do come on, sir. We haven't got time,' Cato urged, drawing back the hood, then wrinkling his nose. 'What the hell is that smell?'

Macro slumped back against the wall, smiling with relief, and the moment's loss of determination set his head reeling again. But he didn't really care. Cato was here, bless the lad. Now if he could just rest a moment . . .

'Sir!'

He was being roughly shaken and his eyes flickered open. Above him loomed Cato, hands tightly grasping Macro's harness.

'Up we go, sir!' Cato said, gritting his teeth with exertion as he hauled Macro to his feet. He supported him with one arm while using the spear to steady them both. Macro stubbornly held on to the standard, which trailed behind them, as Cato dragged him along the side of the market to the next street corner. A quick glance revealed more Germans milling about as their front ranks tried to force a way through to the village square.

'This is no good,' Cato said. 'They're in every street. We must try something else.'

'I have to rest.'

'No, sir! You can't.' Cato shook him until his eyes flickered open again. 'There! That's better. Now then.'

Cato kicked open a door and dragged Macro into a small hut. The centurion was only dimly aware of being led through an assortment of dingy rooms and yards before Cato deposited him beside an earth-faced wicker wall. The lad drew out his sword, slipped off the German's cloak and attacked the wall with all his strength.

'What the hell are you doing, boy?' Macro asked weakly.

'I think the square is on the other side of this house. If we can just get through the wall.'

'Then I can rest.'

'Then you can rest, sir.'

Cato grasped the sword handle with both hands and stabbed away at the wall, loosening great lumps of clay, until he had exposed a large section of the wattle. He wiped his brow once, and attacked the slender intertwined branches with desperate energy. Macro watched listlessly, no longer really caring about anything, slowly giving in to his desire to float off into a deep sleep.

The wattle proved a much tougher prospect than the lathe and Cato's heart pounded as he hacked at the wall with single-minded fury. At last he had cut away enough to start attacking the tightly packed earth and clay on the far side. In moments he had thrust through and a dim shaft of light filtered into the room. Cato worked with renewed frenzy and the gap quickly widened. When it was large enough to squeeze through he gently picked up the centurion and dragged him across to the hole.

'You first, boy,' Macro protested.

'No, sir, it'll be easier to get you through now than drag you out after.'

'Fair enough.'

With Cato half supporting him, Macro thrust his head, arms and shoulders through the wall, dislodging a shower of earth which tumbled down over him. He spluttered for breath, shaking the earth from his head, and then someone swung a boot into his side.

'Bloody Germans are coming through the wall!' someone shouted.

'Easy lads! I'm Roman!'

'Oh! Sorry, mate!'

A rough hand reached down to Macro. Moments later, Cato was helping to prop him up and brushing the dust off his head and uniform. The legionary who had kicked him in the side gulped nervously as he caught sight of the centurion's medalled harness.

'Sir, I didn't know . . .'

'No harm done, son. Just take us to the tribune.'

'This way, sir.' The legionary supported Macro on his other side and, with the centurion's arms over the legionaries' shoulders, the trio made their way past the rearmost ranks of the soldiers holding the entrances to the village square. They found Vitellius standing outside the village chief's hut with the trumpeter and the cohort standard-bearer. From inside the hut came the sounds of muffled cries and screams.

'Stop here a moment, lads,' Macro ordered, before extracting his arm from Cato's shoulder and saluting Vitellius.

'Ah! So you're still with us, Macro! I was told the Germans had you, and the optio here, bang to rights.'

'Yes, sir.'

'Nasty wound. Better get it cleaned and dressed.' Vitellius jerked a thumb at the door to the hut. 'The orderlies are a bit busy right now, but you might attract their attention. And get them to wipe some of that shit off you while they're about it.'

'Where's my century, sir?'

'They're holding the main gate at the moment—' Vitellius moved aside as a fresh casualty was carried past into the hut. 'I had them run the villagers outside between assaults. Can't afford to have troops wasted on guard duty.'

'How are we doing?'

Vitellius frowned momentarily before answering. 'Not well. We're down to less than three hundred effectives. The Germans are trying to force an entry to the square down five streets. The fire has cut them off from all other accesses and we still hold the wall and gate on the other side of the village.'

'Can we hold out until Vespasian gets here?'

'Maybe.' Vitellius shrugged, looking up into the snowy sky. 'If the fire keeps channelling them into a limited number of streets. We're holding them back now, but they can afford to lose more men than us. Once they've got the edge in numbers they'll just push us back into the square. Then we make a final stand here, by the injured.'

'And what if the fire gets to us before the Germans?'

'We'll be forced back to the main gate, and then outside into the tender arms of the waiting German horde.'

To be burned to death or gutted by barbarians, thought Cato. Which would he choose when the time came?

'Get your wound seen to, Macro,' Vitellius ordered. He gestured to the trumpeter and the standard-bearer. 'Come!'

'What about me, sir?' Cato asked.

Vitellius glanced back at Macro. '"Me sir" can guard your standard, Centurion.'

'Yes, sir.' Macro smiled grimly, then held out the Sixth

century's standard. 'Hold this, until they fix the wound. I'll take it once I get out.'

Once Macro had been helped inside, an orderly hurried over to inspect the wound. With a casual nod of the head, he decided that no triage mercy killing was required in this case. He flapped his hands at Cato, shooing him out of the hut. When Cato turned at the doorway to take a last look at his centurion, the orderly was cleaning the wound with a bloodstained rag.

Outside the hut, Cato tried to plant the standard with quick thrusts but the frozen ground defeated his every effort. He eventually gave up and rested it against his shoulder. Although he felt relief at being back with the cohort the fight was not going their way. The tightly compacted melees had turned into a heaving scrimmage whose outcome would ultimately depend on which side had the greater weight. Even so, the odd sword or javelin was finding its mark and the occasional casualty emerged from the rearmost legs of the press. Those who were too badly wounded to make their way out of the maul were simply trampled underfoot.

Slowly, but with painful inevitability, the Romans were forced back down the streets towards the square. Cato knew that the moment the Germans spilled out into the square they would swarm around the Romans, who would be annihilated in short order. Much of the night had already passed but there were still some hours until daybreak and then half a day before Vespasian could reach the village.

But even as the Germans pushed forward the fire began to overtake them, spreading rapidly through the combustible dwellings. Distant horns sounded and from the Germans there came a sudden howl of rage and frustration. The horns blew the retreat more insistently and the Germans reluctantly disengaged with a final desperate exchange of blows as they fled from the fire. And then the cohort was alone. But relief was short-lived. The violence of the Germans was swiftly replaced by the wrath of Vulcan as fire swept up to the village square, burning all along its fringes and out towards the village walls. The Romans recoiling before the blaze were lit up in a terrible red glow that cast their long shimmering shadows far behind them. The heat of the fire withered all before it and the men shrank back behind the shelter of their shields.

A legionary came running up, pointing towards the street that led from the square.

'Fall back! Everyone back to the main gate. Now!'

The cohort limped out of the square, a ragged column of exhausted men, some helping support wounded comrades, and others using shields as makeshift stretchers to carry out those too badly injured to walk. But all were silent and despairing. Too many officers had died and unit cohesion had completely broken down as they trudged wearily and painfully through the red-rimmed silhouettes of German huts. At the main gate, Vitellius threw up a defensive cordon with the wounded clustered behind the rear ranks. Then the remains of the cohort quietly waited for the end to come.

Cato had rejoined the Sixth century, after he had made his centurion as comfortable as possible, and from the gate tower he had a fine view of approaching doom. The wind urged the flames on and now they set about consuming the other half of the village. Beyond the wall Cato saw the clustered German villagers watching as their homes and livelihoods were incinerated. Without food and shelter not many of them would survive the winter and the red glow of the fire lit up the expressions of stricken despair etched on their faces. Cato felt a twinge of guilt as he saw the human consequences of war, even though he knew he would be dead soon, one way or another.

Beyond the villagers, the dark ranks of the German warriors stretched into the night as they waited for the fire to drive their enemy out into the open.

As the night grew old, Cato was surprised to see the men of the cohort succumb to a gentle fatalism. The surviving officers and men exchanged words quietly, without any sense of difference in rank. Imminent death was a great social leveller. It was a strange comfort to be with them now, here – just before the final wild charge into oblivion. A warm sense of serenity flushed through him and Cato found that he was smiling. For a moment his eyes met those of a hard-bitten veteran whose expressionless face suddenly returned the smile. No words passed between them; none were necessary.

As the first hint of dawn appeared on the skyline the fire was almost on them and Vitellius ordered the remaining men to form into a column behind the gate. The tribune paused for a moment to consider the fate of those too badly injured to walk unaided. Most had requested that swords be left with them, to allow them to go down fighting, or at least to deprive the Germans of the terrible amusements they reserved for prisoners. Vitellius wondered if it would be more merciful if he ordered them all to be put to death before the cohort left. As he stood pondering, a sentry on the gate tower called down to him.

'They're moving!'

It seemed that the Germans had allowed themselves to be overcome by impatience. It would end with a brief scrap on the walls then, and no final charge, Vitellius concluded with disappointment. Wearily climbing the steps inside the tower, he emerged on to the watch platform where Cato stood with the sentry. The optio looked confused and a moment later the tribune could see why.

The Germans were on the move all right, but instead of moving forwards towards the gate they were marching round the sides of the village, away from the track that led up the slope towards the forest.

'What the hell?' Vitellius frowned.

'Sir . . . What are they doing?'

'I've no idea.'

The Germans increased their pace and already the villagers were standing in pathetic isolation before the gate. Cato could not quite bring himself to believe what his eyes showed him. Then his ears caught a new sound, a sound that rose above the crackling flames licking at their backs. Sharp and clear on the dawn air came the strident sound of trumpets and on the crest of the hill above the village a line of horsemen rode into view; at their head, a party of officers in red cloaks and crested helmets.

Vespasian, it appeared, had not waited for dawn to break before marching to their rescue.

Chapter Fourteen

The hospital orderly cursed under his breath as the sound of the handbell rang down the central corridor of the Legion's infirmary. The patient was being quite impossible. Constantly demanding that messages be sent out, food and wine sent in, fussing that his leg be positioned just so – and moments later asking that it be shifted once again. If it weren't for the fact that he was a centurion, and outranked everyone in the hospital except the surgeon, the orderly would have taken the bell away and let the man stew. But, because he was a centurion, he was entitled to a separate ward, a bell and the undivided attention of any orderly unfortunate enough to be on duty.

All the other ranks wounded in the recent fracas with the Germans were crammed into five-bed wards with the lack of privileges accorded to those of low status: enough food to get by and a scheduled visit by the surgeon, or one of his orderlies, to change dressings, pour off drainage and monitor their recovery. Those that had been immobilised by their injuries were provided with bedpans which the orderlies emptied three times a day; the centurion had his emptied as and when he was pleased to relieve himself.

The injury to his leg had been messy and might have been fatal had Macro not tied a tourniquet above the wound. The surgeon had stitched together the ends of the torn muscle and then the skin – leaving a small burr in place to aid drainage of pus from the wound. He had ordered the centurion to remain in bed until the wound was cleaned and well on the way to healing. Then he had calmly smiled at the consequent stream of invective and reassured the centurion that at a pinch the Second Legion could actually manage without him for a few weeks. The surgeon appointed a personal orderly and, with a nod of professional satisfaction at his handiwork, he left the fuming officer and moved on to the scores of other patients Tribune Vitellius had seen fit to provide him with. Most recovered in a few days, some died – much to the surgeon's disgust, taking each death as a personal affront to his skills – and the remainder recovered at a slower pace dictated by the severity of their injuries. He was only grateful that there were no Germans to tend to: those that hadn't committed suicide, or been killed by their own side, had been mercifully despatched on Vespasian's orders. So the hospital was quite free of any foul-smelling barbarians.

The same couldn't be said for the settlement outside the fortress, which was now swollen with the survivors from the village. The lucky ones had managed to beg for shelter from distant relatives and friends who now repaid the smug disdain they had suffered for adapting to Roman ways. The unlucky ones would be forced to spend the winter in an ugly sprawl of crude huts that sprang up on the fringes of the settlement. Many of them would not survive the harsh northern winter but there would be little sympathy for them from either the Romans or those who lived in the settlement and now bore the weight of the legionaries' rekindled suspicion of all things German.

The bell rang again, more loudly this time, and the orderly slowed his pace as he walked down the corridor towards the better-ventilated end rooms reserved for officers.

'Get a bloody move on, man!' Macro bellowed. 'I've been waving this fucking bell about for ages!'

'So sorry to keep you waiting, sir,' the orderly apologised. 'But I'm afraid one of the other patients was dying and I wanted to make sure his effects went to the right friends before he popped off.'

'And will they get them?'

'The lads and I will do our best to see that the leftovers are sent on.'

'After you've had your pickings.'

'Of course, sir.'

'Bloody vultures.'

'Vultures?' The orderly frowned. 'Just a perk of the job, sir. Now what is it you wanted?'

'Get rid of this.' Macro shoved a bedpan at him. 'And make the fire up. It's freezing in here.'

'Yes, sir.' The orderly nodded as he carefully carried the bedpan over to a low table and set it down. 'Nice day out, sir. Clear blue sky and still air.'

'Oh, is it? Thanks for letting me know. But it's still freezing in here.'

'Not freezing, sir. Just well ventilated. It's good for you.'

'How can it be good? If the wound doesn't get me, the cold will.'

The orderly smiled at that comforting thought as he placed more fuel on the glowing embers in the brazier and blew gently on them to encourage some flames.

'Right, that's fine. Now take the bedpan and piss off.'

'Yes, sir.' The orderly collected the chamber pot and, holding it carefully, made for the door to the corridor. Without any warning, Cato strode into the room and the orderly nimbly stepped to one side without spilling a drop. He tutted at the optio as Cato closed the door behind him.

The optio stood over the bed and smiled down. 'It's good to see you, sir.'

'For the first time in three days.'

'It's been busy without you, sir. I've been trying to keep the century in good order while you recover. How's the leg?'

'Stiff, and it hurts like buggery whenever I try to move it. But the quacks seem to think I'm well on the mend.'

'You look better than the last time I saw you.'

'That was nothing, just some minor infection. The surgeon reckons it's almost gone.'

'When will you be back on duty, sir?'

The non sequitur and the anxiety behind it were not lost on the centurion. He regarded Cato silently while the wood in the brazier hissed softly.

'I'd have thought a young optio might be enjoying the opportunity of having his first command.'

'I am, sir.'

'But . . .' Macro coaxed.

'I had no idea how much there was to do. There's the drilling to organise, barracks inspections, equipment checks, and then there's all the paperwork.'

'You should leave that to Piso. I do.'

'Yes, he's been very helpful, sir. He insisted on handling it. But we've just had orders to conduct a full inventory of equipment and non-portable personal items. And, to make matters worse, headquarters has ordered all money above ten sestertii to be banked by the end of the week. Is it always as hectic as this, sir?' Cato asked helplessly.

'No.'

So the Legion was to be moved in the near future then. The order restricting personal holdings of coinage was to limit the marching load of a legionary, and all non-portable goods would be inventoried for storage or sale. If the latter, then the Legion's transfer was likely to be long term. Interesting. But then, Macro considered, it was likely that the wounded would have to travel in carts and the prospect of the uncomfortable bumps and jolts that that implied filled him with dread. Marching might be tiring, but it was all good exercise and far more comfortable than jolting around on the flat bed of a legionary transport wagon.

'Any word on where we're being sent?'

'Nothing official, sir, but I've heard rumours that we're going to join an army being assembled to invade Britain.'

'Britain! What emperor in his right mind would want to add that dump to the Empire? Wild, savage and filled with bogs – if what I hear is true. Britain! That's ridiculous.'

'That's what I heard,' Cato said defensively. 'And in any case, what emperor is in his right mind these days?'

'Fair point!' Macro lightened up. 'Look, all this admin you're complaining about. It's what running a century is all about. You're just going to have to cope with it, or get Piso to.'

'It's not really the paperwork that's getting me down, sir,' Cato said uncomfortably.

'What is it then?'

'Well, it's the command side of things. I just can't seem to carry off the business of giving people orders.'

'What do you mean?'

Cato shuffled his feet, shamefaced, as he attempted to formulate the problem. 'I know I'm an optio and that means the men have to obey me, but that doesn't mean that they take kindly to having a – well, if I'm honest – a kid telling them what to do. It's not that they don't obey me, they do. Nobody's calling me a coward any more, but they haven't got much respect for me.'

'I'm sure they haven't. It doesn't come automatically – it has to be earned. It's the same for every new officer. The men will obey because they are accustomed to. The trick is to get them to obey willingly and to do that you need to earn their trust. Then they'll respect you.'

'But how do I do that, sir?'

'You stop whining for a start. Then you begin to act like an optio.'

'I can't, sir.'

'What do you mean can't? Can! Fucking will!' Macro propped himself up on his elbows, wincing as he shifted his leg to a more comfortable position.

'Yes, sir.'

'Now then, put some more wood on that fire – some dry stuff – before the bloody thing goes out. And shut the window.'

'Are you sure, sir? Fresh air's supposed to speed recovery.'

'Maybe air that's not quite so fresh. The only thing that window's speeding is exposure, so shut it now.'

'Yes, sir.' Cato quickly obeyed the order and then carefully selected the driest wood he could find for the brazier.

'Did you notice?' Macro asked.

'What, sir?'

'How you instantly did what I said?'

Cato nodded.

'That's what I'm talking about. It's the tone of voice. You need to practise giving orders a while before it feels natural. But once you're there it's a doddle – comes as easy as breathing.'

'If you say so, sir.'

'I do. Now then, what's the news?' Macro eased himself back on the bed so that he was propped up against the bolster. With the window closed the red glow of the brazier added to what little light there was filtering through the shutters. 'Pull up the stool and fill me in. What else have you been up to?'

Cato shifted uneasily. 'I was summoned to headquarters this morning by the legate.'

'Oh yes?' Macro smiled. 'And what did Vespasian have to say?'

'Not much . . . He's investing me with a decoration, a

grass crown. I'm not quite sure why.'

'Because I recommended it,' smiled Macro. 'You saved my life, remember? Even if you did nearly lose the standard while you were at it. You deserve it, and once you get the phalera attached to your harness I think you'll find the men will go easier on you. All good soldiers respect well-earned decorations. How's it feel to be a hero?'

Cato blushed, grateful that the uncomfortable glow in his cheeks was lost in the flickering orange of the brazier. 'Frankly, I feel a bit of a fraud.'

'Why on earth?'

'I can't be a hero on the strength of one battle.'

'Hardly a battle. More of a skirmish actually.'

'Precisely, sir. A skirmish, and one in which I only managed to injure an enemy by accident. Hardly the stuff of heroes.'

'Killing men in battle doesn't necessarily make you a hero,' Macro gently reassured him. 'Admittedly it does help and the more bodies you pile up the better. But there are other ways to be heroic. All the same, I wouldn't go around blabbing about not having knocked a few Germans on the head if I were you. Look, you didn't have to come back for me but you chose to – against the odds. In my book that takes guts and I'm glad you're with us.'

Cato stared at him, searching for the least sign of irony in his superior's face. 'Do you really mean that, sir?'

'Of course. Have I yet said anything to you I didn't mean?'

'No.'

'There you are then. So take it at face value and don't get sentimental on me. I take it there'll be an investiture?'

'Yes, sir. The legate's holding a parade two days from now. There are a number of decorations to hand out, including one for Vitellius.'

'Oh really?' Macro interrupted sourly. 'I'm sure that'll look good on his CV when he gets back to Rome.'

'Then there's a private dinner in the evening. He's invited all officers who served with the Third cohort that day in the village, those of us who survived, that is.'

'Should be rather cosy and intimate then. Typical of Vespasian; always the grand gesture on the cheap.'

'He insisted that you be there as well, sir.'

'Me?' Macro shrugged and pointed at his leg. 'And how am I supposed to attend?'

'That's what I asked the legate, sir.'

'You did? What did he say?'

'He'll send a litter for you.'

'A litter? That's great. I get to play the invalid all night long and have to chase up some social conversation. It'll be a bloody nightmare.'

'Then don't go, sir.'

'Don't go?' Macro raised his eyebrows. 'My lad, a polite invitation from a commander of a legion carries somewhat more weight than a writ issued by Jupiter himself.'

Cato smiled and rose to his feet. 'I'd better go now. Is there anything I can get you for next time? Some reading matter perhaps?'

'No thanks. Need to give my eyes a break. You might

bring me a jar of wine and a dice set. I need to improve my technique.'

'Dice.' Cato was vaguely disappointed as he disapproved of those who refused to accept that dice fell randomly – straight dice at least. He nodded and made to leave.

'One more thing!' Macro called after him as he strode out of the ward.

'Sir?'

'Remind Piso he owes me five sestertii.'

Chapter Fifteen

Centurion Bestia glared into each face as he marched steadily along the ranks. In many ways inspection was the most onerous aspect of training to most recruits. Marching, drilling and weapons practice required no more than effort and the minimum of thought. Preparing for inspection, on the other hand, required a kind of genius that almost elevated it to the level of art. Every item of kit had to be cleaned, polished – where possible rather than where necessary – and in a perfect state of repair. There were few short-cuts, and since they were all known by Bestia it was a foolish or desperate recruit who resorted to them. Thus it was that Cato stood nervously at attention and prayed to every god remotely relevant to the situation that Bestia would miss the varnish he had applied to his belt and straps. The visit to the hospital had left him no time to buff the weathered leather up into a shine and he had simply painted the varnish on instead, on the advice of Pyrax. Standing stiffly with spear grounded to his right and left hand resting on the rim of his shield Cato was acutely aware of the faint smell of varnish wafting around him. If Bestia touched the tacky leather then

Cato's deception would be uncovered and he would be up on charges.

Four men down the line Bestia suddenly caught sight of his prey and skimmed past the intervening men with barely a sidelong glance.

'Ah! Optio.' He laboured the word. 'So very good of you to join us this morning.'

As always the sarcastic greeting was unfair, since Cato had no choice in the matter and was excused drill on alternate days on orders from the Legion's headquarters.

'So then, it appears that you are something of a war hero, Master Cato?'

Cato kept his mouth shut and continued staring straight ahead, eyes unwavering.

'I believe I asked you a fucking question,' Bestia said, then turned to the optio who accompanied him on inspections through the ranks. 'Didn't I just ask him a fucking question?'

'Yes, sir,' the drill optio replied. 'You asked him a fucking question, sir!'

'So answer me!'

'Yes, sir!' Cato shouted.

'Yes, sir what?'

'Yes, I am something of a war hero, sir,' Cato replied in a low voice.

'I do beg your fucking pardon, son!' Bestia shouted. 'But I must be deaf. I can't hear you. Again! Louder!'

'Yes, I am something of a war hero, sir!'

'Oh really? Young lad like you must have really scared the shit out of the Germans. I mean, just looking at you right now is making me bloody nervous. Next thing you know they'll be chucking fucking foetuses into the front line.'

A ripple of laughter spread across the other recruits.

'SHUT UP!' Bestia bellowed. 'I did not give the rest of you ladies permission to laugh, did I? Well, did I?'

'NO, SIR!' the recruits chorused.

'Well then, war hero, now you've really got something to live up to.' Bestia leaned in very close to Cato's face, so that the latter could see every wrinkle and scar of the veteran's face, as well as the red rim of his nostrils. Cato almost smiled with relief as the centurion stepped back a pace, drew out a dirty piece of linen and sneezed into it.

'What you smiling at, boy? Haven't seen a man with a cold before?'

'Yes, sir.'

'I'll be keeping an eye on you, Optio. Make any mistakes from now on and I'll show you no mercy,' Bestia snarled, and then abruptly strode away.

'So what's new?' Cato muttered once the centurion was out of earshot. The drill optio chuckled as he went by and Cato blanched. But the man just winked and hurried to catch up with Bestia.

That morning Bestia changed the routine. Instead of the scheduled weapons-training the recruits were introduced to the rudiments of camp construction, and were marched outside the walls of the fortress to a prepared area where lines of coloured flags marked out a large square with numerous subdivisions. A supply wagon waited at the side of the track; a brace of oxen grazed with dull expressions as they watched the recruits assemble around Bestia. The centurion had taken a pick and shovel from the back of the wagon and was holding them aloft.

'Any of you ladies care to tell me what I'm holding in my hands?'

The recruits remained silent, not willing to risk the obvious.

'Just as I thought, dumb as ever. Well, these may look like horticultural tools but they're the army's secret weapon. In fact, they are the most important weapon you are ever likely to handle. With these, you can build the most formidable fortifications in the known world. Roman armies get defeated from time to time, Roman fortifications – never! Some of you may have heard on the grapevine that the Legion is about to be relocated.'

A low key buzz of excitement greeted the announcement – the first official confirmation of what had been doing the rounds of the Legion's mess rooms for the last ten days. Bestia let it run its course before continuing.

'Now, you ladies will of course be ignorant of our final destination, unlike senior officers such as myself. Suffice to say we're in for an interesting time. But before you can be let loose outside the base, you're going to need to know how to build everything from a marching camp right up to bicircumvallations.'

Now he had really lost them, only the handful who were familiar with Caesar's account of the siege of Alesia had the remotest idea what he was talking about.

'Ladies, we're going to start small, since you – barring our war hero there – will have problems grasping the tactical defensive potential of anything larger than a ditch. So we begin with the marching camp.

'When the Legion manoeuvres through non-hostile territory it excavates a defensive ditch and turf-mounted palisade. Each legionary, and you ladies, will be issued with one pick and one spade. The yellow flags over there need not concern you – they mark out the tent lines for each century. These red flags mark out the boundary defences. You will dig from that line inwards. You will dig a ditch six feet wide and three feet deep – that's two spades wide by one spade deep – the spoil of which is to be heaped on the inner side of the ditch and then compacted down. Each man digs six feet of ditch, starting with the war hero at the first marker flag. You ladies understand? Then get the equipment issue and get to work.'

Once each man had been issued a pick and spade, for which deductions would be made from their pay, as Cato now knew, and had taken up position along the red-flagged line, Bestia gave the order to dig. A short distance beneath the grass the soil was freezing, if not frozen, and the recruits used their picks to hammer into it with all their might, piling the cold lumps of clay soil immediately beside the ditch. As the morning wore on, the men became oblivious to the chill and sweat poured freely, woollen inner tunics sticking to their backs. Hardened by months of exercise, the recruits nevertheless found the entrenching exhausting, but Bestia allowed them no break from their toils, reminding them that while on the march the Legion would need to make such fortifications every day. Sore hands turned into blistered hands and, when the blisters burst, the palms were rubbed raw by the coarse wood of the wooden handles which would not become smooth through heavy use for some months yet. Cato suffered the agony in tight-lipped silence while those who had joined the Legion from a farming family barely noticed the wood in their calloused hands. As bad luck would have it, Cato was placed immediately next to Pulcher and, while they were out of earshot of the drill instructors, Pulcher resumed his campaign of intimidation.

'War hero? You?' he growled. 'Un-fucking-likely. Who'd you have to be buggered by to get the commendation?'

Cato did not answer, did not even look up from his digging.

'Hey, I'm talking to you!'

Cato ignored him.

'What's this? No manners? And I thought you were so well brought up. I suppose you're too good to speak to the likes of us.' He laughed to the recruit on his other side. 'Seems the war hero's got ideas above his station.'

'Quiet there!' an instructor called out. 'Silence when you work.'

Pulcher fell back to work with exaggerated effort until he was sure that he was no longer being paid any attention. Then he flicked a shovel full of soil at Cato's face.

'You fucking ignore me again, boy and I'll . . .'

'You'll what?' Cato turned angrily, with his pick half raised. 'You tell me what you'll do! C'mon, you bastard!'

Pulcher's hands tightened on his shovel, but some sixth sense warned him to turn back to his ditch just as Bestia strode up to them.

'What's this? Taking a break without orders are we, war hero?'

'No, sir.'

'And why are you covered in dirt, boy?'

'Sir, I . . .'

'Answer my fucking question!'

'I slipped, sir. While I was tossing the soil up into the camp.'

'You tired then, boy?' Bestia asked with an expression of feigned concern.

'Yes, sir, but I . . .'

'Well then, it seems you need a bit more fitness training. You're on latrine fatigues for the next five evenings.'

'But, sir. I'm to attend the legate's party after the investiture.'

'You'll have to shovel shit twice as quick then if you're going to be there on time.' Bestia smiled sweetly. 'And do make sure you're smartly turned out, or Vespasian'll have you on a charge.'

Bestia laughed as he allowed himself to imagine the scene. Then with a hearty clap on Cato's shoulder he wandered back down the line.

'And fuck you, sir,' Cato swore softly at the man's back and then started in horror as the centurion whipped round and pointed a finger at him accusingly.

'Did you say something?' Did you?'

'Just "thank you", sir.'

'You being sarky to me, son?'

'No, sir,' Cato replied, deadpan. 'I'm just grateful that you are offering me an opportunity to improve myself so I can be a legionary you can be proud of, sir.'

Bestia glared at him a moment then whirled round abruptly and strode away, leaving Cato to his digging. Next to him, Pulcher's shoulders rocked with silent laughter.

'I'll remember this,' Cato said quietly.

'Oooh, I'm so scared of you! I'm just pissing my pants,' Pulcher whispered.

Cato stared at him a moment, no longer as terrified of the man as he used to be, only worn down by the anxiety of looking out for Pulcher, wondering when and how the bastard would next find a way to get at him. With an angry sigh he swung the pick back into the ground as hard as possible, then grunted with effort to dislodge the clump of earth. Something had to be done about Pulcher, and soon.

At midday Bestia called for a halt and the men stood at attention as he examined their efforts. The abrupt halt to work allowed the sweat to run cold and clammy beneath their tunics and, in the enforced stillness, most of them were shivering as the drill team strode along tutting at their crude technique. The ditch ran unevenly along its inner side as a number of recruits had forgotten the two-spades-width rule. Others had not yet managed to dig the required amount out of the frozen ground and their sections did not match up to their neighbours. Only a few dozen had performed to Bestia's grudging satisfaction, Pulcher and Cato amongst them.

'Frankly, ladies, I don't think the barbarians out there have much to fear from Rome as long as useless shits like you are manning its legions. If you call this a defensive ditch then I'm a cheap Greek tart. The only thing this'll keep out is the cold. So, ladies, let's fill it in, stop for a quick bite, and then we'll have another go this afternoon.'

Chapter Sixteen

The entrance to the legate's house was brightly lit when Cato arrived, after a fast run from the barracks. He stopped for a moment to catch his breath and place the grass crown back on his head. For the moment, the phalera hung from a ribbon around his neck over the front of his tunic. Later it would be fixed to his harness where it would remain for the rest of his life and be buried with him. Composed, he strode up to the gate where a household steward sat at a desk in the porch behind the two guards. The guards crossed spears to indicate Cato was to halt.

'Name, please?' the steward asked.

'Quintus Licinius Cato.'

'Cato,' murmured the steward as he made a mark on a wax slate with his stylus. 'You're late, Cato, very late. Admit him.'

The spears parted and Cato passed through the gateway to the interior courtyard.

'Straight ahead.' The steward pointed to the main hall, wrinkling his nose and frowning as Cato went by. From the windows above the colonnade came the glow of a brightly lit interior, and the sounds of music and laughter spilled out above the hubbub of general conversation. It was bad form to arrive so late to a party but it would have been unthinkable to have ignored the invitation, just as it was impossible to disobey Bestia's orders to sluice and scrub the latrine channels. Tonight's fatigues had taken longer than usual due to a stomach bug that was going through the Legion at a ferocious rate. Cato had been left with little time to change into his best tunic and run through the fortress to arrive even at this late hour. With a bitter sense of dread for the inevitable interrogation about his tardiness, Cato walked over to the hall at a condemned man's pace. He rapped the door. Instantly the latch leapt up and the door swung inwards to reveal the household's majordomo, hardly able to conceal his irritation.

'There you are at last! You'd better have a good explanation for the legate.'

'I'll apologise as soon as there's a quiet moment,' Cato promised. 'Is there any way I can get to my place unobtrusively?'

'Hardly, young man. Follow me.'

The majordomo shut the door and led Cato through a heavy curtain into a large hall. Though minute by imperial palace standards, Cato mused, the room had been made as comfortable as it could possibly be this close to the ends of the Empire. The hall was brightly lit from scores of oil lamps suspended from the joists. Two long benches ran down each side of the hall, covered with cushions for the diners who ate off the low tables in front of them. Cato was surprised to see that all the tribunes and nearly every centurion was present, together with a number of wives. In the open space between the tables a pair of wrestlers were grunting and straining in a tight embrace as they groped for a decisive hand-hold. At one end of the hall a small group of pipe players strove to be heard above the din of the guests. Cato hurriedly looked for a gap on the nearest bench to quietly slip into, but the majordomo beckoned to him and slowly proceeded down the side of the hall to the head table where Vespasian and his most honoured guests reclined. With horror Cato saw a conspicuous gap between Macro and Vespasian. The legate frowned as they approached, but only for a moment before he forced a smile on to his lips and waved a greeting.

'Optio! I wondered where you had got to.'

'I'm sorry, sir,' Cato replied as he slipped forward on to the couch beside Macro. 'I had some duties I was ordered to complete first.'

'What duties?'

'I'd rather not say over dinner, sir.'

'Not much of that left, I'm afraid. Rufulus! See what you can find for the optio, must be some choice titbits left.'

'Yes, sir.' The majordomo bowed, darting a sharp glare at Cato.

'While you're waiting you might try some of the stuffed dormice.' Vespasian proffered a gold serving dish around which lay an arrangement of tiny baked mice. 'They're filled with some of the local herbs and cheese. Not quite what you're used to at the palace, I suspect, but it's a pleasant enough gastronomic reminder of home. Take one.'

Cato did as he was told. While the mice had been slightly overbaked, they made a pleasant change from standard legionary fare. As Cato happily crunched on the tasty morsels, the legate ordered a slave to bring the late arrival a selection of delicacies.

'Have some wine.' Vespasian pointed out a row of Samian decanters. 'There's a decent Caecuban and a tolerable Massic. I'm saving the last of my Falernian for a toast.'

Cato's eyes glittered at the prospect. 'Your cook has done his Apicius proud. Thank you for inviting me.'

'My pleasure, son. You did well in that little business with the locals. Now I'll leave you to your meal before it goes completely cold. I want to introduce you to a few people later on. Some you will already know.' Vespasian smiled. 'My wife says she is particularly keen to catch up on some of the palace gossip. That is, if I can tear her away from Tribune Vitellius.' He nodded towards the end of the head table where Cato could see the tribune over the shoulder of a slim woman. The pair seemed to be deep in conversation. Suddenly the legate's wife shook with laughter and Vespasian frowned momentarily. He switched his attention back to the waiting optio. 'As I said, that can wait for later. But for now I'm afraid I have to talk shop with the camp prefect. Please excuse me and enjoy the meal.'

The legate turned his back and Cato shifted on to his stomach, feasting his eyes on the spread before him, before he allowed his tastebuds a turn.

'What the hell is that smell?' Macro sniffed accusingly.

'I'm afraid it's me, sir,' Cato replied, filling his cup with a dark red Massic.

'What is it? You stink like a cheap tart.'

'That's because it's a scent Pyrax bought for a cheap tart.'

'You're wearing a scent?' Macro recoiled in horror.

'Had to, sir. I've been up to my knees in shit all afternoon. I cleaned myself down as best I could but there's no shifting the smell. Pyrax suggested I try to cover over it with his scent.'

'He did, did he?'

'Yes, sir. Said it was better to smell like a tart than a turd, or something.'

'That's debatable.'

'How's the leg today, sir?' Cato asked, reaching for another dormouse.

'Getting better. But still a few weeks before I'm allowed back on my feet. I'm not looking forward to spending most of it in a transport wagon.'

'Any idea where the Legion's being sent?'

'Shhh! Keep your mouth shut! We're not supposed to know yet. I think that's why we've all been invited.'

'You think?'

'Why else invite so many if it's just a quiet dinner to celebrate the investiture? There's bound to be more to it than that.'

Flavia laughed politely, but discreetly, at the tribune's joke; one had to be careful when discussing Emperor Claudius. At the same time she wished to probe Vitellius a little further so the amused expression remained on her face.

'That's a good story Vitellius. Very good. But I wonder, do you think Claudius is right for the job?'

'What do I think of Claudius?' He scrutinised her closely before replying. 'It's a bit too early to make a judgement, wouldn't you say?'

'I have friends in Rome who tell me that people are already saying that Claudius won't last long, that he's mad or, at the very least, a simpleton. And that he lets his freedmen run the empire in his name. Particularly that fellow Narcissus.'

'Yes, I've heard that too.' Vitellius smiled, amused by the way in which people discussing the Emperor always voiced their own opinions through the mouths of anonymous friends. 'But it's early days, he's bound to delegate some tasks while he learns the ropes.'

'I suppose you're right,' Flavia replied as she picked a scrap of meat from one of the bones lying on her plate. 'But I wonder how one man can ever be expected to rule the Empire – such a burden. I know I'm only a woman and have a limited perspective on affairs of state, but I would have thought that such a task required the energies of more than one man. Surely there are enough wise heads in the Senate who can be relied on to help the Emperor rule?'

'To help the Emperor rule? Or to rule in his place? And then we're back to the bloodshed of the Republic. Nearly every politician a soldier and every soldier a politician, and once you're in that situation there are no longer any elections – just wars.'

'Not that we have elections any more,' Flavia smiled.

'No. No, we don't. But how long has it been since

Romans slaughtered Romans in the name of their general's political ambitions?'

'As far as I recall, not since the divine Augustus wiped out all his rivals and imposed his dynasty upon us. And, let's face it, the Emperors have rather a lot of blood on their hands. There are many in Rome who suffered at the hands of Augustus, Tiberius and Caligula. And who is to say that the present incumbent won't continue the tradition?'

'Maybe. But how many more might have died if Augustus had not seized control of the army from the Senate and made it the tool of one man?'

'So it's simply a question of the relative death-rates, then?'

'Look here,' Vitellius asked quietly. 'Are you really suggesting that we return to the Republic?'

'No, I don't think so,' Flavia replied sweetly. 'But – just for the sake of argument between friends over a comfortable meal – don't you think a return to senatorial rule would be preferable to the present situation?'

'An interesting question, Flavia. Very interesting. Of course there are arguments that can be made in favour of either arrangement. I'm sure there's a considerable pool of talent that could be drawn on if the Senate had all its powers restored, but I fear that there are rather more senators with designs on accruing power to themselves than there are those who genuinely wish to serve Rome. You only have to look at that nasty business in Dalmatia last year. Poor Claudius had only just been confirmed as Emperor when the mutiny occurred. If a few more legions had joined Scribonianus and the other plotters then who knows how it would have ended? We're lucky Narcissus's agents managed to nip that one in the bud.'

'Nipped in the bud?' Flavia mused. 'That's a nice euphemism for the dozens who were killed. I lost some good friends before I left Rome. I'm sure you did as well. And they're still hunting down the surviving members of the plot. Not a comfortable time in which to live.'

'They brought it on themselves, Flavia. Before you gamble in such affairs you should consider the stakes. It's all or nothing. They lost and Claudius won. Do you think they would have been any more merciful to him if it had worked out the other way round?'

'No. I don't suppose they would.' She nodded thoughtfully.

'Not that there was ever much chance of them succeeding,' Vitellius continued. 'The fools had been old-fashioned enough to appeal to the legionaries' patriotism rather than their purses. The moment Narcissus showed up with Claudius's gold it was all over.'

'It would seem,' Flavia looked him deep in the eyes, 'that the moral of the tale is that the army is only as loyal as the imperial treasury is deep.'

'Why, Flavia!' Vitellius laughed. 'I couldn't have put it better myself! But I'm afraid you are right. At the end of the day it's all down to whoever can offer the troops the most money. Ancestors, wisdom and integrity mean nothing any more. Money is the font of all power. If you have it then the world turns for you, if not then you are quite helpless.'

194

'Well, then.' Flavia sipped at her wine. 'I hope our Emperor can afford to remain in the job. Otherwise, as you say, it's just a question of time before the army looks to a wealthier patron.'

'Yes,' Vitellius said. 'Just a question of time. But enough of politics, for now. You're an interesting woman. I really do wish I'd had the opportunity to share a decent conversation with you before tonight.'

'That would have been nice. I'm afraid Vespasian does tend to try and keep me under lock and key, army bases being what they are.'

'And I'm sure,' Vitellius leaned closer, 'that you're smart enough to run rings round such restrictions, should you want to.'

'Yes . . . should I want to.'

'And is that why you married him?'

Flavia looked up and saw that his eyes were openly appraising her as his lips melted into the smooth smile of a seducer.

'No.' Flavia shook her head. 'I married Vespasian because I love him. And there's more steel in him than you can imagine. You'd do well to remember that.'

The tribune's brow creased and he was quite still as he accepted the rebuff. Then he refilled his glass, without offering to do the same for Flavia, and raised it.

'To your husband,' he said quietly. 'What you say about him may well be true . . . for now.'

Flavia's eyes flickered up and a warm smile flushed across her face as Vespasian rose to his feet. Vitellius quickly glanced over his shoulder and saw the legate approaching with the newly decorated optio at his shoulder. With a sigh of reluctance he eased himself round and stood up.

'I wondered when you would get round to bringing that poor boy over here.' Flavia laughed as she held out both her hands towards Cato. The optio did a quick double take and gulped.

'Lady Flavia?'

'The same. And how's my little Cato? Not so little these days, it seems. Let me have a good look at you!'

'It seems the optio and my wife were friends back in their palace days,' Vespasian explained to Vitellius. 'So it's something of a reunion.'

'Such a small world, sir,' the tribune replied smoothly. 'We seem to live in a time of great coincidences.'

'Yes. I need a quiet word with you. I'm sure my wife would be only too pleased to join the optio and catch up on several years of gossip. My dear?'

'Of course.' Flavia nodded gracefully and led Cato towards the head of the table.

'Lady Flavia, I had no idea you were here.'

'Why should you?' She smiled. 'Officers' wives are seldom seen out of their quarters. And only a lunatic would expose themselves to the ravages of a German winter by choice.'

'Did you know I was here?'

'Of course. There can't be that many Catos joining the Legion from the palace. And as soon as my husband mentioned the – now what was it he said? – the "bookish beanpole", I knew it had to be you. I've been simply dying for a chance to see you again but Vespasian said I had to let you settle in first – the last thing you needed was some interfering woman mollycoddling you in front of the other men.'

'Yes.' Cato winced at the image. 'My lady, I can't tell you how glad I am to see a familiar face in this place.'

'Come, let's sit.' Flavia settled on to her husband's couch and patted the space beside her. Cato looked around but no-one seemed to be paying undue attention. He had been in the army long enough to feel uncomfortable about social intercourse between widely different ranks.

'Now, Cato, you must tell me how it's going. I can't imagine how you, of all people, have ended up here. It must be quite a change in lifestyle?'

Cato, uncomfortably aware of Macro sitting just to his side, phrased his response carefully.

'Yes, my lady, quite a change. But it seems to be a good enough life, and should be the making of me.'

Flavia raised her eyebrows. 'You really have changed, haven't you?'

'May I introduce my centurion to you?' Cato rose slightly to indicate Macro.

'Ma'am.' Macro nodded politely as he wiped the grease from his lips with the back of his hand. 'Lucius Cornelius Macro, commanding the Sixth Century, Fourth Cohort,' he continued automatically.

'Pleased to meet you, centurion. I trust you are looking after my friend?'

'Hmm. No more or less than any other of my men,' Macro replied resentfully. 'In any case, the lad can look after himself.'

'So I've heard. Now then, Cato, you must fill me in

on what's been going on in the palace since I left.'

As Cato talked, Macro hovered on the brink of the conversation until boredom set in. With a shrug he turned back to his food and made the most of the unaccustomed luxury of the feast before him. For her part Flavia listened intently and interrupted Cato with frequent questions about the endless rise and fall of sundry palace officials. At length she had pumped Cato dry of information and leaned back on one arm.

'So, the same seething hotbed of scandal and intrigue that it ever was. That much has not changed.'

'Indeed, it's almost impossible to avoid the gossip.'

'I have to admit I really miss Rome.'

'You could have stayed there, my lady. It's not unknown for legates to leave their wives at home while on active service.'

'True, but I've found Rome a little uncomfortable since that nasty business with Scribonianus in Dalmatia last year. Too many people spending their time denouncing others as conspirators. It's put quite a dampener on the social scene – you have no idea how much of a challenge it is planning a dinner party while the imperial agents are busy whittling down your guest list.'

Cato nodded. 'By the time I left the palace I'd heard that Claudius had already signed over a hundred death warrants. I'm sure there can't be many conspirators left by now.'

'Narcissus has been a busy man, it would appear.'

'And a very important one since Claudius put him in charge of the imperial general staff.'

'Has Narcissus changed much since I left?'

'Not that you'd notice,' Cato replied. 'But most people are careful what they say around him these days – now that he has the Emperor's ear.'

'Does he still look the same?' asked Flavia, absently gazing at her fingers as they stretched the hem of her palla.

Cato reflected a moment before replying. 'A little greyer around the temples but not so different from when you knew him.'

'I see . . . I see. And I trust our little secret is still safe?' she asked softly.

He had been expecting the question for some time and nodded as he looked her firmly in the eye and replied. 'Quite safe, my lady. I gave you my word. It still stands and will until I die.'

'Thank you.'

An embarrassing silence settled between them as they both thought back to the night of a terrible storm raging over Rome, when a little boy, scared out of his wits by the thunder and lightning, had huddled in the corner of a small ante-room where a man and a woman were coupling in the glare of light flashing through the windows. Later, when the man had gone, Flavia discovered Cato trembling in the corner of the room. For a brief moment she had simply stared at him, afraid of the consequences of what he must have seen. Seizing his shoulders, she had sworn him to secrecy. Then, seeing the elemental terror in his expression, some instinct awoke inside her and she'd shielded his small body from the storm as best she could. Afterwards, despite the social gulf between them, she had felt a sense of responsibility for Cato and seen that he was well cared for by the other palace slaves. Then she had left the imperial household and met Vespasian.

Flavia decided to move the conversation on to safer ground. 'Now, Cato, what do you miss most about Rome?'

'The libraries,' he answered without hesitation. 'The nearest I get to a good read here is some weather-beaten army manual. When I left Rome I was reading Livy's histories. It'll be a while before I get a chance to continue them.'

'Histories!' Flavia exclaimed. 'What on earth are you reading histories for? I thought you young men liked poetry – Lucretius, Catullus, Ovid – that sort of thing.'

'Ovid is a little hard to come by, my lady,' Cato reminded her. 'In any case, I'm afraid my tastes are a bit conservative. I've only really bothered with Virgil.'

'Virgil's such a boring old stick,' Flavia complained. 'Not an ounce of feeling, or empathy. It's just turgid elegance.'

'I really must disagree. I find him quite sublime at times – able to put concepts into words in a timeless way. When all today's cheap romantic poets are mere shadows in the memory of men, Virgil will still be a vibrant influence flowing down through the centuries.'

'Most poetically phrased, Cato, but do you speak of time or legionaries?'

'Hardly the latter.' Cato laughed with the legate's wife. 'Literary aesthetics are not foremost in the minds of such men.'

'Pass the mice,' Macro interrupted.

'Yes, sir,' Cato responded guiltily. 'There you are, sir.'

'Do you read much?' Flavia asked Macro. 'I ask only to reassure myself that Cato here is a bit wide of the mark. I can't believe that my husband's officers would ignore the muses.'

'Ma'am?'

'Do you read poetry, Centurion?'

'Not often, ma'am, I'm too busy most of the time.'

'But you do read poetry,' Flavia insisted.

'Of course, ma'am.'

'So who's your favourite?'

'Who's my favourite? Well, let me think. Probably that chap young Cato just mentioned.'

'Really?' Flavia frowned. 'And which of Virgil's works do you rate most highly?'

'Difficult question, ma'am. I think all of his stuff is good.'

'Coward!' laughed Flavia. 'Frankly, I doubt whether you have read anything of his, or any poet, for that matter. In fact, I doubt whether you read at all.'

She laughed again, but Macro looked down at his food in silence and Cato, sensed his centurion's acute discomfort.

'Shhh!' Flavia raised a finger to her lips. 'I think the legate is about to speak.'

Sure enough Vespasian downed the last of his wine and stood up. He tipped a wink to the majordomo who ordered the servants to quickly distribute the decanters of Falernian to all tables. Then he rapped his staff down on to the mosaic floor. The room slowly fell silent as all eyes turned to the head table. Vespasian waited for complete quiet before he began to speak.

'Gentlemen, and ladies, it cannot have escaped your attention that the Legion has been preparing for relocation in recent weeks. I can tonight confirm that imperial staff has issued us with our marching orders. The Legion is to proceed with all due haste to the west coast of Gaul . . .'

If Vespasian was expecting some excited response he was to be disappointed. Many officers in the room looked away in embarrassment, shuffling uncomfortably. One or two polite souls did try and look surprised, as if this was indeed news to them, but they were seen through in an instant, and Vespasian continued with an evident sourness to his tone.

'On arrival we are to join up with elements of four other legions to train for the invasion of Britain. A fleet is being assembled even now and before the year is out a new province will have been added to the empire in the name of and glorification of Tiberius Claudius Drusus Nero Germanicus. The Legion begins moving in two months' time, our fortress to be garrisoned by a mixed auxiliary cohort from Macedonia in our absence. Right, you know the routine. From tomorrow you get straight to it. All that remains tonight is a toast. So, fill your cups and raise them to the Emperor!'

As the orderly and Cato helped lift Macro off the litter into his bed the centurion grabbed hold of Cato's tunic and dragged him close.

'You stay. I want a word in private.' Macro's face was grim.

Left alone with his superior, his mind sharpened by the cold night air, Cato wondered what on earth he could have done to bring on this sudden change in mood. For a moment Centurion Macro stared up at Cato intently before he could nerve himself to say what was on his mind.

'Cato, can I trust you?'

'Sir?'

'Can I trust you with a secret? Something I dare not tell anyone else?'

Cato gulped nervously, and instinctively took a step away from the centurion's bed. 'Well, that depends, sir. I mean, naturally I'm flattered, but you know how it is, some men do and some don't. It just happens that I don't, sir. No offence or anything.'

'What the fuck are you going on about?' Macro frowned as he raised himself up on an elbow. 'If you think, for one moment, that I'm some kind of arse bandit then I'll take your fucking head off. Understand?'

'Yes, sir.' Cato relaxed. 'So how can I help?'

'You can help . . . You can help by teaching me to read.'

'Read?'

'Yes, read, damn it! You know, all those bloody words and stuff. I want to learn how it all works. All right, that's a bit too strong. I don't want to read any more than the next man. Fact is, I have to read and write, if I'm going to stay a centurion. And that bitch of woman nearly had me by the short and curlies tonight. But some day it'll come out and, when it does, I'll get busted back to the ranks. Unless I learn my words.'

'I see. And you want me to teach you?'

'Yes. And you promise not to tell a soul. Will you do it?'

Cato thought it over a moment and inevitably his nature led him to the answer. 'Of course I'll teach you, sir.'

Chapter Seventeen

The winter wore on towards spring and the snow melted; for several weeks frequent heavy showers of rain turned all unmetalled roadways into muddy quagmires. The only traffic in and out of the fortress was the constant stream of imperial staff messengers rushing to the far-flung Second Legion with the latest instructions for the impending relocation. Having delivered the despatches they returned burdened with requests for permission to buy draught animals, fodder and slaves to cover the spring campaign.

Anticipating the assent of the staff corps in Rome, the Legion had hired a cadre of muleteers to buy up the necessary livestock from the towns and villages in a wide sweep south of the Rhine. The men were hand-picked and could be trusted to select only the fittest animals for the long journey ahead. They could also be trusted to haggle for the lowest possible price and, as long as the cost remained reasonable, those in authority generally overlooked the unofficial 'commission' that found its way into the purses of the muleteers. So it was that the mules, and other draught animals, arrived to swell the ranks grazing in the pastures hastily constructed outside the fortress.

Inside, most of the space between the walls and the barracks was filled with the Legion's transport vehicles. Each century was allocated a wagon for engineering tools, administrative baggage – namely, the centurion's tent and all the personal items he desired to make the campaign comfortable – and the pointed entrenchment stakes. Then there was the medical convoy for the carriage of sick and non-walking wounded, the artillery company with their carriage-mounted catapults and bolt-throwers, large grain wagons for the portable food reserve of barley, the vast headquarters baggage train and, finally, the staff officers' convoy of personal effects. Even as things stood the Legion was travelling light. No time could be spared for foraging and so a number of grain dumps had already been established along the route.

Within the fortress the imminence of events was palpable, even to those soldiers who lived a day at a time, and desperate legionaries were trying to offload their non-portable goods to the merchants who gathered like vultures to take advantage of such occasions. Word of the Legion's relocation had spread far and wide and, over the following weeks, the settlement around the fortress swelled to accommodate the Empire's peripatetic merchants, in search of the bargains that every such buyer's market attracted. Disconsolate legionaries trudged from dealer to dealer with all manner of goods, sentimental, ornamental or simply superfluous, and haggled bitterly for the few coins that escaped the tight purses of the merchants, who made small fortunes every time a major military formation was relocated.

One crisp, clear spring afternoon Cato came

wandering through the hastily erected market, on the lookout for some basic reading matter for Macro.

'Nothing fancy, mind,' Macro had warned him. 'None of your poncy literature. Just something simple you can teach me with.'

'But we'll need to go through some literature eventually, sir.'

'Eventually, but for now let's keep it simple, understand?'

'Sir.'

'Now, there's a month's pay there, so make sure you get me value for money.'

'Of course I will, sir.'

'And you keep this quiet. If anyone asks, just tell them I want something to read in the wagon. Catching up on my military histories, whatever. But just you remember – not one mention of reading lessons.'

'Yes, sir.'

And so it was that Cato pushed his way through a buzzing throng of soldiers and merchants on a cold and windy afternoon. Clutching his military cloak tightly about him Cato made his way down the lines of merchant wagons piled high with a bewildering array of goods; fine Samian ware, lyres and other musical instruments, a variety of chairs, chests, tables and portable libraries.

In one wagon sat a slender slave girl in a thin well-worn tunic, shivering miserably, a For Sale sign leaning against her legs. She must have been sixteen or seventeen, with jet black hair tied back. Perched on the driver's board, she rested her pointed chin on her knees, hugging them tightly and trembling from the cold. She glanced up and Cato was stopped dead in his tracks by a pair of startling green eyes. For a moment he simply stared, then, aware that he was making a fool of himself, he tore his eyes away and scurried off down the line of wagons.

He soon found what he was searching for. The tail of one wagon was piled high with scrolls and, as Cato rummaged through them, a shrewd old Phoenician dragged himself away from his small brazier to greet his customer. In view of the soldier's age and inexperience, the trader tried to interest Cato in a nicely illustrated set of pornographic manuals which, while not anatomically accurate, were at least conceptually diverting. Eventually Cato managed to persuade the Phoenician that his interests were strictly limited to historical studies and they parted company with Cato carrying an armful of books, as the trader added yet more coins to his swelling purse.

Books were not uppermost in Cato's mind as he made his way back down the line of wagons. He found himself drawn back to the girl sitting on the driver's board, driven by the simple desire to set his eyes on her once more. That was all. What else could possibly come of it? And yet he felt his heart quicken as he approached the place he had seen her earlier.

The wagon was still there, piled high with goods, but there was no sign of the girl. Cato pretended to browse through the wares of the next trader, making sidelong glances at the nearby tents set behind the wagons. Casually reversing direction, he sifted through some chipped Samian ware with his spare hand.

'Looking for anything in particular, noble sir?'

Cato looked up quickly. A swarthy merchant in an unseasonally bright cloak stood at his side.

'Oh no! Nothing. Just looking.'

'I see.' The merchant continued to watch him closely, a hint of a smile on his dark lips. 'Just looking, then?'

'Yes. You, uh, you had a girl here earlier.'

The merchant nodded slowly.

'Is she yours? I mean is she family?'

'No, sir. A slave. Bought her from a tribune this morning.'

'Oh, really?'

'Yes. And I just sold her a few moments ago.'

'Sold her!' Cato's heart jumped.

'To a lady, there, sir.' The merchant pointed through the throng to where a tall, slender figure was about to enter the fortress gate. At her side, following her new mistress like a dog, was the girl he had seen earlier. Without another word to the merchant Cato set off in pursuit, not sure of any reason for his behaviour other than a powerful desire to see the girl again. And so he hurried through the crowd, eyes locked on the pair of women ahead as he quickly closed the distance. At the gate, the woman turned to look back and Cato instantly recognised her as the legate's wife. Before he could react, Flavia's eyes met his and she instantly waved a greeting.

'Why! It's young Cato!'

Trying hard not to blush, Cato hurried over, managing to avoid looking at the slave girl as he made his greeting.

'Good morning, my lady.'

'Been buying books I see, rather a lot of books.'

'Not for me, my lady. For my centurion.'

'Ah yes,' Flavia smiled. 'It must be quite pleasant having an officer who shares one's tastes in poetry so completely. Did you find anything for yourself?'

'No, my lady.' Cato let his eyes shift to the slave girl and flushed with embarrassment when he saw her smiling back at him. 'Can't afford any books, my lady.'

'Really? That's too bad. But look here, Cato. I have to leave some of my books behind since there's so little room to spare in the wagons. They might not be to your taste, but you're welcome to have the first pick.'

'Thank you, my lady. That's most kind.'

'Call round to the legate's house later on and we'll see. Do you two know each other?'

Cato had found himself responding to the slave girl's smile while the legate's wife had been speaking and now he snapped his eyes back.

'Oh no, my lady! Never!'

'You could have fooled me!' Flavia laughed. 'You look like a pair of lovestruck puppies. Honestly, you youngsters only ever have one thing on your minds. You're worse than rabbits.'

'No, my lady!' Cato's blush deepened to a most unbecoming crimson. 'I assure you I had no intention—'

'Peace, Cato! Peace!' Flavia raised her hands. 'I didn't mean to offend you. I'm sorry. There, I've embarrassed you. I apologise. Do you forgive me?'

'Yes, my lady.'

'Oh dear! I really have upset you. I just hope I can make amends when you call round later on. Can't leave you walking around the base with that look on your face, it'd damage morale.'

'I'm all right, my lady.'

'Of course you are. Well, I'll see you later on then.'

'Yes, my lady.'

'Come, Lavinia!'

Lavinia. Cato savoured the name a moment and, as he watched Flavia lead her new purchase away, the slave girl glanced back and winked at him.

Chapter Eighteen

The legate's house was in turmoil, packing cases lay strewn about his private quarters and the household slaves laboured to bed down every breakable item between layers of straw. The slaves, fearful of Flavia's wrath – she had a fierce temper when provoked and was not above having a slave flogged when the circumstances warranted it – handled the pottery and china with as much care as possible. Besides the breakables, Flavia had to make arrangements for the packing of the linen and personal items of furniture – all of which was being shipped back to Vespasian's house on the Quirinal in Rome. Flavia and Titus were to accompany him as far as the Gaulish coast and return home once the campaign was launched. By that time the witch-hunt for the surviving members of the Scribonianus conspiracy should have died down and some sort of normality would have returned to the social scene. And Rome was the best place for Titus since they must begin thinking about his education in the near future. Vespasian favoured a strictly vocational training in law and rhetoric and wanted Flavia to begin looking for a tutor as soon as possible.

Through the tangle of packing cases and piles of straw

weaved a maid-servant, trying to catch Flavia's eye.

'What is it?'

'Someone to see you, mistress. One of the soldiers,' she said with evident distaste.

'Who?'

'An optio.'

'Cato?'

'Yes, mistress, that's what he said his name was.'

'Very well. I suppose I could do with a little break from all this packing.'

A nearby slave raised his eyes heavenwards.

'Show the optio through to the study. I'll be there in a minute. Make him at home and offer the boy something to drink.'

'Yes, mistress.'

'I was just thinking about you,' Flavia said as she breezed into the study, wearing a light silk stola. The room, like most rooms in the legate's house, was heated by a hypercaust system and Cato was relishing the warmth it provided in the moments before Flavia's entrance.

'You're fortunate that those fools haven't packed up my study yet. Do sit down.'

Cato resumed his seat as Flavia wafted over to a large shelved cupboard with dozens of scrolls neatly stacked in sections. She paused a moment and fondly ran her hands over some of them before she addressed the optio.

'You're welcome to whatever you want, or at least whatever you can carry. You can take the Philippics – bombastic delivery but with flashes of wit – and the Georgics – fertile reading matter – and here's a few volumes of Livy. Would you like some poetry?'

'Yes, my lady.'

Nearly an hour later a pile of scrolls lay on the couch beside Cato and he was engaged in the heart-breaking task of deciding which of Flavia's offerings he would be able to fit into his marching pack. Flavia watched him thoughtfully as he mentally weighed up each book before deciding which pile to place it in.

'You were quite taken with Lavinia, weren't you?'

'My lady?' Cato looked up, scroll poised in hand.

'The slave girl I bought this morning.'

'Oh, her!'

'Oh, her, indeed. You're not fooling me, young Cato, I know the signs. The question is, what do you want to do about it?'

Cato stared back, mind reeling with shame at the transparency of his feelings and a desire to see Lavinia again, to stare into those emerald eyes.

'Well, maybe I was wrong then,' Flavia teased him. 'Maybe you don't want to see her again.'

'My lady! I . . . I . . .'

'Thought so,' laughed Flavia. 'Honestly, I can read you men like a book almost every time. Don't worry, Cato, I'm not going to stop you seeing her – far from it, but give the girl some time to settle into the household and then I'll see what I can arrange.'

'Yes, my lady . . . Thank you.'

'Now you'd better take those scrolls and leave. I'd love to talk but there's too much work still to be done. Another time, soon. And maybe Lavinia can join us?'

'Of course, my lady. I'd like that.'

'I bet you would!'

As she watched Cato's back disappear down the Via Praetoria Flavia smiled to herself. A lovely boy, she thought, and far too trusting. If she cultivated him carefully he might well be useful to her some day.

'So what is all this stuff?' asked Macro suspiciously as Cato handed over the scrolls, each one neatly encased and labelled.

'Essays and histories mostly.'

'No poetry?'

'None, sir, as you ordered,' Cato replied. 'There's some pretty exciting material here—'

'Exciting? Look, I just want to learn enough to read. That's it, as far as I'm concerned – all right?'

'Yes, sir. If that's what you really want . . . Now then, sir, how have you been managing with the letters I showed you?'

Reaching under his bed, Macro brought out a wooden wax tablet and handed it over to his subordinate. Cato flipped it open and scanned the contents. To the left-hand side of each tablet were the letters of the alphabet that he had neatly inscribed on the wax-coated surface. Immediately to the right of this were the centurion's rough attempts at copying – straggling lines and curves that occasionally bore a passing resemblance to the original.

'It wasn't easy writing on my lap, you know,' explained Macro. 'Bloody thing kept sliding all over the place.'

'So I see. Well, it's a good start. Have you managed to remember what each one sounds like?'

'Of course.'

'Then would you mind going through them with me, sir? Just for practice. Then we'll try a few words.'

Macro ground his teeth. 'Don't you think I can do it?'

'I'm sure you can, sir. But practice makes perfect, as you keep telling me. Shall we?'

As Macro stumbled through the alphabet, Cato kept his comments to a minimum and all the while images of Lavinia trickled into his mind's eye, to be expelled with considerable reluctance. In the end, even Macro could see that the young man's attention was not fully engaged with the task at hand. Abruptly he snapped the tablets shut so that Cato nearly fell off his stool.

'What's on your mind, boy?'

'Sir?'

'Even I know I got some of those words wrong – and you're just sitting there nodding like a chicken. What's so bloody important that you can't concentrate on this?'

'Sir, it's nothing. Just a personal matter. It won't happen again. Shall we continue?'

'Not if your problem's going to get in the way.'

The lesson had become boring and Macro was not keen to continue. Moreover, the boy's evident reluctance to explain the cause of his distraction had provoked Macro's curiosity.

'Spit it out, lad!'

'Really, sir,' protested Cato. 'It's not important.'

'I'll be the judge of that. Speak. That's an order. I'm not having my men walk around like daydreamers. You youngsters spend all your time worrying about bullying

216

and women. So which is it? Who's been having a go at you?'

'No-one, sir.'

'Narrows things down a bit then, doesn't it?' Macro winked salaciously. 'So who's the woman then? It better not be the legate's wife. Might as well write out a suicide note right now.'

'No, sir! Not her,' Cato said, with a look of horror.

'Then who?' Macro demanded.

'A slave girl.'

'You want to get her in the sack, I take it?'

Cato stared at him for a moment and then nodded.

'So what's the problem? Offer her a few goodies and you're in. I've never known a slave woman who wasn't prepared to part her legs for the right gifts. What's she like?'

'Quite beautiful,' Cato replied softly.

'No, you idiot! I meant what does she like?'

'Oh, I see.' Cato blushed. 'I don't really know that much about her.'

'Well, find out. Ask her what she wants in exchange and you're away.'

'It isn't like that, sir. I feel something more than just lust.'

'Lust? Who's talking about lust? You want to screw her, right? So that's your objective. All you need now is deployment of the appropriate tactics to manoeuvre her into an advantageous position and then secure your conquest. Then it's just a question of mopping up.'

'Sir!' Cato, who thought he had become inured to the crude humour of the army, was caught off guard and blushed. 'It's not like that.'

'What are you talking about, lad?'

Cato tried to elaborate, but found it excruciating to talk about his feelings for Lavinia. It wasn't that there were no words – his mind reeled with well-remembered lines from any number of poems – but none seemed to quite capture the essence of the horrible aching pain that twisted his stomach and tore at his heart. Poets, he decided, were poor mirrors of mankind's soul. Precious little pen-scratchers pouring out their petty banalities in order to impress their pals. His feelings for Lavinia went some way beyond mere verse. Or did they? Perhaps Macro was right and his motives were somewhat more prosaic than he thought?

'What's so different about this woman? Spit it out.'

'I think you have to see her to understand.'

'Bit of a looker, eh?'

'Yes, sir.' Cato smiled.

'So let her know you're interested and that you'll pay what it takes to have your way – within reason of course, no sense in inflating her price for the lads who come after you – give her one and be on your way.'

'I was hoping for something a little more meaningful and long-lasting.'

'Don't be so bloody ridiculous.'

'Yes, sir!' Cato replied hurriedly. There was no speaking to the man on such issues, he now realised. 'Shall we continue with the letters, sir? We've quite a long way to go.'

'And some of us are hoping to go all the way,' Macro smirked.

'Yes, sir. The letters, sir?' Cato held out the waxed tablets.

'All bloody right then! I can see you don't want to talk about the woman – that's your business, right?'

'Shall we continue with the letters, sir?'

'Fair enough,' Macro said sulkily, 'bloody letters it is.'

Chapter Nineteen

By nightfall on the eve of the Legion's departure every vehicle had been checked for roadworthiness and all wheels freshly greased with tallow. Now they stood in long ranks loaded with the Legion's equipment and assorted baggage. In their pens outside the fortress the animals contentedly chewed on the last of the winter feed. Most of the headquarters staff, their work done for the next few weeks, were on a serious bender amongst the tents and grimy halls where the locals sold a heady brew that the garrison had grown accustomed to in the years they had been stationed on the Rhine frontier. The more sober-headed veterans were busy waterproofing their boots and making sure that the nail-studded soles were in good shape for the three hundred miles that lay between the Second Legion and the coast.

At headquarters a small staff still laboured over final details in large chambers that echoed with an eerie emptiness now that all records had been carefully ordered and packed in filing chests and loaded on wagons. Sundry debts owed to local traders were still being settled and travel permits written out for those officers' families immediately heading south to Italy. A detachment of the

Legion's cavalry had been assigned to escort the convoy as far south as Corbumentum before turning west to rejoin the Legion.

As Vespasian passed a row of desks where a team of five clerks were bent over their work, writing by the flickering light of oil lamps, he glanced down at the papers strewn before them.

'What's this?'

'Sir?' The senior clerk quickly rose to his feet.

'What's this stuff you're working on?'

'Copies of a letter we're writing for Lady Flavia, sir. They're for slave agents in Rome requesting details of any infant tutors they might have in their catalogues.'

'I see.'

'She said it was on your orders, sir.'

The resentment in the tone was unmistakable and Vespasian felt a twinge of guilt that these men were labouring into the night while their comrades were free to indulge themselves to excess.

'Well, I doubt that a night's delay will ruin her plans. You and your men can finish the letters another time. Off you go then.'

'Thank you, sir. You heard the legate, lads.'

The papers were eagerly shuffled into order, ink pots stopped up and pens wiped clean before the clerks rose to leave the room.

'Wait!' Vespasian called out and they turned towards him anxiously. He fumbled in the purse hanging from his belt and tossed a gold piece to the senior clerk. 'For you and your men – have a few drinks on me. You've done a good job these last few days.'

The clerks mumbled their thanks and hurried away, voices loud with excitement, leaving Vespasian gazing wistfully after them. It seemed a lifetime ago that he had enjoyed a night out with the lads as a newly appointed tribune. Dusty memories of wild nights and hideously painful hangovers amidst the fleshpots of Syria filtered into his mind and Vespasian felt a pang for the sweetness of youth that seemed over almost before it had begun. Now he was forever separated from these men by age and, more fundamentally, by rank.

Vespasian slowly made his way towards the gate of the headquarters building, pausing only to nod as he passed by the door to Vitellius's office where the tribune was still toiling over some paperwork by lamplight. Vitellius had been spending a great deal of time in headquarters of late – more than was required by his duties and more than enough to make Vespasian curious. But he could not ask him outright the reason for his new-found diligence; tribunes were supposed to be diligent and any questioning of the man might look like paranoia, or worse. If Vitellius was indeed up to something, any undue attention would alert him to the legate's suspicion. More curious still was the fact that the tribune had taken on a bodyguard. It was a right due to his rank, but one rarely claimed these days. But there he was – shadowing his master about the base – a stocky thick-set man with the manner of professional killer. It would be sensible to keep a closer eye on Tribune Vitellius from now on.

Since Lavinia had been taken into Vespasian's household,

Cato had had no chance even to speak to her and was only able to catch fleeting glances from time to time as he loitered outside the legate's house after he had finished with his duties for the day. He contrived to visit Flavia a few times in the hope that Lavinia might be present while they reminisced about life in the palace. But she remained out of sight and Cato was loath to reveal the true purpose of his visits, to the barely concealed amusement of the legate's wife. Finally, one day, Flavia could not help laughing.

'Really, Cato! You should be more inventive.'

'What do you mean, my lady?'

'I mean these excuses you have for coming to see me,' she smiled, 'or should I say coming to try and see Lavinia.'

Cato flushed and stammered out a garbled protestation that only provoked further laughter. He frowned.

'Please don't get cross! I'm not making fun of you. Really I'm not. If you wanted to see the girl then you should have said and I'd have arranged something for the two of you. Would you like to see her now?'

Cato nodded.

'All right then. But in a moment. We need to talk first.'

'What about, my lady?'

'I take it you know very little about Lavinia?'

'I only met her the same day you bought her,' admitted Cato.

'So she said.'

'The merchant who sold her said that she used to be owned by one of the tribunes.'

'Yes,' Flavia nodded. 'Plinius. Nice man, very intelligent – a quality that is totally wasted on the army.'

'Why did he sell her? Why did he leave her nothing more than those rags?'

'The answer to that depends on who you listen to.'

'What do you mean, my lady?'

'Plinius let it be known that he had sold her because Lavinia was useless as a house-servant. He said she was lazy, dishonest and incapable of learning her duties. The last straw, so he tells the tale, is that she stole one of his silk nightshirts.' Flavia leaned forward and continued, quietly. 'But the story being touted around the officers' wives is far more interesting. They say that Lavinia was something more than a house-servant. With her looks, anything else would be a sheer waste. Anyway, word has it that Plinius bought her from a sex-slave trader and was trying to groom her to while away the long winter evenings.'

'A concubine!'

'Not quite. Our Plinius wanted someone more sophisticated than that. Someone he could converse with afterwards. So, for the last few months he's kept Lavinia hidden away in his quarters teaching her how to read and write so he could introduce her to some literature. Bit of an uphill struggle apparently.'

'Hardly any reason to throw her out like that.'

'Quite.'

'So what happened, my lady?'

'What always happens. While looking up from her studies her head was turned by another tribune, somewhat more handsome and personable than Plinius.

And definitely more cunning and versed in the ways of subterfuge and seduction.'

Cato thought for a moment. 'Vitellius?'

'Who else? He had to have Lavinia as soon as he slapped eyes on her. Being rather new to the game Lavinia hadn't quite cracked playing hard to get and caved in with distasteful celerity – she must have been quite taken by Vitellius. In any event, *she* was taken, quite a few times if rumours are to be believed. Until one day Vitellius over-extended his tryst and in walked Plinius, fresh from a hard day's work and just itching to get stuck into some elementary grammar tuition. Well, you can imagine the scene and the consequences you already know about. He almost gave her away to that merchant.'

'Poor Lavinia.'

'Poor Lavinia?' Flavia's eyebrows arched. 'My dear boy, that's what she was raised for. You must have come across her type at the palace in all those years? They were virtually a fixture under the last two Emperors.'

'That's true enough,' admitted Cato. 'But my father did his best to keep me away from them. He told me to save myself for something better.'

'He did? And you think Lavinia's something better?'

'I don't know what she is, all I know is how I feel about her. Am I making any sense, my lady?'

'Oh yes. It's your first experience of infatuation. Sounds like you've got it bad – but don't worry, it'll soon pass. It always does.'

Cato glared at her and said with bitterness, 'Do all older people think like that?'

'Not all. But young people do. That's their charm and

their curse.' Flavia smiled. 'I understand your feelings, really I do. You'll see that what I say is true in a few years' time. You won't thank me for it now, or then. But let's try another perspective. What do you think Lavinia thinks about you?'

'I don't know,' Cato admitted. 'She hasn't got to know me yet.'

Flavia smiled gently and kept quiet for a moment.

'All right, my lady – I haven't got to know her either.'

'Good boy, you're beginning to see reason. It's important that you try to keep a clear head over this situation. My husband thinks you show promise, so don't do something rash which might return to haunt you later. That's all I'm trying to say. Now then, do you want to see her again?'

'Yes.'

Flavia smiled. 'Just as I thought.'

'You're disappointed with me, my lady.'

'On the contrary. A man who has a passion that overrides logic can be trusted in his principles. Only a fool values logic above feeling; sophists can reason themselves to accept any and all principles and therefore cannot be trusted. You have a heart as well as a mind, Cato. Just be careful how you use it. I will say what I believe to be true: that Lavinia can only hurt you, given what you are and she is. I'll say no more, for now. Just leave it with me. It won't be easy to arrange a meeting; there's not exactly much privacy available in the middle of a legion. In any case, my husband has rather traditional attitudes concerning the handling of his property.'

★ ★ ★

When the eagle and the other standards were removed from the fortress strong-room at dawn the next day, the legate and his staff breathed a sigh of relief. Soldiers, being the superstitious lot that they were, interpreted any problem in moving the eagle at the start of a campaign as an ill omen of the worst kind. But today the eagle emerged smoothly from headquarters and marched down the Via Praetoria to take its place in the colour guard at the front of the First cohort. The significance of the moment was observed by all those within sight of the eagle: the Legion was about to go off to war for the first time in years – minor border skirmishes excepted. An expectant hush settled over the fortress as every soldier, muleteer and camp follower waited for the order. Only the animals, insensible as ever to the affairs of mankind, moved; hooves scraped on cobblestones, bits jingled on harnesses and tails flicked to and fro in the spring morning.

The legate lowered his arm and the Legion's senior centurion snapped his head back to bellow out the order.

'First century! First cohort! Second Legion! Advance!'

In fine order, the red-cloaked ranks of the First cohort stepped out along the Via Praetoria, past the vast vehicle park and through the west gate where the rising sun caught them in its light so brightly that their cloaks glowed like fire. Close on the heels of the First cohort marched the headquarters company led by Vespasian and the tribunes mounted on smartly groomed horses.

Cohort followed cohort and then the ponderous lines of baggage trundled into their appointed place in the line of march. The last cohort, assigned for rearguard duties, followed the baggage train out of the fortress and the end of the column crawled up the slope away from the west gate. Many of the locals from the settlement watched the Legion depart with genuine sorrow. The Second Legion would be missed, particularly since they were to be replaced by a mere thousand auxiliary troops, two cohorts from Spain whose poor quality made them fit for garrison duties only. The auxiliaries, not being Roman citizens, were paid only a third as much as the legionaries. The local economy was going to be hit hard in the following years, and even as the final ranks of the Legion disappeared from view, a desultory column of civilians was already heading south to find new army bases to live off.

Chapter Twenty

'Halt!' The command was quickly relayed down the column. 'Packs down!'

The legionaries of the Sixth century shuffled to the side of the road and slumped to the freshly churned grass along the verge, far enough from the road to allow quick access for any messengers passing along the column. With a loud sigh, Macro slumped down and rubbed his leg. He had been discharged, at his own request, after the first two days on the road. Hospital wagons were as comfortable as it was possible to make them but, even so, the regular bone-rattling movement punctuated by jarring crashes from potholes was more than he could bear. Enforced lack of exercise made the march difficult but the dogged determination that came with the post of centurion carried him along. And now, some ten days later, Macro was almost back to his previous good health. The scar was still a livid red welt straddling his thigh but it had healed well enough and, apart from an aching stiffness and itch, it troubled him no more than all the other scars he carried.

'Water-carriers coming up, sir.'

'Any stragglers, Cato?'

'Two, sir. Both been placed on a charge.'

'Good. All right, boy, take a break with the rest of us.' He patted the grass at his side. 'The legate's setting a killing pace. It's a wonder we haven't had any more drop out. That's only seven since we set off.'

Cato glanced down as Macro rubbed his thigh again. 'How's the leg today, sir?'

'Fine. Just takes a bit of getting used to.'

A pair of slaves came down the line, pouring watered wine from animal skins into the mess tins held out by eagerly waiting legionaries. The water-carriers were part of a contingent of slaves Vespasian had brought along to carry out menial duties that might slow the Legion down on its quick march to the sea. They moved swiftly from man to man, pausing just long enough to half fill each mess tin. Once they had passed, Cato gratefully sipped the sour-tasting mixture of water and cheap wine. His legs ached terribly and the yoke from which his kit and non-fighting equipment hung was intolerably heavy. He had only managed to keep his place in the line of march through the fear of being seen as weak and unable to keep up with the veterans – the men whom he outranked by virtue of patronage, not merit.

Macro regarded the young man for a moment as he sipped another mouthful from his mess tin and swilled it around his tongue to fully appreciate the refreshing flavour. Cato sat leaning forwards, forearms resting on his knees and hands hanging limply as he stared fixedly into the mid-distance with a strained expression. Macro smiled with almost paternal affection for the boy. Despite all his earlier fears, Cato had turned out well. There was no doubting his guts and his coolness of mind under pressure. And, at last, he was beginning to sound like an officer. Words of command were coming easily now, albeit stiffly and without humour. But that would come in time. He was proving to be an excellent subordinate; conscientiously carrying out every order Macro issued and able to use his initiative when faced with unanticipated situations.

Macro had more cause to be grateful. At the end of each day, Cato freely gave up time to continue the reading lessons, as discreetly as circumstances allowed. Macro was pleased to find there was less to this literacy lark than he had feared. Those dreadful, indecipherable marks were slowly yielding up their secrets and Macro was able to follow the more simple texts in a halting way, dragging his finger from word to word along the scrolls as his lips framed sounds, and gradually extended them into words.

'Packs on!' The cry repeated itself down the line to the Sixth century where Macro stood to repeat the order at parade-ground volume. The century wearily picked itself up from the roadside and shouldered their yokes while the few men with enough energy to indulge in some ad-hoc foraging ran back from the surrounding countryside with knapsacks crammed with fruit and any small livestock they had managed to buy, or steal, from the local farmers. The century stood in line, while up ahead the column rippled into motion as the lead elements moved forward. They were off again, trudging down the paved road that led from Divodurum to the west of Gaul.

Cato, unseasoned as he was, suffered terribly in

comparison to the grim-faced veterans. The afternoon's march was agony, particularly since the blisters he had acquired early on the road had burst and he was only just getting over the agonising rawness of the last few days. He had found that the best way of coping was to try and think of other things, examining the gently rolling landscape they were marching through, or turning his gaze inwards to try and occupy his mind. And there lay the problem. As much as he tried to concentrate on matters military there was always Lavinia lurking on the periphery of his consciousness.

That evening, after the century had been fed and the miscreants assigned their extra duties, just as Cato was yawning with arms at full stretch, a slave entered the flickering gloom of the oil lamps lighting the centurion's tent. He glanced about him, message tightly grasped to his chest.

Macro looked up from his desk, where the benefits of acquiring rudimentary writing skills were counterbalanced by the tedious paperwork he could now cope with. He held out a hand. 'Here!'

'I'm sorry, sir,' replied the slave withholding the scroll protectively. 'This is for the optio.'

'Fair enough,' Macro said. He watched curiously as Cato tore off the seal and unrolled the message. The contents were brief and Cato dipped his pen and quickly scribbled a reply, thrusting it back into the hands of the slave before ushering him out of the tent.

'That looked rather dodgy,' said Macro.

'It was nothing, sir.'

'Nothing?'

Nothing to do with you, thought Cato, but he managed to smile before replying, 'Just a personal matter, sir. That's all.'

'A personal matter? I see.' Macro nodded with a maddeningly amused expression on his face. 'Nothing to do with that slave girl, then?'

Cato blushed, grateful for the orange hue cast by the oil lamps, but kept his tongue still.

'Have you finished your work for the night?' Macro asked pointedly.

'No, sir. There are still some ration requisitions to complete.'

'Piso can finish them.'

Piso abruptly looked up from his desk in annoyance.

'Off you go, young Cato. Right now. But don't over-exert yourself.' He winked. 'Remember there's another long day ahead.'

'Yes, sir.' Cato forced a smile and then dashed out of the tent, burning with embarrassment.

'Boys, eh?' Macro laughed. 'Same the world over, since the dawn of time. Takes you back a bit, doesn't it, Piso?'

'If you say so, sir,' grumbled Piso, and then he sighed at the heap of scrolls spread out in front of him and looked at his centurion reproachfully.

Chapter Twenty-one

Vespasian smiled, even as he rubbed the red marks on his wrist where Titus had sunk his teeth in. That little boy could use some firm discipline, he decided. He simply had to stop biting, throwing things at people and running off with articles he was forbidden to touch. Earlier in the evening the little terror had burst into the nightly briefing of the tribunes. Scampering under the table he had raided the confidential papers safe-box and run off with Claudius's scroll. If it hadn't been for Plinius barring the tent flap, Titus would have got clean away. As it was, the tribune grabbed the boy and swung him up into his arms to return him to an embarrassed Flavia, who had appeared from the legate's personal quarters. The boy swung his hand out and caught Plinius on the chin, just as his mother wrestled the scroll from Titus's grip. Laughter rolled around the tent as the exasperated mother momentarily lost the scroll in the folds of her gown before handing it to the injured tribune and leaving with the writhing, giggling Titus pinned to her chest.

'May I have that scroll please?' asked Vespasian as evenly as possible.

After a cursory – but not openly curious – examination

Plinius returned it to his legate.

'Thank you.' Vespasian restored it quickly to the safe-box and returned to the matter at hand. 'As you gentlemen know, there have been rumours that the army gathering at Gesoriacum is on the verge of mutiny. I had a message from General Plautius late this afternoon, brought to me by a household slave. I'm afraid there's some substance to the rumours.'

He looked up and met the surprised, and anxious, expressions of his officers. There was a silent pause, broken only by the sound of Titus playing somewhere nearby. The officers shifted uneasily. Many careers were riding on the success of the invasion. If the campaign failed, all those associated with it would have blotted reputations. Worse still, for those with an appreciation of the wider political implications, the authority of the Emperor himself would be questioned. Claudius had survived one attempted coup already and until he won the acclaim of the mob in Rome and of the armies spread across the Empire, his hold on power would be tenuous. A successful invasion would tie down a large body of troops and distract the legions from their recent distasteful interest in politics.

'Six days ago a cohort from the Ninth Legion refused to embark on to ships bound for a squadron reconnaissance of the British coast. When the centurions tried to force the men aboard there was a brief struggle which left two centurions dead and four wounded.'

'Has word of this got out to the rest of the army?' Vitellius asked.

'Of course,' Vespasian said with a smile. 'What did

you expect? I've seen at first hand how well soldiers keep secrets.'

Some of the tribunes blushed as Vitellius continued. 'Do we know why that cohort mutinied?'

'It seems that someone has been stirring up the superstitious fears of our troops about what they may encounter when they land in Britain. The usual stuff and nonsense about fire-breathing monsters and other demons. I know it's rubbish but, even if we don't believe it, most legionaries do. As things stand, the troops have refused to go on any ships, even for training purposes.'

'What's being done about it, sir?'

'We're to continue marching towards Gesoriacum but have been ordered to stop ten miles short, in a holding area, until the mutiny is quelled – with or without our intervention. The new chief of the imperial staff was at Lugdunum when the news broke. He's making for the army at top speed and we're to supply an escort from Durocortorum. Apparently he has asked for men from our unit since they have not yet been contaminated by the mutiny.'

'Contaminated?' Plinius raised his eyebrows.

'His words, Tribune, not mine.'

'Sir!' Plinius protested. 'I didn't mean to imply—'

'That's all right. Narcissus is not the most tactful of men at times, but there we are.'

'Narcissus?' Vitellius muttered, just loud enough to be heard by the others.

'Narcissus.' Vespasian nodded. 'You don't seem to approve, Vitellius.'

'I'm not sure I approve of any man who wields power

disproportionate to his social standing, if I may be so bold, sir.' Some of the other tribunes – those unaware of their legate's provincial origins – laughed.

'What I meant to say, sir,' Vitellius continued, 'is that I'm not sure why the Emperor would find it necessary to send his freedman . . . his chief secretary, to deal with the situation in person. It's not as if it's something the army can't handle for itself.'

'It's a big operation,' Vespasian replied. 'I would have thought Narcissus would want to make sure it ran as smoothly as possible, for the Emperor's sake.'

'Nevertheless, it is peculiar, sir,' Plinius added quietly.

Vespasian leaned back from the table. 'There is nothing peculiar in this. You know the man's reputation – he's more gauche than sinister. Narcissus will be escorted to the coast and that's the end of it. If he's playing a deeper game then it's one I'm not aware of. Or perhaps some of you gentlemen are privy to information that is being withheld from me. Well?'

No one dared meet his eye, either through guilt or fear of seeming guilty, and Vespasian sighed wearily. 'I'm getting just a little sick of high politics at the moment, gentlemen. Whatever our futures hold, we happen to be soldiers under strict orders which I intend to obey to the best of my ability. All other considerations should be pushed from your minds. Do I make myself clear? Good! Now, I don't need to remind you of the need for strict secrecy in this matter. If word of the mutiny spreads to our men then the entire army is as good as useless. Jupiter knows how it'll end. Any questions?'

The tribunes remained silent.

'Your orders for tomorrow will be passed to you before morning assembly. Dismissed.'

Later, with an empty tent to himself, Vespasian lay back on the couch and closed his eyes. From all around came the sounds of the Legion settling in for the night; the shouts of sentries and duty officers, the hubbub of men relaxing after the day's exertion, even some laughter. That was good. As long as the men were happy he could be sure that they remained loyal to the authority that bound them all together. Mutiny was the one thing that a commander feared above everything else. After all, what was it that compelled thousands of men to bend their efforts to his will, even to the point of death? The moment the common soldiery decided to disobey their officers the army ceased to be.

The news from the coast was bad, and by now would be spreading east down the roads. It was only a matter of time before the Legion ran into the rumours seeping out from Gesoriacum. Then he would have to proceed with the utmost caution; a fine balance would be needed between upholding the harsh discipline of everyday army life and not provoking the men into open revolt. He wondered about the loyalty of the rank and file. They seemed to respect him well enough and had done little to disappoint him on the march so far. The grizzled senior centurion had assured him that there were far fewer stragglers than normal for such a hard march. And yet he couldn't help wondering how fickle those men outside his tent headquarters might prove to be if given the chance. The mutiny had to be quashed so the invasion could proceed. Narcissus had better be as good an operator as his reputation suggested. Certainly Flavia believed he would be up to the job, when the matter had been quietly discussed over dinner.

Then there was the other issue. The second part of the message brought to him that afternoon had confirmed the presence of a conspirator in his Legion. But he was to be reassured by the fact that the imperial agent would be able to deal with the traitor. The imperial agent's identity would remain a secret to all but the Emperor's inner circle. This, the message assured him, was to ensure that Vespasian could concentrate on the business of running his Legion.

'As if . . .' Vespasian grumbled. He found that he now thought hard about every word spoken in front of his senior officers for fear of alerting the conspirator, or of voicing thoughts that the imperial agent might possibly construe as disloyal. Although he had his doubts about Vitellius, there was as yet no proof, or any overt indication, that the tribune was plotting against the Emperor. For all Vespasian knew it might just as easily be that bookworm Plinius. The distracted academic behaviour might well be a clever front for his real activities. Try as he might, Vespasian could not picture Plinius as a spy. Yet, in the absence of proof, he had to suspect everyone – not just his senior officers.

The presence of the imperial agent was far from reassuring. Vespasian was certain that the man's job was to keep as close an eye on the Legion's commander as it was to track down any unknown traitors. And he wondered who that agent might be; in the current political turmoil it might be any officer under his command. For that matter, it might well be that youngster who had joined the Legion straight from the imperial palace. He made a mental note to have the lad closely watched and then swore out loud.

Of course he wouldn't do that. Otherwise where would it all end? A legion riven by men spying on men spying on men. A mental image of the Legion marching into battle with every soldier casting suspicious sidelong glances at his neighbour sprang up into his head and he laughed.

Well then, let someone else worry about the espionage. He would try and concentrate on making his Legion fight well in the coming campaign. That was bound to enhance his reputation far more than plotting in dark corners. He smiled at his own naivety and went to bed.

Chapter Twenty-two

Although winter was gone, the spring night was cold and Cato's exhaled breathing plumed into the air as he clasped his cloak about him. The note he had received from Lavinia, or at least on her behalf, had arranged for them to meet at the rear of the headquarters' tentage shortly after the trumpeter sounded the change of watch. A roped-off area surrounded the staff baggage vehicles and two sentries marched slowly around the perimeter. Cato waited until they had passed each other, then he padded softly between them over the beaten-down grass and slipped under the rope, before weaving in among the dark forms of the wagons looming up all around. Some of the tents glowed from the light of lamps still burning within and Cato quietly picked his way through the baggage train until he emerged to find a long wall of leather sidings stretching out before him. It was here that Lavinia had arranged to meet him. And yet, there was no sign of her. He stood quite still and waited, annoyed that his heart pounded so quickly as he strove to listen for any movement. But there was none from the immediate area. Perhaps she had lost her nerve? Or been kept busy with some household task?

His shoulder was suddenly grasped from behind. Cato jumped round and a sharp cry of surprise escaped his lips before he could stop himself.

'Shhh!' Lavinia whispered. 'Quick, under here!'

She tugged his arm, pulling him beneath the wheels of a large wagon. He followed automatically and rolled into her side.

'What—' he whispered, but she pressed a hand to his lips and told him to keep quiet and still. He marvelled at the softness of her skin as it brushed his lips and caught a momentary scent of something fragrant.

'Who goes there?' a voice called out from nearby. 'Come on out, sunshine!'

Cato froze and held his breath, scared – and at the same time excited by the physical closeness of Lavinia. A warm glow flowed into his loins.

'What's up?' another voice called out from slightly further off.

'Think we've got a thief. Heard someone over here.'

A pair of legs and a spear butt appeared in front of the wagon and paused. A moment later the other sentry arrived on the scene.

'Found anything?'

'Not yet.'

Cato fumbled for Lavinia's hand and held it tight as he carefully pulled her body into his with his spare arm. She stiffened in protest for an instant and then allowed herself to be embraced.

'Seems quiet enough.'

'I'm telling you I heard something.'

'Could have been from inside the tent.'

'I don't think so.'

Cato's lips moved across her hair and down her cheek until they met hers. With a delirious sense of pleasure – even in this dangerous situation – Cato kissed her gently, relishing the warmth of her breath and the pounding of his chest against her breasts. Lavinia returned the kiss softly for a moment and then darted her tongue into his mouth. Cato felt a ripple of ecstasy sweep through his body.

'Look, there's no-one here now,' the second sentry said impatiently.

'Maybe.'

'Well, there's no point in stumbling around in the pitch dark looking for someone who's scarpered. We'll just do ourselves an injury. Let's forget it.'

The second sentry marched off. After a short pause, the first reluctantly turned away from the wagon and stamped sourly back towards the perimeter rope, muttering dark curses at his companion.

Under the axle, Cato was wallowing in the throes of a passion he had never experienced before. His right hand slowly slid over the silken curve of Lavinia's hips towards the inside of her thighs. She clamped them together and twisted away from him.

'No!' she hissed.

'Why?'

'Not here!'

'What's wrong with here?' asked Cato desperately.

'It's too cold and uncomfortable. Mistress has found a place where we won't be bothered.' She squeezed his hand tightly. 'Somewhere more cosy where we can get to know each other properly. Come on.'

'Flavia?' Cato wondered aloud. 'Flavia arranged this? Why?'

'Shhh!'

Lavinia tugged his hand and led him out from under the wagon. They paused at the edge of the line of vehicles to make sure all was still, before quietly crossing to the back of a tent. She had unlaced a join to provide a small opening in the heavy leather. The gloom inside was almost impenetrable, but Lavinia seemed to know her way well enough, and led him on by the hand. Underfoot, the grass gave way to a sectioned wooden floor which Cato managed to trip over, almost flattening Lavinia in the process.

'Sorry,' he whispered. 'Where are we going?'

'The quietest place we could find.'

'We?'

'The mistress and me. This way – come on.'

They passed down a long corridor with rolled-down flaps, leading to private sleeping chambers, and came to a large space dominated by the dark forms of a campaign table and various seats and couches. No more detail than that was available in the darkness. Cato found himself being pushed down on to a soft couch and, with a small chuckle, Lavinia collapsed on top of him. Immediately his lips sought hers again and he kissed with a burning passion that flowed to every extremity of his body. As Cato held her close he untied a silk ribbon and ran his hand through the long flowing hair. Suddenly Lavinia pushed herself upright so that she was sitting on his stomach.

'What?'

'Shhh! Lie still.' She placed a finger against his lips and, with her other hand, reached behind her and felt for his crotch.

She giggled as she discovered his excitement. 'Do you want to do it?'

Cato choked out a yes.

'All right then. I hadn't planned to let you. First I need to get something.'

'What do you mean?'

'Something to prevent babies.'

'Do we have to stop now?' Cato asked desperately, stroking and squeezing her thighs with his hands. 'Please.'

'Typical man!' She slapped his hands gently to show she was only joking. 'You don't have to live with the consequences, we do. And I don't want to get pregnant.'

'I don't have to, you know, come inside you,' Cato said shyly.

'Oh sure! That's what you all say. *I can control myself – really I can* but when it comes down to it – wallop! Then what's a poor girl to do?'

'Don't be long,' Cato said, somewhat startled by her forwardness.

'Relax. I'll be right back.'

Lavinia climbed off his chest, gave him a final soft kiss and padded away into the darkness, leaving Cato alone in a thrill of expectation. He lay still, eyes closed, heart pounding, letting his mind dwell on that last kiss and the shocking excitement of the touch of her hand on his crotch. He wanted to treasure this moment for ever and opened his eyes to take in as much of the detail of the chamber as possible. Now that they were fully accustomed to the dark, his eyes could discern more of the surroundings and they passed curiously over the trappings of command.

Lavinia had been gone a little while now and a tinge of doubt slowly swelled in his mind. He wondered if he should go and look for her.

Surely she shouldn't take as long as this? Unless she planned to use the most extreme form of birth-control and not turn up at all. That wasn't funny, he decided. Suddenly some sixth sense made him aware that someone else was in the chamber. He was about to whisper Lavinia's name when he realised that the sound of a tent flap being pushed aside was coming from an altogether different direction to the one Lavinia had taken.

He froze, hardly daring to breathe, and strained his ears and eyes towards the far side of the chamber where a dark form eased itself in through a gap in the sidings. Once the shape was inside the room it paused a moment, crouching down, poised for action. Cato was suddenly afraid for Lavinia and for what the intruder might do to her when she returned. But the night was quite still.

Then the figure moved stealthily towards the table, strewn with the evening's paperwork. Round the table he came and now Cato could see that the man wore a hooded cape over his short and stocky frame. He moved with the balanced agility of a cat. In his hand was the unmistakable shape of a legionary's short sword. Cato only had a dagger, sheathed in a scabbard under his left thigh. The intruder, no more than ten feet away, turned his back and groped blindly beneath the table. He grasped something and pulled. Slowly an awkward dead weight was dragged clear – the man pausing every time it grated on the wooden floor panels – Cato saw that it was a chest. He lay rigid with fear, hardly daring to draw breath as his blood pounded in his ears. Leaning over the box, the intruder worked on the iron lock with faint clicks until the mechanism clunked open. The man rummaged inside – he was clearly after something specific.

Cato suddenly realised that the man would turn round in a moment. He could hardly fail to see his body stretched out flat on the couch. Cato slid his left hand under his thigh and pulled at the dagger handle. It was wedged under him firmly enough to require a sharp tug, and he shifted his buttock to make the task easier. Too much. The blade rasped from its scabbard into his hand. The intruder spun round and raised his sword in one motion, momentarily forgetting his basic training – that a few inches of point is worth any length of edge. The sword slashed down and struck the edge of the couch above Cato's head with a loud splintering crack.

Cato thrust his dagger at the shape looming over him and the weapon penetrated cloth and something a little more yielding beneath.

'Fuck!' The man grunted, leaping backwards. He crashed against the table. Cato ran blindly to the left, towards the flap through which Lavinia had deserted him, and smashed his shin against a low stool. He thrust his arms out as he flew headlong over the stool on to the floor. The intruder came after him in a low crouch, taking care not to repeat his previous mistake. Cato felt an agonising shooting pain along the front of his leg and paused an instant too long before trying to rise. His attacker, recovered from his surprise now, rushed at him, sword point aimed at his throat.

'Help!' Cato cried out and instinctively rolled under the table. 'Help!'

'Quiet, you little fucker!' The man hissed and for a moment Cato was taken back enough to still his tongue – but only for a moment. The sword swiped at him and he rolled against the couch and shouted again.

'Help! In here!'

Groggy voices of men disturbed from sleep sounded in the chambers down the adjoining corridor. With relief Cato heard someone call out the guard. The intruder heard as well and paused, twisting about as he looked for an escape route. A glow suddenly appeared at the front of the tent as a sentry shouted, 'Here! This way!'

The intruder ran fast to the side of the tent flap and raised his sword as Cato leapt to his feet by the table. A spear tip swept the tent flap to one side and suddenly the chamber was flooded with the flickering glow of a torch as a sentry stepped inside. Out of the shadows to his left the intruder swung his sword.

'Look out!' Cato shouted.

The sentry turned to the source of the shout and, an instant later, was struck a savage blow to the back of his head. With a grunt he slumped to his knees and pitched forward as Cato looked on in horror. Sparks flew as the torch thudded down on to the wooden flooring and rolled up against a loosely arranged pile of maps. When Cato looked up the light was fading and he saw the back of the intruder as he dashed from the room. Without any hesitation he followed, sprinting out of the legate's tent into an antechamber lined with collapsible tables for the scribes. Ahead, to the right, the intruder slashed at the tent siding and hurled himself through. From the left came the flares of approaching torches and the shouts and thudding footsteps of those carrying them. Cato stopped at once, panting in a blind terror.

He ran back to the legate's tent and saw that the maps were now alight, orange and yellow flames eagerly lapping across their surfaces. From the other side of the canvas he heard the voices of those roused by the commotion. There was no escape there. He fell to the floor at the opposite end and heaved at the heavy leather siding. A peg suddenly gave and he rolled underneath. He found himself in a kitchen area with trampled grass beneath him – no luxury wooden floors for the slaves then. Terrified by the proximity of the cries behind him, Cato rushed across the kitchen to the far wall and rolled out under the side of the tent.

He was outside, on his back looking up at the stars peacefully twinkling from the serene inky depths of the night sky. Then he was on his feet, running for the gap behind the tribunes' tents and the artillery train, weaving in between them until the headquarters tent was no longer visible. Leaning against the side of a ballista carriage, he paused to catch his breath. His heart pounded as his breathing came in sharp, shaking gasps. Over in the direction of headquarters a tinge of orange was visible and then a stab of flame as voices shouted for water and more guards.

It would be bad to be discovered anywhere near

headquarters, Cato realised. He turned away, hurrying through the artillery train until he emerged on the far side of the camp, into the space in front of the turf wall and palisade. Drawing his cloak around his shoulders, he turned left and headed for his century's line of tents, at what he hoped was a steady pace. If anyone stopped him now he knew he could not trust himself to give a plausible reason for his presence.

The sentries on the wall were turning to look back into the camp but the distance between them, and the darkness, protected Cato and he walked steadily on. After a nerve-shredding age, he reached the cohort standard and then hurried to the tents of the Sixth century. Off in the night, a trumpet sounded the call-out of the watch cohort. Without a glance back over his shoulder, he entered the eight-man tent of his section and lay straight down on his blanket roll, without removing his cloak or boots.

'That you, Cato?' Pyrax asked sleepily from the darkness.

Cato lay still and silent.

'Cato?'

It was no good ignoring Pyrax. Better say something. 'Yes?'

'What's going on out there?'

'How should I know?'

'You've just come in.'

'Just been to the latrines, that's all. Seems like there's some kind of fire up at headquarters.'

'Careless twats,' Pyrax yawned. 'Wake me if it spreads to our tent line. Night.'

'Night then,' Cato muttered sleepily. But there was

no sleep possible as he lay quietly staring up at the roof of the tent in absolute terror.

Chapter Twenty-three

With hands on hips and head thrown back, Vespasian looked up into the starry night, through a large scorched hole in the roof of his tent. Lowering his eyes he stared at the silent ring of men standing around the table. The sentries looked down in shame.

'So how do you suppose our thief managed to gain entry to this tent? If you were as conscientious in your duties as you claim.'

'Sir, we were keeping a good watch, as always,' the centurion explained. 'Four men at the entrance, another four patrolling the outside of the tentage. I've checked round and we've found two places where the tent sidings have been slashed open. I suspect our man used those to get in and out, sir.'

'You suspect that, do you?' Vespasian said bitterly. 'That's brilliant Centurion, quite brilliant. And while our man was busy cutting his way in, where were the rest of you?'

'Please, sir, we were being spoken to by the tribune.'

'Which tribune?'

'Gaius Plinius, sir. Duty tribune for the night. Came up and demanded a full inspection.'

'And why did he do that, do you suppose?'

'Begging your pardon, sir, but we were talking about the invasion.'

'Oh, were you? What were you saying?'

'Well, sir—' the centurion was embarrassed. 'Some of the lads have heard that there's monsters living on the islands.'

'And where might they have heard such nonsense?' Vespasian asked, trying not to reveal his anxiety.

The centurion shrugged. 'Just the grapevine, sir.'

Vespasian drew a breath. 'So then, Plinius was disciplining you for talking like a bunch of old women, and that's when you think the intruder made his way into my tent?'

'Yes, sir.'

'Right, well, you and the watch will be up on charges. And you're demoted to a line century. Now get out of here.'

As he watched them shuffle out Vespasian knew that the latter punishment was the more telling since the headquarters guard was rightly seen as a cushy number under normal circumstances; better food, lighter duties and a relatively safe position in the line of battle. And now one of them was lying in the hospital tent critically injured. The man had been unconscious and bleeding heavily from a slash wound to the back and side of the head. He was alive, just, but the surgeon had not been convinced that he would survive the night. It was too bad, since the man might have seen his attacker and be able to provide an identification. And that was what

Vespasian desperately needed at the moment.

Upon entering the room, half dressed like the others who had been woken by the crashes and thumps coming from the command tent, the first thing he had checked was his document safe-box. One glance was all he needed – the small scroll bearing the confidential seal of Claudius had gone. Everything else remained; that meant the thief knew precisely what he was after, and now he had it. Someone in the camp had possession of a priceless piece of political intelligence that might be used to help topple the Emperor. Not that Vespasian needed the document – he had long since memorised the contents and made his plans. But now someone else had access to the information it contained.

And what would happen to him once word got back to Rome, to Claudius, that he had allowed someone to steal the scroll? No excuse would be accepted, the responsibility was his, and that was why he had punished the sentries harshly; they had to share in the suffering they had caused him.

At least the thief had to be near. Someone in the Legion, more than likely the traitor Plautius's letter referred to. There might yet be time to recover the letter before the Legion reached the coast and merged into the mass of units gathering for the invasion. Some blood had been discovered near the couch, with more splatters around the table, leading from the tent to the churned-up soil where the trail was lost. The man had been wounded, then. Which struck Vespasian as most odd. Since the sentry had been struck from behind in the doorway to the tent it seemed likely he had been surprised. In which case the intruder must have been injured by someone else.

What had happened to Lavinia? Inwardly Cato squirmed with fear and worry. She had never come back, but surely she wouldn't have encountered the intruder while he lay waiting in the tent? He prayed that she was alive and unhurt. He couldn't risk going near headquarters to try and see her for a while. That guard had got a clear look at him and would surely be able to pick him out without any problem. He would have to get word of Lavinia from Flavia; a message must be got through to her as soon as possible. But he did not know how much the legate's wife would know about the situation and how far she could be trusted. If Vespasian discovered that he had been in the tent, then all the evidence would point to him being directly involved in the theft of whatever it was the intruder had taken from the chest. He was in deep trouble and needed an ally. If he could see Flavia – tell her everything he had seen – then maybe she could protect him. She had befriended him and now he needed her. In the morning he would try and see her.

Next morning Cato was rudely woken from a troubled sleep by a rough shaking of his shoulders. He looked up blearily into Pyrax's face. 'W-what?'

'Centurion wants you right away.'

Cato propped himself up on his elbows and, looking out of the tent-flap, saw that the sun had risen for some time. He shook his head and scrambled up.

'How long since morning call?'

'A while.' Pyrax shrugged. 'You missed breakfast and

we're about to strike the tents.'

'Why didn't someone wake me?'

'You're a grown-up now, lad, it's up to you to look after yourself.'

'Where's the centurion?'

'In his tent. I'd get over there smartish if I were you. Macro doesn't look too chuffed with his lot—' Pyrax glanced down at Cato. 'What happened to your hand?'

Following his gaze, Cato saw that the thumb and forefinger of his hand were smeared with dried blood.

'Oh that! I, er, managed to get a cut of meat from a beast some of the muleteers slaughtered last night. Roasted it on their fire.'

'Nice of them,' Pyrax said grudgingly. 'But you might have cleaned yourself up afterwards.'

'Sorry,' Cato mumbled. 'I have to go.'

He punched through the half-open flaps and washed his hand with some water from a skin hanging on the tent frame. The blood from the intruder had caked on and had to be scratched off with his nails and wiped clear. With a shock he realised that his dagger must be bloody as well and drew it to find the blade heavily soiled by dried blood. That took somewhat longer to clean and by the time Cato pushed his way into Macro's tent the centurion was steaming. Piso stood at the back of the tent, eyebrows raised in warning.

'What took you so bloody long? I sent for you ages ago.'

'I'm sorry, sir.'

'Well?'

'Sir?'

'Why were you late? Explain yourself.'

'I was in the latrines, sir, something I ate last night.'

'Well, take more care over what you eat in future,' Macro said impatiently. 'Now then, we've got work to do. The legate's detached our century from the Legion to perform escort duties. I was given the orders at the morning briefing. We're to advance ahead of the Legion to Durocortorum and meet up with some staff bigwig. Then we're to escort him to General Plautius's headquarters at Gesoriacum. That's all, and since we have to get moving ahead of the column we're going to have to rush. I've already given the orders for the wagon to be loaded and hitched up. I want you to requisition some wine and treats for our guest. The quartermaster's been notified. Piso, you go and get the men moving; I want tents struck and loaded and packs ready before the next watch call. Now get out of here, both of you.'

Outside Cato looked at Piso enquiringly.

'Bad morning,' Piso whispered. 'Some dodgy business up at headquarters last night.'

'Dodgy business?'

'Some thief tried to rob the legate. Managed to knife a guard and get away. Now Vespasian's blowing his stack at the officers for not having their men keep a good enough watch.'

'Oh. Did anyone say what was stolen?'

'Nothing of value, apparently. But the poor sod who discovered the thief won't live long.'

'That's too bad.' Cato tried to sound concerned while his heart lifted slightly at the news, and then, as his cursed imagination summoned up an image of the blameless

257

sentry lying bandaged and scarcely alive, he felt ashamed and guilty.

'Don't take it too badly, son.' Piso laid a hand on his shoulder. 'It happens. Just your good fortune it wasn't you.'

The tribune rested his chin on the palms of his hand and stared across to where Pulcher sat on a folding stool nursing his leg. The upper thigh had been punctured to a finger's depth and had bled profusely until he had got far enough away from the tent to apply pressure on the wound. Pulcher had limped back to the tribune's quarters, where he now sat applying a fresh bandage to the area. Luckily, the wound was high enough that the bandage would be concealed under his breeches and no-one need know that he had been injured. But the day's march would be agony, the tribune reflected with a smile. That would encourage the man not to cock it up next time – if there was a next time. Vespasian had issued orders to double the guard from now on and access to the command tent would be almost impossible. The man opposite did not yet know that another attempt would be required.

'I expect you'll be looking forward to returning to Rome,' the tribune asked as he poured the man a cup of wine.

'Too right!' Pulcher grunted. 'I've had enough of this undercover nonsense. I want to get back to soldiering.'

'I hardly think the Praetorian Guard counts as soldiering,' said the tribune mildly.

'It's the kind of soldiering I like.'

'But you did volunteer for this.'

'True. But for the sum of money we arranged anyone would volunteer.'

'But not everyone has your unique talent for ensuring things happen, encouraging loquacity in the tongue-tied, making people disappear – that sort of thing. Speaking of which, are you sure you can't put a face to the man you saw in the tent, the one who managed to pigstick you so efficiently?'

'No.' The reply was laced with anger. 'But when I do find out who it was, they'll suffer before I let them die. That's something I'll take care of for no extra fee.'

'Well, be sure that you do find him. If he knows who you are, he might manage to make you implicate me.'

'There's no chance of that.'

'Don't ever underestimate the power of effectively applied torture to loosen tongues,' the tribune warned him. The other merely sniffed with derision before the tribune continued, 'Now, I'm afraid I've got some bad news for you.'

'Eh?'

'You've not done your job.'

'What do you mean?' Pulcher jabbed a finger at the scroll. 'That's what you wanted, and that's what you've fucking got.'

'Oh no,' replied the tribune. 'You don't really think I took the trouble of bringing you all the way up from Rome to get a piece of stationery.'

He flattened the scroll out for the other man to read. But there was nothing to read, it was completely blank.

'It seems someone is a step ahead of us. Looks like

Vespasian was smart enough to use his safe-box as a decoy. Or, someone else here has beaten us to the scroll and left this in its place.'

Chapter Twenty-four

The departure of the Sixth century well ahead of the main column caused some little excitement to those who witnessed it, not least the men of the century itself. In the normal course of events no common solider would dare march out of the camp before the senior officers and the colour party. Therefore it was clear to all that the Sixth century was being detached on a special duty. What that duty was remained known only to the centurion, his optio and secretary; the common soldiery could only wonder as the century's baggage wagon creaked out of the main gate and followed the line of men stepping out down the road towards Durocortorum. The curiosity of the onlookers soon disappeared as their officers drove them back to work, preparing to strike the tents for the day's march.

The Sixth century's excitement was palpable and the men noisily speculated about the task before them. At the head of the column Macro could hardly fail to overhear the conversation conducted behind him at a level calculated to attract his attention. He allowed himself a small smile at their all-too-obvious angling for information. Let them have their fun, they would know soon enough. In the meantime there was little to be gained from ordering them to quit babbling like small children and march in silence. While they were happy he was prepared to indulge them. The centurion was glad to be detached from the Legion; no more looking at the same backs he had followed for the best part of two hundred miles. No more frustrating delays for distant bottlenecks, and waiting patiently to be led to and from tent-area allotments by members of the colour party puffed up by their sense of self-importance.

Ahead was an empty road, stretching out in a more or less straight line towards the horizon. Above him the sky was clear and deep blue, while the air was filled with birdsong. In short, it was the kind of morning that filled Macro with an inner glow of delight at simply being alive.

Which made it all the more strange that the optio marching to one side and slightly behind him cast his eyes down to the road surface with a grim expression of concentration, quite oblivious to the general sense of well-being in the world.

Macro dropped back a step and clapped him on the shoulder.

'What on earth is the matter with you this morning, Cato?'

The boy was quite startled by this abrupt intrusion into his thoughts. 'Sir?'

'I asked you what the matter was.'

'Matter sir? Nothing's the matter.'

'Exactly!' Macro beamed. 'So, smile and enjoy life. It's not often you'll get an independent duty. Even if,' he lowered his voice, 'even if all we're told to do is nursemaid some staff officer to army headquarters.'

'If you say so, sir.'

'I do say so, lad. And believe me, I know what I'm talking about. Now be a good sort and try to enjoy things a bit more. You take life too seriously, young Cato.'

The optio fixed him with a bitter glare. 'That's because I find life rather too serious at the moment, sir.'

'Still mooning about over that slip of a girl?' Macro laughed, before giving him a sharp nudge in the side. 'So how did last night go then?'

Cato was startled into breaking his stride for a moment, until a low curse from the front rank of the column made him skip forward again to his position at the centurion's side.

'Well?' Macro winked. 'Did you score?'

'No, sir.'

'Why on earth not? Don't tell me you came over all poetic and romantic. You didn't, did you? Please tell me you didn't.'

'No, sir.' Cato looked down, not trusting himself to mislead Macro effectively. 'We were interrupted before we could . . . get down to anything.'

'Oh that's too bad.' Macro nodded sympathetically. 'So what happened?'

'We had arranged to meet in the wagons behind the legate's tents. We were getting on rather well when all this shouting and commotion broke out. We would have ignored it and carried on with things but Lavinia heard her mistress calling for her.'

'Should have gone for a quickie,' Macro suggested.

'Not even enough time for that, sir,' Cato said

regretfully. 'She had to rush off, without even arranging our next meeting. And now I'm sent off on escort duty and she's stuck back there.'

'Never mind, lad, I'm sure she'll keep it warm for you.'

'Yes, sir.'

'So you were there when that thief was discovered? Did you see anything?'

'Nothing, sir. Nothing at all. Just got out of there and went straight back to my bed.'

'Looks like you missed all the fun.'

'Yes, sir,' Cato replied, quietly enough that Macro mistook it for the boy's continued pining for his first love. A degree of sensitivity was called for to distract young Cato from his woes. Macro grasped at the first idea that crept into his head.

'Let's see how my words are coming on. You say a word and I'll spell it. All right?'

'Whatever you want, sir.'

As Macro stumbled through such tests of his new-found skill as 'rampart', 'sentry' and 'javelin', Cato was consumed by anxiety. If that sentry recovered from his head injury it would only be a matter of time before the investigation closed in around him. And then what? Torture, a confession extracted, and certain humiliating death. But if Lavinia was safe then she would be sure to back up his version of events. Unless – a rather nasty thought struck him – unless she feared that she might implicate herself. And what of Flavia? After all, she had arranged the meeting. She might deny Lavinia's statement for precisely the same reasons. While the century was detached from the Legion he would not know how the situation developed.

'Cato?' The centurion had quickly grown tired of spelling tests.

'Sir?'

'This man we're going to meet.'

'Narcissus?'

'Keep it down,' Macro hissed. 'That lot back there aren't supposed to know.'

'Sorry, sir. What about him?'

'Did you ever run into him at the palace?'

'Yes, sir. He was a close friend of my father, or at least he was until he struck it rich.'

'What's he like?' Macro asked, then noticed the curious expression on his optio's face. 'I just need to know before we meet so we don't start off on the wrong foot, that's all. If we're to guard him for the next few days then I don't want to risk pissing him off, given that he's one of the Emperor's inner circle. Not that I'm afraid of him or anything, after all the man's only a bloody freedman. Just want to make sure he's happy while in our care. Won't harm our futures any if he gets to like us. So then, tell me about him.'

'Well sir—' Cato paused for thought. This wasn't going to be easy. What he knew of Narcissus was far from flattering, and he had been wise enough to keep what he knew to himself. The cold shoulder Narcissus had turned to Cato's father in the latter years of their friendship had left Cato in no doubt that he could expect few favours from the leading figure of Claudius's inner council. After Narcissus, only Messalina – the Emperor's carelessly ambitious wife – wielded more power under the Emperor.

'Well?'

'He's a good man – I mean a brilliant man – sir. Might seem a bit cold and distant at first, but that's probably because he has a lot on his shoulders. They used to say in the palace that he had more brains and worked harder than any other man in the Empire. We all respected him,' concluded Cato tactfully.

'Well, that's all very nice, but what I want to know is what he's like as a man. What should I do to get on with him?'

'Get on with him?' Cato raised his eyebrows.

'Yes. I mean, is he a man's man? That kind of thing. Does he like a good joke? There's plenty I could tell him.'

'No, sir. Please don't try to be funny,' Cato begged, visions swimming before his eyes of a cosmopolitan sophisticate being regaled with the boorish humour of the ranks. 'Just be yourself, sir. Be professional and keep out of his way as much as possible. And be careful what you say.'

Chapter Twenty-five

Just after dawn, Flavia was sitting at her portable writing desk going through some papers. From the next tent she could hear Titus squealing with laughter as his nurse struggled to feed him his morning meal. Flavia intended to catch up on some correspondence she had been meaning to write since the Legion had set out from the Rhine. She had already despatched a letter to a distant relative commanding a cavalry unit that was joining the invasion force, hoping to meet up with him when the Second Legion arrived in Gesoriacum. Then there were people in Rome she needed to inform of her return. And there were instructions to be issued to the majordomo of the house on the Quirinal, as well as to the steward of Vespasian's villa in Campania. Both establishments needed plenty of warning to ensure that they would be ready to receive Flavia and her retinue.

But the writing of those letters must wait until the present task was meticulously completed. She dipped the tip of her stylus in the inkwell and continued writing with deliberation, pausing occasionally to copy some detail or other from the map on a scroll lying open before her. A salute was shouted outside her tent and Flavia quickly pushed her paperwork into a roughly ordered pile as Vespasian entered. Flavia smiled and laid her stylus down as she rose to give him a kiss.

'I'm afraid you'll have to begin packing in a moment,' apologised Vespasian. 'Even the legate's wife is not permitted to delay the Legion.'

'Surely, after last night's rumpus, you'll allow us time to recover?'

'Recover from what? Lost sleep is a fact of life in the army.'

'I'm not in the army,' she protested.

'No, but you're married to it.'

'Brute!' Flavia scowled. 'I knew I should have married some fat old senator with a consuming interest in viniculture. Instead of roughing it out here in the barbaric wilderness with a man who thinks being a soldier matters.'

'I never forced you to,' Vespasian said quietly.

Flavia took his face between her hands and looked deep into his eyes. 'Just joking, you idiot. You know why I married you. For love – as unfashionable as that may be.'

'But you could have married better.'

'No, I couldn't.' Flavia kissed him. 'One day, you'll be powerful beyond your wildest dreams. I guarantee it.'

'That's reckless talk, Flavia. Please don't. It's too dangerous to even think such things these days.'

Flavia looked deeply into his eyes for a moment and then smiled. 'You're right, of course. I'll be careful what I say. But mark me, history won't remember you merely for commanding a legion. I'll see to that if no-one else will. You really should be more ambitious, or do you still cling to that deep-seated Republican modesty of yours?'

'Maybe.' Vespasian shrugged. 'But right now I think I'll be lucky if I retain command of the Second until the end of the month.'

'Why dear? What's the matter?'

'That incident last night—'

'The fire?'

'The person who caused the fire. The thief. He stole something quite precious – something that Narcissus had trusted me to keep secret. Once Narcissus finds out that it's been stolen I don't think he'll be in much of a mood for any excuses.'

'It's not your fault it was stolen,' Flavia protested. 'Whatever "it" was. He can't replace you just for that.'

'He can. He will. He has to.'

'Why? Whatever can be that important?'

Vespasian allowed himself a small smile. 'That I can't tell you. The orders were quite explicit on that point at least.'

'Were they?' asked Flavia, her face momentarily flushed with anxiety. 'When we join the rest of the army, let me have a word with Narcissus. He was a good friend of mine back at the palace.'

'I'd rather you said nothing to him. Let me continue the investigation here in the Legion. We'll find the thief sooner or later.'

'How is the sentry?'

'Not good. The surgeon says he's lost a lot of blood. He's in no shape to travel and today's journey might just finish him off.'

'Well, why can't we leave him at Durocortorum until he's well enough to follow the Legion – if he lives?'

'We could, with a few men to carry a litter once he's up to it. I had thought of that. But he won't be under the care of the surgeon.'

'Good thing too – if half of what I've heard is true. Look here, why don't I leave Parthenas to care for him? He's a trained physician. I've seen him at work on the other slaves and he seems competent enough.'

'All right,' Vespasian nodded. 'The man would have a far better chance of survival lying still in a bed rather than bouncing along the road in a hospital wagon. Now, if it's not too much trouble, I'd be greatly obliged if you would arrange for your personal effects to be packed immediately.'

'Very well.'

'Oh! One other thing.'

'Yes?'

Vespasian reached inside his tunic and drew out a small silk ribbon. 'I wonder if you've ever seen this before?'

'Let me have a look.' Flavia examined the ribbon a moment before replying. 'This is Lavinia's. Where did you find it?'

'In my command tent, on my couch. Yet there's no reason for her to have been in there and I don't recall seeing it when I left the tent last night. Odd, don't you think?'

'What's odd?'

'Lavinia has no cause to be in my tent. Do you know anything about this?'

'Why should I? It's your tent.'

'She's your maid.' Vespasian looked up, a strange expression on his face – one that alarmed his wife.

'Whatever's the matter?'

'Probably nothing. But I think I might have a word with that girl. There's something funny going on.'

Chapter Twenty-six

'And, if I'm not mistaken, lurking under that monstrously oversized helmet is young Cato.' Narcissus smiled and held out his hands. With an instinctive reluctance Cato responded and Narcissus held the young man's hands in a tight grasp while he stared searchingly into Cato's eyes. 'It's good to see you. But what you are doing dressed up as a solider is quite beyond me.'

'It's because I am a soldier – sir,' Cato said formally. 'As you may recall, I was given my freedom on condition I agreed to enlist.'

'I seem to vaguely recall some such detail,' Narcissus replied airily, as if trying to remember a snack he had once eaten. 'So how are you finding the army? I'd wager a boy of your age would be relishing the outdoor life.'

'Can't complain, sir,' Cato said, bitterly swallowing the indignity of being referred to as a boy in front of his centurion. 'Of course, it is more physically demanding than living in the palace.'

Narcissus produced a thin smile. 'You're right about that, I'm afraid – haven't exercised in years. Policy-making is more my metier these days. But no matter.

272

I'm glad to see you again, my boy. I trust that he is giving satisfaction, Centurion?'

'Yes, sir. The lad's got the makings of a fine optio. You must be quite proud that the palace can turn out lads as good at soldiering as young Cato.'

'Refresh my memory, if you'd be so kind. What exactly is an optio?'

'Why, he's my second-in-command, sir,' Macro replied, shocked by the civilian's ignorance. 'And good at the job too.'

'It's most gratifying that even the army can appreciate the worth of a good education.'

Macro produced the required flush of anger.

'Just my little joke, Centurion. No harm intended.'

Narcissus took him by the arm and led him into the lodge of the imperial staging post. The imperial secretary was well into his middle years and his eyes peered out of crow's-feet lines formed by a lifetime's worth of smiling. There was no stoop in the way he carried himself and the mobility of his expression clearly matched the speed of his thinking. And yet that dry, caustic wit indicated a mind practised in the art of putting others down. Macro pressed his lips together; as long as the man was under his protection he would have to endure the inevitable slights and barbs. Narcissus, he concluded, was typical of his kind. He treated social superiors as intellectual inferiors and – as his treatment of Cato had shown – he was inclined to treat his intellectual equals as social inferiors. One just could not win with that kind of man. Best try and ignore it.

'What are your orders, Centurion?' Narcissus asked

him when they were alone inside the lodge. 'Your precise orders?'

'To escort you as far as the main body of the army and then wait for the rest of the Legion in a holding area yet to be specified. That was it, sir. Other than to render you assistance should you require it.'

'In other words, you're to obey my orders.'

'Yes, sir,' Macro conceded reluctantly. 'That's about the size of it.'

'Good.' Narcissus nodded. 'Glad to see that Vespasian managed to get that right at least.'

Macro stiffened at this unwarranted slur on his commander's aptitude. Coming from a Roman citizen that would be bad enough – but to hear a freedman speak in this manner was a clear breach of the most basic social etiquette.

'Centurion, we must get on the road immediately,' Narcissus ordered, poking Macro's chest to emphasise the point. 'I have to reach Gesoriacum as soon as possible. Much depends on it. In fact, I can tell you that the entire campaign depends on it, and more. Do we understand one another?'

'I'm not sure what you want me to understand, sir,' Macro replied frankly. 'Why the hurry?'

'That information is given on a strictly need-to-know basis.'

'But a whole century to guard one man?'

'Suffice to say that some political miscreants would prefer me not to make it to Gesoriacum – and that's all you need to know.'

'Yes, sir.'

'Right then,' Narcissus resumed brightly. 'Let's be off. I'm travelling light; just my litter bearers and a personal bodyguard. A number of my porters have succumbed to some local ailment and I'll need a few of your men to replace them. There are two chests outside the stables. See to it now, please, and I'll join your line of men in a moment.'

The grinding of Macro's teeth was almost audible as he emerged from the lodge and approached Cato.

'Detail five men for the freedman. He needs some porters.'

'Porters?'

'You deaf? Just get on with it. The men can stow their yokes on the wagon.'

'Yes, sir.'

'Apparently we're in a bit of a hurry to reach the coast, so we're going to have to give our leisurely stroll through Gaul a miss. Might as well have stayed with the Legion,' Macro grumbled.

Narcissus's litter turned out to be a light travelling model with screens, carried by eight huge Nubians who moved with a strength and litheness born of a lifetime's experience at the job. The litter took up position in the middle of the century, immediately followed by the two chests carried by the five bitterly resentful legionaries who had joined the slave porters. The latter were quite enjoying having someone brought down to their level. Beside the litter stood the bodyguard: a huge, muscular figure with a highly polished black cuirass and short sword. His knotted ponytail, savagely scarred face and black eye-patch announced to the world a long experience in the arena. Suddenly a hand emerged from the leather screen and clicked its fingers to attract the bodyguard's attention.

'You! Polythemus! Tie these back. Might as well see some of this benighted land while we march. Right then, Centurion!' Narcissus called out. 'When you're ready.'

Macro sourly gave the order to advance and the century moved off, marching through the main gate of Durocortorum, along the plumb-line straight road that passed through the town to the far gate and the road to Gesoriacum. As they crested a low ridge, Cato glanced back and saw, far to the rear, the advance units of the Legion emerging from the forest road, heading towards the town they had just left. He felt a twinge of anxiety as he thought of Lavinia, then vivid memories of the previous night flooded into his mind and he turned away, filled with dread.

Chapter Twenty-seven

By midday the baggage train and rearguard of the Second Legion had passed through Durocortorum and Vespasian gave the order for a short rest period. Progress had been slow because some of the local children had taken it into their heads to sling stones at the oxen pulling the artillery carriages. One viciously aimed shot had struck a larger than average beast in the testicles, causing it to try to turn in its traces as it bellowed with rage and pain. Seeing the small crowd of urchins responsible the beast had plunged after them, toppling the bolt thrower and its carriage into the street. While the beast was pacified and the wreckage cleared, word had to be passed up to the front of the column and back down to the rearguard, ordering a halt. Eventually the carriage and the bolt thrower were pushed down a side street where a detachment of engineers set about making repairs and the column started moving again.

Vespasian, riding back to investigate the delay, had cursed the shortage of draught animals that had necessitated using temperamental male oxen. The beast, comforted by a muleteer, was led away to join the small herd of lame animals destined to provide the column's fresh meat, while the young boy concerned was given a thrashing he would remember for the rest of his life. Not that that in any way comforted Vespasian as he raged inwardly at the delay. Nor was he in an improved mood when the Legion halted at midday. Seated at a table, he gave the order to see his wife's new maidservant.

As he snacked on some tough cold chicken washed down with a nameless local wine – when would these Gauls ever learn the art? – Lavinia was brought before him. His mouth full, he indicated that she should stand by the table where he gazed at her while his jaws worked hard to break the chicken down. She was quite a beauty, he decided, now that he had the chance to look her over properly. Completely wasted as a serving maid; a tidy sum could be fetched for her in Rome as a courtesan.

After a quick sip of wine to clear his palate he was ready to begin. He extracted the ribbon from his tunic and laid it down on the table. He was gratified to see that it was instantly recognised.

'Yours?'

'Yes, master. I thought I'd lost it.'

'And well you might, it had nearly slid down behind a cushion on my couch.'

Lavinia reached for it but Vespasian still held it in his grip and her hand dropped back.

'What I'd like to know,' Vespasian smiled, 'is why it was there in the first place?'

'Master?'

'What were you doing in my tent last night?'

'Last night?' Lavinia asked, all wide-eyed innocence.

'That's right. The ribbon wasn't there when I left for

bed. So tell me, Lavinia, and tell me straight, what were you doing there?'

'Nothing master! I swear it.' Her eyes pleaded with him to believe her. 'I just went in there to lie down for a moment. I was tired. I wanted somewhere comfortable to rest. The ribbon must have come off then.'

Vespasian stared long and hard at her before he continued. 'You just wanted to rest on my couch? That's all?'

Lavinia nodded.

'And you didn't take anything from the tent?'

'No, master.'

'And you didn't see anything or anybody while you were there?'

'No, master.'

'I see. Here.' He pushed the ribbon towards her and leaned back in his chair, while he considered her claims. She might be telling the truth or she might tell an altogether different tale if a little physical persuasion was applied. But almost as quickly as the thought of torture entered his head, Vespasian dismissed it. He did not doubt its efficacy in loosening tongues, it was just that he had seen too many victims offer up the version of events they knew their tormentors required of them. Hardly an effective way of finding out what had really happened. A new tack was required.

'You've only recently joined the household, according to my wife.'

'Yes, sir.'

'Who did you belong to before then?'

'Tribune Plinius, master.'

'Plinius!' Vespasian's eyebrows shot up. That changed things. What was a former slave of Plinius doing in his household? An agent? A spy trying to gain access to his safe-box? Yet, looking at her, it was hard to imagine that she could manage the guile required for the job. Another facade? It was impossible to tell at this stage.

'Why did Plinius sell you?'

'He grew tired of me.'

'You'll forgive me if I find that hard to believe.'

'It's true, master,' Lavinia protested.

'There must be more to it than that. Speak up, girl, and mind it's the truth.'

'There is more, master,' Lavinia admitted and bowed her head, as Flavia had told her to do, before she continued. 'The tribune wanted to use me . . . in certain ways.'

I bet he did, thought Vespasian.

'But he wanted more than that, he wanted me to have feelings for him. I couldn't bring myself to and he grew angry with me. And when he discovered I loved someone else he flew into a rage and hit me.'

Vespasian tutted in sympathy. 'And who might this other person be, the one you loved?'

'Please, master,' Lavinia looked up, tears glistening at the corners of her eyes. 'I don't want to say.'

'You have to tell me, Lavinia.' Vespasian leaned forward to pat her arm comfortingly. 'I must know who this other man is. It's vital that I know. I can command you to tell me.'

'Vitellius!' she blurted out, and broke down in tears, clutching her hands to her face.

Vitellius. So she loved Vitellius. Enough to do his bidding? A further thought struck Vespasian.

'Have you been seeing Vitellius since you joined our household?'

'Master?'

'You heard me. Are you still seeing him?'

She nodded.

'Did you see him last night? In my tent?'

Lavinia looked up at him with a shocked expression and shook her head.

'But you were planning to. Weren't you?'

'He never turned up, master. I waited, but he never came to me, as he had promised. I waited in the dark and he never came. So I went to bed. I never noticed the ribbon was missing until this morning.'

'I see. Did Vitellius ever ask you to tell him anything about me? Did he ask you anything about my household?'

'We talked,' Lavinia replied carefully. 'But I can't remember much of what we said about my lady Flavia and you, master.'

'And he never asked you to steal, or borrow, anything from my tent?'

'No, master. Never.'

Vespasian stared into her eyes for a long time, trying to determine if she spoke the truth. Lavinia just stared frankly back at him, until she could no longer meet his gaze and stared down at her feet instead. Certainly her story had the ring of truth. But if she still loved Vitellius it was conceivable that she might be persuaded to steal for him, or arrange access to the general's tent so that the senior tribune could steal the secret scroll after she had given up on him and gone to bed.

'You may go now, Lavinia.' Vespasian waved his hand. 'But I want you to remember this: if Vitellius ever asks you for any information about me again, or arranges another meeting, I want to know about it. And I warn you, the consequences of not telling me the truth from now on will be very painful. Very painful indeed. Do we understand one another?'

'Yes, master.'

'Good. Now leave me.'

'So how did it go?' Flavia asked Lavinia that evening as they waited for the tents to be erected.

'I think he believed me, mistress. But why did I have to say that I was meeting Vitellius in the tent that night?'

'Would you rather have told him the truth and got Cato involved?'

'No, mistress. Of course not.'

'Well then, if we're to keep Cato out of the frame we need to put someone else into it. Vitellius fits the bill nicely. Very nicely indeed.'

Lavinia glanced at her mistress in surprise. Clearly there was more to this than simply saving Cato's skin. The pleased expression on Flavia's face as she idly watched the legionaries struggling with the guy ropes went beyond relief for saving the young optio and Lavinia could not help wondering if she, and Cato, might well be small pieces in a deeper game. Flavia suddenly switched her gaze to the slave girl.

'You must remember to stick to the story we agreed,

Lavinia. Stick to that and we're all safe, understand? But don't ask me for any further explanations. The less you know, the more honest you will appear. Trust me.'

'Yes, mistress.'

Chapter Twenty-eight

The Sixth century marched through lush Gaul countryside bursting with the fresh buds of spring. The legionaries joked and chatted happily – with occasional raucous bursts of lewd singing to while away the day. And this mode persisted despite the pace that Macro had set, for he was eager to reach his destination as soon as possible and offload the imperial secretary before the latter tempted Macro to some act of violence. Narcissus had lost no opportunity to make barbed comments about the army in general, and its soldiers and Macro in particular. The centurion would dearly have loved to smack the smug bastard in the mouth just once, to emphasise the fact that you simply did not behave in such a fashion: 'When in Rome do as the Romans do, but when you're in the army keep your mouth shut and show some fucking respect.'

He smiled at the thought but knew it could never be voiced aloud, let alone face to face with a close friend and confidante of the Emperor. And so he had to sullenly endure the sarcasm and criticism in apparent good spirit – the fate of all those exposed to insecure arrivistes. Cato fared somewhat better at the hands of their tormentor since their common background provided a basis for conversation, even though Narcissus made it perfectly clear that, whatever the past, a huge social gulf now existed between them. Fortunately, the only opportunity for conversation occurred at rests in the march and at the end of the day when the century camped for the night. In between, Macro and Cato led the column from the front, though a smoother-tongued, more ambitious officer would have marched by the imperial secretary's litter to engage him in conversation and use every opportunity for flattery. After the first day, Macro insisted that he inspect his troop's equipment at each break in the march. The men regarded this zealous display of duty with curiosity, silently shaking their heads as the centurion tugged at equipment straps and checked that their weapons were being properly maintained.

On the evening of the third day of their escort duty Macro calculated that they would reach the coast the following evening, thanks to the extended length of the marching day that had been possible for the small formation. If they started just before dawn and really pushed the pace they should make the main body of the army by nightfall.

'Very good, Centurion.' Narcissus nodded approvingly. 'And an arrival in the darkness will attract less attention. That would be better in the present circumstances.'

Cato and Macro exchanged a look; precisely what the present circumstances were was still a mystery. Narcissus had said nothing to enlighten them over the last three days and Macro was a good enough soldier not to question his orders. He was also human enough not to want to give the imperial secretary the satisfaction of turning down a direct request for information. A more subtle tactic was required, thought Macro.

'More wine, sir?' He held out the jug, with a forced smile.

This time it was Cato and Narcissus who exchanged a look, surprised at the transparency of the centurion's approach. Narcissus laughed.

'Yes please, Centurion. But I'm afraid it'll take more wine than we have with us to loosen my tongue. You'll just have to wait.'

Macro's blush was visible even by the glow of the fire. The night air was still chilly and the fire and hot meal at the end of each day was greatly appreciated before the men turned in. The food that Piso had managed to wangle for the century had come from the staff officers' stores, as Vespasian was anxious to create a good impression on the distinguished guest. A rich stew of venison and spring vegetables was being mopped from the silver plates that Narcissus's bodyguard produced from one of the chests. Macro had eaten a double portion and smacked his lips before wiping them on the back of his hairy hand. He caught the disapproving gaze of the other two and shrugged as he knocked back the last of his wine before refilling the cup.

'It's good to see a man enjoy his food,' Narcissus remarked with a sly smile. 'Even if it is only such rude morsels as are provided for the common soldiery. I must say, I almost feel like one of you as we share the hardships of the march, iron rations and outdoor living in the wilds of untamed Gaul.'

'Untamed Gaul?' Macro's eyebrows rose. 'What's so untamed about it?'

'Did you notice any theatres as we passed through Durocortorum? Have we passed any great landscaped estates? The only things I've seen are a handful of struggling farms and a few shabby inns. That's what I mean by untamed, Centurion.'

'Nothing untamed about inns,' Macro replied gruffly.

'Not as such, no. But look at that foul beverage they sell as wine. I wouldn't even use it as a salad dressing.'

'You're drinking it now,' Macro pointed out.

'Only under the strictest sufferance. And you did rather force it on me. Maybe I'll reveal all to avoid inflicting any more on my poor stomach.'

'So make it easy on yourself, sir,' Cato said with a grin. 'And tell us why you're going to Gesoriacum. It can't be to oversee the invasion – all the plans for that must have been made months ago. Something's gone wrong, hasn't it?'

Narcissus looked at him, carefully weighing his thoughts. 'Yes. I can't say too much. I won't. But everything is at stake. I have to reach Gesoriacum – alive. I have certain information for General Plautius. If anything happens to me, I doubt that there will be an invasion, and if there's no invasion then there might be no Emperor in short order.' Narcissus saw the incredulity that his words produced, and he leaned closer to the others, half his face thrown into flickering shadow. 'The Empire is in great danger, greater than it has ever been. Even now there are still some fools in the Senate who think they're capable of running the

Empire. They never cease trying to undermine the Emperor – that's why I have to get to Gesoriacum. There are some who say Claudius is a cruel simpleton.' He smiled sadly. 'I'm sorry if it surprises you to hear me say that. And it might even be true. But he's the only Emperor we have and the Julio-Claudian dynasty may well end with him.'

'I've heard some people argue that it might be as well if it did,' Cato said.

'And then what?' Narcissus asked bitterly. 'A return to the Republic? How would that benefit us? Back to the old factions fighting it out in the Senate with words, and then letting it spill out on to the streets with violence, until the whole of the civilised world is torn apart by civil war. To read the pious nonsense republican historians write you'd think that the days of Sulla, Julius Caesar, Mark Antony and their breed marked some kind of golden age. Well, let me tell you, those "heroes" marched into history over the bodies of three generations of Roman citizens. We need the Emperors, we need the stability of one authority dominating the state. We Romans are no longer capable of anything else.'

'We Romans?'

'All right, we freedmen and the Romans,' conceded Narcissus. 'I admit that my fate is bound up with the Emperor's. Without his patronage, some senator or other would rouse the mob and I'd be torn apart in a matter of days. My destruction would just be the start. Even you people out here on the frontier would suffer the consequences.'

'Makes no difference to me who is in power,' said

Macro. 'I'm just a soldier. There will always be an army and that's all that matters.'

'Maybe. But what kind of an army? If Claudius falls you'll still get your war – but it'll be fought against Romans. You may even be called upon to fight men you now regard as friends. Maybe even each other. Think about it. And then give thanks for the Emperor.'

Cato looked across at his centurion, whose eyes glinted in the light of the fire. The optio smiled unsteadily as he turned back to Narcissus.

'You're testing us, aren't you? To see how we respond.'

'Of course I am,' Narcissus readily admitted. 'A man has to know where other people stand on the fundamental issues.'

'Just as well we kept our peace,' Macro laughed.

'Silence can be every bit as incriminating as the spoken word, Centurion. But I doubt whether you, or the optio here, constitute much of a threat to the Emperor. So you're both safe . . . for now.'

Macro glanced nervously at his optio for reassurance that the imperial secretary was joking with them. But the frozen stare of the young lad was enough to still any attempt at obsequious laughter.

'Anyhow, enough of that.' Narcissus drained his silver cup of the last remnants and set it down in front of the flask of wine. 'One last drink for the road and then to sleep. You know, it's quite a liberating thing to be away from all the intrigues of Rome. A man could get used to this life of yours. I propose a toast,' he said as Macro half-filled the cup proffered to him, and then the centurion filled his to the brim.

'To the good life!' Narcissus raised his cup. 'To the army, who—'

An arrow whistled out of the darkness and the imperial secretary screamed as his cup flew off into the night to clatter down against a rock. Narcissus held his drinking hand tightly against his chest as his face contorted with agony.

'What?' Cato began.

'To arms! TO ARMS!' Macro roared, throwing down his cup. He sprang to his feet and ran to gather his shield and sword propped up against the litter. Only a handful of men had risen to their feet around the century's camp fires when a shower of arrows descended on them. Several were aimed at Narcissus but mercifully missed him, their feathered ends sprouting up in the grass about the fire – and one thudding against a glowing red log, sending a plume of bright sparks swirling into the blackness. The imperial secretary had recovered sufficiently to be aware of the immediate need for self-preservation and he rolled away from the light of the fire towards the century's baggage wagon where he lay flat between the protection of the wheels.

As Cato snatched up his shield and drew his sword, an arrow took a legionary in the back as he struggled to pull his chain-mail shirt over his head. The man grunted as the breath was knocked from him by the impact and he toppled forwards, hands desperately scrabbling for the shaft sunk deep beneath the shoulder blade.

Shield held close to his body, Cato ran over and saw that the injured legionary was starting to cough up frothy gouts of blood.

'Leave him!' Macro shouted and pointed to the other men. 'Get them formed up around the wagon!'

In the flickering red light of the fires, Macro raced through the century kicking men to their feet and pushing them towards the wagon. Some were still dazed and had to have a shield and sword thrust into their hands before they recovered their wits and stumbled off in the direction of the wagon. Two more men had been hit by the time Cato had formed a rough perimeter around the century's baggage wagon, under which the imperial secretary lay, wide-eyed at the action around him. The legionaries knelt down behind their shields as they had been trained to do in the face of missile fire. Except now they wore no armour, merely woollen tunics that would stop neither arrow nor spear-thrust. Most had not been able to strap helmets on and kept their heads ducked down as the arrows continued to whirr in from the darkness, striking shields with a splintering crack. From the nearly flat trajectory, Cato knew their attackers had to be close and tensed himself for a sudden rush. Looking around he saw that he had twenty or so men with him, and more were straggling up from the main line of tents, driven on by Macro.

Suddenly the volley of arrows ceased and, an instant later, there came the wild roar of a battle cry from the darkness all about them. Dark shapes flew out of the night and, in the mid-distance, could be heard the deep thrumming of many hoof beats.

'Stand by to receive cavalry!' Cato shouted. 'Close up on me!'

His little body of men compacted around the wagon

just as a score of huge men burst into the lurid glow of the fires, bearded faces contorted by their screams. They wore thick black cloaks, pointed helmets and carried curved cleaver-like swords. They moved into attack with a fierceness few of the Romans had seen before. The first three crashed into the shields and tumbled to the ground in a tangle of cloaks, shields and flailing limbs and were quickly despatched by the other men around them. The rest of the attackers arrived as one body and a desperate fight began in the flickering red and orange light.

The Roman line dissolved at once into a mass of desperate one-on-one fights and Cato, no longer in command of a cohesive body of troops, found himself facing a large, powerfully built enemy, face twisted into a snarl. Sizing up his young opponent in an instant, the attacker screamed as he feinted forward. Cato flinched momentarily, but kept his position, shield raised and short sword poised by his side. Seeing that his attempt to scare Cato into fleeing had failed, the man laughed and swung his sword in an arc at Cato's head. The raised shield took the blow at an angle and the blade clanged off into the ground, gouging up a long divot of turf. The shock of the blow shot pain down Cato's arm from fingertips to shoulder and he cried out. Then, as the momentum of the blow carried the man forward, Cato went down on one knee, twisting to one side to avoid being crushed by his enemy. Savagely, he thrust his sword deep into the warrior's side. He fell forwards on his face with a dull moan, yanking the sword from Cato's hand. Cato thrust his foot against the man's back and tried to jerk the blade free, grimacing with the effort as the dying warrior groaned in agony. But it was no use, the blade was tightly wedged in the man's ribs and would not come free easily. Glancing around, Cato saw that most of the attackers were down, together with a number of Romans.

Close by, one of his men had lost his shield and could only raise his arm against the sword about to be smashed down on his head. With a howl that bordered on an embarrassing scream, Cato threw himself behind his shield into the attacker's back, sending both of them headlong into the grass. By the time he had risen to his feet, the man he had saved had thrust his dagger into the attacker's throat.

As suddenly as the attackers had burst upon them they were gone, and the surviving Romans stood, bewildered by the speed of events.

'What the fuck are you doing?' Macro shouted from close at hand as he ran up to the wagon with the remainder of the men. 'You heard the optio! Close up to face cavalry!'

For a moment, Cato had forgotten about the horses but now they were close and the legionaries hurriedly closed ranks around the wagon, shields interlocking, with swords and javelins held ready.

As suddenly as the first attack had come, the second raced out of the night; a line of horsemen in the same equipment, some still holding horse-bows while others carried long spears, thrusting out from under their arms, all of them crying out their terrifying battle-cry. Macro quickly looked across at Cato to make sure the optio was unhurt.

'Pick up a fucking sword, you idiot!'

Cato realised that he was unarmed and hastily snatched up the nearest weapon – one of the attackers' curved cleavers. It felt strange to a hand used to the weight and balance of the legionary's short sword, but reassuringly heavy.

'Hold steady, lads!' Macro called out. 'Hold steady and we'll live.'

When the horsemen were almost on them they drew up; those who still carried bows drew arrows and waited for a chance to pepper any Roman foolish enough to expose himself while the spear-carriers moved in on the ring of shields. They brought their horses slamming up against the shield wall, throwing the legionaries back against the wagon, while stabbing down with their long bladed spears. The bulk of their horses and fear of the archers kept the Romans crouched down through sheer instinct for self-preservation. A few of them took every chance to thrust their swords into any part of man or horse that came within reach and an occasional cry or shrill neigh told when a blow had struck home. But time was not on the Romans' side; already four men were down on the ground around the wagon and blood was making the grass slippery.

It was all too obvious to Macro what the outcome of the fight would be if they fought defensively; a whittling away of their numbers and one final rush that would overrun the survivors. Just as he realised this, fate intervened in a peculiar way. Two of the horsemen suddenly spied the imperial secretary sheltering beneath the wagon and hurled their horses through the Romans.

Leaning down from the saddle, they thrust under the wagon. Narcissus rolled away from their spear tips with a scream. Up jumped Macro, teeth parted in a savage snarl, as he automatically leaped to the imperial secretary's defence. He caught one man by the arm and hauled him bodily from his saddle. A slash of the sword into the man's eyes left him helpless as the centurion snatched up the fallen spear and plunged it into the small of the other attacker's back.

Then Cato, too, was on his feet, kicking at the men nearest him. 'Up and at 'em! Come on, get up! Charge!'

Now all the Romans were running at their attackers echoing Cato's call to the charge. The attackers were momentarily shocked into stillness – a fatal failure of nerve, as it turned out. Moments later, the Roman infantry were in amongst them, knocking them from their saddles and finishing them off as they lay helpless on the ground. The bloody skirmish was quickly over, only a handful of the enemy managing to break away and flee into the night.

Cato leaned on his shield, blood pounding through his veins as he breathed heavily. All about him bodies were strewn around the century's camp fires. Legionaries quickly moved among the prostrate forms to finish off the wounded enemy.

'Stop that!' Narcissus shouted as he scrabbled out from under the wagon. 'Don't kill them!'

The shrill tone of his voice caused the men to pause in their grisly work, swords poised, waiting for Macro to countermand this ridiculous instruction.

'Don't kill them?' Macro was astonished. 'These

bastards were about to gut you. And us!'

'Centurion, we must have prisoners! We must find out who is responsible for the attack.'

Macro could see the sense of what Narcissus was saying. He wiped his sword clean on the cloak of one of the attackers before sliding it back into his scabbard. 'Lads! If any of these bastards are still breathing drag them over here. Section leaders! Call the roll of your men, all returns to the optio at once!'

Later, while the Roman injured groaned and cried at the rough first-aid that was meted out to them by their inexpert comrades, Macro gazed down angrily at the three warriors sitting sullenly at his feet. Cato emerged from the night.

'What's the butcher's bill?'

'Eight dead and sixteen wounded, sir.'

'Right. Get the seals off the dead and tell off a burial detail.'

'What about my litter bearers? My bodyguard?' asked Narcissus, nursing his injured hand.

'One dead, one missing and the bodyguard's still unconscious – someone said he'd been kicked by a horse.'

'Right then, you bastards,' growled Macro, and as he kicked the nearest one on his broken arm a shrill scream of agony split the air. 'Eight of my men are dead. Don't think for a moment you aren't going the same way. But we can make it quick for you, or slow and painful. Depends on how you answer this gentleman here.'

He jerked a thumb at Narcissus and stepped to one side. The imperial secretary stared hard at them, hands on hips, but stood beyond arm's reach.

'Who ordered you to kill me?'

'Kill you?' Cato asked. 'I thought they were bandits.'

'Bandits!' Macro laughed harshly. 'Ever heard of bandits attacking a full century? No? Well then, don't be stupid. Besides, look at them, look at the clothes and armour. This lot belong to something far more organised.'

'Like an army unit?'

'Maybe.'

Narcissus raised a hand for silence and asked his question again. 'I said, who ordered you to kill me?'

None of the three looked up, even when he repeated the question more forcefully.

'Centurion?'

Macro stepped up and delivered another kick, this time to the head. The man went down on his back with a sharp cry.

'Well, are you going to tell me?'

The man who had escaped the kicking thus far glared up through bushy brows and said something in a language Cato had not heard before. He emphasised his point by spitting on to the hem of Narcissus' tunic. Macro drew back his boot.

'No!' Narcissus raised his hand. 'There's no need for that. I think I know this tongue. They're from Syria. If they're who I think they are, they won't talk for a while.'

'I wouldn't bet on that, sir,' Macro replied coldly. 'There are ways . . .'

'I haven't got time. We mustn't be delayed in reaching the army. These men will come along as prisoners. When I get to Gesoriacum there'll be plenty of time to go to work on them. See that they're securely bound. They can march behind my litter tomorrow.'

When the century set out the next morning, the full scale of the action became clear. Twelve more bodies were found, as well as the Roman dead, and all were buried in a hastily dug trench before the unit broke camp. Macro had ordered his men to march in full battledress and they moved wearily down the road to Gesoriacum in a box shape around Narcissus's litter and the wagon now carrying the Roman wounded. All surplus baggage had been abandoned to make room for the wounded. That had not endeared the prisoners to the centurion, who had them tied to each other by the ankle, and fastened the line to the back of the wagon. There was no stop for a rest, despite the weariness brought on by a sleepless night, as the column picked its way along the road to the coast. A pair of horsemen appeared in the distance from time to time as they shadowed the century, evidently frustrated by the lack of opportunity to continue the action. Shortly before dusk the horses wheeled away and disappeared over the brow of a narrow ridge that ran alongside the line of the road. As night fell the century's pace quickened and the men glanced nervously into the shadows looming around them, fully expecting the ambush to be renewed the instant darkness could provide enough cover for their strange attackers.

At last they marched over the brow of a hill and Cato let out a gasp of astonishment. Below them was a vast military camp stretching, it seemed, for miles, lit by thousands of camp fires and braziers. Four full legions were concentrated in the area, together with an equal number of specialist auxiliary cohorts, engineers, ship-builders and staff planning-officers – over fifty thousand men all told. But as they approached the gates Macro sensed that something was wrong. Small pockets of men roamed outside the camp, unarmed and out of uniform, others played at dice or just sat drinking themselves insensible.

Before the Sixth century came within speaking range of any of the other legionaries they were intercepted by a staff officer on horseback, escorted by several centurions, who commanded them to halt. Once the identity of the imperial secretary had been confirmed, the officer issued immediate orders for the removal of the prisoners to a secure place, while he escorted the imperial secretary to army headquarters. And that was the last Cato and Macro saw of Narcissus. They received no thanks for their success in preserving his mission and no acknowledgement of the lives that had been lost in his cause.

The camp prefect of the Ninth arrived to arrange for the movement of the wounded to the Ninth Legion's hospital. Then he led the remnants of the century out of the camp to a cleared area some miles distant where the lines for the Second Legion had already been laid out.

The Sixth century set up its tents as quickly as possible and, once the pickets had been positioned, the men fell into an exhausted sleep.

Chapter Twenty-nine

Two days later the Second Legion marched into the site and the vast area was overrun by thousands of soldiers struggling to erect tents. In strict accordance with military protocol, the legate's camp was put up first, followed by the senior officers' and only then was the common soldiery allowed to begin work on their own, far more basic, quarters.

Vespasian sat in his command tent at a small table, screened off from the household slaves as headquarters staff scurried to and fro, laying down wooden flooring and unpacking furniture and other items. Above it all, he could hear Flavia issuing orders and driving them on to greater speed. He knew she was glad the tiresome journey was over and that the hardships of life on the march could be pushed to the back of her mind for a few weeks at least, though soon she would have to undertake the even longer journey south to Rome.

Vespasian was much less content – even though the missing scroll had been returned to him by Flavia a few days earlier. She had found it amongst the toys in Titus's travel chest and saw that it was addressed to her husband. The boy told her he had found it on the floor, so she said, and was incapable of being any more specific, given his age. Vespasian had hugged his wife and immediately locked the document away in the darkest recess of the safe-box. It seemed that whoever had stolen the scroll must have dropped it while fleeing from the command tent. Vespasian was appalled by the breach of security that could have occurred. What if someone else had discovered the scroll before Titus? Jupiter! It didn't bear thinking about. But Vespasian's joy at the recovery of the scroll was now tempered by the forbidding situation that existed beyond the confines of his command tent.

A day's march from Gesoriacum they had been met by a messenger from Plautius with new orders. In the army commander's opinion – and here Vespasian detected the hand of Narcissus – it would not be wise to use the Second Legion to put down the mutiny. It would be more efficacious for the mutiny to be settled by negotiation rather than direct action. For the army to go into a major campaign with the memory of bloody repression fresh in their minds would be foolhardy. A delay in crossing the thin strip of sea between Gaul and Britain would have to be tolerated as the price to be paid for quelling the mutiny.

Worse news, as far as Vespasian was concerned, followed: the Second Legion would not be included in the first wave of the invasion. Two other legions had been training for amphibious operations for several months and to them would fall the honour of fighting their way ashore and establishing a beachhead for the rest of the army. Vespasian knew that if the Britons decided to meet the invaders on the beaches then all the glory and political capital would go to the commanders and officers of the spearhead units. He gloomily foresaw a long period of mopping-up operations stretching ahead of him; a nasty process of attrition that would win no garlands and be a mere footnote to the epic tales of victory that would be told on the streets of Rome.

If the mutiny could be put down, he reflected.

As he had made his way through the main camp to report to Plautius, it had been heart-breaking for the legate to see the collapse of discipline in the other legions. Few of the soldiers he rode past bothered to salute and, although no-one had actually said anything to him, the look of defiance in their eyes – daring him to try and exercise his authority – enraged Vespasian. Only the army commander's personal bodyguard and the officers remained in full uniform, carrying out their normal duties as far as they were able to.

Vespasian was shown into the wooden headquarters building dominating the centre of the huge army camp, where Narcissus was seated at a great map table with General Plautius. Vespasian had known Plautius socially before he had joined the army and he was shocked to see the weary, beaten expression on the general's face.

'Good to see you again,' said Plautius with a smile. 'It's been a long time. I just wish it was under happier circumstances. Have you met Narcissus?'

'No, sir, though his reputation precedes him.'

'A good reputation, I trust?' Narcissus asked.

Vespasian nodded, not willing to perjure his true opinion.

'I must thank you for your unit's protection, legate.'

'I'll pass word of your gratitude on to the men concerned, if you haven't already thanked them.'

'You are most kind.'

'Now, your report please, Vespasian.' Plautius waved him to a seat. 'How is your legion?'

'They are still responding to orders, if that's what you mean, sir.'

'For the moment maybe. In a few days they'll be just like the others.'

'Have you found the ringleaders of the mutiny yet?' Vespasian asked.

'Thanks to Narcissus we have the names. Tribune Aurelius, two centurions and twenty or so legionaries. All were transferred to the Ninth from the Dalmatian legions, complete with their previous loyalties, as you'd expect.'

'Have they made any demands?'

'Only that the invasion be abandoned. They've managed to persuade the others that demons and certain death are the only things waiting for them on the other side of the ocean.'

'Not that it's much of an ocean,' Narcissus added. 'But the word has a certain depressing effect on the imagination of military types. Present company excepted, of course.' He smiled. 'I'm afraid we are dealing with some quite well-thought-through treason, gentlemen. More sophisticated than anything that Tribune Aurelius and his little band of mutineers could come up with. You see, Vespasian, the general and I have already decided to eliminate this group. But first we must try and discover the identity of their masters back in Rome. Aurelius and his men were only exposed when my agents intercepted a message en route to his masters in Rome. Unfortunately, the courier expired before he could be induced to divulge the name of the intended recipient. Such is life – or not, in his case. Then there is the little matter of the ambush on the road from Durocortorum. Evidently the opposition got wind of my travel arrangements and the purpose of my journey. It appears that someone on "our side" is not quite what they seem.'

'I had news of the attack. I heard that you had prisoners. Have they said anything yet?'

'Not much, I'm afraid, before they died,' Narcissus replied, with regret at the inconvenience. 'The interrogators were quite thorough, but only managed to confirm that they were Syrians, supposedly a group of deserters raiding the area. That's all we got before I had their throats cut.'

'A raiding party?' Vespasian shook his head. 'Doubtful enough. But to attack an army unit . . .'

'Quite,' Narcissus replied. 'It's not remotely possible. Their loyalty to their masters does – did – them credit. But there's a more worrying factor. I've had news that a few days ago an entire squadron of Syrian horse-archers supposedly deserted from an auxiliary cohort that was marching from Dalmatia to join this army.'

'Dalmatia?' Vespasian pondered. 'From Scribonianus's command?'

'Exactly.'

'I see. Whose unit?'

'Gaius Marcellus Dexter,' Narcissus replied, watching the legate closely.

'The name's familiar, my wife might know him. Do you think the men who attacked you are from that unit?' Vespasian asked.

'We'll know soon enough. The cohort is due here in three days' time. The bodies will keep until then and someone should be able to identify them.'

'If they are from that unit,' Plautius added, 'then this plot spreads far wider than we first feared. The question is, can we stamp it out in time for an invasion this year?'

'We have to, my dear Plautius,' Narcissus said firmly. 'There's no question of the operation not proceeding. The Emperor himself has arranged to join the army in Britain.'

'Has he?' Vespasian turned to Plautius. 'But I thought you were to be the supreme commander, sir?'

'Apparently not.' Plautius shrugged. 'The Emperor's right-hand man here has told me to summon the Emperor to our "rescue" once the army stands outside the Trinovantes's capital.'

'Relax, General,' Narcissus said with a gentle pat of Plautius's hand, which the other man withdrew as if it had been slithered over by a snake. 'It's just good public relations. You'll be in charge right through the campaign. Claudius is there to act as a figurehead, to lead the triumphant army into their capital, hand out the gongs and then rush back to Rome for the triumph.'

'If the Senate awards one,' Vespasian reminded him.

'It's already in the bag,' Narcissus smiled. 'I like to plan ahead as far as possible, keeps things simple for the historians. So Claudius gets his triumph, the Empire gains a new province, we all avoid a nasty civil war, and our careers are safeguarded for the foreseeable future – which, I admit, is never quite as long as one would like. It all comes up roses, provided—'

'We end the mutiny and get the legions on to the ships,' Plautius finished wearily.

'Precisely.'

'And how,' Vespasian broke in, 'do we achieve that?'

'I have a little plan.' Narcissus tapped his nose. 'Can't let anyone else in on it if it is to stand a chance of working. But, trust me, it's a corker.'

'And if it doesn't work?' asked Vespasian.

'Then I'll save you a space on the cross next to me.'

Once the Second Legion had settled down for the night and the sentries had been issued with strict orders not to permit any men to move in or out of the camp, Vespasian summoned Macro to make his full report. He had received a preliminary account earlier but, in the present hush-hush atmosphere dominating army headquarters, Vespasian wanted to glean as much information as possible. Night had long fallen when the centurion was quietly ushered into the tent and stood at attention before the legate's desk. Vespasian was catching up on some paperwork by the guttering light of a pair of oil lamps. Once the leather tent flap had fallen back into place, the legate set down his stylus and closed the ink pot.

'Tough journey, I hear?'

'Yes, sir.'

'Lose many men?'

'Eight killed, six of the wounded are still in the Ninth's hospital recovering.'

'The losses will be made up from the recruit pool.'

'Yes, sir.'

'Now I want the full story, Centurion. Leave nothing out and tell it just as it happened, no embellishments.'

With Macro standing at attention and staring at the back of the tent above the legate's head, the tale of the march, the ambush and the final day's journey to Gesoriacum was delivered in a prosaic monotone while Vespasian listened attentively. When the centurion had finished Vespasian looked sharply at him.

'And you told no-one the nature of your mission?'

'No-one, sir. The orders were very clear on that.'

'So we can assume that your attackers were not acting on inside information?'

'Yes, sir.' Macro nodded before committing his own opinion on the matter. 'They were no ordinary bunch of thieves and crooks. Those men laid on an excellent ambush and fought like regulars. It was clear they were after the imperial secretary.'

'I see.' Vespasian nodded, hiding his disappointment; nothing the centurion had said added significantly to what he already knew. If Macro was to be believed then Narcissus's attackers had acquired information about his route from outside the Legion. That should narrow things down for the imperial chief secretary – if the centurion was telling the truth.

'Centurion, may I ask you for a personal opinion – strictly off the record?'

Macro shifted uneasily. He would like to have replied 'It depends', but a soldier did not set conditions for his response to a superior officer, so he had to agree – while emphasising his reluctance as far as possible. 'Yes, sir, I suppose so.'

'Do you consider the invasion of Britain to be wise?'

'That's state policy, sir,' Macro replied warily. 'Far too high up for me. I guess the Emperor and his staff have thought it all through and made the right decision. I don't even have an opinion.'

'I did say it was off the record.'

'Yes, sir.' Macro inwardly cursed his legate for placing him in this tortuous situation. Nothing a subordinate ever said was 'off the record', if a superior chose to change his mind later on.

'So?'

'I simply don't know enough about it to voice an opinion that would be useful to you, sir.'

So, that line of enquiry was stalled, Vespasian realised. A more indirect approach was needed, one that would absolve the centurion of responsibility for what he said.

'What are the men saying about it?'

'The men, sir? Well, some of them are worried, quite naturally – none of us likes to be any nearer to water than the next drink. Anything could happen at sea. And then there's stories about the dangers waiting for us.'

'You're not afraid of their army?'

'Not afraid as such, sir. Only concerned, as much as any man facing a new kind of enemy should be. It's, well, more to do with the druids, sir. Them and their kind.'

'What about the druids?'

'The men have heard that they have the power to summon up demons.'

'And you believe this?'

'Of course not, sir.' Macro was offended. 'Anyone with half a mind can see it's a load of bollocks. But you know what the men are like with their superstitions.'

'Not so long ago I believe you were one of the men.'

'Yes, sir.'

'But you're not superstitious? Like them?'

'No, sir. I gave most of that up when I became a centurion. A centurion hasn't much time for that sort of stuff.'

'Where did your men hear about these druids?'

'Some of our foragers ran into men from the main camp yesterday, sir. They told them about the druids, then they let on about the mutiny.'

'They called it a mutiny?' asked Vespasian. 'Be quite sure about that.'

'Well, no, sir. They said they were still loyal to the Emperor and that the invasion must be some crackpot scheme of Narcissus's that no sane man would pursue. Call it what you like, it's still mutiny to me, sir.'

'And the other men feel as you do about this?'

'As far as I can tell, sir.'

'Very good, Centurion. Very good.' Vespasian eased himself back in his chair. So far so good. For the moment at least the Legion was loyal. But, unless Narcissus's little scheme worked its magic, then it would only be a matter of time before the Second Legion was riven by the same contagion that had hit the other units. However, as long as the officers like Macro acted their part, the spread of the mutiny might be contained for a few weeks at least.

Chapter Thirty

While the men of the Sixth century watched the rest of the Legion settle in around them, Cato left the tent lines and hurried between the mass of men, animals and transport wagons to the area allocated for the legate's quarters. The headquarters staff and the wagons allotted to Vespasian's household were just entering the area set aside for vehicles behind the tent site. Since summer was fast approaching and the Legion would only be encamped for two months at most prior to the invasion, the army staff officers had marked the camp out for tents rather than wooden barracks.

Cato kept far enough back from the wagons to avoid attracting attention and looked for any sign of Lavinia. The wagons were drawn up alongside each other by heaving, cursing muleteers. Their passengers climbed down to begin the tiring process of unpacking the travel chests, carrying them into the large tents being hauled up on tall tent poles by teams of legionaries straining on guy ropes. Cato's eyes alighted on the household wagons and his frantically searching gaze was finally rewarded by the sight of Lavinia descending from the legate's personal coach with Titus clenched under one arm. Cato resisted the temptation to wave or call out, and tried to look as inconspicuous as possible as he stood still amongst the crowds of legionaries toiling away. He watched Lavinia follow her mistress as Flavia marched into one of the erected tents. Cato stared at the entrance for a long time before he turned and walked slowly away.

He wandered through the Legion until dusk when the meal call was sounded and he realised he was hungry. Cato had had no appetite at midday as he nervously anticipated the arrival of the Legion and news of Lavinia and the injured sentry; an odd mix of heartache and dread that was peculiarly painful. By the time he had rejoined the century the sun had set and the shapes of men and tents were grey and indistinct against the pale glow of the horizon. Cooking fires had been lit and the first faint odours of yet another stew wafted into the rapidly cooling air. Cato had been assigned to the second watch and wanted a full belly before he had to follow the senior watch officer on his rounds, collecting the tokens from each station on the walls and gates. As he sat by the section fire and mopped up the last remnants of his meal with some freshly baked bread, Macro squatted down by his side.

'Where've you been?'

'I just went for a walk, sir.'

'A walk, eh? I don't suppose you happened to pass the general's quarters?'

Cato smiled.

'I suppose it's that woman of yours. Still carrying the candle for that little bint?' Macro shook his head wonderingly. 'What did I tell you about all this before –

back at the base? A soldier who lets his feelings cloud his thinking is a soldier distracted, and the army can't afford distraction. Put her out of your mind, boy. As a matter of fact, I might be able to help out in that direction. Some of the lads and I are heading into the town later on tonight – I've wangled a pass to purchase barley supplies for the cohort. We've been told where to find a nice little inn that offers something a little more tasty than the local brew. You might want to join us once you've finished your watch.'

'Is that an order, sir?'

Macro stared coldly at him. 'Well, fuck you, lover boy. I'm just trying to help out. But if you want to sit and sulk rather than have a drink with some mates and get your end away, then it's your funeral.'

Cato knew he was in the wrong. The sour note of his reply had been impulsive and now he regretted the offence it had caused.

'Sir. I'm not ungrateful for the offer. I just don't feel like it right now. I can't help it.'

'Can't help it?' snorted Macro. 'Suit yourself then.'

He quickly rose to his feet and stormed off, with one final black look at Cato before entering his tent.

While he waited for his watch to begin, Cato sank into a mood of despair. Perhaps the centurion was right? What kind of romance could he carry on with a girl he could never see? She was, moreover, a dangerous girl to know, given that she could testify that he'd been in the legate's tent that night. If for any reason she was indiscreet, then both of them would be up in front of Vespasian. And the truth, about the other man, was hardly likely to be believed. The best move would be to forget her, forget about love and get on with life. Perhaps he would join Macro and the others after all.

Shortly after the change of the second watch, when all but a few diehards were sound asleep, the sentry on the main gate saw two figures walking down the road towards the camp. He called out for the password and, when he received no immediate reply, he lowered his javelin point and challenged them again.'

'Relax soldier!' a voice called out. 'We're friends.'

'Password!'

'We're friends, I tell you! From the other camp.'

'Keep your fucking distance!' the sentry shouted, slightly relieved that the strangers spoke Latin.

'We want to speak with your commander. We have a pass signed by General Plautius himself. Let us in.'

'No! Stay where you are.' The thickset sentry took a pace back and pointed his javelin at the two figures scarcely ten feet away. Now, by the dim light of the stars, he could see that one man was tall and thin, wearing a dark, hooded cloak. The other was a giant of a man who wore a sword in a scabbard at his side. 'Optio! Optio of the watch! Come down here quick!'

The side-passage gate opened and the optio marched over, munching on a hunk of bread soaked in wine.

'What is it? Better not be another false alarm, I'm still bloody eating.'

'This man wants to speak to the legate.'

'Has he given you the password?'

'No, sir.'

'Then tell him to fuck off – you should bloody well know the regulations by now.'

'If I might interrupt?' The taller figure took two paces nearer.

'Stay exactly where you are, pal,' the optio growled.

'I have business with the legate,' the man insisted, then he brought out a small slate from his cloak. 'See here, I've a pass authorised by Aulus Plautius.'

The optio approached cautiously and quickly took the slate held out to him, before retiring towards the open side-gate, which provided just enough light to read the message. The pass was in order and the ring seal pressed into the wax surface bore the eagle of a commanding general. Still, the optio considered, it might just be a fake. Given the strictness with which camp regulations and restrictions of movement to and from the gates were being enforced, the legate and his senior officers were clearly jumpy about something.

The optio paused: a person bearing a pass authorised by Plautius himself must hold some kind of rank. 'Please wait here, sir.'

'Commendable security you have here,' Narcissus said, somewhat later, as he accepted a drink from Vespasian. 'It was quite difficult persuading the senior watch officer to let us see you, even with the general's pass. Your soldiers are sticklers for the rules.'

'No rules – no order – no civilisation – no Rome.' Vespasian trotted out the old adage and raised his glass to Narcissus. 'But I'm glad you came, for whatever reason of your own. I needed to speak to you alone.'

'Then our interests happily coincide.'

'What about him?' Vespasian nodded at the imperial secretary's bodyguard looming in the shadows, still and silent.

'Ignore him,' said Narcissus. 'I take it we're safe in here?'

'Absolutely. All entrances are well guarded.'

'Oh yes?' Narcissus took a small sip of wine as he fixed Vespasian with his eyes. 'That's not what my sources tell me.'

Vespasian coloured. 'Your spy told you about that?'

'I was informed that a sentry had been injured by an intruder. I take it nothing was stolen. Nothing important that is.'

'Nothing.' Vespasian said firmly, forcing himself to keep his eyes fixed on those of Narcissus.

'So what happened?'

'As far as I know, a slave girl was due to meet her lover in my command tent. He didn't show and she waited a while and then left. Shortly afterwards the guards came across someone in the tent. He injured a sentry and fled the scene. A dropped torch set fire to the tent, but we managed to get it out without too much damage being done. And that is all there is to tell.'

Narcissus stared at him and slowly took another sip. 'You tortured the girl?'

'It wasn't necessary.'

'Really? There are some officers who get a kick out of that sort of thing.'

'If you think—' Vespasian half rose from his chair and the figure in the shadows moved quickly forwards. Narcissus waved the bodyguard back.

'I think nothing of the sort. I just wondered if you had managed to get any more information out of her.'

'Just what I said.'

'And the man's name? The one she said she had arranged to meet.'

'Look here, Narcissus, I run my Legion, and if there are any problems to solve then I'll sort them out. You're a freedman, you don't give orders to a legate. This isn't Saturnalia, you know.'

Narcissus gave him a curious smile. 'It's funny you should say that. But no matter . . . I want the man's name.'

Vespasian did not reply immediately. Much as he disliked Vitellius he was reluctant to give information that might lead an innocent man to his destruction. An innocent man now – but possibly a political rival later. Or an ally. Nothing was written in stone.

'It would be best that you tell me now,' Narcissus said quietly. 'Before I get Polythemus to ask you.'

'How dare you?' Vespasian recoiled in shock. 'You threaten me in my own tent? Why, man, I could call out for my guards now and have you, and your brute there, crucified just like that!' He tried to snap his fingers with a crack but his damp hand made no sound.

The failure of the gesture was not lost on Narcissus and he allowed himself a small smile of satisfaction before he continued in a more conciliatory tone.

'I fear you misunderstand our relative worth in the eyes of the Emperor. Aristocrats with pretensions to political greatness are ten a sestertius. Some undoubtedly have considerable talents – you are such a one – but they are freaks within their own class. Generations of inbreeding have produced nothing more than idle, arrogant idiots. We – the Emperor – can replace you easily enough. I, on the other hand, am irreplaceable. How do you imagine a mere freedman has been able to rise to become the Emperor's right-hand man? There is more intelligence, more cunning and more cruelty in my little finger than in your whole body. Remember that, Vespasian. Remember it before you even think to upbraid me.'

Vespasian clamped his mouth shut to stop up the torrent of rage churning inside him. He gripped the edges of his chair tightly and swallowed.

'Excellent.' Narcissus nodded slowly. 'It's good that you're smart enough to accept an unpalatable truth when it is presented to you. You will grow to understand the importance of that when you return to Rome. I'm glad I was right about you.'

'And how were you right about me?' Vespasian asked through clenched teeth.

'Your brain rules your heart, and your pride knows its place. Now, be a good fellow and tell me the name of the man the slave girl was supposed to meet in your tent.'

'Vitellius. She said it was Vitellius.'

'Vitellius? Now that is very interesting, wouldn't you say? A senior tribune engaged in a liaison with a slave girl in the legate's command tent where, no doubt, some very sensitive documents were being stored. I find that very interesting. Not to mention suggestive. Don't you?'

Vespasian just stared coldly back.

'Do you still have the letter?'

'Yes.'

'You're clear about what has to be done?'

'Of course, but finding a wagon dumped in a bog a hundred years ago won't be easy.'

'Then you'd better get some good men for the job. Keep the numbers down – the less who know what's going on, the better – and make sure they are discreet.'

'I have a few men in mind.'

'Fine. That chest has to be located and once you've got it, guard it with your life. When the Emperor arrives with the reinforcements the chest will be passed over to a special unit of the Praetorian Guard for shipment to Rome. And then you will forget that you ever knew about it. You and those men you choose to carry out the mission.'

Narcissus pushed his cup away and rose to his feet. 'Now, I'm afraid I must go. Thanks for your hospitality, Vespasian. And relax. I'm sure the Emperor will be deeply gratified when I report how co-operative you have been.'

'Before you leave, tell me one thing.'

'Yes.'

'Who is the imperial spy in my legion? I must know who I can trust once we arrive in Britain.'

'Then he would lose his value to me.'

'Like being able to report on me, for instance?'

'Of course.'

'Then, at least tell me who the traitor is,' Vespasian asked. 'I need to know which direction to guard myself against.'

Narcissus tried to look sympathetic. 'I don't know. I

suspect, but I can't be sure yet – I need further proof. If I say anything that causes you to treat the people around you differently then the other side's spy will know we are closing in. Nothing must be done to alert suspicion. You speak to no-one about this matter. Not even your wife. Understand?'

Vespasian nodded. 'I understand that you're putting me in danger.'

'You're a soldier. Get used to it.'

With that, the imperial chief secretary turned his back on the legate and left the tent, summoning his bodyguard from the shadows with a waggle of a finger. Alone, Vespasian fumed with silent frustration. He had managed to get himself off the hook for the theft of the letter, for the moment. But he was no nearer finding a way out of the dark threads of intrigue that bound him so tightly.

Outside, Narcissus paused. There was no sign that Vespasian had ordered them to be followed. He turned to his bodyguard.

'Make sure that I'm not tailed. If I call out, come as quickly as you can.'

He walked off quietly, and a few moments later the bodyguard followed, hugging the shadows and keeping a keen eye on his master. Narcissus walked down the line of tribunes' tents, then paused outside an entrance flap. When he was sure he was unobserved, he entered hurriedly. Inside, the imperial spy was waiting for him, as had been arranged earlier in the day by secret messenger. He rose from his campaign seat to greet the imperial secretary.

'Keeping well, sir?'

Narcissus grasped the hand that was extended towards him and smiled. 'Yes, Vitellius, very well. Now, we need a little talk about that scroll I told you about a few months ago. Moreover, I'm curious to know why you omitted to tell me about your arranging to be in the legate's tent the night it was burgled.'

Vitellius frowned. 'But I wasn't in the tent.'

'That's not what Vespasian says. He questioned some slave girl who said she had arranged to meet you in there.'

'It's not true. I swear it's not true.'

Narcissus watched him closely and then nodded in satisfaction at the response. 'All right. I believe you . . . for the moment. But if it's not true, then why would she say so? Or why would she be told to say so?'

'Told? Who by?'

'That, my dear Vitellius, is what you were sent here to find out.'

Chapter Thirty-one

'Cato! How on earth did you get in here?'

'Brought a report from my centurion to headquarters, my lady. Somehow I lost my way trying to get out. And here I am.'

Flavia laughed as she rose from the floor. She had been busy packing a campaign chest for her husband and the wooden flooring was covered in neat piles of tightly folded clothes. 'You look awful. Rough night?'

'Yes, my lady. I went into Gesoriacum.'

'When will you youngsters learn? Still, I don't suppose you've come here to explain yourself to me. So you might want to go and inspect progress on the nursery I'm having built for Titus.'

'My lady?'

'I've put Lavinia in charge of some household slaves to spruce up the nursery. She wanted a word with you. And I dare say you wouldn't mind seeing her again.' Flavia winked. 'Now run along and let me get back to work. Go out that flap, it's the third entrance on the left. Oh, and don't let anyone catch you in here.'

As Cato walked slowly the way Flavia had indicated, his mind raced. Desperate as he was to see Lavinia, there were still questions in his mind about that night in the legate's tent. He needed to know if she had said anything to anyone about him. Clearly Flavia knew he had been there, but who else? He paused at the entrance to the nursery.

Cato steeled himself and stepped inside. The interior was cluttered with children's toys and clothing. Squatting amongst the mess were several of Flavia's household slaves, busily striving to make a comfortable place for a child to play. Sitting to one side, happily painting a farm animal on to a small screen, was Lavinia. She had not seen Cato enter and jumped when he softly called her name from a few feet away.

'Now look what you've made me do.' She laughed, pointing her brush at the screen. 'There's a tail on my cow's head.'

'Cow?' Cato could have sworn it was a horse.

Lavinia turned to face him. For a moment her expression was serious and his heart sank. Then she reached out for his hands and smiled.

'I was worried about you, after I heard about that sentry.'

'Why didn't you come back?'

'I couldn't. When I got back to my quarters, my lady Flavia said she needed me, said Titus was ill. I couldn't see anything wrong with him but she told me to stay with him while she went to find some medicine. By the time she got back everyone was shouting. I'm glad you got out before that nasty business with the guard happened. I can't tell you how worried I've been. I felt really bad about leaving you alone in the tent. I'm sorry I did, truly I am.'

Cato squeezed her hands. 'It's all right. I'm just glad you were safe. When that man came into the tent I was afraid you'd walk right into him when you came back. I think he'd have killed you.'

'Other man?'

'Yes, you didn't think it was me who attacked that sentry?'

'No . . . but who?'

'I don't know. When he discovered I was there he nearly did for me. I shouted for help and, when the sentry appeared, the man attacked him and vanished. I got out as quickly as I could.'

'I see.'

'Anyway, I was so glad to see you safe when the wagons arrived at the camp.'

'Were you glad? Really?'

'Of course.'

'That's so sweet.' She leaned forward and kissed him on the mouth. 'You do care for me, don't you?'

He said nothing and kissed her back, for longer this time, his heart pounding against the warm softness pressed against his chest. When their lips parted he looked into her eyes, feeling cheap for what he was about to ask.

'Has the sentry identified anyone yet?'

'He's dead. He died back in Durocortorum. My mistress only had word of it this morning. He never spoke a word – so you're safe.'

'Does anyone, apart from Flavia, know that I was there that night?'

'No. But the legate knows I was there. He found my hair ribbon.'

'What did you say to him?' Cato felt a finger of ice trace its way down his spine.

'I told him I was going to meet someone else there and that when he didn't show up I went to bed. That's all I told him. I swear.'

'I believe you. Who did you say you were going to meet?'

'Tribune Vitellius.'

'Why him?' Cato felt uneasy about Vitellius being fitted up in this manner. A vision came to mind of the tribune issuing orders in the flames of the German village. It would be a low thing to do to cast suspicion on him.

'Because my mistress told me to say so. Apparently her husband doesn't like him, and thinks there's something suspicious about him. He seemed the natural choice, she said.'

'It doesn't seem quite right.' Cato started to protest but Lavinia pulled him close and kissed him again.

'Hush! It doesn't matter. As long as no-one suspects you. That's all that matters to me. Now then,' she continued, pulling him to a screened-off area of the tent that was to be used as a changing area, 'we haven't much time and there's a lot we have to catch up on.'

'Wait. What do you mean, we haven't much time?'

'My mistress is returning to Rome soon. She's taking me with her.'

Cato felt sick.

'I'll try and wait for you in Rome,' she said gently.

'I might never return. And even if I do, it might be years from now.'

'It might be . . . It might not. Either way there's not much we can do about it right now.' Lavinia gently took his hand. 'We haven't got long, so come with me.'

'What about them?' Cato nodded at the other slaves.

'They won't mind us.'

She pulled Cato through a pair of curtains into Titus's sleeping chamber and drew the curtains behind them. A soft pile of folded materials had been neatly arranged over the floorboards, and Lavinia gently pushed Cato down on to his back. As he lay still, heart pounding, his eyes travelled down her body to where her hands were lifting the hem of her tunic.

'Now then,' said Lavinia, 'where were we?'

Chapter Thirty-two

A few days later, the cohorts of the three mutinous legions were gathered in the turf amphitheatre that had been built outside the camp. They were guests of Plautius and Narcissus, who had paid for a day's gladiatorial entertainment in the name of the Emperor, and sat with Vespasian and other senior officers in the comfort of the box. Throughout the morning and into the afternoon a lavish display of beasts and men shed their blood on the sand in the arena. The men's enjoyment had been lubricated by a generous issue of wine and a cheerfully boisterous mood filled the amphitheatre as the spectacle drew to a close.

Down on the sand, the last gladiatorial fight reached its inevitable conclusion. As usual, the Retarius had had the best of it and now stood over his victim, trident poised at the throat of the heavily armoured Mirmillo helplessly enmeshed in his net. The Retarius looked towards the audience for a decision. Against the odds, the Mirmillo had put on a decent show and all around the arena thumbs were raised to have him spared. After the briefest hesitation, Narcissus turned his thumb down. The men instantly roared out their disapproval and surged towards the box where the senior officers were sitting. Right on cue, Plautius jumped to his feet and raised his arm high for all to see, thumb up. The howls of outrage abruptly turned into cheers of approval and the crowd turned back to the arena where Narcissus was alarmed to see the Retarius already taking a bow. The fool! If the legionaries got the slightest inkling the thing had been set up . . . but far too much wine had flowed and all but the sharpest minds were dulled to the elaborate performance that was being enacted before them.

Narcissus suddenly rose to his feet and, without any warning, jumped over the edge of the box. Making his way to the centre of the arena, he raised his hands for silence.

The legionaries had not been expecting this and quickly fell silent, waiting with curious expectation, still in high spirits. A few were whispering, but were hushed by their comrades as Narcissus waited for absolute quiet.

When all was still Narcissus raised his arm in a dramatic gesture.

'My friends! Romans! Legionaries! Hear me!' he called out in a deep rolling voice. 'You all know me. I am the Emperor's secretary and, while I do not speak in Claudius's place and am only a freedman, I count myself as being as Roman as any of you.'

A small murmur of disapproval rippled through the audience as Narcissus blatantly assumed the mantle of Rome and ignored the sensitive distinction between Roman citizen and mere freedman.

'I say again, my heart is as Roman as any man's here!' At this, he ripped his tunic open and bared his thin white chest to the audience. A few could not help but titter at the sight. 'And because I am Roman in all but name I come here to say to you that I, Narcissus, am sickened by what I see. That men who I count as fellow Romans should rise in mutiny against the heroic generals of Rome, who you are privileged to serve and to whom you should be honoured to lay down your lives for, chills my blood to ice! That a great man, from one of our greatest families – Aulus Plautius!' Narcissus thrust his hand out towards the general. 'That he should suffer the shame and ignominy of your treacherous mutiny makes me weep!'

Narcissus half turned and buried his face in a fold of his tunic while huge sobs wracked his body. Some of the men were laughing openly now at the freedman's histrionics.

Narcissus took a deep breath and swooped round to face his audience, tears streaming down his face. 'COWARDS! Ungrateful cowards who dare call yourselves Romans! If you shall not follow the brave and honoured Plautius then lend your arms to a man who will! I shall invade Britain! Alone, if I must. So lend me your arms!'

The imperial secretary held out his hands imploring the audience to give him their weapons.

'All right, you old bastard, have this!' A legionary stood and tossed his sword at Narcissus, who ducked back in alarm. Then all at once others followed suit and swords and daggers rained down on to the arena, as Narcissus dived backwards for his own safety, accidentally stepping on the hem of his torn tunic and rolling over backwards. The legionaries roared with laughter.

Vespasian smiled and then forced himself not to laugh as the imperial secretary went down again. His face burning with embarrassment and anger, Narcissus jumped to his feet and snatched up one of the swords.

'Laugh at me? You dare to laugh at me? I'm the one who's prepared to fight. I'm not sitting on my fat arse doing nothing. I'm the only one here worthy to carry the sword and glorious eagles against the barbarian hordes!'

Some of the men were crying with laughter at the ludicrous spectacle, and Narcissus rushed to the front of the stage and swung his sword at them, totally misjudging the swing. He spun round and the sword dug into the sand at his feet. Panting, he struggled to regain his wind.

'Weak, am I, from a lifetime serving Rome, and yet I would do what you are afraid to, and you call yourselves Romans! Why should I beg you to go back to your officers? Why should I even ask? No – I order you to end this mutiny. I command it!'

This was too much for the troops, who hooted with laughter and, from somewhere in the crowd, a voice called out, 'Ho Saturnalia! Ho Saturnalia!' The cry of the public holiday when social ranks were reversed was taken up by others, and spread quickly until all of them chorused, 'Ho Saturnalia!' and pelted the arena with whatever refuse was to hand. With a last shake of his fist and some inaudible cry of defiance, Narcissus turned and ran from the arena.

For some time the legionaries still shouted 'Ho Saturnalia' until it was clear that Narcissus had left the stage for good. Then slowly the men dispersed, trickling, then streaming, out of the amphitheatre and back towards the main camp.

'Well, I hope it's worked,' said Plautius.

'A fascinating team-building exercise,' Vespasian reflected. 'It'll be interesting to see if Narcissus has managed to shame them back to their duties. Can you imagine how the rest of the army will react when word gets out that a freedman has spoken to them like that? Now, if you'll excuse me, sir?'

'What? Oh, all right. Whatever you will. I need a drink.'

Vespasian left his superior and hurried down to the holding cells at the side of the amphitheatre.

'Anyone seen the imperial secretary?'

'Here I am.' A voice piped up and Narcissus emerged from the dark recesses. 'Safe to come out?'

'Only just!' laughed Vespasian. 'That was quite a performance.'

'Thank you.'

'I'm just curious. Is there no indignity you wouldn't suffer to further your cause?'

'My cause? That humiliation you just witnessed wasn't for me. I did it for the Emperor and Rome. One day you'll learn, Vespasian,' Narcissus continued bitterly. 'One day you'll realise that the only thing that keeps any state running is the number of bureaucrats who are prepared to eat shit to keep it going. That's the measure of their commitment. And the fact that they are never mentioned by historians is the measure of their success. You'd do well to remember that.'

'Oh, I will. But what made you think of trying that strategy?'

'It's a cynical age,' Narcissus replied. 'A direct appeal for patriotism was bound to fail, so a different approach was needed. I just pray to the Gods that it's enough. Do you think it'll work?'

'We'll have to wait and see.'

'Yes. Can I take shelter in your camp tonight?'

'No-one else will have you,' said Vespasian with a grin. 'Do you want an escort back to the camp?'

'I need to have a word with someone first. There's still a little matter that needs sorting out. See you later.'

The imperial chief secretary threw a military tunic over his torn clothes, then scuttled off back towards the main army camp. Vespasian returned to his headquarters and passed the word for Macro to be brought to him.

Shortly afterwards a hastily spruced-up centurion was standing to attention in front of the legate's desk.

'Centurion Macro, in view of your proven fighting qualities and discretion over that escort business, the imperial chief secretary and I have got a little job for you once we land in Britain . . .'

The festival atmosphere deriving from the afternoon's events in the amphitheatre lasted well into the night until the riotous soldiers had drunk the army base dry and returned to their quarters to sleep it off. Those too drunk to stand found themselves a quiet corner and slumped down. And so, in the dark hours before dawn, few were around to witness what followed.

A small detail of centurions, led by Vitellius and Pulcher, accompanied a wagon as they made their way through the base arresting men named on a list supplied by Narcissus. Most of the victims were veterans who had joined the eagles in the last years of Augustus's reign and despised the moral decline that had followed when first Tiberius, and then Caligula, became Emperor. Most were too drunk or tired to put up a fight as they were dragged out of their tents. Pulcher saw to it that they were securely bound before being thrown into the back of a wagon. When one of the more alert tried to shout for help, Pulcher promptly cut his throat and threatened to do the same to the very next man who muttered a single word. And so, as the sky lightened in the east, the little procession silently passed through the gates of the camp and made for a distant forest where it halted in a clearing well beyond earshot of the slumbering legions.

While Vitellius went to report back to Narcissus, the bound men were rolled off the back of the wagon and dragged into a rough line. They knelt fearfully eyeing Pulcher as he slowly walked up and down, a dreadful smile fixed on his scarred face. Once the line was complete he casually drew his dagger.

'Right then, traitors, you've had your fun. Now it's my turn. I need names. I need to know who gives you your orders from Rome. Now, while I appreciate that most of you will not be in the know over this, frankly I don't care. If I get names – you live, if I don't – you die. That's all there is to it.'

Pulcher approached a grey-haired veteran at the end of the line.

'You're first. Names?'

The man pursed his lips and spat on Pulcher's feet. Without the slightest hesitation Pulcher grabbed a fistful of hair and yanked the man's head back. The dagger flashed across his throat and a sheet of crimson splashed on to the forest floor. Pulcher let go and the man collapsed, writhed a moment, and then was still.

'Okay, who's next?'

Shortly after dawn, Pulcher returned to the camp of the Second Legion to find Tribune Vitellius. He presented a list of names scratched on to a waxed tablet. Grim-faced, Vitellius ran his finger down the list – there were few surprises – until his finger stopped abruptly.

'Are you sure about this last one?' he asked sharply.

'That's what the man said.'

'That explains how the opposition got to know about Narcissus's visit so speedily. Who gave you this name?'

'Aurelius, senior tribune of the Ninth. He's well connected in Rome.'

'I know that, thank you,' Vitellius replied testily. 'I don't suppose there's any chance of having a word with Tribune Aurelius?'

Pulcher shook his head. 'You said they were to disappear. I've been my usual thorough self, I'm afraid.'

'That's a pity. I would have liked to confirm this name myself. But we'll just have to accept that Aurelius's information is accurate.'

'Should we tell Narcissus?'

'No, I don't think so. Not just yet at any rate.'

'Right. I'd better get back to the woods then. Need to arrange a bit of digging.'

As the mid-morning sun shed its warm glow on the sentries at the main gates of the camp, a wagon emerged from the treeline of the immense forest that stretched inland from the coast. It was escorted by a party of grim-faced centurions, with Pulcher whistling contentedly in the driver's seat. As the wagon passed into the base the sentries saw that it carried just a few picks and shovels – and a dark stain smeared across its wooden boards.

Chapter Thirty-three

The late afternoon sun slanted across the deck, sliced by the shadows of the mast and rigging of the army transport. In the bows, a sailor was casting a weighted line out ahead of the vessel and reading off the depth as the line touched bottom. The ship eased its way through the entrance of the channel as the captain ordered two more reefs to be put in the sail. While the sailors climbed aloft and spread out along the yardarm, Cato gingerly made his way forward to the base of the stubby bowsprit.

As soon as the transport had drawn out of the port at Gesoriacum and met the gentle swell of the channel a wave of seasickness had engulfed him. Cato had joined several other men at the side of the ship as they spewed their guts up into the foaming sea sweeping past the gently rolling vessel. Macro took the opportunity to munch his way through several pastries he had bought from the harbour market shortly before boarding. He couldn't resist offering the last one to his optio and burst out laughing at the look of pure evil that answered his gesture.

As soon as the transport entered the sheltered waters of the anchorage, Cato felt the terrible nausea subside and, with one hand on the stay, he gazed out over the channel where the invasion fleet lay at anchor. Hundreds of vessels crowded the shimmering surface of the sea; sleek warships with their high crenellated towers rising above the banks of oars lining each side, wide troop transports with shallow drafts wallowing close by the shore and hundreds of smaller craft ferrying in supplies and equipment from Gaul.

The legionaries crowded the sides of the transport to get a better view and were pushed and cursed by the sailors, who still had to handle the vessel as it slowly made its way towards the mainland under a slight breeze. The mysterious fog-ridden island of Britain, so long a part of Roman folklore, lay revealed as a dull coastline basking in the heat of a clear midsummer's day. Excitement was therefore tinged with a sense of disappointment at the gently rolling landscape of farms, fields and forest that stretched away into the distant haze. Here and there, small columns of legionaries spread out across the country while far off the faint dust cloud of the rearguard marked where the main body of the first two legions had pressed ahead inland.

During the last two days the men had heard only the sketchiest details of the progress of the invasion. The crew of the transport who had returned for the second division of the army could only report that the first two legions had managed to land unopposed. As Cato could see, there were no signs of heavy fighting, no funeral pyres of fallen comrades, no bodies of the enemy – in fact no sign of the natives whatsoever. It was hard to believe. Caesar's account made great play of the hazards of invading Britain and recorded that the first landing had been bitterly opposed by an enemy who met the Romans on the beach and almost fought them to a bloody standstill in the pounding surf. This, on the other hand, looked almost identical to the last amphibious exercise with which Plautius had engaged the army on the coast of Gaul barely two weeks earlier: Plenty of Romans but a non-existent enemy.

With a shout from the captain, the transport altered course. The great sail was hauled round at an angle to the deck and the bows swung in from the centre of the channel. The bows steadied on a gap in the lines of shipping close to the shore that had been marked out with large red pennants which lifted lazily in the dying breeze. A number of transports carrying elements of the Second Legion had already landed and Cato could see a group of horsemen riding up the beach and into the flattened grass beyond. That would be Vespasian and his command party rushing ahead to mark out the area where the Legion would assemble for the night before moving off in the wake of the Twentieth and the Ninth Legions.

Except that he would not be marching with them, Cato reflected with a sudden tremor of excitement and fear. While the rest of the Legion marched to meet the enemy, he would be with a small detachment under Macro's command carrying out a special duty. As yet the centurion had not confided the details of the mission and sat apart from his men, at the stern of the vessel staring down into the heavily silted sea. As Cato looked aft, Macro spat into the water and turned forward, immediately catching the eye of his subordinate. He paused a moment, then made his way towards the bows through the tightly packed mass of legionaries in the waist of the transport.

'Not so terrifying after all, is it?' He waved a hand at the shore.

'No, sir,' Cato replied. 'Quite pleasant, really. Looks like it'll make decent farm land once we've settled on it.'

'And what could a palace boy possibly know about horticulture?'

'Not much,' admitted Cato. 'Only what I've read of it from Virgil. He makes farming sound quite fascinating.'

'Quite fascinating,' mimicked Macro. 'Real farming's a hard life – there's no poetry in it. Only townie tossers paying the odd visit to their estates could make it sound good.'

Macro immediately regretted his harsh response and smiled as he patted his optio on the arm. 'I'm sorry, that was uncalled for. It's just that I've got things on my mind right now.'

'What things, sir?'

'Things that concern ranks higher than yours. I'm sorry, Cato, I can't say anything until we're well away from the Legion. Those are my orders.'

'Orders from whom, I wonder,' Cato said quietly. 'Our commander – or Narcissus, perhaps?'

'No use fishing for information – I can't tell you. Just be patient. I'd have thought at least the army would have taught you that by now.'

Cato frowned and turned to look at the approaching fortifications that rose above the beach and the surrounding land.

When Vespasian had issued his orders he had placed great emphasis on the need for utmost secrecy. Of the eleven men Macro had selected for the mission Cato alone had been told about it, and even the optio knew only that he had been selected for a dangerous detached duty. As Macro gazed at the slowly approaching shoreline he recalled the previous evening in Vespasian's tent. The legate had regarded him by the dim light of an oil lamp, as rain pattered on the canvas overhead.

'You will, of course, need a cart for the return journey.'

'Yes, sir.'

'So make sure you draw one from the transport pool – I'll have a clerk make up the necessary orders.' Vespasian drained his cup and carefully contemplated the centurion. 'I trust you appreciate the importance of this mission?'

'Yes, sir. With that kind of money you need someone you can trust, sir.'

'Quite.' Vespasian nodded. 'But there's more to it than that. The Emperor desperately needs every scrap of gold and silver that he can find. The only thing that's keeping him in power at the moment is the support of the army, and more importantly those greedy bastards in the Praetorian guard. Claudius will last only for as long as the donatives flow to the troops. Understand?'

'Yes, sir.'

'So it's vital we recover the chest, and' – Vespasian continued with added emphasis – 'the men you select for the job must know *nothing*. It is likely that the Emperor's enemies have already got wind of this and we dare not show our own hand too openly. If one word of this leaks out to the wrong set of ears, you won't be the only ones after the chest. You have to locate it first. I think you'll find that you have enough danger to face from the natives without worrying about your own side.'

'May I ask exactly who I have to worry about, sir?'

Vespasian shook his head. 'I suspect a few of our comrades-in-arms, but right now I have no evidence.'

'I see.' Macro could see all right. He could see that this mission had an additional agenda: to expose those members of the Legion who might constitute a threat to the Emperor – even if that meant staking Macro and his men out as bait. 'And what happens when—'

'If.'

'If we come across these people? What happens then, sir?'

'Then you prove to me that I've selected the right man for the job. You succeed, in either task, and I promise you that you will not find me, or the Emperor, ungrateful.'

Macro allowed the corners of his mouth to lift in appreciation. A desperately dangerous mission then, but one that should pay off well if it went according to the simple plan Vespasian had outlined. Too simple, Macro reflected.

He was to lead a small party of men and a cart south to the marshes, way beyond the protection of the main army. All contact with natives and Roman army scouts was to be avoided. Once at the marshes he was to use the map Vespasian had provided him with to locate the remains of a wagon sunk in a bog almost a hundred years earlier. Having located the wagon, the detachment was to retrieve a chest and load it aboard the cart for the return journey to the Legion where it was to be handed over to the legate in person. Under no circumstances was the chest to be opened. The sight of the treasure that lay within might well corrupt the minds of the common legionary. And if the inevitable curiosity of his men was not enough to contend with, then there was the prospect of having to fight his way through enemy territory against both the natives and men supposedly on his own side who were playing a deep political game.

'Is there anything else you need to know, Centurion?'

'One thing, sir. What happens if we fail to locate this wagon?'

'Don't even think about it,' Vespasian said simply.

'I see.' Macro nodded.

The legate was glad that he didn't see. Should the mission fail, then the chest would remain in the marsh, waiting for someone else to find it. There was no guarantee that the original map Narcissus had supplied him with was the only one, and now that he had entrusted the centurion with a copy there was no guarantee that further copies would not be made. If the mission failed, then it would be very inconvenient to have a handful of soldiers around with even the slightest inkling of what lurked in the marshes. But that contingency was taken care of.

'If that's all, Centurion?' Vespasian asked, and Macro nodded. 'Then you had better go and prepare your men. We shan't speak again until you return to the legion with the chest.'

'Yes, sir.'

'Good luck. And goodbye.'

Once Macro was out of the tent he carefully folded the map and tucked it inside his harness, more than a little uneasy about the tone of finality with which he had been dismissed by the legate. But the mission was now in motion and there was no turning back.

The transport's captain shouted to the crew to let go the sheets and the remaining sail was gathered in. The vessel had just enough way on her to glide forward and a slight tremor could be felt through the deck as she grounded a short distance from the beach.

From the stern the captain cupped his hands and shouted. 'Landing ramp out!'

The legionaries gave way as the crewmen lifted a long, hinged ramp and ran it forward, well beyond its fulcrum, until the end was only a few feet from the shore. A seaman gave the signal and the ramp was allowed to fall with a messy splash into the sea. The rear of the ramp was then pegged into place with two iron rods driven through the ramp into sockets on the deck.

'There you are!' The captain clapped Macro on the shoulder. 'Safely delivered across the ocean by yours truly. Hope you enjoyed the voyage.'

'It was all right,' Macro replied without enthusiasm. Like most soldiers, he thought that land was the proper place for men, and the sea was for fish and any idiots who cared to traverse it. 'But thanks.'

'My pleasure. Just make sure you give the natives a good kicking.'

'We'll do our best.'

'Now I'd be grateful if you'd get your men off my ship. We're returning to Gaul straight away. Some horses to bring over for a Syrian cohort tonight.'

'Tonight?' Macro was surprised. 'I thought you sailors never went to sea at night if you could help it.'

'Normally, no.' The captain smiled affably. 'But we're being paid by the trip and there's money to be made. So, if you wouldn't mind?'

Macro faced forward towards the expectant eyes of his men. 'Okay, lads, off you get. Make sure you don't leave anything on board or you won't see it again.'

In single file the legionaries picked their way down the boarding ramp and, lifting their equipment clear of the sea, they jumped into the waist-deep water and surged on to the beach. By the time Macro and Cato had reached the line of shingle along the high-water mark, the ramp was already being stowed as a team of seamen strained on a long thick pole to push the transport free.

'What's the hurry?' Cato nodded at the ship.

'Money.'

'What men won't do for it!' Cato laughed. 'You'd think there was nothing more important in this world.'

'There isn't.'

The hard-edged expression on his centurion's face caught Cato by surprise and, as Macro turned to call the century to order, Cato stared at him. The man was understandably tense, as every officer had been, even after the mutiny slowly crumbled. Word of Narcissus's extraordinary performance quickly spread through the legions causing great hilarity whenever impromptu renditions of the bureaucrat's bravado were performed. As the wily freedman had intended, the joke could be shared by one and all and the atmosphere of mistrust and betrayal soon evaporated in the mysterious absence of Tribune Aurelius and his associates. Plautius had further soothed the situation by having the retinue of exiled British chiefs and princes let slip tales of the great wealth to be found in Britain; gold, silver, slaves – and women, just begging to be taken from the arms of a handful of benighted savages who insisted on fighting in the altogether. Their fearful appearance – painted bodies and hair stiffened into wild spikes of white – and the endless shouting all counted for little in the thick of battle. The great warriors of the legions would sweep them aside with ease and seize the fruits of victory. A firm resolve to do what legionaries do best gripped the army in the last few weeks of preparation for the invasion.

It was well after dark when the final tent had been raised and the men of the century settled down to a light supper of barley gruel and coarse loaves of bread prepared in Gaul and already stale. Around the campfires the talk was about the progress of the campaign, based on snatches of information gleaned from messengers and forward-supply orderlies returning from the front. As yet the only contact with the enemy had been a handful of skirmishes between scouts and, from all accounts, the native charioteers had so far bested the Roman cavalry. The old hands of the Legion grumpily told the new recruits that it would be a completely different story once the heavy infantry of the Romans managed to close with the Britons.

Inside the centurion's tent, Macro quietly addressed the men he had picked for Vespasian's mission. In addition to Cato, he had selected the best ten legionaries of his century for the task. They sat on the grass as he outlined the special duty they had been selected to perform.

'As some of you may have observed, our legion has been honoured by the presence of a number of the local royalty, who have been taking advantage of Roman hospitality in recent years due to some misunderstandings with their subjects.'

The men grinned at this description of the Emperor's clients. It was the same throughout the Empire; the local people threw out their despots, who fled to Rome to plead their cause, only to discover that Rome granted asylum at a high price – perpetual obedience.

'As it happens,' continued Macro, 'one of our friends – Cogidubnus by name – had been a little indiscreet in his earlier years when he first approached Rome to discuss a treaty. Apparently he was so impressed by what he saw that he pledged to completely surrender his nation to the Emperor should the Empire extend to Britain. Well, as you can see, it now has. But Cogidubnus seems to have forgotten his earlier good intentions and is holding out for an improved deal from Rome. Unfortunately for him, when he was thrown out by his people, the wagon carrying his personal papers managed to get lost in a marsh near here. Luckily, the general's spies have found out where that wagon is and it's our job to recover his personal document chests and bring them back to the safety of the Legion. Once Plautius has a record of the man's earlier promises to sell his people out to Rome he will be able to hold Cogidubnus to his word – if he gives us any problems we can threaten to let his people see precisely what he thinks of them. A neat double bind, I'm sure you'll agree.'

Macro paused, quite pleased with himself for making this complete fabrication sound so plausible. 'But first we have to retrieve those documents. And that's where we come in. The twelve of us have been detached from the legion to recover the chest.'

'Sir!' One of the legionaries raised a hand.

'Yes?'

'Is someone really expecting us to go wandering off right in the middle of hostile territory. Twelve men alone?' The soldier spat contemptuously on to the ground. 'It's nothing short of suicide.'

'Let's hope it's something short of that.' Macro smiled reassuringly. 'Vespasian said that the scouts have found very little sign of resistance since the first two legions landed. We should be all right if it's a quick job. No more than a couple of days.'

'When do we leave, sir?'

'Tonight. As soon as the moon rises.'

Chapter Thirty-four

A damp clinging mist rose from the ground during the night and, by the time the second watch was sounded, a thin veil of white cloaked the ground. The watery red smudges of campfires silhouetted the forms of Vitellius and his bodyguard, Pulcher. The tribune handed Macro a small tablet.

'There's your authorisation. It's countersigned by the general so you won't have any trouble with our pickets, though I doubt this will hold much sway over any Britons you may encounter.'

Macro did not smile as he tucked the tablet inside his knapsack. Bloody typical of a staff officer to make fun of men he might well be sending to their deaths.

'Well then, Centurion, I trust you will succeed in your mission – whatever it may be.'

Macro nodded.

'Good luck.'

Macro saluted and turned back to the still shapes of his men waiting like shadows in the ghostly mist. The rearmost man was hissing abuse at the pair of mules detailed to pull the cart. Disturbed from a well-deserved rest after a traumatic day at sea, the mules were not on their best behaviour and their long ears twitched nervously as steamy breath plumed from their nostrils. Macro gave the signal to move off and the driver tapped the lead mule on the rump with a javelin butt. With a grunt, both beasts strained against their harnesses. The cart had been stripped bare of any loose attachments and the axles thoroughly greased so that the only sound came from the soft crunching of the ground under the wheels. The mist further deadened the sounds of the night and to the men of the detachment the swishing of their footsteps through long wet grass seemed abnormally loud. Behind them, the fires of the Second Legion faded into nothingness and before long theirs were the only man-made sounds to break the night.

For Cato, born and raised in the world's greatest city, the quiet was dreadfully oppressive: his keen imagination magnified every owl hoot or faint rustle of grass into a deadly Briton silently stalking the Romans until the moment was ripe for the kill. He marched behind his centurion and, not for the first time, envied the way Macro strode about his business with a confident air of invulnerability – which was ironic, given the number of scars that he bore.

Macro's little column marched on, quietly calling out the required password when they were challenged by a sentry on the picket lines who looked curiously at the looming bulk of the cart gently rumbling along behind. Then the strange patrol was abruptly lost in the clammy fog, and very quickly even the sounds of the cart were swallowed up.

★　★　★

It was only when the picket came to be relieved that word of the strange detachment filtered back to headquarters. Vespasian was confronted by a puzzled senior watch officer who wanted confirmation that Macro was acting under orders.

'Twelve men and a cart, you say?' Vespasian asked irritably – since there was a more pressing matter that needed immediate attention.

'Yes, sir.'

'That's very strange. Doesn't sound like a reconnaissance patrol to me.'

'No, sir. That's what I thought.' The watch officer nodded. 'Want me to send a cavalry patrol after them?'

'No point. Anyway we can't spare the men right now. The scouts have lost contact with one of the British columns – we need every cavalryman we've got to track them down.'

'I see. So what should I do, sir?'

'Enter them in the watch log, of course. Until we know otherwise, I think it's best that we regard them as deserters.'

'Deserters?' The watch officer almost laughed at the ridiculousness of the idea. 'But they'll be cut down by the very first Britons they come across, sir.'

The cold eyes of the legate warned him against uttering another word.

'Deserters is what I said. And if they're caught then I want them brought straight to me. They're not to be seen or spoken to by anyone.'

'Yes, sir.'

Once the watch officer had left, Vespasian frowned.

He felt guilty about branding Macro and his men as deserters. But if they failed to complete their mission they would have to be silenced to prevent any word of the wagon's existence reaching other ears. The legate tried not to give the centurion and his mission any further thought. At present, the movements of the British were a source of considerably more worry. As soon as the invasion force had landed Plautius had sent out his cavalry scouts to locate the natives' army and keep him supplied with precise information on its size and movements. But the dense fog of last night and the lingering mist at dawn had allowed a large British force of chariots and infantry, some nine or ten thousand, to slip away from the Roman scouts and the army's cavalry commander had been desperately struggling to re-establish contact throughout the night. Word had just come to Vespasian that the missing column was believed to be under Togodumnus – brother of Caratacus, the leader of the British forces, and no fool, if the British émigrés accompanying the Roman army were to be believed.

A shaft of orange light fell across the papers in front of him and Vespasian looked up to see that the rising sun had found a chink in the tent. It was going to be a difficult day but, once he found time, someone was going to answer for the shoddy way the tent had been erected.

As the distant skyline lightened with the coming of dawn, Macro softly ordered a halt and the men slumped down along the side of the track. The night march had taken a heavy toll on their nerves and the men were glad to see the darkness beginning to dissolve into the glow of the coming sunrise. After leaving the pickets behind, they had twice had to hurry from the track at the sound of approaching horses, but none could tell whether it had been Roman or British scouts passing as the hooves thundered by in the darkness. For the rest of the night they had marched along the track as quietly as they might, fully expecting to be attacked at any moment. The first shafts of orange light fell upon Cato's worn expression as he chewed on a strip of dried pork. He turned to Macro.

'Much further to go, sir?'

'Should be there by nightfall. See there.' He pointed out across the rolling countryside into the distance where a low, flat expanse still lay underneath a blanket of fog, save for the odd hummock of land that rose like an island from a sea of milk. 'That's where the marsh begins.'

'And how are we supposed to find the wagon amongst that lot, sir?'

'We follow this track, until we find a depression in the track where it enters a small copse. The wagon's hidden in the marsh by a burned-out oak stump. Shouldn't be too difficult to locate.'

Looking down the track to the point where it finally disappeared into the bank of fog, Cato somehow doubted that the search would be as easily resolved as that. The distant marsh waited for them with a cold, sleepy inertia that filled Cato with sudden superstitious fear. This was the vision of the underworld that he heard of as a child on his father's knee. Wraith-like shadows curled about the darker shapes of dimly seen trees as the thinning mist shifted on the lightest of airs.

Macro stared intently down the track and then quickly scanned the surrounding countryside for any signs of movement. To the left, the land rolled gently away and in the distance the sea shimmered, off to the right the sparsely cleared farmland gave way to a distant forest. Nothing moved. The Britons had made sure that all farm animals had been swept from the invader's path and every store of grain had been torched. Well then, Macro decided, it was safe to move. He stood up.

'On your feet, you idle buggers. There's work to do.'

Rising wearily from the grass the men formed up. The centurion strode off down the track and his men followed, tired and tense. The track sloped down towards the marsh and the mules had to be tightly reined in to prevent the cart from gathering speed. At the edge of the marsh, the track narrowed so that the cart's wheels crushed the grass on either side. The ground beneath was soft and Cato could feel it give slightly under his boots as the little column moved into the mist. In a short space of time the vistas of the British countryside had vanished and an indefinite white horizon hemmed them in on all sides. At their backs, the sun struggled to make itself felt through the dense haze and the air was cold and clammy on their skin. No-one spoke and the only sounds were the snorts of the mules as they hauled their burden through the soft peat sucking at the cart's wheels.

The narrow track wound its way through the marsh. Where the ground was too soft for vehicles to negotiate, a thin corduroy road of logs had been laid down and covered with shingle. With annoying regularity, first one wheel of the cart, and then the other, stuck in the black oozing muck on each side of the path. The legionaries had to down spears and shields to lay their shoulders to the thick wooden spokes and strain every sinew to break the cart free and roll it back astride the track. Soon the men were covered in foul-smelling mud and desperately tired. Macro allowed them a short break and they hunched down miserably on a small mossy hummock surrounded by a dank expanse of shallow water. From the angle of the pale yellow disc hovering over the mist Macro realised that it was nearly midday, yet looking at the exhausted men slumped around him he knew that he could not march them much further and still expect them to dig out the wagon once it had been found. It should be near now, if the directions he had been given were accurate.

A sudden lightness in the air caused him to look up and he saw that the sun was at last making an impact on the mist. Patches of brightness began to break up the white swirls, and here and there the air cleared for two or three hundred paces.

'Cato!'

'Sir?'

'Get up on that mound over there. See if you can spot that tree trunk.' He indicated a mossy lump beside the track and Cato rose reluctantly. Tentatively placing a foot on the soft green surface, he tested it to make sure it would bear his weight.

'Don't fuck about lad!' Macro said irritably. 'Get up.'

With arms stretched out to break his fall Cato tensed his knees and slowly straightened up. The surface beneath the moss was surprisingly firm and he stood erect and stared at the haunting landscape about them. Ahead the track wound down a small slope and all but disappeared into a particularly foul black morass. Even at first glance it was clear that the cart had come as far as it could along the track. Macro wasn't going to like that.

'See anything that looks like our trunk?'

'No, sir.'

'What about that, over there?' Macro pointed to where a gap had opened in the mist to reveal several dead trees, starkly black and crooked against the thick white backdrop.

'I'm not sure, sir.'

'Well look bloody harder then!'

Cato squinted his tired eyes, but it was difficult to make out much detail and the mist was closing in around the dead trees once again. Instinctively he leaned forwards to try and see better. With a muffled crunch the moss suddenly gave way beneath him and Cato pitched headlong on to the track, arms outstretched. He came down hard and the breath was momentarily knocked out of him.

'All right?' Macro leaned over to help him back on to his feet.

'Yes, sir.'

'You know, Cato,' Macro smiled, 'I've met some clumsy soldiers in my time, but you . . .'

'It wasn't me, sir! Bloody ground just gave way.'

'I see.' Macro turned to look at the place Cato had fallen from. A large section of moss had collapsed to reveal a crumbling round mass of decayed vegetation.

'There, sir. See?' a piqued Cato protested. 'The whole thing's rotten.'

He fell silent for a second, and then curiously pulled a clump of moss away, and then another, tossing them excitedly to one side.

Macro smiled. 'No need to take it so personally.'

Cato ignored him and continued to clear the moss away until, a few moments later, the rotten remains of a tree stump became visible. He stood up and quickly glanced around; there were several other similar mounds covered in moss on either side of the track. He hurried over to the nearest and kicked the moss away to reveal the remains of another ancient tree stump, then looked up at Macro with a grin.

'What on earth?' The centurion was startled by the young man's actions, which were eccentric even by his normal standards of behaviour.

'Sir! Don't you see?'

'I see you've finally gone mad.'

'They're tree stumps, sir! Tree stumps!'

Cato paused, waiting for his comments to provoke a reaction, a wide grin splitting his mud-spattered face. For all the world, Macro could not help feeling a pang of paternal affection. Cato looked like a little boy – it was impossible to be angry with him.

'Tree stumps?' Macro replied instead. 'Yes, well, I can see that they're tree stumps. Probably been cut down for use on the track.'

'Exactly, sir! Exactly. Cut down. How many of them would you say?'

Macro looked around. 'Ten, twelve or so.'

'Do you think that ten or twelve trees might be enough to constitute a copse?'

Macro stared at him and a familiar cold tingle traced its way down the back of his neck. 'Everyone on their feet!'

The legionaries, tired and filthy, could have looked even less excited had they put their minds to it, but rose to their feet nonetheless.

'The optio thinks we're at the right spot. Start looking for the remains of the cart off the side of the track.'

The legionaries looked at the dull, gloomy morass surrounding them, and then back to their centurion as if waiting for more helpful directions.

'Well, get on with it!' Macro said firmly. 'It's not going to bloody well find itself!'

Without waiting for the others, the centurion started attacking the nearest mound of moss at the side of the track, wrenching away handfuls of the moist growth and hurling them to one side. The others reluctantly followed suit and soon the pleasant little hummock of grass was well on the way to utter ruin. Clods of moss and earth flew through the air and yet more filth adhered to the legionaries as they struggled to unearth any sign of the lost wagon. The sun slowly declined from its midday position with little further effect on the mist that clung to the vast expanse of marsh. The legionaries had found nothing and one by one they sat down and surveyed the dark brown debris of peat and rotten wood that was all they had to show for their exertions. Macro let them stop without a word and squatted down on his heels, fixing Cato with an accusing stare.

'I only said it might be the place we're looking for,' Cato said guiltily. 'I mean, it seemed a reasonable guess, given the way things are going.'

'Guess?' Pyrax muttered angrily. 'You seemed pretty damn sure of yourself earlier on!'

'Maybe it was a mistake.' Cato shrugged. 'But where else can the wagon have gone? From the look of the track up ahead there's no way it can have gone any further than this, and how many other trees have we passed? None. It has to be close by.'

'Where then?' Macro swept his arm round at the excavations. 'We've looked.'

'Well, we just haven't found it yet.'

'Fuck this!' Pyrax stood up angrily. 'Look, Centurion, the wagon isn't here. Any fool can see that. Either we've missed it earlier on the track, or it was never here in the first place. Why don't we just get back to the Legion?'

The other legionaries grumbled in support.

Macro looked down between his feet and thought for a moment before he rose stiffly. 'No, not yet at least. The lad's right. If it is anywhere then it has to be here. We'll have a rest and then have another dig. If we find nothing by dusk we'll head back.'

Pyrax swore and spat at Cato's feet. His fist clenched.

'That's my decision, Pyrax,' Macro intervened firmly. 'Now back down and have a rest. That's an order. Understand me?'

Pyrax remained silent, glaring coldly at the optio. Then he turned towards Macro for a moment and nodded.

'I asked if you understood me?'

'Yes, sir!'

'Good. Now sit down.'

With a last glare at the optio, Pyrax turned away and slumped down with the other legionaries who all looked angrily at Cato.

It was more than the young optio could bear for the moment and he wandered down to the edge of the swamp to escape the immediate aura of hostility assaulting him from all sides. The remains of a sapling protruded out of the dark surface at the edge of the hummock and hung at an angle towards the track. With a deep sigh of frustration Cato leaned back against the sapling, firmly intending to empty his mind of immediate concerns and take in the view, such as it was. The moment the mass of his weight fetched up against the sapling it gave way with a loud creak and fell down on to the grass bank of the hummock. For a moment Cato felt himself toppling forwards for a second time, but a frantic windmill gesture kept him on his feet.

'Cato!' Macro shouted out. 'Oh, for fuck's sake! Can't you keep on your bloody feet for a little longer? I swear I have seen completely pissed sailors less clumsy than you.'

'Sorry, sir. I thought this tree could bear my weight.'

'Tree?' Macro asked, then looked down in the grass where Cato indicated. 'That's no bloody tree.'

He bent down and examined the long shaft of wood. Under the lichen, grime and scraps of moss the wood was far too smooth and regular for a sapling. At the end of the shaft he wiped away the dirt and exposed an iron cap. A little more work revealed a foot-long iron collar with two handles protruding on opposite sides of the shaft.

'Well, Cato,' he began, 'you may not be the most agile lad to have joined the legion, but your clumsiness has its moments. Do you know what this is?'

Cato shook his head, still a little bemused that his sapling had managed to sprout ironware.

'It's a wagon shaft end. And where there's a wagon shaft end it's reasonable to suppose that there might be a wagon. Let's see.'

Macro picked the shaft of wood up and raised it above his head, following its line down to where it disappeared in the marsh. He gave it an experimental tug, but even though the shaft rose up and down it was clearly fixed to something at its base. Macro let it drop back into the grass and turned to face the other legionaries who were watching him with weary curiosity.

'Last time then, lads! On your feet and get over here. Seems the optio was right after all. Not that I ever seriously doubted him.'

Were it not for the unreasonable fact that assaulting a superior officer was a capital offence, Cato would have hit him.

Chapter Thirty-five

Dusk was fast approaching and there was still no sign of Togodumnus's force. By now the cavalry scouts of three legions had been joined by two auxiliary cavalry cohorts and the surrounding country was being systematically swept for any trace of the Britons. Until they were found, the Second Legion would be highly vulnerable and Vespasian was loath to quit a fortified position while the location and strength of the enemy were still unknown. His imagination readily visualised the consequences of his men being attacked in force as they were strung out along the line of march. A determined attack, pushed through resolutely, could cripple the Second. That was why he had placed the scouting sweeps under the direct command of Vitellius. Even now, the tribune was somewhere out there in the British countryside with orders not to rest until Togodumnus was located.

Meanwhile, General Plautius was relentlessly pressing the enemy back and had sent messengers racing to the rear to call up the two fresh legions – the Second and the Fourteenth – and have them rush to the front to sustain the offensive's momentum. A swift crushing blow was required, he told his subordinates. If the four legions could catch the Britons before they managed to place a major river between themselves and the Romans, the resulting battle would surely see the destruction of the Britons' field army. After that, it would just be a question of picking off the odd hill fort and mopping up the surviving forces. The legate smiled bitterly as he had read that. What the general had not mentioned – perhaps had not anticipated – was the guerrilla war that would inevitably follow for many years before the new province could be considered pacified.

Vespasian wished that he could share the general's confidence in the smooth progress of the campaign. But orders were orders and Plautius wanted the Second Legion on the move at daybreak on the morrow. Vespasian could only assume that the general was aware of the risk.

As far as Vespasian could tell from the latest scout reports, the tracks leading west to the front were clear of the enemy and the land to the south had been searched as far as the marsh – which, his British émigrés had told him, was impassable for a force of any size as the old tracks had been abandoned for many years and were all but swallowed up by the bogs. That left the heavily wooded region to the north of the line of march; a rolling mass of trees and thickets criss-crossed by numerous tracks well known to the natives. If an attack came, it was sure to come from that quarter.

The sun was sinking into the rolling banks of mist by the time Macro and his men had cleared away enough of the slimy foul-smelling peat to reveal the bed of the wagon. The men were caked in mud that sucked at them as they struggled, waist deep. Finally they had discovered the chest they had been sent to retrieve. Once it was cleared of mud, Macro excitedly examined the heavy wooden box bound with iron. Aside from the inevitable staining and the dampness of the wood, the chest was in remarkably good condition and still fastened by a heavy lock. The other men, now that they had something to show for all their exertions, shared his excitement and eagerly helped drag the chest to more solid ground. It proved to be far heavier than they expected and nearly sank back into the mud several times before it was heaved on to the grass bank leading up to the track.

'Right, lads, there's no time to waste. We have to load it on to the cart and get back to the Legion.'

Cato looked up at the sky. 'It'll be dark soon. We won't make it back before nightfall, sir.'

'No. But we'll get out of this place at least.' Macro grasped one of the iron handles. 'Come on! Let's get on with it.'

The twelve men struggled around the chest and hauled it up the bank. Then, with a final back-breaking effort, accompanied by loud hisses of strain and exertion, the chest was pushed on to the back of the cart, which creaked under the load. The men leaned against its sides gasping for breath. Cato found himself shivering as his body was overtaken by a degree of tiredness he had never experienced before. His leg and arm muscles ached abominably and the strenuous labour of the previous hours had left him feeling sick. Looking at the faces of the other men he realised that they were all quite done in, and it would be as much as they could manage to haul the cart clear of the marsh by the time night fell.

Macro rested his arms across the top of the chest. He was tired, but elated that he had succeeded in his mission. Once the chest was in the legate's safe keeping, Macro could rest assured that he had at least one friend in high places who might smooth his path to further promotion. He had reached the pinnacle of a career based solely on competence and ability. Further advancement depended on a mix of guile, intelligence and personal connections. Macro knew himself well enough to be aware that he was somewhat lacking in the first two of these qualities; the third he had just taken care of. He patted the chest affectionately.

'Well done, Centurion!' a voice called out of the growing gloom of mist and dusk.

Macro snapped round, his hand going straight to the pommel of his sword. The other men were on their feet in an instant, alert, some with swords already drawn.

A vague shape slowly emerged from the mist and took the form of a Roman staff officer – Tribune Vitellius. Behind him several more figures materialised, men in Syrian garb leading horses. At sight of them, Cato felt a cold chill of recognition and slowly drew his own sword. And there, holding the bridle of the tribune's horse, stood Pulcher.

Vitellius walked up the track towards them and stopped ten paces from the cart.

'I take it that is the chest you were sent to retrieve?'

Macro was still recovering from the shock of the tribune's sudden appearance. He frowned with suspicion, but made no reply.

'Well, Centurion? Is that the chest?'

'Yes, sir. But what . . .'

'That's a job well done. I congratulate you and your men.'

'Thank you, sir—'

'And now I'll take charge of things. The chest needs to be returned to the legate as quickly as possible.' Vitellius turned his head back to the waiting horsemen. 'First two men – here!'

Vitellius walked over to the cart and patted the chest with a smile. 'You must be exhausted. I expect you'll be glad to be relieved of this. Get some rest before you follow us back to the Legion.'

Macro nodded while his mind worked quickly to frame his next words as carefully as possible. He could see the credit for his achievement slipping away. 'Sir, our orders were to hand the chest over to the legate in person.'

'I know. But the orders have been changed.'

'The legate was quite specific, sir. To him in person.'

'Are you questioning my authority, Centurion?' Vitellius asked coldly. 'I'm telling you that the orders have been changed. Now you will hand over the cart to my men, understand?'

Macro stared at him, eyes cold with bitter resentment that his superior was about to snatch the prize from his grasp.

'Tell your men to stay away from the cart, sir,' Macro said quietly.

'What?'

'Tell your men to back off. You're not taking the chest.'

'Centurion,' Vitellius tried to sound reasonable, 'there's nothing you or I can do about it. I'm obeying a direct order from Vespasian.'

'My orders come from Aulus Plautius,' Macro bluffed. 'We're not giving up the chest until I get different orders from the general, in person.'

Vitellius stared at him silently, and his men – sensing a confrontation unresolved – stopped short of the cart. Then Vitellius smiled and backed away a few paces as he spoke.

'Very well, Centurion. You keep the chest for the moment, but this isn't the last you'll hear of the matter – I swear it.'

He turned and beckoned his two men to follow as he retreated from the cart back towards the waiting horsemen. As he watched, Cato saw the tribune move to one side of the track, casually moving out of the line of sight between his men and the cart. A sudden movement from the figures in the mist caught Cato's attention and his eyes returned to the tribune. Vitellius had flicked the cape off his sword arm and was looking back towards the cart. Cato's eyes widened in sudden realisation of the danger.

'Down! Get down!'

He hurled himself at his centurion and they rolled on to the muddy track behind the cart. The other legionaries followed suit as a flight of arrows whistled through the air. One man reacted too slowly and, with a sickening thud, a dark feathered arrow buried itself in his throat. The legionary slumped to his knees, gurgling blood, as he desperately struggled to wrench the barb free from his neck. Two arrows from the second volley caught him in the face and chest and, with a cry he went down.

'Behind the cart!' Macro shouted. 'Get behind the cart!'

The legionaries crouched down in the filth behind the cart as further arrows landed around them. Two men were wounded and gasped in pain as they tried to wrestle the arrows free.

'Leave them!' Macro shouted, only too aware of the damage barbed arrows caused on extraction. If they lived, the arrow heads would have to be cut out by a surgeon.

If they lived.

The Syrians were already fanning out on either side of the track, as far as the marsh would allow, in order to minimise the effective shelter of the cart. The legionaries huddled tightly together. Most had left their shields down on the grass bank and only a couple had leaned them against the cart. Now these were hurriedly passed to the side to protect the men's flanks and deflect the arrows with a harsh clatter. Even so, arrows were finding their mark and another man had been wounded in the leg.

'What the hell are they doing?' Pyrax asked. 'They're on our fucking side.'

'Apparently not,' replied Cato. 'Whatever's in that chest must be bloody priceless.'

'How many of them are there?' Macro asked. 'Did anyone see?'

'I counted eight,' Cato replied. 'Vitellius, Pulcher and six Syrians.'

'Then we're even. If we try and rush them.'

'Rush them?' Pyrax repeated shocked, as he pressed

himself into the ground. 'Sir, they'd cut us down before we could get near them.'

'Only while their arrows last.'

'If we live that long.'

A sudden piercing shriek caused Cato to jump. One of the mules had been hit in the flank and now it bellowed with pain and reared and wrenched in its traces. For a moment it looked as if the animal might panic enough to drag the cart clear of the sheltering legionaries but the other animal had frozen and gazed at its comrade with wide-eyed terror, and the cart stayed still.

'Careful, you fools!' Vitellius screamed out a short way off. 'You're hitting the mules. Pick your targets – only the men!'

'Thank you, Tribune,' Macro said bitterly as the arrows struck the cart and shields with splintering thuds. He caught Cato's eye and gestured towards their attackers with his thumb. 'I'm getting a bit sick of those Syrians. About time we did something about them.'

'But not right now, sir,' Cato implored him. 'Please wait until the odds are a little more even.'

The arrows continued to fall, but at a diminishing rate as the Syrians conserved ammunition. Individually they had closed the distance and were now taking pot shots whenever a target made itself available. But the narrow strip of the hummock made it impossible for the archers to enfilade the legionaries. So, after a little while, it became apparent that a stand-off had been reached. The legionaries, stripped of armour and with only two shields between them, dared not rush the archers; and the archers, lightly armed and a poor match for well-trained heavy infantry, dared not take the legionaries on hand-to-hand. The Syrians only hope was to incapacitate enough of Macro's force to make their numbers decisive.

The arrow fire ceased, but the legionaries remained under cover in case it was a ruse.

'Macro!' Vitellius called out. 'Macro! Still with us?'

'Yes, sir!' the centurion shouted out, automatically responding to his superior.

'That's good. Now look here, Macro, I will have that chest in the long run. You're trapped where you are and I've sent for more men. It'll take them a while to arrive. We can spend that time sitting here staring at each other or you can give me the chest and I'll let you and your men go.'

'Fuck off, sir!' Macro shouted back. 'If you want it, you'll have to fight for it!'

'Hear me out, Centurion! If you make me wait then there will be no mercy. We will over-run you and you'll be killed. Give me the chest now and you'll live. You have my word on it.'

'His word?' Cato raised his eyebrows. 'What kind of idiots does he take us for?'

'My thinking exactly, Optio,' replied Macro.

'Macro!' the tribune called out again. 'I'll give you a few moments to talk it over with your men. Then you choose; delay the inevitable and it's death for all of you, or give me the chest and walk out of here.'

Macro turned back to his men. 'Well?'

'There's no way he's going to let us live,' Pyrax said firmly. 'No matter what we decide.'

'You're right.' Macro nodded. 'So what do we do? A charge is out of the question.'

'Unless we can hit them from two sides,' Cato suggested.

'And how do we achieve that?'

Cato rolled over and propped himself up on an elbow so he could point out directions as he talked.

'Some of us go back down the track. The grass is long on either side, so if you keep low enough you should be screened. Then, where it dips into the marsh, you swim round in a wide arc until you come back on to the trail behind them. Then we charge from both sides – hopefully the surprise should be enough to put them off their aim for just long enough.'

Cato finished, but saw that the others were still looking at him expectantly. 'Sorry, that's it.'

'That's a plan?'

Cato nodded.

'Fair enough. It's that or die, I suppose,' Macro said. He looked around the surviving members of his squad. 'Right then, you take Pyrax, Lentulus and Piso. When you get round behind them you charge and make as much noise as you can.'

Cato shifted with embarrassment. 'Sorry sir, but someone else has to lead the other party.'

'Why?'

'I can't swim.'

'You told Vespasian you could. That night you joined the Legion.'

'I'm afraid I was exaggerating, sir. Sorry.'

'Lying, you mean.'

'Yes.'

Macro glared at him. 'Well, that's just terrific, Optio. Now I'll have to bloody do it.'

'Yes, sir. I'll make sure I learn as soon as we get back to the Legion.'

'Fine.' Macro unfastened the clasp on his cloak and nodded to the others to do the same. The small party checked that their swords and daggers were firmly attached to their belts, then Macro led them down the track away from the Syrians, closely hugging the ground and slithering along the muddy surface. Once they had eased themselves into the water and swum off into the gloomy mist, Cato risked a quick glance round the side of the cart. The Syrians stood as before and, to one side, the unmistakable shadow of Vitellius sat atop a small mound close to where Pulcher tended their mounts. There was a sudden blur as an arrow flew close by and Cato ducked back down. The three other men, still unwounded, held their draw swords tight in their hands and crouched expectantly.

For a while it seemed nothing was happening, all was still and quiet as before. As the light failed Cato began to wonder what had become of his centurion. Then Vitellius stood up and called out impatiently.

'Time's up, Centurion. Surrender the chest now or die. What's it to be?'

Cato looked round at the other legionaries.

'Well, Centurion?'

'Say something!' one of the men hissed.

'What? Say what?' Cato asked helplessly.

'Anything, you fool!'

'That's it, then,' Vitellius concluded angrily. 'You'll bloody well die and like it.'

With a roar of fighting rage, Macro and his four men rose up from the shadows immediately behind the line of archers and raced down the track. The noise momentarily surprised Cato as well, but he recovered in an instant and was up on his feet running for the nearest Syrian, shouting at his party to follow. As he saw Cato running towards him, teeth bared in a feral war face, the Syrian dropped his bow and reached for the cleaver at his side. He fumbled as he unsheathed the blade and it fell to the ground. Cato shouted as loud as he could and the man ran for it leaving his weapon lying in the mud. Cato thrust his sword at the Syrian's back but the point barely penetrated the cloak and caught him in the buttock instead. The man yelped and sprinted down the track as fast as his feet could carry him, frantically weaving round Macro and the others who were mercilessly despatching his comrades.

Frustrated by the enemy's escape, Cato turned wildly about to look for another foe and saw Pulcher heaving Vitellius up into the saddle.

'Over here!' Cato cried out. 'Don't let him get away! Quick!'

Without waiting for the others, Cato dashed towards Pulcher, sword raised high above his head. At the last moment, Pulcher turned and drew his weapon, faster than Cato would have believed possible.

Firmly standing his ground, the stocky legionary aimed the tip of the blade squarely at Cato's throat. Cato instinctively tried to dodge the blade and, to his horror, found his feet losing their grip on the slimy peat. He went down on his knees, sliding in under Pulcher's blade and thrusting up into his guts as hard as he could. His momentum slammed him into Pulcher's legs and both went down in a sprawling heap. Cato pulled himself clear with unbloodied sword still in hand. The thrust had not penetrated Pulcher's armour, only winded him badly, and now he rolled away fighting for breath. Before Cato could finish him off, a sudden swish through the air, close to his ear, caused him to duck. Vitellius loomed above him, raising his sword arm. When it came, Cato had just enough time to raise his sword to parry a jarring blow.

'Here! Quickly!' he cried out.

Vitellius was about to move in for the kill when several shouts close at hand alerted him. Swearing bitterly, he charged his horse at Cato. The optio dived to one side, but not fast enough to avoid being sent sprawling by a blow from the animal's flank as it swept past, and he crumpled to the ground.

With hooves sliding and slithering in the mud, the horse weaved through the loose line of legionaries and pounded down the track, past the cart where the wounded mule still bellowed its pain, and on into the gathering gloom.

Macro hurried over to Cato and hauled him on to his feet.

'You all right?'

'Will be . . . once I get my breath back. Did we get them?'

'Near enough. Five down and three did a runner.

Shame we didn't get that bastard Vitellius.'

Cato quickly looked about but there was no sign of Pulcher either.

'Yes, sir.' Cato drew in a deep lungful of air and felt his chest. Aside from bruises all seemed in order. 'What are we going to do?'

'There's no point in going after him, if that's what you mean. We have to get the chest back to Vespasian as soon as possible. Before the tribune comes after us with more men.'

Once the legionaries had harnessed four of the horses up to the cart, the others were tethered to the back, along with the remaining mule. Concerned that the other mule might attract unwelcome attention with its hoarse bellowing, Macro had led the animal down to the side of the marsh, cut its throat and tipped it into the mire. With the wounded loaded aboard the cart, the small party began to retrace its steps along the track towards the edge of the marsh. Night closed in around them as they drove the horses onwards, grateful that they no longer had to labour at hauling the cart out of every muddy rut along the way.

As they neared the edge of the marsh and could see the dark swell of land rising up above the mist, Macro heard the sound of a horse approaching behind them.

'Halt,' he called out softly. 'Grab your shields and spears and follow me.'

He led them back down the track a small distance and detailed four men to hide each side in an extended line to be sure of providing the approaching rider with no means of escape. Cato lay down close to the ground, too tired by the day's action to be anxious any more. Moments later the dark shape of a rider and horse loomed out of the mist and cantered into the middle of the trap.

'Now!' Macro shouted, and eight shadows detached themselves from the grass on either side of the track and converged on the horseman. Startled by the sudden movement, the horse reared, whinnying in terror, and the rider struggled to regain control of his mount before tumbling to the ground. Macro pounced on him, slamming a punch into his face before hauling the man to his feet.

'Well now!' He laughed. 'What a fucking surprise it is to see you again, sir.'

Vitellius wiped his bloody nose on the back of his hand. 'Get your hands off me, Centurion!'

'Get my hands off you?'

'You have to let me go. I've got to get back to the Legion.'

'Listen, you bastard, if you think—'

'There's no time for this!' Vitellius shouted. 'There's a bloody army coming down the track. Nearly rode right into them. I don't think they saw me, but they'll be here soon. I have to tell Vespasian!'

'He's lying, sir,' Pyrax growled. 'Kill him, and let's go.'

'Wait!' Cato interceded. 'We don't even know what he was after yet.'

Pyrax raised his sword. 'Who needs to know?'

'Lower that sword legionary!' Macro ordered. 'Now!'

'Please!' Vitellius begged. 'You have to let me go. I

have to warn Vespasian. We've found Togodumnus! If that column surprises the Legion we'll lose thousands. Thousands of our comrades.'

'Comrades!' Pyrax spat at him. 'Comrades don't fucking kill each other.'

For a moment they stood in silence, a tableau of crisis and indecision, Vitellius on his knees, Macro with his fist twisted into the tribune's cloak, a look of bitter contempt etched on his face.

'If there is a column,' Cato said softly, 'the legate has to be warned.'

'There's no fucking enemy column!' Pyrax thumped the butt of his spear down. 'He's just trying to save his skin.'

'Then why ride back towards us?'

'He got lost. Why are we even wasting time on this?' Pyrax turned to Macro. 'Kill him, sir!'

Macro glared down at the tribune for a moment, face hardening into a look of pure disgust and resentment at the predicament the tribune's reappearance had placed him in. Then he thrust his fist hard against Vitellius's chest and the tribune went down flat on his back in the mud.

'Go and warn the Legion. But, make no mistake, when this is all over I'll see to it that the general himself knows what you did here. I'm sure he'll be most keen to find out why a senior officer should want to kill his own men to get hold of that chest. Now go! Go, you bastard, before I change my mind.'

Vitellius scrambled to his feet, jumped on to his horse's back and snatched the reins back from the legionary who stood at the beast's side. Without any delay he kicked his heels in and raced up the track, past the cart, and disappeared into the night.

'Right then! Let's move. If he's told us the truth, there's no time to waste. Let's go!'

'Of course he's not telling the truth!' Pyrax snorted.

'You questioning my decision?' Macro asked coldly.

'I'm telling you, we should have killed him.'

'You call me sir when you address me, legionary!'

'Quiet!' Cato raised his hand. 'Listen!'

The small party froze, every ear straining in the direction Cato pointed. For a moment there was nothing to disturb the soft sounds of the night. Then came a distant whinny, then another, accompanied by the unmistakable crack of a whip as someone shouted a Celtic curse.

From somewhere on the track not far behind them.

Chapter Thirty-six

It was clear that the Britons would be upon them before they even made the ridge. There was no hope of outrunning the enemy, that much was evident to Macro as he frantically scanned the immediate area, and found a faint possibility of hope.

'Over there!' He thrust his arm out to one of the larger folds in the land away to the left of the track. In the dim light of a new moon the mist forming in the dip had a cold luminosity that was far from welcoming, but it offered the only hope of quick concealment. 'Get the cart off the track, quick as you fucking can!'

As the men turned the horses into the long grass and hurried across the slope towards the hollow, Macro followed and tried to conceal the worst of the grooves the cart had crushed into the wet grass. Praying that the marks would be missed in the dark, and fearing that the Britons might march into view at any moment, Macro dashed after the cart which had reached the rim of the dip and was being man-handled down the reverse slope. The thrumming of shod hooves in the near distance spurred him on and when he reached the dip he threw himself down and lay there for a moment, panting.

The slope was steep and the cart was well below the level of the mist that covered the ground in a thick unbroken layer. Ordering the others to stay with the wagon and make sure the animals and the injured remained silent, Cato scrambled up the slope to join the centurion.

'We were lucky there, sir. Wagon nearly went over when we came down this.' He thumped the slope.

'Really?' Macro said, and yawned before he could help it. Then he flipped himself over and propped his chin up with his hands. 'Keep down, and do nothing . . . absolutely nothing. On my orders only.'

Cato nodded and lay as still as he could, waiting nervously for the enemy to emerge from the swamp. And then, suddenly, a small column of cavalry trotted into the dim moonlight barely a hundred paces away, a blend of man and horse in the dark shadows. Cato was surprised to see British cavalry since Caesar had claimed that they preferred to use their animals for chariots. Either the Great General was wrong or the Britons had finally discovered the value of cavalry. The horsemen fanned out on either side of the track and trotted up towards the ridge. The left-flank scout passed within twenty paces of their hiding place and Macro and his optio pressed themselves into the ground, hardly daring to breathe. Their tired eyes strained to detect any sign that the passage of their cart across the slope had been discovered. But the scout passed by without breaking his pace.

From the swamp came the sound of jingling and a dark mass of chariots and infantry spilled out on to the track and snaked their way up the slope. The chatter of their queer lilting language carried softly to the ears of the terrified Romans and Cato found himself comparing the sound favourably with the harshness of the German he had grown used to. A sharp order was given as a chariot passed down the line, and the column obediently fell silent until the chariot had passed beyond the line of scouts and over the brow of the hill, then laughter rippled down the line and they continued talking as before.

There seemed to be no end to the soldiers streaming from the marsh, and now the head of the dark mass had passed over the hill. On and on they came, until at long last the rearguard emerged from the swamp. Macro and Cato watched as the last ranks of the enemy marched over the crest of the hill and merged into its dark silhouette as they passed out of sight down the reverse slope.

'How many do you think there were, sir?' Cato whispered, as if afraid his words might yet carry to the ears of the Britons.

Macro looked down at the small stones he was clutching in his hand and quickly counted them up. 'Say the equivalent of twenty cohorts, that's . . .'

'Nine thousand!' Cato whistled.

Macro silently did the necessary maths for himself and nodded. 'More than enough for Vespasian to worry about. Not to mention the chariot force. If that lot gets the drop on the legate . . .'

'Then it's up to Vitellius.'

'Yes,' Macro replied simply. 'Vitellius . . . Look, we'd better get moving. With that lot on the scene we'd better abandon the cart. Bury the chest here, lose the cart somewhere else and use the horses to circle round the column and rejoin the Legion.'

'Bury the chest? After all we've been through?'

'You want it to be captured? Or worse, you want to be captured with it?'

'No, sir.'

'Well then, we'll have to leave it here and return for it, if we ever get back to the Second in one piece.'

It was clear that the horse was badly winded and would drop if he drove it any further. Vitellius swerved off the track and dismounted in the shadows of an ancient grove whose leaf-laden branches stretched out on all sides. While his mount snorted and gasped at the cool night air, Vitellius cursed in anger and frustration. That bloody chest had nearly been in his hands. An emperor's ransom – enough to fund the most lavish of political careers; an endless source for buying the favours of senators and soldiers alike. Maybe enough to buy him the loyalty of the Praetorian Guard. Certainly the services of the Praetorian agent Pulcher had been reasonably priced and the man had been sufficiently impressed by gold to rid himself of any inconvenient principles. And buying the services of the Syrians earlier that day had been easy, once Vitellius had passed himself off as a close friend of Scribonianus.

It was quite astonishing just how much the prospect of riches bent a man's will in new directions. Only a few months earlier he had been a loyal servant of the Emperor, so loyal in fact that Narcissus had shared a good many more secrets with him than was strictly necessary, or wise. But as soon as Narcissus had told him about the chest, deeply repressed ambitions began to whisper sinister thoughts to him. The recovery of the chest was supposed to be a test of Vespasian's loyalty to Claudius, and Vitellius had been ordered to watch the legate closely for signs of treachery. However, Vespasian had behaved impeccably and in his strict adherence to duty Vitellius had found his opportunity. Secure in the knowledge that the legate would do all in his power to carry out his instructions, it simply remained for Vitellius to be equivocal in his reports to Narcissus. Once the treasure disappeared the finger of blame would unswervingly be directed at Vespasian whose every protestation of innocence would condemn him all the more. And Vitellius, armed with his fortune, would watch quietly and bide his time.

That had been the plan up until a short while ago.

Rosy dreams of that future were now dashed, and he impulsively swore out loud, then nervously glanced about – but the night remained quite still. Vitellius sighed. He had failed and, worse, he had left witnesses to his failure. Once that squat little centurion and his precocious optio got back to the Legion he would be compromised. If only there was some way of ensuring that they never made it back alive. It was possible that the column of Britons he had run into back in the marsh had already caught up with the cart and massacred its escort; Vitellius sincerely hoped that they had. But he knew it would be foolish to count on it – that fellow Macro had just about enough luck and guile to see him through any peril.

Memories of the desperate fight in the German village flooded back into Vitellius's mind, particularly the vision of the centurion bleeding from a savage spear wound. If only that bloody German had paused long enough to take a proper aim.

While Vitellius reflected on his circumstances, his horse had recovered enough to graze contentedly on a patch of grass at the fringe of an oak tree's boughs. Suddenly it lifted its head and stared intently into the night. It was a moment before the tribune was aware of the horse's change of mood and then he hurried over and placed a reassuring hand on the animal's neck. The horse flinched.

'What is it, girl?'

Nostrils flaring and ears twitching the horse took a step back into the shadows. As Vitellius looked into the night he saw a thinly spread line of horsemen approaching along the treeline, barely a hundred paces away. His heart raced as he silently struggled to get up on his mount but the horse, already nervous, reared back with a loud whinny.

'Stupid bastard!' Vitellius yanked the reins savagely as he steadied the horse and hauled himself on to its back. Already there was shouting from a short distance off and Vitellius kicked his heels into the flanks of his mount, turning it away from the dark figures hurrying in his direction. Panic and the desire to flee gripped him and, shouting at his mount, Vitellius galloped away into the night, dimly aware that the direction he was heading in would take him away from the Second Legion. Very well, he'd try and make for the Fourteenth instead, already well down the road as it marched to join Plautius. Vespasian would have to deal with the enemy column on his own and Vitellius would live to be a hero another day.

At the foot of the oak tree where the tribune had taken shelter the dark shapes of his pursuers watched the figure fleeing as fast as his horse could gallop – the drumming of the hooves clearly audible.

'Who the hell was that?' asked a legionary. 'Thought he looked like one of ours.'

'Probably some idiot messenger,' his decurion replied. 'Got himself lost most like.'

'Should we go after him, sir?'

The decurion thought about it a moment and shook his head. 'Nah! Not worth it. If he's one of ours he'll find his way soon enough.'

'What if it's one of them, sir?'

'Then he's had a lucky escape. I'm not risking breaking any of our necks on some wild chase in the dark. Anyway, we'd best get back to the Legion.'

The decurion turned his squadron round and led them at a walk back towards the Second Legion, somewhat concerned about the negative report he would have to give to Vespasian. There had been no sign of Togodumnus and his forces. Frankly, the decurion doubted whether there had ever been any enemy column attempting to flank the army. It was probably just some paranoid staff officer over-reacting. The decurion shrugged wearily. So far the campaign had been a huge disappointment; no enemy, no spoils and no women. It had hardly been worth turning up for, and he had already resigned himself to the fact that Plautius and the vanguard legions would have defeated the Britons long before the Second could get into the action.

Shame, he thought. A nice little battle would have been most welcome, especially in view of the promotional opportunities provided by combat deaths. But, he sighed to himself bitterly, there wasn't going to be a battle, because there wasn't a single bloody Briton for miles.

For Macro and his men, the ride through the night was proving to be a disaster. The Syrian horses were light frisky things; ideal for darting in and out of the fringes of a battle while their riders loosed off volleys of arrows, but totally impractical for carrying more than one man at a time. In the end, after much swearing and kicking of heels, Macro ordered the men to dismount and use the horses just to carry the wounded. His legionaries were far more content on foot in any case.

So the small group quietly made their way through the night, trying as far as Macro could guess the route, to march round the British column and locate the Second Legion before the Britons. Macro had decided to keep his party to the seaward side of the enemy, to be as near as possible to the fortified beachhead. With luck they might even be picked up by a patrol and escorted back.

Vitellius might already have reached the Legion and raised the alarm, so their comrades would at least be safe from surprise attack. Even so, Macro's gut instinct told him that Vitellius would be planning a nasty surprise for them on their return and he cursed himself for letting the man go. They should have slit his throat and dumped the body in the marsh. That was more than the treacherous bastard deserved. The question plaguing Macro's mind was why the tribune had been there in the first place. Vespasian had assured him that the real reason for the mission was a closely guarded secret. Yet, not only was Vitellius in the know, he had also had time to enlist his band of helpers – presumably the same bunch of Syrians who had jumped Macro's century on the road to Gesoriacum. Someone was playing a deep game and Macro was uncomfortably aware that he was just a small thread in a much greater tangle of conspiracy.

He forced himself to concentrate; this was not the time to let his mind wander. Every fibre of his body must be bent towards ensuring that his men returned safely to the Legion. Looking round he could see that the legionaries were completely done in – he had to keep his mind clear and his eyes and ears open as they passed through this hostile landscape. Even as he thought this, a warm aching weariness was flowing through his limbs. In a moment he knew his head would begin to swim. He rubbed his eyes, momentarily rocking on his feet, and then felt a hand grasp his elbow and hold him steady.

'Careful, sir!' Cato whispered. 'You almost fell over. You need to rest.'

'No – I'm fine.'

'You could sit on one of the horses and let me lead the way for a while, sir.'

'I said no. I can't do that.' Macro wanted to explain that no officer could even think of doing such a thing, but he could not frame the words and merely mumbled his thanks, freeing himself from Cato's grip.

As the night wore on, the small band of legionaries carefully picked their way through the shadows of the rolling countryside. They dared not pause for fear that an irresistible desire to sleep would overwhelm them the moment they stopped. They were all aware of the danger they were in, cut off from the Legion and wandering through the dark in hostile country. On they trudged until, just as the sky was beginning to lighten away to the east, they reached the top of a small hill. In the distance they could see the mass of small fires that identified it as the marching camp of a Roman legion. In the glow of the distant light tiny figures moved about in a frenzy of activity.

'Just in time it seems,' Macro grinned wearily. 'Looks like they're already on the march. Vespasian always was an early bird. No rest for us today.'

Cato smiled at Macro.

But Macro was no longer looking at the camp. He was staring fixedly away to that part of the horizon furthest from the coming of dawn. Disappearing into a dense wood that bestrode the Legion's line of march was a thick black shadow of men, horses and chariots moving with the silent stealth of a serpent stalking its prey.

Chapter Thirty-seven

Vespasian had left orders that he be woken well before dawn; the Second Legion was about to move through enemy territory and, although the staff officers had issued orders to every unit, there was still a host of details that needed his personal attention. That, he smiled to himself, was the biggest burden of command. The public in Rome pictured their generals as masters of the battlefield, heroically charging into overwhelming odds at the head of the legions. The mass of paperwork and petty bureaucratic tasks that were also part of the job remained largely invisible, yet it was this dedication to discipline and order that made the army work. Whatever the public may think, the secret of being a good general was having a good army, and the very best armies were composed of men who could wage war with methodical efficiency.

Rolling out of his camp bed, Vespasian pulled on a robe and sat at his desk. His personal slave had left a cup of heated wine and bread soaked in olive oil on a small silver tray and Vespasian gratefully gulped both down as he cast an eye over the latest papers. The century returns were initialled and thrust to one side before he scanned a few requisitions awaiting his approval. Finally he read through the night log. Still no sign of Togodumnus, and the thinly spread cavalry patrols had been shifted to the west and north. It was most puzzling – unless of course there was no column. That possibility looked increasingly likely, but Vespasian was wise to the tricks of fate and refused to discount the existence of the Britons just yet. And so the orders to march closed up would stand, however much the men grumbled. It was far better to be cautious than reckless – like that idiot Vitellius who had ridden off with the scouts and completely disappeared, together with a squadron of badly needed auxiliary cavalry. No doubt he was floundering about in the dark, scared out of his wits. Serve him right.

Having completed the paperwork, Vespasian summoned his armourer and stood still, pensive, as the man fastened the contoured breastplate and carefully looped the ribbons at the front. While the man fussed over the final accoutrements, the legate's eyes wandered across the cameo images of his wife and son on his desk and a nagging sense of guilt caused him to frown. It had been some days since he had last paused to even think about them; the sheer volume of the demands placed upon the commander of a legion in the field left no room for any private thought or deed. Vespasian was suddenly aware how much he missed them. It was only ten days since he had seen them set off on the wagon convoy to Rome, yet so much time seemed to have passed already. And the prospect of a long campaign meant it might be years before he saw them again. Titus would be a young boy, no longer the little toddler with his awkward sentences and manic humour. Flavia . . . what would

Flavia be like? More strands of grey in her hair? An extra crease around her eyes and mouth when she smiled? Suddenly he wanted to hold them both close to him and never let them go for as long as he lived. For a moment he was unaware of the stinging sensation in his eyes, then he quickly blinked before tears could betray his inner feelings.

'Too tight, sir?'

'What? Oh no, it's fine. You can leave me now.'

'Yes, sir.'

Once he was alone Vespasian pinched his arm painfully. That had been close – a moment more of wallowing in his homesickness and he would actually have shed tears in front of a bloody slave. He burned with shame at the thought that even now the slave might be confiding with his cronies about the legate's moment of sentimentality. All the work that had gone into constructing an image of a hard, disciplined commander with a heart of stone, coldly aloof from his men, all of that was for nothing if he allowed his emotions to show. Well, he was damned if he would let it happen again. Angrily he snapped shut the hinged likenesses of Flavia and Titus and made a mental note to have his slave stow them at the bottom of a travelling chest for the duration of the campaign.

His foul mood persisted long after dawn and the surly way in which he snapped out his orders was not entirely an attempt to undo the damage of his earlier moment of weakness. As the headquarters tent was packed away none dared even meet the eye of the legate, such was the dark expression that knitted his brow together and twisted down the corners of his mouth.

After a quick meal of barley gruel the legionaries hurriedly packed their equipment. As the sun struggled above the horizon, the men formed up into their centuries ready to march.

The instructions for the order of progress filtered down to the centuries and the men groaned inwardly. Vespasian had elected to march in two divisions, either side of the baggage train, with a cohort at each end to act as vanguard and rearguard. The veterans quietly cursed their commander's excessive caution and then patiently explained to the new recruits that, although the baggage train would have a nice easy passage along the track, the poor sods on each flank would have to negotiate all the obstacles that nature threw in their way. By the end of the day, the flank columns would be scratched, tired and wet, and all because the legate was worried about a few poxy Britons.

'Now then, you stop for nothing, understand?'

Cato nodded and tried to steady the horse.

'You get to Vespasian and tell him it's a trap. Tell him their numbers and tell him where you last saw them entering that wood.' Macro had severe misgivings about sending the lad but none of the others were up to it.

'What about you, sir?'

'Don't worry about me, lad. Just warn Vespasian. Well, what are you fucking waiting for? GO!'

Macro slapped the horse's rump as hard as he could and the animal started forwards, nearly throwing Cato from its back. At the last moment the optio grabbed the reins and pressed his thighs and heels into the horse. He stayed on, after a fashion. With a last look over his shoulder at the little knot of men gazing anxiously after him, Cato urged his horse down the slope towards the Roman camp in the distance. Cato had never been terribly good in the saddle and now he just knotted his fingers in the flowing mane and pulled sharply on the reins to alter direction. For its part, the horse reacted much to be expected having been parted from its usual rider. It didn't respond easily to his commands and man and horse continued at a slow gallop each regarding the other with antipathy.

As he reached the bottom of the hill Cato looked up in a panic and saw that the camp had disappeared from sight. However, a quick check on the direction of the sun and the lie of the land convinced him that he was still heading in the right direction and he kicked his heels in. As he rode, he wondered if Vitellius had managed to reach the camp ahead of him and if this wild gallop was a waste of time. But unpleasant as this ride might be, Cato could see that it was vital to alert Vespasian to the peril ahead. Visions of the grateful reception of his news filled his imagination and Cato drove his little horse on as he clung to the reins.

A movement to the left drew his attention. To his horror, he saw several horsemen in the wild attire of the Britons racing at an angle to intercept him. They were scarcely a quarter of a mile away and urging their horses on to cut in front of Cato before he reached the top of the next hill. With a savage kick at the flanks of his horse, Cato shouted at it to run, run fast as the wind, run for its life. The beast sensed the new urgency, pricked its ears back and lowered its neck as it burst into a headlong gallop up the side of the hill. Cato glanced again to the left and saw that the Britons had closed the distance. With a chilling clarity he knew that he would not make it, the camp was just too far away, and in a few moments he would be dead – already he anticipated the sensation of a sudden spear thrust from behind.

The crest of the hill was barely more than a few hundred feet away and Cato begged his horse to make more speed. But even as he did so, he could sense that it was running on its last reserves of strength. Cato looked over his shoulders. His pursuers were right behind him, close enough for him to see their feral expressions of triumph as they too realised that he would not escape them. It would be over in moments. Then his horse carried him on to the crest of the hill – two miles away lay the Roman camp, two miles too far. Cato let one hand fall from the reins to draw his sword. Fear had gone now, in its place was a frustrated rage. There was no escape now and death was certain, but he would not let them take his life without a brief, bitter struggle.

Cato looked over his shoulder again, fully expecting to see the Britons hefting their spears, but to his amazement he saw that they were reining in, the leading man pointing his spear directly beyond Cato. He looked ahead and saw what the Britons had already spotted. At the base of the hill, a small patrol of infantry were marching back towards the camp. Heart thumping with a surge of joy, Cato slapped the sword on the horse's rump and pounded down the hill. Looking back he was surprised to see the Britons had gone, vanishing over the crest of the hill as their prey escaped.

The men of the patrol heard the approaching sound of hooves and turned quickly, shields to the front and javelins held ready. A short distance from the patrol Cato reined in a few feet from the rearmost men. Slipping from the horse's back, Cato ran into them.

'Who the hell are you?' demanded the optio in command.

'Doesn't matter,' Cato panted. 'Have to see the legate! Now!'

'Who are you?'

'Quintus Licinius Cato, Optio, Sixth Century, Fourth Cohort. I have to report to Vespasian.'

'Report?'

'The enemy are preparing an ambush, ahead in the woods.'

'Enemy? Where?'

'They were right behind me. You must have seen them.'

The optio shook his head.

'But they were there!' Cato pointed to the top of the hill. 'Right behind me. Someone must have seen them!'

The men of the patrol watched him in silence and Cato stared back in disbelief.

'How could you not have seen them? Look, I have to see the legate.'

He turned and reached for the horse's reins and was about to throw himself up on to its back when the optio grabbed his arm and pulled him away from the horse.

'Not so fast! You're coming with us.'

'What? Look, you don't understand! I have to warn Vespasian!'

'I'm sorry, but I have my orders. Now, you're coming with us.'

As Cato stood in numbed disbelief the optio ordered one of his patrol to take charge of the horse, and then Cato was pushed into the centre of the patrol and forced to march with two men behind him to guard him.

'What the fuck is going on?' he shouted at the optio.

The patrol's commander stepped closer, so that his words would not be overheard.

'You're not to speak to anyone until we get back to the camp.'

'Why? What's this all about?'

'All patrols have been ordered by headquarters to look out for you and your mates, and told to bring you in quietly. Between you and me, it seems you're in deep shit. Now, don't make it worse. One more word out of you and I'll have you knocked on the head and thrown over that horse for the rest of the way to camp. Clear?'

Cato opened his mouth to protest and the optio raised his eyebrows in warning. Cato just nodded.

As the patrol approached the camp, Cato saw that the bulk of the Legion had already moved off towards the forest. Only the rearguard remained, forming up and ready to depart. Unless Vespasian was told about the Britons lying in wait, the disaster was unavoidable. Cato searched for any sight of the legate, but in the milling mass of soldiers, artillery trains and baggage wagons there was no sign of the Legion's commander. The patrol wound its way through the turmoil to report to the officer commanding the Legion's rearguard. Tribune Plinius looked up from his campaign desk as the patrol approached.

'What have we here then?'

'Captured a deserter, sir,' replied the optio. 'Rode right into us on some horse he stole.'

'I'm not a deserter!'

'Seems the boy wants to deny the charge. Well?'

'We're not deserters, sir,' Cato said quietly. 'We were on a secret mission for the legate.'

'A secret mission for the legate – I see.' Tribune Plinius let his amusement show, and winked at the optio. 'So you were on a secret mission, were you? What kind of a mission?'

'It doesn't matter, sir. I have to warn the legate. Before it's too late!'

'Too late for what?'

'There's an ambush, sir, right up ahead in the forest.' Cato pointed desperately at the back of the column disappearing into the trees. 'Togodumnus and his column are right there waiting. Thousands of them, sir. We have to warn Vespasian now!'

Tribune Plinius stared at him in silence for a moment, weighing up the information. There was no reason why he should believe the wild tale told by the boy. How could Togodumnus possibly have evaded the cavalry screen?

'You've seen these Britons personally?'

'Yes, sir! I beg you to tell the legate—'

'Silence!'

Whatever the boy had seen was clearly enough to scare him into this state, Plinius reasoned. But what if it turned out to be a false alarm? What damage would that do to his career? On the other hand what would be the damage of not acting on the information should it prove to be accurate? The reputation of a tribune could not be allowed to weigh against the safety of a legion.

'Very well, get on your horse and go after the legate as fast as you can. Tell him I'm getting the rearguard formed up for battle and will close up with him as soon as I can.'

'Yes, sir!' Cato's heart lifted, and he immediately turned to retrieve his horse from the patrol.

'One last thing!' Plinius called out.

'Sir?'

'If this proves to be a false alarm then I will personally crucify you on the nearest tree. Understand?'

Chapter Thirty-eight

The Second Legion had advanced well into the forest and the vanguard and colour party moved steadily down the track towards General Plautius and the three other legions. The artillery and baggage followed as the two flanking divisions formed a line of march fifty yards either side of the heaving mass of wagons, carts and draught animals. Even as they moved out, it was clear to Vespasian that the order of march was going to run into immediate difficulties. Ahead on the track, trees closed in on either side so the path was constricted to a width of less than thirty paces. Vespasian had foreseen the problem and instructed the senior centurion of each division to thin the flank divisions down to permit as swift as possible a passage through the wooded area. It might well leave the Legion temporarily vulnerable but it was that or face a long march around the forest and Plautius's instructions had required his legates to bring the legions up to the front by the speediest possible route. As the vanguard moved into the forest, the flank cohorts were ordered to form a column of twos to avoid any entanglement with the baggage train.

The manoeuvre was carried out without problem and

Vespasian took pleasure in seeing his troops perform with the effortless ease of an elite unit as they funnelled into the forest. Although Plautius's engineers had done a good job of clearing the foliage from the track, they had not had time to clear it the regulation distance of an arrow shot. Once the men had emerged from the trees the double files would be halted, formed back columns of regular width and moved forward to wait for the rest of the Legion to catch up. Routine as the task was, and the legionaries had carried out many such drills on training marches, the fact that they were in hostile territory lent a tense edginess to the officers as they hurried their men through the forest, eager to return their units to a more secure formation.

Although it was midsummer, when the forest should be bursting with wildlife, a gloomy silence hung in the trees and the dark shadows beneath their boughs. Vespasian was keenly aware of it as he rode forward along the column to check that the units were maintaining cohesion.

By the time he had travelled the length of the column Vespasian was content that all was going tolerably well. He allowed himself to relax, with the confidence that the rest of the day's march should be a formality. Even the legionaries had brightened up and some greeted him as he rode past. The sky was a deep blue that reminded him of the Mediterranean; brilliant white clouds towered above the horizon and the sun blazed down on a myriad of flowers alongside the track. Beyond the lines of men, the green woods shimmered in the sunlight and a faint breeze stirred the topmost branches into a soothing rustle. It was a good day to be alive and the thrill of it all flowed through his veins, so Vespasian was delighted when a stag suddenly plunged out of the trees ahead and froze as it encountered the thousands of men marching towards it along the forest track.

'Look!' Vespasian pointed, the severe facade of a legate momentarily slipping to reveal a boyish excitement.

His staff, who had suffered his foul temper for most of the morning, were keen to make the most of his sudden change of mood and eagerly followed his direction. The stag raised its antlers high and sniffed the air to its front and rear, undecided which way to run. Vespasian was struck by the grace of the animal and its lofty air of natural superiority.

'Bound to be some good meat on that one!' one of the officers said. 'Sir, may I?'

Vespasian nodded. It would be a shame to break the spell of the moment, but after all one couldn't eat spells, and the prospect of a venison supper was too alluring to pass up.

The officer spurred his horse on and yanked the reins round to head for the stag, the line of legionaries hurriedly parting to let him by. Pausing only to snatch a javelin from one of the men, the officer charged off in pursuit of the stag. The animal stood its ground for a moment before it sprang into the air and bounded into the trees. Shouting out his hunting call, the officer raced after the beast and disappeared into the shadows, and Vespasian smiled as he heard the crackle of small branches as the officer crashed through the undergrowth to get at his quarry.

Then the excited cries of the young man were suddenly cut short and, with one last crack of breaking branches, the forest fell silent. The staff officers exchanged looks of alarm. Vespasian craned his neck and stared into the darkness of the forest.

'Shall I go after him, sir?' someone volunteered. 'Sir?'

But Vespasian was no longer listening. His eyes were fixed on the space beneath the broad boughs of the trees. Shadows were moving there, moving all along the treeline. As the cold certainty of realisation clutched at his heart, he knew that he and his men were in the gravest danger. And, in damning proof of the foolishness of the Legion's dispositions, the enemy emerged from the forest into the bright light of day with a silence that was more shocking still. Before Vespasian could respond, a horn sounded and the Britons unleashed a volley of arrows that arced up into the clear sky and swept down on to the Romans. The legionaries dropped their marching yokes and desperately snatched at the shields slung across their backs. Some were too slow and slumped to their knees as they were struck down by the rain of arrows which rattled down on shields and carts and pierced their unprotected skins.

Then the danger was over for a brief instant as the Britons notched arrows ready for their next volley. Vespasian turned in his saddle to see that, miraculously, his staff remained uninjured. Already, the centurions and other line officers were bellowing at their men to form up and face the enemy. Their endless training paid off as the legionaries hurriedly turned from column to line and presented their broad rectangular shields to the enemy, even as a second, ragged, volley fell on to the Legion. Those who had been hit in the first shower, men and animals, were now mercilessly exposed and many were struck again, some killed outright. The area between the cohorts and the baggage train was littered with the still bodies of the dead, and the writhing, screaming forms of injured men and beasts. But the men who had formed up and now sheltered behind their shields were comparatively safe. Vespasian hurriedly issued orders for the north-facing cohorts to prepare to advance and staff officers spurred their horses to each end of the division. Looking across the baggage train to the other cohorts Vespasian was relieved to see that their officers had already formed them up and were clearing gaps in the baggage to allow their men to pass through to the other side. With the legionaries in position, they would be able to make short work of the lightly armed archers. Now that the initial shock had run its course, Vespasian found himself looking forward to the coming fight and inevitable victory.

That was when the Britons unleashed their real attack.

At the very moment the southern cohorts were forcing a way through the baggage train, a deep note blasted from a horn behind them in the forest, and the sound was taken up by other horns up and down the length of the track. And with an ear-splitting roar, the Britons erupted from the forest and hurtled towards the disorganised cohorts, who had frozen at the sound of the horns and now gaped in terror at sight of their impending doom. Some centurions with presence of mind shouted out a string of orders and bodily turned their men to face the charge, but the coherent battle line so typical of the Roman army had simply disintegrated. Vespasian watched in horror as the screaming wave of Britons engulfed his men in a shattering crash. The impact immediately drove the legionaries back on to the baggage train and scores were cut down as they tried to escape through the gaps between the vehicles. Those who turned to face the enemy fought in isolation and, with the Britons still pouring from the forest, the legate could see that the unequal numbers would lead to a massacre of his men unless a battle line could be established within the next few moments.

'Out of the bloody way!' Cato shrieked as he desperately yanked at the reins and the exhausted horse swerved round a legionary who had stepped into his path. Ahead he could see Vespasian amongst his staff. The group had stopped and were looking into the forest on the right-hand side of the track. Suddenly Cato was aware of movement all along the treeline as the Britons emerged from the shadows.

An icy dread washed over him as he realised his warning had arrived too late.

A war horn blasted out and the air was filled with a whirring sound. Before Cato could react, his horse let out a piercing shriek and threw him to one side as it tumbled. Cato scrambled away from the animal and, looking back, saw that it had been struck in the neck by two arrows and now thrashed about in agony. Other victims littered the ground as more arrows thudded down pitilessly. Some men had already abandoned their yokes and were running back down the column towards the camp.

But Cato had no intention of fleeing. He crouched down and glanced around. He felt vulnerable out of armour and hurried over to a dead legionary, quickly stripping the body of shield, helmet and sword. Thus protected, Cato plunged into the nearest mass of men still struggling to organise a resistance against the enemy. It was a desperately unequal fight since the legionaries were not formed up and were engaged in hand-to-hand combat against superior numbers. Only those men who managed to form shield to shield in little knots stood a chance against the sweeping, hacking strokes of the Britons' long swords. Two utterly different fighting styles were in play and as long as the Britons could maintain a loose melee the shorter swords of the legionaries were badly outranged.

Cato rushed into battle, screaming a savage war cry he was not even conscious of. Exhausted to the point of delirium, bitter at his treatment and driven by a keen awareness that this was a fight for survival, he sought the nearest enemy. A tall man of his own height and stature stood in his path, long sword raised and face painted to resemble a many-fanged mouth. Lowering his point and raising his shield Cato deflected the blow and thrust his sword deep into the man's guts. The Briton went down with a piercing cry as Cato wrenched the blade free and knocked him flat with the shield boss. He quickly glanced round, looking for the next target alert to the danger. Three paces ahead of him a Briton stood over a prone legionary whose sword arm had almost been hacked through. The Briton raised his sword to despatch his enemy but before the sword reached the zenith of its arc Cato caught him high in the back between his shoulder blades. With a puzzled expression the man toppled to one side of his intended victim.

'Here!' Cato grabbed the legionary's good hand and, covering them both with his shield dragged the man a short distance to where a group of Romans had formed a tight line with their backs to a pair of wagons. At the centre of the line stood Bestia, bellowing out encouragement to the others in his best parade-ground voice. Cato flung the man he had rescued down with the other injured and turned to take his place among the legionaries.

'Cato!' Bestia shouted, snatching a sidelong glance. 'Time for you to show me what you're really made of.'

Cato nodded grimly as he faced the enemy, thrusting out at any Britons who came close enough, and deflecting the blows of the wicked long swords that carried enough momentum to cut through a man's head in one blow. Indeed, as he fought shoulder to shoulder with his comrades, Cato saw a Roman lean down to finish off a wounded enemy, oblivious in his moment of triumph to the Briton standing to one side, sword raised high in the air. It flashed down, straight through the legionary's neck, before the tip buried itself in the bloody grass beside the track. The legionary's helmeted head shot forward and, with a rattling thud landed several feet away as arterial crimson exploded into the air from the stump of the man's neck.

It was a detail lost in an instant as Cato stabbed at

the Britons surrounding the little group. Now that the initial momentum of the charge had subsided, the two sides were locked in thousands of individual struggles whose minutest details would be etched forever in the minds of those who survived. Centurion Bestia laying about with all the ferocious efficiency of a veteran – an anguished expression on an enemy's face – the exotic pattern of the Britons' body paint – the stiffened spiky hair and strangely patterned tattoos. All these impressions burned into the mind's eye even as they passed in a flash. For Cato, an inner calmness seemed to consume him as his mind divorced itself from his body and he fought by instinct. For the first time he felt he really belonged to the Second Legion. If the rearguard arrived in time he might even live to enjoy the feeling.

The battle was going badly and Vespasian saw that the southern line of cohorts – if it could, in truth, be described as a line – would completely disintegrate at any moment unless it could be strengthened. Two cohorts who faced the archers had been ordered forward to clear the treeline and deny them any further opportunity to pepper the Romans. The two remaining cohorts of the main force, some eight hundred men, were all that was left to him now and he hurriedly formed them into a double line facing the baggage train. Then, as their comrades fell back through the tangle of wagons and draught animals, gaps were made in the lines to permit them passage to the rear, where staff officers were hurriedly reforming the survivors of the southernmost cohorts into a reserve.

As things stood, Vespasian knew that the battle could only have one outcome. Sheer weight of numbers, and the loss of a third of his command, meant that the Britons would eventually overwhelm even the stoutest defence. For a moment he considered ordering his men to break formation and flee into the forest to the north but, scattered and lost, they would be easy pickings for the inevitable pursuit. The destruction of the Legion would take place more quickly if they stood their ground, but they would take more of the enemy with them. Then, at least, his posthumous reputation would be salvaged and the name Vespasian would not be linked to that of Varus, who had led three legions to a similar fate many years ago in the dark depths of the German forests.

The reserve line held steady as their comrades were forced back through the baggage train, slowly yielding ground before the enemy onslaught. Once the retreating Romans were safely within javelin range, Vespasian nodded to the trumpeter who blared out the prearranged signal. The men of the two cohorts readied their javelins.

'Release!' Vespasian roared out and the centurions instantly echoed the command. Eight hundred arms hurled their javelins in a high-angled arc over the heads of their comrades, beyond the baggage train, where they fell on the lightly armoured bodies of the Britons massing on the far side. From the volume of cries and screams, the Romans knew that they had hit the enemy hard and the men exchanged grins of satisfaction as they readied their final javelins. The second volley caused a fresh crescendo of screams and cries to rend the air. The legionaries drew their swords, waiting for the Britons to resume their attack on the thin Roman lines. The Legion had shot its bolt and now prepared to renew the vicious hand-to-hand fighting that would decide the matter.

Dismounting from his horse, Vespasian undid the clasp at his shoulder and let his legate's cloak slide to the ground in an untidy heap. An orderly held out a shield and Vespasian slipped his left hand through the strap, took a firm hold of the iron handle and drew his ivory-handled short sword. He drew himself up to his full height and pushed his way forward until he stood in the middle of the front rank of men facing the enemy. If this was the day ordained for his death, then he would go down as his breeding and respect for Roman tradition dictated he should: with his face to the enemy and a sword in his hand.

Chapter Thirty-nine

From the crest of a hill at the southern edge of the forest, Macro stood at the base of a vast oak tree and stared up through its leafy branches. The track from the marsh had brought them to this point and Macro could wait no longer to find out how things stood with the Second Legion.

'Well?'

'I can't quite make it out, sir,' Pyrax called down to him.

'Just tell me what you can see.'

'I can see the baggage train right enough, but there's men all over it – can't tell who's who though.'

Macro balled his hand into a fist and struck the rough bark in frustration. 'This is no good,' he muttered and then, grabbing a low branch, he began scaling the broad trunk. He reached Pyrax, sitting astride a limb growing perpendicularly from the trunk.

'Next time I need information,' Macro gasped, 'I'll bloody well do the job myself, and not get somebody who's half blind.'

Beside Pyrax, Macro had his first view of the distant battle and saw with horror that the thin scarlet lines of the Legion were engulfed by a multicoloured wave of enemy troops. Only the rearguard retained any appearance of order. Vitellius and Cato had failed then and Vespasian had unwittingly led his men into an ambush. From the look of things, the ambush was about to become a massacre.

'What shall we do, sir?'

'Do? What can we do?'

'Should we try and find one of the other legions, sir? Or maybe head back to the fortress on the coast.'

'Well, we're hardly going to reinforce that lot,' Macro said bitterly and jabbed his thumb towards the forest. 'But we'll wait. Something might happen.'

'Like what, sir?'

'Haven't got a fucking clue. So we wait.'

They sat in silence, watching their comrades, men they had known for most of their lives, as they were gradually pushed back from the baggage train. It was a struggle for survival, the bloody intensity of which they could only helplessly imagine. It was almost more than Macro could bear and he tried to stop tears forming in his eyes as he witnessed the death of the Second Legion.

'Sir?'

'What?'

'Over there. Look.' Pyrax pointed to the west of the forest, eyes straining to make out the detail in the extreme distance. Following the direction of his finger Macro saw the dark mass which had escaped his attention earlier, when he had been battling to fight back his tears. But now as he looked, the dead hand of fate closed its fingers on any last hopes he may have entertained for the Second

410

Legion. A second column of Britons was flowing down the forest track to seal the Legion's fate.

The hard-pressed men of the Second Legion had been forced to steadily yield ground to the Britons and now their backs were almost up against the treeline from which the archers had emerged. The last reserves of Cato's strength had almost run their course; the weight of the shield on his arm seemed to have increased tenfold and now he could barely raise it off the ground. His sword thrusts had been reduced to feeble jabs at the faces of the enemy and he could barely parry the blows that were aimed at him. But still he fought on, determined to resist to the last. And that time, he knew, was fast approaching. Bestia had fallen, cut down when three of the enemy had jumped him together and he now lay on the bloodied grass, face laid open to the bone. The fact that the legate was fighting alongside his men was eloquent proof that he too believed that the Second Legion was about to be wiped out. Separated from vanguard and rearguard by the cleverly worked ambush, the cohorts of the main column fought on alone. The ground before them was covered with the fallen and the moans of the injured mingled with the overall cacophony of war cries, shouts of rage and the incoherent roars of men who had surrendered to the blood-lust of battle. There were no cries from Roman wounded, any who fell to the ground at the mercy of the Britons were quickly despatched with the bitter anger that is reserved for all invaders. All around the grass was splashed with slippery crimson gore that presented yet another peril to the men

411

engaged in the deadly struggle waged all along the forest track.

To Cato's left, the Second's legate fought with a savage abandon that filled those around him with surprise, so used were they to the quiet-mannered disciplinarian. But with death so imminent, Vespasian saw little point in preserving any sense of decorum. What the men needed now was not the cold reserve of aristocratic command, it was an example of fighting spirit to sustain them to the end. So he threw himself at all comers, hacking and slashing at the enemy with wanton disregard for his own safety. Yet he still lived, apparently charmed against the blows of the enemy, while men about him were struck down.

In spite of the fact that the Romans showed no signs of breaking, and only seemed to fight harder the more they were pressed back, the Britons scented victory. After the initial surprise of the ambush, the Legion had exacted a terrible toll on them such that only the complete destruction of every Roman would suffice. Vespasian saw a chariot careering along behind the Britons. It carried a richly dressed man of some stature who was wildly exhorting his men, driving them onwards as he pointed his war spear again and again at the Roman lines. For a moment, the legate considered leading a small group against the Britons' commander, in the hope that the elimination of Togodumnus would knock the fight out of them. But every Roman was already committed to the battle and could not be extricated to form such a force. Vespasian despaired as he watched the chariot pass by unharmed and then, his rage further inflamed, he

412

slammed his shield into the body of a Briton engaged with the legionary next to him and thrust a sword into the man's side. No doubt Togodumnus would be considered a great hero by his own people when the day was out, and the thought spurred Vespasian on to fight with even greater ferocity.

When the Roman line finally gave under the relentless pressure, the Legion broke into small groups fighting independently of each other, no longer a part of any coherent military formation, simply fighting to live a little longer yet – and make the enemy pay for the privilege.

Cato found himself in a knot of fifty or so men holding off several times that number of Britons. As he dragged himself round to face the latest attacker he was suddenly confronted by a huge man, naked but painted in strange Celtic patterns from head to toe. With a roar, the man swung a great two-handed sword at Cato's head. Summoning up all his energy, Cato jerked his shield up just in time. With a terrible jarring crash the sword splintered the shield and instantly numbed Cato's shield arm from his fingertips through to his shoulder. His grip failed him and the shield slipped from his useless fingers leaving Cato at the mercy of the towering British warrior, who laughed into the face of his helpless victim. He brutally shoved Cato backwards and the optio sprawled on the ground, the force of the impact winding him as his sword fell beyond his reach. Raising the great sword up for the final blow, the Briton bellowed his war cry. But before he could strike Cato saw a figure come between them – Vespasian. With a snarl the legate thrust himself forward, coming in under the Briton's sword and warding it off with his shield. Then he thrust out, and up, at the Briton's throat, but the warrior reacted with a lithe sidestep that bespoke a mastery of close combat. Pulling back, each man sized the other up, ready to spring to the attack in an instant.

For a moment a stillness surrounded the pair as Britons and Romans alike watched for the outcome of the fight between the giant Briton and the legate. The decisive moment of the battle had been reached. But even as they paused, they became aware of a new sound – the blare of distant instruments. Both men heard the noise though their eyes remained firmly fixed on each other. Lying on the ground, Cato wondered at first if his tired ears had deceived him, but he saw that his comrades shared his reaction. Could it be possible?

The sound was repeated almost at once and Vespasian felt his heart lift – there was no mistaking the trumpet call for the charge. Help was at hand, but from whom? The thought was over in an instant as the British warrior stepped back a pace, instinctively following the rest of his comrades, who broke contact with their enemy as the first terrible doubts began to sow themselves. Seizing the opportunity of the moment, Vespasian thrust his sword-point deep into the Briton's throat and quickly ripped it free. Dropping his sword, the British warrior grabbed at his wound in an attempt to stem the flow of blood. Vespasian ignored him and craned his neck in the direction of the trumpets, now definitely closer at hand. Then, over the heads of the Britons, far down the track, a line of horsemen appeared, cloaked in red, at their head the unmistakable silhouette of a Roman standard.

And from the other direction came the roar of the Second Legion's rearguard as they renewed their attack from the other end of the forest track.

A palpable shiver of anxiety rippled through the Britons as the cavalry began to roll up their flank. A handful of men began to retreat towards the southern treeline. As others followed their lead, the chariot bearing Togodumnus raced up the line and the Britons' leader shouted harshly at his men to hold, but the infectious sense of fear was already turning to panic and his men swept by him. Seeing that a hard core of Britons were holding their ground, Vespasian raised his sword high above his head. No eloquent speech was needed, and none came.

'Get them! Get them!'

The Roman line surged forward in pursuit of the men who, a moment ago, had been utterly assured of victory. Now they ran like rabbits, bolting for the safety of the forest on the far side of the track, all sense of arrogant self-belief gone in an instant. Cato, still lying on the ground, could only marvel at the suddenness of the change in circumstances.

Vespasian kept his eye on Togodumnus and, collecting a handful of men about him, he launched himself through the bloody pursuit, straight at the chariot. But the Britons' leader was no fool and knew when he had lost control of a battle. He barked an order at the driver and, with a crack of a whip, the chariot turned round and raced back down the forest track, away from the rapidly approaching cavalry. Vespasian could only watch in despair as the chariot accelerated away from him, the driver recklessly mowing down everything in his path to ensure that Togodumnus reached safety.

The legate called his men to a halt at the side of the baggage train and climbed on to the driver's seat of the nearest wagon to try and get an overview of the battle. Everywhere he looked, the Britons were on the run and, from the west, the Roman cavalry he had spied moments earlier, mercilessly swept along the forest track slaughtering all the enemy before them. As they approached, a tall figure on a white horse tore itself away from the pursuit and made his way over to Vespasian.

'Vitellius?' Vespasian muttered to himself doubtfully. But a moment later the likeness was clear enough and Vespasian shook his head in surprise. Vitellius reined in by the wagon and saluted.

'What the hell are you doing here, tribune?'

'It's a long story, sir.'

'I bet it is. And once this little lot's over I want a full report.'

High on the hill overlooking the forest, Macro almost fell out of the tree with excitement. He bobbed up and down on the bough, smacking his fist into his other hand as he saw the lead elements of the Fourteenth – it could only be the Fourteenth, he surmised – plough into the enemy surrounding the Second's vanguard, just as the Second's rearguard rushed at the other flank of the fleeing Britons. As soon as the enemy broke, the cavalry was released for the merciless pursuit that followed, the troopers sweeping all before them as panic flooded through the enemy who turned and streamed from the battlefield.

'Brilliant! Bloody brilliant, I tell you!' He slapped Pyrax on the shoulder.

'Easy, sir!' Pyrax shouted as he desperately grabbed the bough.

Macro just smiled at him and then continued his rejoicing. 'Bastards are all over the place! Look at 'em running from the forest. They must have gone through the trees like shit through a goose!'

'Some of them are running this way, sir,' Pyrax observed quietly.

'Of course they are. They're going to try and reach the marsh while they can. Oh . . .' Macro looked down through the branches to the track below that meandered over to the forest in one direction and the distant marsh in the other. 'I see what you mean.'

'We'd better not be here when they come by. I don't imagine they'd be too chuffed to encounter any more Romans.'

'Point taken.' Macro nodded to the men lying in the grass at the foot of the oak tree. 'You'd better go down and get them up here. And lose the horses, they're no good to us now.'

'Right, sir.' Pyrax quickly clambered down and left Macro to watch the final phase of the fight unfolding panoramically before him.

The pursuing cavalry and rearguard troops were emerging from the forest to run down the rearmost Britons as they attempted to stumble for safety. Some dropped their weapons and threw themselves at the mercy of their pursuers, but few were spared. Those taken alive were swiftly rounded up and herded together under the watchful eyes of a handful of sturdy men appointed for the task. Pyrax had been right, many of the figures fleeing from the Romans were heading up the track leading back to the marsh they had used to outflank the Second Legion and they would be passing under the tree in a few moments. Macro looked down and saw that his squad was scrambling up into the oak tree, the uninjured hauling up their less fortunate comrades until all were hidden in the leafy boughs.

Satisfied that they were safe from the Britons, Macro once more watched the pursuit. His eye caught a movement from the edge of the forest nearest the remains of the Second's marching camp and saw a chariot tear round the edge of the trees and head directly up the hill towards the track. As the charioteer thrashed his horses, Macro saw that the man standing behind him, clutching at the wicker handholds, was a superbly built individual in richly decorated robes, sporting a gleaming bronze helmet. Clearly he was a warrior of some significance. A pair of Roman cavalrymen took advantage of the slope and charged after the chariot. Nimbly knocking aside the cavalryman's spear-thrust, the Briton smashed the heavily weighted butt of his spear into the man's face and he tumbled from his horse. The second cavalryman was equally reckless and he paid for it with his life as the British chieftain ran him clean through then ripped his spear free.

As the chariot lumbered up the slope, Macro could see that its present course would take it under the oak tree.

'We'll have him! That bastard there!' He pointed out

the chariot and ordered those of his patrol who were still armed and uninjured to follow him down to the ground. Breathing heavily, with swords drawn, they crouched low and waited. A handful of British infantry ran by but took to their heels with a fresh burst of energy as soon as they saw the grim-faced huddle of legionaries with glinting short swords. Then the pounding of hooves and rattle of wheels heralded the approach of the chariot and Macro tensed, ready to pounce. The harsh shouts of the charioteer rose above the din and Macro risked a peek round the tree trunk to make sure of his timing.

'Ready, lads? Go for the charioteer and the horses first. Then we'll deal with the big one.'

He waited until the chariot was almost level with the oak tree.

'Now! At 'em, lads!'

Macro rushed out, directly into the path of the horses, and made a grab for the traces. The men on the chariot were taken completely by surprise and had no time to steer round the Romans. Macro pulled down hard and the horses stumbled to a halt. Pyrax took down the charioteer with a quick thrust before the man could even drop the reins. He fell off the chariot and his head was crushed under a wheel as his nervous horses sidestepped. The chieftain recovered his wits and leaped down, spear in hand, and made for the broad trunk of the oak tree. He turned, presented his spear and dared the Romans to fight him with a harsh laugh. Macro looked at him admiringly; the fellow was certainly game for a fight, whatever the odds.

'Spread out!' he ordered his men. 'And watch that bloody spear!'

As the half circle of legionaries cautiously approached, the Briton kept the tip of his war spear on the move, thrusting it at one man after another as they crept too close. With a howl of pain, one of Macro's tired men was stabbed in the guts and tumbled to the ground, bleeding profusely.

'All right then!' Macro called out, keeping his eyes firmly on the Briton. 'We'll rush him. Ready? Now!'

Six men threw themselves at the Briton and, with a wild stab, he caught one man in the leg before the others crashed into him, knocking him flat. But, hopelessly outnumbered as he was, the Briton hurled two men to one side, grabbed a Roman sword and rolled on to his feet, crouching low, with the unaccustomed blade held ready to slash at his enemies.

'Leave him to me!' Macro waved the others back. 'Bastard wants a fight, then he can have one with me.'

Readying his short sword, Macro bent his knees and slowly circled the Briton, sizing him up. And all the time the chieftain stared back, coldly assessing the stocky Roman.

'Fancy yourself, don't you?' Macro said quietly. 'Big bastard you may be, but you haven't got a bloody clue how to use that sword. Designed for thrusting . . . it's not a bloody cleaver.'

He feinted forwards and, as he had anticipated, the Briton swung the sword up above his head, rushing at Macro with a savage howl of rage. Macro simply dropped to his knee, straightened his arm and let the Briton's momentum do the rest. With a grunt the man doubled over the sword and flung his arms forward, his hands searching for Macro's neck. He got a grip and pressed down on the windpipe. Gasping, Macro tumbled on to the ground with the Briton on top of him, huge hands grasping ever more tightly on Macro's throat. Their faces were less than a foot apart and Macro saw the man's eyes brighten in triumph as he gritted his teeth and tightened his grip. The sword was still in Macro's grip and he worked it furiously inside his opponent trying for a vital organ. His head felt as if it would explode under the pressure of the man's grip until, at last, the fire in the Briton's eyes faded and after a last spasm, the man's grip loosened. Macro wrenched the hands from his throat and desperately gulped down air. He heaved the body to one side and struggled on to his feet before fixing his men with an angry glare.

'Why the fuck didn't you help me?'

'You told us not to,' Pyrax protested.

Macro rubbed his neck, wincing at its tenderness. 'Well, next time use your bloody initiative. If some sod's about to croak your centurion you get stuck in and stop him, whatever you've been told to do. Get it?'

'Yes, sir.'

'Right then, might as well put the chariot to good use. Load the wounded on, and sling him over one of the horses. Then, my lads, it's back to the safety of the Second Legion and the drinks are on me, if anyone's still awake tonight.'

Chapter Forty

The Second Legion moved no further that day as the surviving officers re-formed their units and took stock of their losses. They had answered grievously for Plautius' orders to join him as quickly as possible. Nearly a third of the Legion had been killed or injured and half the baggage train destroyed or immobilised by the loss of draught animals. A rough perimeter was in the process of being erected around the survivors although no-one seriously believed that the Britons would be able to regroup enough men to mount another attack. In any case, Togodumnus had been slain and his body was displayed, spread-eagled across his chariot, in front of the pen holding the British prisoners. They gazed at the body of their commander in sullen silence and wept, quite unashamed.

The Roman wounded lay in long rows waiting their turn for treatment as the Legion's hospital orderlies moved amongst them, sorting out the triage cases from those that stood a good chance of surviving their injuries. The air was filled with their moans and cries. To one side of the track, a huge pyre had nearly been completed and a growing pile of Roman bodies was being heaped on top: the pyre would be lit once night fell. In front of the hastily erected headquarters tent the pile of identity seals taken from the dead was mute testament to the price the Legion had paid. The dead Britons were unceremoniously thrown into a series of pits dug along the length of the track. Although a victory had been won, the men of the Second Legion had no desire to join the rejoicing of their comrades in the Fourteenth, whose distant cries of celebration could be heard from their camp at the edge of the forest.

In Vespasian's tent, an altogether different mood pervaded. He sat at his desk staring at the three men before him – Vitellius, seated, with a sickening hint of a smile playing about his lips as he listened to the account being given by the centurion and the optio standing to one side. Every so often he was aware of the hate-filled glances shot at him by the other two, but it only seemed to amuse him all the more as be bided his time.

Macro, filthy and exhausted, tried to make his report as clearly as possible but the intense weariness of the last few days clouded his mind and every so often he would turn to his optio to clarify a point, or to recall a detail. Cato stood stiffly at attention, his arm in a sling, still numb and useless from the blow he had received earlier.

The pair looked quite done in, reflected Vespasian, but he was secretly delighted with them. They had recovered the chest from the wagon in the marsh and even now the Legion's cavalry squadron had been despatched to retrieve it from its new hiding place. Not only that, but Macro had brought the body of

Togodumnus into the camp and the corpse was identified by one of the British exiles accompanying the Fourteenth legion, a vile rat-faced man by the name of Adminius. With Togodumnus dead, only his brother Caratacus remained to co-ordinate the British resistance to the invaders. All in all, the legate decided, a disaster had been neatly averted, and had in fact been turned into something of a victory. In that light, his career was safe.

But there remained the sticky problem of the accusations being made against Vitellius by the centurion and his optio. As they spoke of Vitellius's attack on them in the marsh, their words were spoken with the simplicity of truth and all the doubts that Vespasian had ever entertained about the tribune seemed to be vindicated.

Macro finished his report and, after a moment's silence, Vespasian weighed up the evidence, while he stared intently at each of the three in turn.

'Are you quite sure about this, Centurion? Do you really wish to prefer charges against the tribune here?'

'Yes, sir!'

'What you say will sound quite incredible in a court of law. You know that, don't you?'

'Yes, sir.'

'Very well then. Very well. I will give your statements the fullest consideration and let you know my decision at the earliest convenience. You two are dismissed.'

'Sir?'

'What is it, optio?'

The young optio paused to consider his next words carefully. 'I still don't quite understand why we were listed as deserters, sir.'

'The charges have been dropped,' Vespasian said curtly. 'No harm done.'

'Yes, sir, but why were the charges made in the first place? Who—'

'A mistake, Optio. Leave it at that. Now you're dismissed.'

As Macro and Cato made for the tent flap, Vespasian called after them. 'One last thing. You have my thanks for alerting the rearguard. I doubt we'd have lasted long enough for the Fourteenth to rescue us, if Plinius hadn't been able to hold that end of the column. Now, make sure you get some rest. Wait outside and I'll have my orderly fix you and your men some hot food.'

'Thank you, sir,' Macro replied.

Alone in the tent with Vitellius, the legate considered his next interview carefully. Already the established version of events had Vitellius down as the hero who had single-handedly found Togodumnus's column. Unable to fight his way back to warn the Second Legion, he had caught up with the Fourteenth causing them to turn and intervene, just in time to save the Second Legion from annihilation. Consequently the tribune had won fulsome praise from nearly all quarters for his gallant action. Yet the two men who had left talked of treachery and betrayal.

'I take it you will not be pursuing their wild claims any further, sir?'

'It's quite a story. Wouldn't you agree?'

'Yes, but still a story. And, like all the best stories, there isn't a shred of truth in it.'

'But if the rest of their patrol says the same then you're in a bit of a fix.'

'Not at all,' Vitellius protested smoothly. 'It's my word against theirs. The word of the son of a consul against a bunch of squaddies. Who do you think a court will believe, especially after I've risked my life to save the Legion from certain defeat? At best it'll look like sour grapes. At worst, it will look like a political prosecution and that's hardly likely to go down well with the plebes in Rome – they're rather partial to heroes, I understand. I'd let it go if I were you.'

Vespasian smiled. 'Even heroes still have to call their superiors "sir",' he said quietly.

'My apologies – sir.'

'Let's, for the moment, agree that the centurion spoke the truth. How did you find out about the chest?'

Vitellius did not reply immediately as he sized up the legate. 'You know, I could deny all knowledge of the chest. I was, after all, acting on your orders to scout for sign of Togodumnus. I could say I just happened to be in the marsh at the same time as your little team. A thick mist, a case of mistaken identity . . . all perfectly understandable.'

'Understandable, but not true.'

'Of course it's not true, sir. But it doesn't really matter.'

'Why?'

'Because nothing will ever come of it. Not one word of what passes between us now will ever be uttered outside this tent.'

'And why might that be, tribune?' Vespasian smiled.

'I'll come to that, in a little while. Since you seem to be quite keen to know the truth about things then I'll indulge you. Actually, Narcissus told me about the chest.'

'Narcissus?'

'He told me before we'd even left the base on the Rhine. You see, I'm the imperial spy you were told about. He wasn't entirely sure about you and wanted me to keep an eye on the operation. Of course, I was only too happy to oblige.'

Vespasian managed to smile at the irony of the situation. Even the cunning Narcissus had his blind spots. Motive and alibi had been handed to Vitellius on a plate.

'But while he told me about the wagon, he didn't tell me where it was. That's why I needed to see the map on that scroll. Unfortunately someone beat me to it. Not only that but they tried to frame me for its theft. Still, it was simple enough to have Pulcher follow your men down into the marsh and send for some assistance the moment they started digging. I genuinely hoped to avoid any bloodshed, amongst my men that is. If I'd managed to persuade Macro to give up the chest we'd only have had to kill them afterwards. As it was, he demonstrated an unfortunate penchant for the most resourceful soldiering in adverse circumstances. And so the chest has been won for Claudius.'

'But why would you want the chest in the first place?' Vespasian asked. 'You couldn't possibly have hoped to use such a vast sum without attracting attention.'

'Absolutely. I hope you don't take me for that much of a fool, sir. I never intended to spend the money on myself.'

'Then why go to such lengths to obtain it?'

'For the same reason the Emperor wants that chest.

427

Gold is power; and with that kind of wealth I could buy the loyalty of pretty much any, and every, man I wanted to.'

'I see.' Vespasian nodded. 'Then that would make you the traitor Narcissus warned me about. It never occurred to me that the imperial spy and the traitor were the same person. I think Narcissus will be equally surprised when I tell him.'

'Me the traitor? Is that what you think?' Vitellius laughed. 'Hardly! As it happens, I am still the imperial spy – always have been. At least that's what Narcissus believes.'

'So why try to kill him?'

'Kill him?' Vitellius frowned. 'Oh, that business on the road to Gesoriacum. Not guilty, I'm afraid. And anyway what could I possibly gain from his death? I needed him to get to the army and help crush the mutiny. After all, how could I hope to get to the chest unless the invasion went ahead? No, that ambush was the work of someone else. My guess is that the person behind the ambush wanted to prevent the invasion. You know as well as anyone how important it is for Claudius to win approval for his elevation to Emperor. With Narcissus dead, the mutiny in full flow, the invasion abandoned, and the fortune in the chest denied him, how long do you think Claudius would last? Believe me, until I could get my hands on the chest I was only too keen to further the Emperor's aims.'

'And what then?' Vespasian asked. 'You could hardly produce such a large fortune all at once.'

'Of course not. I don't need it right now. I'm just

planning for my future. Claudius won't last for ever and someone has to be Emperor – why not me one day?'

'You?' It was Vespasian's turn to laugh.

'Why not? Come to that, why not you?'

'You can't be serious?'

'I'm serious. Deadly serious.'

'But Claudius has heirs, a family to ensure someone succeeds him.'

'That's very true,' agreed Vitellius. 'But you must have noticed how easily members of the imperial family succumb to all manner of peculiar deaths. They're quite a tragic lot. And if something is to happen to them, I intend to be there when the vacancy is announced. But I'm in no hurry just now. I can bide my time and make sure that I move only when I have the resources to buy the necessary support. Thanks to those two outside I'll just have to wait a little longer.'

Vespasian was shocked by the tribune's naked ambition. Was there no limit to what the man would do in his desire for power? Yet there was a more immediate question that demanded an answer.

'If you aren't the spy acting for the traitors, then who is?'

'I was wondering when you would ask that.' Vitellius leaned back. 'The truth is, it took me a long time to find out. I should have known much earlier, certainly before my man Pulcher beat it out of the ring-leader of the mutiny.'

Vespasian suddenly recalled the way in which Plinius had looked at the scroll he had retrieved from Titus that evening back in the command tent, and the convenient way Plinius had distracted the guards at just the moment when the thief had been searching through his document chest. 'Plinius?'

'Plinius!' Vitellius laughed. 'Him? Oh, do be serious, sir.'

'If not Plinius, then who?'

'I would be wary about someone much closer to home if I were you.'

'What do you mean?' Vespasian felt a cold, sick feeling rise in his throat.

'If what Narcissus tells me is true then it seems that someone was trying to frame me over that business in the tent.'

'You deny that you tried to steal the scroll?'

'No,' admitted Vitellius. 'But the scroll I had Pulcher steal from you was blank. Someone had made the switch before I could get to it.'

'It couldn't have been blank,' Vespasian countered with a smile. 'Because it couldn't have been switched in the first place. It was already out of the safe-box, Flavia found it, she said Titus had . . .' Vespasian felt his blood turn icy cold.

'Flavia found it. How convenient.' Vitellius smiled at the legate.

'It's not possible,' muttered Vespasian.

'That's what I thought at first. You have to hand it to her, Flavia is a slick operator.'

'But . . . but why?'

'Why? I can't pretend to fully understand her motives. I don't suppose for a moment that she's half the Republican she pretends to be. I'd say it was more likely

430

that she was easing the way for you, to advance your career.'

'Me?' Vespasian was shocked.

'My dear legate, you may think that your moral integrity does you great credit, and that to serve the Emperor unquestioningly is the first duty of your office, but the very fact that you don't suspect your wife makes you all the more useful as a political pawn. What better candidate to step into the gap following Claudius's fall than a man who honestly believed he had served the old boy to the fullest extent of his ability and loyalty. The plebes would love you. I bet you could have given Antony's funeral oration over Caesar a run for its money.'

'How dare you?' Vespasian said quietly, struggling to control his rising temper. 'How dare you suggest that Flavia – could even begin to do the things you accuse her of?'

'You never suspected? I suppose that's to your credit as a husband. And I'm sure you'd make a great statesman, but you'd be a lousy politician. The men who attacked Narcissus came from a cavalry unit commanded by Gaius Marcellus Dexter, one of Scribonianus's officers and, as it happens, a distant cousin of your wife. You don't think that's a coincidence, I hope. Face it, Flavia's cover is almost blown. I'd have a word with your wife very soon. Encourage her to cease her meddling in power games and Narcissus might just miss her part in all this. If you want to keep your wife in good health, I suggest you make sure that I never feel the need to tell anyone about her extra-curricular activities. I haven't yet told Narcissus what I know. You give me your silence about all that we've said in here and I give you Flavia's life. A fair bargain, wouldn't you say?'

Vespasian stared at him, his mind still trying to deny the evidence his memory relentlessly reassembled from the events of the last few months. That moment in the tent when she fumbled the scroll she had retrieved from Titus. It had been deftly swapped, he now realised.

'Sir, I don't expect you to agree to my offer right now. But think it over carefully. I won't deny that I've been rather careless in many respects. And I might just be able to persuade Narcissus that any charges you bring against me are unfounded, or even unscrupulous. But the merest suggestion that I have been anything but the good and faithful servant he believes me to be, will surely undermine my position. So you see, if you force all this out into the open we'll both suffer the consequences. Moreover, I'll be forced to reveal what I know about Flavia. I'm sure you'll accept that it's in all our interests to be discreet about every detail of the last few months.'

Vitellius waited for a reply but Vespasian was looking down, wrapped in a growing despair and oblivious to the tribune's final comments. He raised a hand to rest his head on, still shattered by the revelations.

'Oh, Flavia . . .' he whispered. 'How could you?'

'Now, sir, if I may go? I have my duties to attend to.' Vitellius rose to leave the tent. 'And I trust we'll hear no more about Centurion Macro's charges against me.' For a moment Vespasian struggled for words to continue the interview. Words to express his shame and fear – and rage at the smug superiority of the tribune. Some words to put Vitellius in his place. But no words came and he simply nodded in the direction of the tent flap.

Outside, Cato and Macro were sitting on some forage left out for the staff horses. Macro was fast asleep, head bowed down on his chest and snoring heavily, having finally surrendered to a terrible need for rest. The loud snores drew disapproving glances from passing orderlies bustling in and out of headquarters. The peat-soiled clothes, grimy skin and dark dried blood of Togodumnus smeared over his hands and face had reduced the centurion to a pitiful state. Yet Cato regarded him with affection as he recalled Macro's honest delight at finding him alive and well on his return to the Second Legion. The sense of belonging that Cato had been so clearly aware of during the battle had remained with him and he sensed that this was how it felt to be a legionary, at one with his comrades and the unforgiving way of life he had been thrust into. The army was his home now. He belonged body and soul to the Second Legion.

And it was as well, he reflected, as he looked up and caught the eye of one of the hundreds of Britons sitting quietly in the prisoners' pen, spoils of war destined to be shipped back to Rome and sold into slavery. But for his late father's request, Cato might still have been a slave, like that poor savage in the pen. A lifetime of the worst kind of slavery awaited them all. Back-breaking agricultural labour on some huge estate, or a faster death on a chain-gang in a lead mine was all that uncivilised prisoners taken in battle could expect.

Yet there was something in the prisoner's eyes that spoke of an unbroken spirit, of a will to fight to the bitter end at any cost, of a fire that burned within as long as one man bore arms against the invaders. Cato knew that the campaign to subdue these people was going to be a long and bloody struggle.

Also by Simon Scarrow

Centurion

Roman army officers Cato and Macro have survived
many dangerous missions together.

They look out for one another. They're faithful to
their Emperor. And from their men they demand
bravery and ruthless efficiency.

With the news that Rome's old enemy, Parthia, is poised
to unleash its might against the border kingdom of
Palmyra, Cato and Macro must embark on a desperate
quest to protect the Empire.

Outnumbered, deep in treacherous territory
and besieged, they will have to endure a pitched
battle that will test their courage and loyalty as
never before . . .

978 0 7553 4836 7

headline

Also by Simon Scarrow

The Gladiator

The friendship between Roman Centurions Cato
and Macro is as solid as a rock.

Returning to Rome from a harrowing campaign
they are shipwrecked when an earthquake strikes
the island of Crete.

Struggling ashore they discover panic, devastation
and a slave revolt. Led by a gladiator called Ajax,
the slaves are driven by a bloodthirsty desire for
revenge that renders them almost invincible.

Taking control of the shaken men of the local
garrison Cato and and Macro must save the
province, before the rebellion can threaten the
Empire itself . . .

978 0 7553 2779 9

headline

Embark on a journey with Cato and Macro and find out about their other exploits across the Roman Empire.

www.catoandmacro.com/the-books